A Trick of Fate

Brandon Brothers - MAX

STELLA RILEY

Copyright © 2019 Stella Riley
All rights reserved.

ISBN: 9781695965836

Cover by Ana Grigoriu-Voicu, books-design.com

CONTENTS

Chapter One	1
Chapter Two	16
Chapter Three	31
Chapter Four	42
Chapter Five	55
Chapter Six	68
Chapter Seven	83
Chapter Eight	97
Chapter Nine	113
Chapter Ten	124
Chapter Eleven	136
Chapter Twelve	149
Chapter Thirteen	166
Chapter Fourteen	180
Chapter Fifteen	192
Chapter Sixteen	203
Chapter Seventeen	219
Chapter Eighteen	232
Chapter Nineteen	244

	Page
Chapter Twenty	254
Chapter Twenty-One	268
Chapter Twenty-Two	283
Chapter Twenty-Three	297
Chapter Twenty-Four	309
Chapter Twenty-Five	320
Chapter Twenty-Six	332

CHAPTER ONE

'My lord?'

'Yes?' Leaving his finger marking a place part-way down a column of figures, Max Brandon glanced absently across at his secretary and then froze when he saw the younger man's expression. 'Oh – for the love of God. Not *another* one?'

'Two,' replied Mr Balfour, shoving back a strand of fiercely red hair.

Max cursed under his breath and threw his quill across the desk.

'What is it this time?'

'A pearl bracelet from a jeweller in Bedford, valued at a hundred-and-twenty guineas. And four nights' accommodation at a hostelry in Lichfield, totalling seventy-five.' The secretary scanned the second of two sheets of paper. 'Judging by the consumption of food and wine, either our friend entertains lavishly or he has a voracious appetite and hollow legs.'

Ordinarily, Max might have smiled. This, however, was no laughing matter. What had originally seemed to be nothing but a couple of random, inexplicable errors had, in the course of the last month, escalated into a problem.

It had begun at the turn of the year. Max had lingered in London far longer than originally intended – first for his sister's wedding to Julian Langham and then, at the insistence of his mother, for that of his cousin Elizabeth to the Earl of Sherbourne. December weather had made the journey back to Yorkshire a nightmare and they had arrived at Brandon Lacey only three days before Yule and with barely enough time to finalise the arrangements for Mama's traditional Twelfth Night Ball. The first 'mistake' had turned up two days later; a polite reminder for the trifling sum of fifteen guineas – being the cost of hiring a post-chaise for a journey between Buckingham and High Wycombe.

Max pushed his chair back and stood up. 'How many is it now?'

'Including these two? Eight.' Duncan Balfour's pleasant countenance hardened – as, despite the soft Scottish accent, did his tone. 'As well as becoming more frequent, the sums are getting larger.'

'I'd noticed.'

So far, in the absence of any better plan, Max had let Duncan deal with the matter by letter – explaining that some confusion must have occurred since Lord Brandon had not left his Yorkshire estate since Christmas and was thus not responsible for whatever charge from elsewhere was being laid at his door. Although this approach had inevitably generated further argument, the various tradesmen had eventually accepted that they had been hoaxed and nothing could be done about it. But Max was beginning to get the uneasy feeling that sooner or later one of his so-called creditors was going to turn up on the doorstep accompanied by a magistrate ... which would prove deuced awkward since he himself was the magistrate for the Boroughbridge and Knaresborough district.

He said, 'What the devil am I going to do, Duncan? Whoever is doing this is constantly on the move. The last bill was from Oxford and the one before that ...?'

'Aylesbury.'

'Aylesbury. And now Staffordshire. So even if I sent someone to Lichfield to try tracking him, he could be in Wales by now.'

'Perhaps,' suggested Mr Balfour slowly, 'it's more than one person.'

Max stared at him. 'More than one fraudster running about the country racking up bills in my name? Am I supposed to find that comforting?'

'No – I meant more than one fraudster targeting other gentlemen as well as yourself.'

'Oh. Well, that's marginally better, I suppose. But why me, for God's sake?'

'No idea, my lord. And the fact that it *continues* to be you strikes me as odd. After all, if one expects to get away with this kind of game, one doesn't dip repeatedly into the same well.'

'I agree. But the fact that he *is* going to the same well doesn't help us stop him, does it?' asked Max irritably. 'And this can't go on. Thus far, I've kept it from the family in order to spare my mother anxiety and I hope to go on doing so. But if it gets closer to home – if someone to whom I supposedly owe money decides to collect in person – it's all going to come out.' He stopped, shoving a distracted hand through his hair. 'And then there's the other side of it. All *I'm* suffering are rising levels of annoyance. The *real* victims are those whose bills aren't being paid ... and I'm becoming less and less comfortable with that.'

'Understandable,' said Mr Balfour. 'But what do you suggest? That you pay them?'

'I – yes, I think so. Some of them, anyway. The goldsmith, for example. Through no fault of his own, he's seriously out of pocket.'

'So, to one degree or another, are the other seven we've heard from – none of them through any fault of yours, my lord. I recognise that the unfairness of it sits badly with you. But if you pay one, how do you justify not paying others? Where do you set the bench-mark? And if you once begin, how long before your conscience has you paying all of them?'

Max loosed a long breath. 'I don't know. But I don't think I can go on as we have been ... and settling the goldsmith's bill may make me feel a little better.'

'Even though – forgive me – you'll likely have bought a gift for some doxy? Even though, in taking responsibility for the debts, you'll be doing exactly what this fellow seems to want?' Mr Balfour waited and then murmured, 'The decision on how to proceed must be yours, of course, but perhaps --'

'Pay the goldsmith,' said Max abruptly. 'And try thinking of a way to stop this clown – though I don't see how we're to do it. But right now, I'd give a lot for the opportunity to put his bloody head through the wall.'

It was unfortunate that the door opened at that precise moment and his mother walked in. She said calmly, 'Such language, Max! Whatever has put you out of temper?'

He hauled in a calming breath, thought fast and said, 'Padgett says one of the men has been smoking in the weaving sheds.'

Louisa nodded. 'Ah. The fire risk. Of course. But I'm interrupting. Perhaps you will join me in the drawing room when you are less busy?'

'No, Mama. Duncan and I were more or less finished.' He gestured to the bills in Mr Balfour's hand and said, 'Deal with those as we've discussed and make finding a solution to the other thing a priority, please. We can give it further consideration later.'

'Very good, my lord.' Exchanging a brief, meaningful glance with Max and bowing slightly to Lady Brandon, the secretary made a brisk exit.

Sitting down and spreading out her blue moiré skirts, Louisa said, 'What a very admirable young man he is. I'm so glad you let me persuade you to take him on.'

'His mother being your dearest friend left me little choice,' he returned dryly. 'However, I'll agree that it was a good decision – though I'll be glad when he stops my-lording me. As the son of an earl, I'm not sure he doesn't outrank me.'

'The *fourth* son of an earl ... and you know he doesn't.' She laughed suddenly. 'It's a pity, really. If he had a courtesy title, you could my-lord him back.'

'And sound like a bad play? I don't think so.' With his burst of temper firmly locked away, Max smiled at his mother and said, 'Now, Mama ... what may I do for you?'

'It is merely that I have had a letter from Belle. Around the middle of May, Julian has three engagements in Paris followed by a further two in Vienna. Belle wants to go with him but has concerns about leaving the children in the charge of the boys' tutor and Ellie's governess for several weeks. So she is hoping we will have them here.'

'She *knows* we'll have them. I don't understand why she's even asking.'

'Manners, dearest. I hope all my children have some of those.'

'Don't say that as though you're not sure,' he retorted. 'However ... are she and Julian bringing the terrible trio here themselves?'

'They are not at all terrible and there's no point pretending that you find them a trial. I know differently. As to how they will get here ... that is the other thing I wanted to discuss with you. Lord Sherbourne is to bring Lizzie for a visit to her parents at around the same time, so they have volunteered to escort the children.'

'Herd them, don't you mean?' Max laughed. 'Do you think anybody has warned Sherbourne that Rob is travel sick?'

'Probably not,' agreed Louisa, her eyes twinkling. 'But they won't have to ride in the same carriage, so his lordship should be spared the worst of it. However, it was of Sherbourne and Lizzie that I wished to speak. They will have a valet, a maid, a coachman and a groom with them, as well as two coaches and their horses – all of which can't possibly fit into the vicarage.'

'So you want them to stay here. At the same time as the children.'

'Yes. It would seem the only solution – and Lizzie could still spend as much time as she wishes with her family. What do you think?'

'I think,' replied Max, 'that you've already made up your mind and have also probably discussed it with Aunt Maria – thus making my thoughts superfluous. So it's fortunate that I've no objection, isn't it?'

'Thank you, my dear. And you will be here yourself during the visit?'

'In May? Yes, of course. With Adam in France and my best land steward still managing Julian's estate, I don't envisage going anywhere at all until the harvest is in.'

'No. I suppose not. And after it?'

'I haven't given the matter any thought – though I might consider spending a few weeks in London in the autumn.' Catching a gleam of something very like speculation in his mother's expression, Max said suspiciously, 'Why do you ask?'

'Why do you think?' she sighed. 'I'm asking because you are thirty years old, still unwed and likely to remain so unless you put yourself in the way of meeting suitable young ladies. Marriage may not be a concept to which you've previously given any thought – but it's high time that changed.'

Once upon a time, for eight short weeks before his hopes had come crashing down around him, Max had thought of nothing *but* marriage ... and had paid for it with months of silent, gut-wrenching misery. But Mama was unaware of that and he had no intention of enlightening her now. So at length and managing to inject some humour into his tone, he said, 'Why is it that as soon as sons leave their twenties behind them, mothers everywhere become inveterate matchmakers?'

'Because we want to see our boys happy.'

'And they can't be happy without a wife and children?'

'Perhaps some of them can,' conceded Louisa, rising and shaking out her skirts. 'But not you. Family is the centre of your being and always has been, even before we ... before we lost your father and you devoted all your energies into filling his shoes. No – please don't argue. You knew I could not contemplate marrying again and you did everything in your power to ensure that I need not do so. I also know that you would move mountains for Belle and die for both Adam and Leo. But much though you love us all, we *are* not and *should* not be enough. You need a family of your own, my dear.' Smiling, she reached out to pat his hand. 'I've seen you with Julian's orphans. And I have always known that the lady who wins your heart will be fortunate. But it is you who must go and find her.'

* * *

Although he suspected that his mother might be right, Max put her words to the back of his mind. In addition to his various business interests, the day-to-day running of Brandon Lacey and dealing with the tenants was sufficient to fully occupy his time even without the added problem of the nomadic fraudster.

For six days nothing more happened. Then, on the seventh, his butler informed him that he had a visitor.

Max looked down at the visiting card and then up at Hawkes.

'Sir Desmond Appleby? I've never heard of him.'

'No, my lord. But he insists upon seeing you and appears somewhat ... agitated.'

Max felt a sense of unease creeping over him.

God, he thought. *What now?*

'Then you'd better show him in, Hawkes.'

The butler bowed. 'Will you be requiring refreshments, my lord?'

'I doubt it. But I'll ring if I need you.'

Hawkes bowed and withdrew. With reluctance, Max rose from behind his desk and waited. Every instinct warned him that what lay ahead wasn't anything good.

The door opened again and the perfect epitome of a country squire – heavy-set, red-faced and wearing an old-fashioned wig – advanced into the room, his expression pugnacious.

'You've got my horse,' he said by way of greeting.

Max stared at him. 'I beg your pardon?'

'My horse. Chestnut gelding with white socks on the forelegs. You've got him.'

Max knew what was in his stables. Shaking his head, he said, 'You appear to be labouring under a misapprehension --'

'No I'm not.' Appleby dragged a sheet of paper from his pocket and slapped it down on the desk. 'Read that. It's clear enough, ain't it?'

Your missing chestnut has found a new home, sir. Look for him at Brandon Lacey.

Max read the words and then read them again. A chill ran down his spine and he found it necessary to keep a grip on his temper. If the note was a lie ... if Appleby was wrong ... a visit to the stables would soon prove it. But if, as seemed all too likely, malice and mischief were at work, the reverse would be true. And that would implicate his youngest brother – since it was he who had overall charge of the stables.

He said slowly, 'How did you come to ... mislay ... your horse, Sir Desmond?'

'I didn't mislay him, damn it! I rode into Wetherby to – well, it's of no consequence *why* I went. But when I'd completed my business, I found Percival gone.'

Percival? thought Max involuntarily. 'I see. And when was this?'

'Two days ago. Then this morning that note turned up.' Appleby scowled across the desk. 'Comes to a pretty pass when a man of your standing --'

'Stop!' snapped Max. 'If you are wise, you will draw the line at accusing me of stealing your horse. I can assure you that I won't take it well.'

'That's as may be but --'

'*If* your horse is in my stables, I am not aware of it – nor do I know how he might have got there. But if I had to hazard a guess, it would be that he was taken by the person who wrote that very helpful note and who then had him brought here. Did that possibility not occur to you?'

'No. Why would anybody do something so damned silly?'

'I have no idea. So by all means let us attempt to find out.'

Throughout their silent walk to the stables, there was only one thought in Max's head.

Leo ... if you've bought the horse without knowing where it came from, I'm going to murder you.

He found his brother in the yard, conversing with the head groom. Sending the older man away with a jerk of his head, Max said curtly, 'Leo – allow me to introduce Sir Desmond Appleby.'

Not appearing in the least discomposed, Leo smiled and held out his hand.

'Pleased to meet you, sir. Come to see how Bucephalus is doing, have you?'

'Bew-*what*? His name's Percival,' began Appleby.

'Never mind his name,' growled Max, seeing the ground opening up before him. And to his brother, 'Where is he?'

'In the end stall. Barker's grooming --'

Max stalked off, hotly pursued by Appleby. Having caught the expression in his brother's face, Leo watched them go and debated making himself scarce. Then, realising that this probably wasn't a good idea, he set off slowly in their wake.

'Percy!' said Appleby, joy and relief transforming his previously gruff tone. 'Percy, my boy. Here you are – safe and sound.'

'Did you imagine we'd turn him into dog-meat?' muttered Max, taking in the glossy chestnut coat and white socks Appleby had described. 'Leo! Get yourself over here and explain to Sir Desmond and me how *Percival* comes to be lodging with us?'

'A stable-hand brought him over on a leading-rein yesterday,' replied Leo, by now more than a little alarmed. 'He said that Sir Desmond was reducing his stables and --'

'I'm doing no such thing! And even if I was, I'd *never* part with Percy!'

'Go on,' said Max, his eyes boring into his brother's skull.

Leo avoided that look by turning to the squire.

'I thought the fellow worked for you, Sir Desmond. He said you were determined that Buceph-Percy must go to a good home and that the Brandon stables have that reputation.' And risking a reluctant glance at his brother, 'Honestly, Max, it all seemed perfectly above-board. So we agreed a price and he left.'

'How much did you pay him?'

'Fifty guineas. Obviously I assumed --'

'*Fifty*?' exploded Appleby. 'Percy's worth twice that!'

Leo blinked. 'Ah. Yes, well ... as I was saying, I assumed the money would be going to you, sir. But it appears that I misread the situation and --'

'And bought a stolen horse.' Max turned his chilly stare on Appleby. 'I hope we can agree that my brother made a stupid but innocent mistake which has cost him fifty guineas. And for what they may be worth, you have my regrets for any anxiety or inconvenience this has caused. As for you, Leo ... I believe you owe Sir Desmond an apology of your own, along with whatever assistance he requires to take Percy home. I'll see you in my study later. Meanwhile,' he made the merest suggestion of a bow, 'I'll ask you both to excuse me.' And walked away.

Slanting a sly but not unkind glance at Leo, Sir Desmond said, 'I reckon your brother's going to have something to say to you, young man.'

'Oh yes,' agreed Leo equably. 'Not a doubt of it.'

It was a further half hour before he joined Max and found himself greeted with, 'You bloody idiot. Haven't I *told* you not to buy from men who just come knocking at the gate?'

'You told me not to buy from tinkers or gypsies – and I don't,' replied Leo calmly. 'It's a pity because they often have a better eye for horseflesh than most dealers ... but I recognise there's always the risk of --'

'Of something like this?'

'Yes. But the fellow who brought Percy here claimed to be Appleby's groom and --'

'And you believed him?'

'Why wouldn't I? It's not --'

'Perhaps because you had no proof that he was who he said he was? Did it even *occur* to you to ask if he had something in writing from Appleby?'

'Well, no. But our stables are --'

'That isn't the point!'

'Yes it is. Our stables are known to be the best and largest in this part of the county – so when a gentleman has good bloodstock to sell, we're the obvious --'

'I'm aware of that – but it doesn't excuse what you did.'

Leo stood up. 'Since you're not going to let me finish a sentence, there's no point in continuing this. But you can rest assured that I'll be more careful in future.' And he walked out.

Max dropped his head in his hands. He tried telling himself that it was just coincidence; that some fellow had stolen a horse and taken it to where he might expect the best price. Unfortunately, the business of the note stopped him from believing it.

* * *

Three days later, Max returned from the quarterly meeting of the Merchant Adventurers in York to find his mother all but dancing around a stone nymph some four feet high which had apparently taken up residence in the hall during his absence. He said, 'Mama? What on earth is that doing in here?'

Louisa tucked a hand into his arm and laughed up at him.

'Don't tease, you wicked boy. She's exactly the centre-piece needed for my garden and I love her. Isn't she beautiful?'

'Very pretty.' He recalled that she'd had a plinth placed in the middle of the small walled garden to the south of the house but hadn't yet found a piece of sculpture to occupy it. 'Are we keeping her inside in case it rains?'

'Don't be silly. I just wanted to enjoy her while I waited for you to come home.' Reaching up and simultaneously tugging him towards her in order to kiss his cheek, she said, 'I don't know where you found her – but she's quite perfect! Thank you.'

Caught unawares, Max said, 'I don't ... I didn't ...' And then stopped, as understanding of exactly what this meant hit him like a punch in the stomach.

'Didn't what?' asked his mother, her attention still largely fixed on the statue.

He cleared his throat and tried to think past the enormous thing filling his head.

'I didn't know if – if you would like it or might prefer to choose something --'

'I could never have found anything lovelier than this lady, Max.' Louisa's eyes grew decidedly misty. 'And the fact of you having been thoughtful enough to buy her for me ... well, that makes her even more special.'

Max felt sick. Controlling his voice as best he could, he mumbled, 'I probably owe you a gift or two. However ... I'm glad you like her. And now, if you'll excuse me, I'll have to leave you to keep her company. I need a word with Leo.'

Having sent a footman to find his brother, Max stood staring blindly down at his desk and tried to get a grip on both his temper and precisely what that bloody statue was shrieking at him.

It had been specifically chosen to occupy the place Mama intended to put it ... which meant that the person who had bought it had seen the empty plinth. The bastard had been in the walled garden, mere yards from the house. But the knowledge that made Max want to smash something was the realisation that he'd let an opportunity slip through his fingers by assuming that Sir Desmond's so-called stable-hand was just hired help; a mere tool, paid for his trouble. But he hadn't been, had he? It had been the man himself ... wandering freely about Max's property. And it had taken three days for Max to see it.

Leo stuck his head around the door. 'You wanted to see me?'

'Yes. Come in and shut the door.' He waited until his brother was facing him, his forearms resting lazily on a chair-back. 'Tell me about Appleby's so-called groom.'

'God, Max – we're not back to *that*, are we?'

'Not in the way you mean. Describe him for me.'

Leo sighed and shrugged. 'Misshapen hat, shabby brown coat --'

'Not his clothes – *him*. What did he look like?' demanded Max, before suddenly recalling his brother's remarkable, if generally useless, talent. 'Better yet, sketch him.'

Leo's eyes narrowed and he straightened, folding his arms. 'Why?'

'Why do you think? He was in the district three days ago. If he still is and you can come up with a good likeness, we may have some chance of finding him.'

'I doubt that. Horse-stealing is a hanging offence. He'll be long gone.'

'Perhaps – perhaps not.' Max shoved a sheet of paper across the desk. 'Draw.'

'Not until you tell me what this is all about.'

'You *know* what it's about, damn it!'

'I don't think so. You wouldn't be wound tight as a coiled spring if it was just fifty guineas and a small amount of embarrassment. And then there's the question of how Appleby knew the horse was here.' He waited through a sudden, deafening silence. 'Well?'

'Christ.' Max dropped wearily into his chair. 'Leo ... just for once, could you please stop asking questions and simply do as I ask?'

'No. Percy hadn't been on the property twenty-four hours before Appleby knew exactly where to find him.' And when his brother still didn't answer, 'I'm not letting it go – so you may as well tell me. How did Appleby know we had his horse?'

With another muffled curse, Max said resignedly, 'He had a note.'

'What?' Leo gaped at him. 'From whom?'

'I imagine from the man who stole the horse in order to sell him to you.'

'But that doesn't make any sense.'

'In normal circumstances, no. But this ... I'm fairly sure this is part of something else. Something that has been going on for a while.' Max drew a long breath and said, 'I suppose I'd better start at the beginning – but not a word of it to Mother. Not one word!'

'That goes without saying.' Leo sat down. 'Now ... spit it out.'

So Max related the whole sequence of events, from the hired chaise at Buckingham to the nymph in the hall. And at the end he said baldly, 'In the beginning, I thought it was simply about money. But it isn't. It's personal.'

'Yes.' Leo surveyed him coolly. 'When were you going to tell me about it?'

'I wasn't. There didn't seem any need. Though I suppose --'

'No *need*? Really? Let's think about that for a minute, shall we? How about because I'm your brother ... or because if I'd known all this, bloody Percy wouldn't have been in our stables ... or because I'm your brother ... or because you need help ... or because --'

'You're my brother. Yes. I got that bit. If it's any comfort, Adam doesn't know either.'

'Adam isn't here,' retorted Leo. 'I am. And in case you haven't noticed, I came out of short coats a long time ago.' He paused regarding Max somewhat balefully out of normally guileless blue eyes. 'You will have told Duncan, I presume.'

'Everything except the horse and Mama's statue. But that's no reflection on --'

'Good. At least you haven't been trying to deal with this *completely* on your own. Do the two of you have a plan?'

'Not much of one,' admitted Max. 'Duncan suggested finding a thief-taker but as yet he hasn't had --' He stopped as Leo stood up and headed for the door, 'Where are you going?'

'To fetch my sketch pad. You wanted a likeness, didn't you?'

* * *

While Leo drew, Max told Duncan Balfour about Sir Desmond's horse and the newly-arrived nymph. The secretary listened carefully and, at the end, said, 'Do you still have the note, my lord?'

Max handed it to him. 'It's anonymous of course, but a

sample of his handwriting may come in useful. And the next time you *my lord* me, I'll dismiss you without a character.'

'He won't,' remarked Leo absently.

'I know.' Mr Balfour smiled but returned to the business hand. 'We can hope he didn't disguise it but shouldn't overlook the fact that he may have done. However ... an educated hand, wouldn't you say?'

'I thought so, yes.'

'And do you have *any* theories about why he's doing this?'

'None. There's no obvious link to anyone I can think of nor anything that points in a particular direction. Belle didn't leave a trail of broken-hearted suitors behind her; Adam hasn't killed anybody yet; I haven't offended anyone that I'm aware of ... and Mother never offends anyone. Leo?'

'I take after Mother,' said Leo without glancing up.

Max gave a derisive snort and Duncan, a choke of laughter. They fell silent for a while, watching the artist at work but knowing better than to go and look over his shoulder. Then Duncan said tentatively, 'Is there any possibility that the fellow Leo met *isn't* the man we're after? That he was paid to steal the horse, bring it here and snoop around a bit?'

'No.' Max let his head drop back against the chair, refusing to dwell on what Mama's pleasure in the seeming gift made him feel. 'Instinct tells me he did this himself. For whatever reason, he's been targeting Brandon Lacey specifically and the business with the horse was so he could get a closer look – which, clearly, he did.'

For a further ten minutes, the only sound was that of charcoal on paper. But finally Leo stood up, rolled his shoulders and tossed his sketch on Max's desk, saying, 'That's him.'

Max and Duncan pored over it, shoulder to shoulder. It showed a man of around thirty with long, lightish hair casually tied, and an amiable expression. Narrow, straight brows; a slight bump in an otherwise ordinary nose; a suggestion of hollows beneath the cheekbones and a square jaw. Taken all in all, it was a face plenty of ladies might call handsome.

Neither Max nor Duncan needed to ask how accurate it was.

Leo had excellent recall for faces and frequently drew from memory. Now, while the two men studied his efforts, he said, 'His eyes are brown, his hair is dark blond verging on the colour of very weak tea and his skin is tanned, as if he spends a great deal of time outside. He's shorter than me but maybe an inch taller than Duncan. He has a pleasant smile, an easy manner and is altogether plausible. I'd guess that most people he meets like him.'

'That could be a hindrance,' muttered Max. He looked up at his brother and added, 'But this will help, Leo – in fact it gives us an immense advantage. Would it take very long to make three further copies?'

'No. Why do you want them?'

'One for each of us and a spare. Then we can split up and hawk them around every inn and tavern within a five-mile radius of both Wetherby and here. We may not actually find the fellow but there surely must be *somebody* who'll recognise him and set us on the right track.'

CHAPTER TWO

It was a long and largely frustrating day spent riding from inn to inn and sometimes from shop to shop, showing Leo's sketch to everyone they met. But at the end of it, they had each unearthed a somewhat tenuous lead.

Max eventually found the inn – a shabby out-of-the-way place near Coneythorpe which he nearly missed – where *Mr Barnaby*, as he'd styled himself, had stopped for a meal around noon three days ago.

Presumably, thought Max grimly, *just after he took Leo for fifty guineas.*

'Ever so charming, he was,' sighed the serving-girl. 'A proper gentleman, sir. And we don't get many of them around here, more's the pity.'

'I take it that means he paid you?'

'Course he did – *and* gave me an extra shilling. Why ever would you ask a thing like that, sir? A real gentleman *always* pays.'

'Very true,' agreed Max aridly. 'And did you happen to see which direction he took when he left here?'

Sensing the possibility of another shilling, she said, 'I might've done.'

Max dropped a coin into her ready palm. 'And?'

'He carried on towards Flaxby. Said he'd business in Harrogate.'

Which, Max decided, probably meant he was heading in precisely the opposite direction. But he smiled, tossed the girl another shilling and left.

* * *

While Max was following his instincts and trying the York road, Leo struck lucky with a second-hand clothes dealer in Wetherby. Mr Parkin had sold their quarry what Leo had no difficulty in recognising as the stable-man's clothing.

'Said he was on his way home from visiting friends but his servant'd had some sort of accident and his clothes had got ruined, so he needed summat to tide him over, like. All sounded a bit rum, if you ask me. I mean, if they was travelling, stands to reason this servant of his'd have had a change of clothes with him, wouldn't he? And then there was the thing about 'em being much the same size. Very convenient that, I thought.'

'Very,' agreed Leo. 'What were his own clothes like?'

'Smart and not cheap – but not flashy, neither. Black tricorne, dark green wool coat wi' no braid nor trimming and a plain grey silk vest. He *looked* like a gentleman. He *sounded* like one an' all ... but for all his easy chat and smiles, I knew there were summat not right about him cos he was telling me a tale when there were no call for it.' The shop-keeper eyed Leo shrewdly and with a hint of sardonic amusement. 'Then again, I don't reckon you're looking for him because he's somebody's long-lost friend.'

'No, I'm not.' Leo grinned and handed over a florin. 'You're a very shrewd fellow, Mr Parkin. Did you notice anything else I might find useful?'

Mr Parkin scratched his bald head. 'Not much that picture don't tell you. Face and hands brown from the sun and his hair streaked blond. *That* didn't happen in Yorkshire.'

* * *

It was Mr Balfour who eventually located the comfortable inn at Kirk Deighton where *Mr Grey* had spent the two nights prior to his appearance at Brandon Lacey.

'Reserved my best room with the private parlour and supped here both evenings,' said the landlord proudly. 'A very particular gentleman. Very particular *indeed*.'

'Really?' said Duncan, managing to sound impressed as well as interested.

'Oh yes, sir. Knows his wines, does Mr Grey and insists on the best of everything. A gentleman of rare discernment. *Rare* discernment. Of course, he was a bit put out about his valet falling sick just when he's on his way to visit his uncle the marquis.'

'Most understandable. But I daresay his uncle's household will be able to supply a temporary replacement. And this would be the marquis of ...?'

'I don't know,' replied the landlord regretfully. 'Mr Grey never said. He was always polite and affable but he didn't encourage conversation. Not to be wondered at, of course. A gentleman is entitled to his privacy, after all – and bandying his uncle's title about wouldn't be seemly.'

'Indeed not.' Duncan hesitated briefly and then said, 'Did Mr Grey pay his shot?'

'To the penny, sir!' came the shocked reply. 'Why would you suppose he might not?'

'Because he often doesn't – something you might care to bear in mind if he passes this way again.'

* * *

Tired, dusty and, most of all, thirsty, the three gentlemen gathered in the library at Brandon Lacey little more than an hour before dinner. Having furnished each of them with a well-earned glass of wine, Max dropped into a chair and said, 'So ... what do we have? And let's make it quick. We need to wash and change before Mama sees us and asks questions we can't answer truthfully.'

Briskly and without unnecessary elaboration, each of them shared their findings. Mr Balfour made notes and, at the end, gave a lawyerly summing up.

'When he needs to give his name, he uses a different one each time. Max's tavern wench found him charming; the Kirk Deighton inn-keeper considers him a gentleman of rare discernment; and Leo's clothes-seller didn't believe a word he said and wondered why he'd bother to lie when there was no need for it.' He looked up, a faint smile touching his mouth. 'The clothes-seller is also our only source of new information. From him, we know a little about ... for the sake of convenience, let's call him Grey ... we know the style of dress he favours and that he's presumably been spending time in sunnier climes than here. From all three sources, we know that he rarely – if ever – tells the truth. I think your instinct was right, Max. If Grey told the girl he was going to Harrogate, he was absolutely *not*. In fact, the only semi-honest thing he's done is pay his shot at Kirk Deighton – and he'll have done that with Leo's fifty guineas.'

'Thank you for pointing that out,' muttered Leo.

'None of this helps though.' Max left his chair to prowl frustratedly towards the hearth. 'He could be anywhere by now. Oh – I know we never expected to actually catch up with him but I hoped we'd at least find something that would enable us to pick up his trail. As it is, we're as much in the dark as we were yesterday and he's free to continue persecuting me, secure in the knowledge that there's not a damned thing I can do about it.'

'Sooner or later, he'll make a mistake,' said Duncan calmly. 'And meanwhile, we wait for his next move and hope it gives us an opportunity to put him in check.'

* * *

Three days later, the bill from the stonemason arrived. On first sight, it was extortionate – until, that was, Max saw that it was demanding payment for not one but *two* pieces of sculpture.

'But where's the other one?' he asked Duncan, uneasily. 'I suppose it's too much to hope that he's kept it for himself and had it sent to his home.'

'Probably. But there's no harm in writing to ask the stonemason if he was required to deliver it – and, if so, where.'

'Do it, then. But don't hold your breath.'

On the following morning Max had barely finished breakfast when Hawkes informed him that Viscount Ripley wished to speak with him. This, since he and the viscount were barely on nodding terms, was surprising.

It was even more surprising when Lord Ripley stalked in and, sending Max staggering with a mighty blow to the jaw, said furiously, 'Just what the hell are you playing at, Brandon? How *dare* you send gifts to my wife! You must be bloody insane!'

Head ringing and grateful he had crashed into his desk rather than ending flat on his back, Max cautiously investigated his throbbing face before risking speech.

The viscount didn't wait. His voice shaking with temper, he said, 'We're scarcely back from our bridal trip and you send Letty – who has never so much as clapped *eyes* on you - that disgusting object? Why? She's in hysterics. Is that what you wanted? Or had you some idea of making me doubt her? I ought to slap a glove in your face, by God!'

Taking care to move his jaw as little as possible, Max said, 'It's as well that you didn't. I can overlook a punch but I'd have had to respond to that. However ... a statue, is it?'

'You know damned *well* what it is.'

'No. I'm guessing. Your wife has received a statue that you and she believe was sent by me.'

'It *was* sent by you. The delivery note said so plainly enough.'

'Of course it did,' sighed Max. And then, 'What *is* the statue?'

'You know that too,' growled Lord Ripley. 'It's a damned obscenity. A – a male nude.'

'Ah.' Despite the ache in his jaw, Max felt a distant quiver of amusement at the notion that perhaps the sculpture was better endowed than the viscount himself. '*Sans* fig leaf, I take it?'

'*Sans* everything, blast you. Why did you do it? If it's your idea of a joke --'

'It isn't. I have just received a bill for two pieces of sculpture I didn't buy. One of them is here. It appears that you have the other – which solves one mystery, if not the most pressing one.' He drew a steadying breath. 'The important point, Ripley, is that I did not send it. I give you my word on that.'

The young man opened his mouth, closed it again and finally said, 'That sounds like nonsense. If you didn't send it – who did?'

'I can't answer that. Yet. Put simply, you and your wife have been drawn into something I have been attempting to unravel for some time – and for which you have my sincere apologies. As to the ... obscenity ... I suggest you send it back whence it came.' He paused and thought for a moment. 'Unless you've an inclination to take an axe to it?'

* * *

The bruise on Max's jaw had taken some explaining. He'd told his mother that it was the result of a moment's carelessness whilst installing the new loom at Scar Croft. Duncan and Leo heard what really happened. Leo, inevitably, found it amusing.

A week went by. March slid into April and nothing untoward arrived at Brandon Lacey either in person or by post. Praying that Grey had tired of the game, Max applied himself doggedly to his usual routine.

He visited various tenants, inspected cottages needing repair and gave the necessary orders; he discussed possible improvements to the weaving and dyeing sheds with their respective overseers; and he spent the best part of a day haggling over the purchase of a small, currently unworked coal mine.

He received the usual monthly progress report from Ben Garret, still on loan to Julian's estate in Nottinghamshire. The land was now in full production and the quantity of livestock had been increased. Finally, repairs to the estate cottages were beginning to tempt new tenants to fill the vacancies. Max sent his congratulations and told Garret to remain in place until he was confident that the fellow he was training to take his place was up to the task.

He paid calls on some of his neighbours, went riding with Leo, escorted his mother to Lady Hanwell's dinner-party in Harrogate and spent an evening playing cards with friends in Knaresborough. And bit by bit, he felt the tension that had been building in his muscles start to ease.

Then a letter from the Rothwell Steam Company politely reminded Lord Brandon that the three thousand pounds owing in respect of shares purchased was still outstanding. Perhaps his lordship could deal with the matter at his earliest convenience?

Max swore, briefly but with dedication.

'Quite,' agreed Mr Balfour, still perusing the other paperwork which had accompanied the lawyer's missive. 'But at least it appears that the company actually exists.'

'Since, if it didn't, I could simply ignore it, I don't see how that makes it better.'

'Point taken. But Mr Royston has included copies of the company information in case you have mislaid the ones you were given ... and you'll like the sound of it.' Duncan looked up, smiling faintly. 'Under licence from Messrs Watt & Boulton, Rothwell – basically an iron-foundry – manufactures and distributes Mr Watt's new steam engine.'

'Ah.' Max's expression brightened. 'This would be a good time for that. The old Newcomen engine is what the majority of mines still have because they can be adapted to Watt's design – but most of them will have been around for anything up to seventy years. Then again, working directly in conjunction with Watt himself will give Rothwell a distinct advantage on --' He stopped abruptly and stood up. 'Wait a minute. Rothwell. That's Leeds, isn't it?'

'I believe so. Why?'

'Write to them, inviting the company officers to visit me. Don't bother with explanations – those will be easier given face to face. And don't make any promises. I'm interested but I won't make a decision until I know more.'

* * *

Mr Whitby and Mr Royston of the Rothwell Steam Company accepted Lord Brandon's invitation and were shown into his library four days later only to stop dead just past the threshold, their faces imprinted with confusion.

Mr Whitby looked from Max to Duncan Balfour and back again. Finally he said uncertainly, 'There appears to be some mistake, sir. *You* are Lord Brandon?'

'My butler certainly thinks so,' agreed Max, with what Duncan privately considered unhelpful levity. 'But I'm aware that it was not me you expected to meet today.'

'No, sir. It was another gentleman entirely.'

'Perhaps we misunderstood, Geoffrey,' suggested Mr Royston. 'I don't precisely recall it … but perhaps the gentleman we met previously was speaking *on behalf of* Lord Brandon.' And to Max, 'Was that the case, sir?'

'I'm afraid not. To be perfectly honest gentlemen, I don't know *who* you met. All I *do* know is that he has recently been making free with my name … and had no intention whatsoever of investing in your company.'

'He hadn't?' Mr Whitby frowned. 'Are you sure about that?'

'Perfectly.' Max held out Leo's sketch. 'I take it that this is the man in question?'

'Oh dear. Yes – that is he, is it not, Henry? But I am at a loss to understand what he expected to achieve with this – this --'

'Hoax?' supplied Max. 'I wish I knew. I also wish I could get my hands on him – as, presumably, do you.'

'Very much so,' said Mr Royston curtly. And fixing Max with a suddenly very acute stare, added, 'However, since this imposture could have been explained to us by letter, may I ask why your lordship invited us here?'

Wincing, Mr Whitby said, 'Easy, Henry. I'm sure Lord Brandon has his reasons.'

'I do,' agreed Max. 'But perhaps we might begin by sitting down?' He ushered his guests to chairs by the hearth and when they were seated, said, 'I wanted to meet you because it is possible that all is not lost. Our anonymous friend was never going to invest in your company. I, on the other hand, might.'

Both men stared at him, apparently stunned into silence. But finally Mr Whitby said, 'That is ... most unexpected, my lord.'

'It shouldn't be.' Taking his own seat and waiting for Mr Balfour to re-join them, Max said, 'I understand that you are manufacturing the Watt steam engine under licence from Mr Watt himself. This alone puts your company in a very strong position and at what may well be the optimum time. Does Mr Watt take any ongoing practical interest?'

'Why, yes.' Mr Royston leaned forward, elbows on his knees. 'He remains in regular communication – as does Mr Wilkinson who devised the method by which the cylinder of the engine is bored.'

'Yes. I read about Wilkinson's invention in one of the scientific journals.'

Seeing the gleam of interest in Max's eyes, Mr Balfour seized the opportunity to deflect it. He said, 'May I ask if you have a specific reason for seeking further capital at this time?'

'Yes, sir. Monthly turnover is rising and we're already working to capacity. If the current trend continues – and we've reason to suppose that it will – we'll soon need to expand, which will require additional space, equipment and workers. Mr Whitby and I are agreed that we should begin setting these matters in hand sooner rather than later.'

Max nodded but once again Duncan spoke first.

'I'm assuming your quarterly figures support this?'

'Naturally,' said Royston stiffly.

'Would it be possible to see them?'

Messrs Whitby and Royston exchanged glances.

'If Lord Brandon is serious in his interest ... by all means,' said Mr Whitby.

'Good,' said Max. 'We can come to that later. For now, I'd like to hear more about --'

He stopped as a tap at the door heralded the butler. 'Yes, Hawkes?'

'My apologies for disturbing you, my lord,' said Hawkes uncomfortably. 'A young lady has arrived and is demanding to see you.'

Max rose and moved slightly away from his guests. 'A lady? *Here*?'

'Yes, my lord. She is unaccompanied and she refuses to give her name. I have explained that you are occupied with other company but she will not leave and --' Which was as far as he got before the door burst open and a dark-clad tornado erupted into the room to whirl to a halt three feet from Max and stare at him out of eyes filled with a mixture of wrath, accusation and something oddly like well-deep sadness.

'*You*!' she spat, breathless with some overwhelming emotion. 'It *is* you. All the way here I prayed that it wouldn't be – prayed that it was a mistake – that it *must* be, even though I couldn't see how it was possible. I wanted to believe you would never – *could* never do this.' Two strides brought her close enough to slam her fists repeatedly into his chest, making him stagger. 'Yet you did. You *did*, didn't you? How *could* you?'

Time stopped. Four men looked on, frozen in horrified embarrassment.

Max stood like a stone, unable to move or speak or even, just for a few seconds, to breathe. He stared unblinkingly into furious gold-flecked blue eyes ... he saw pale skin, faintly dusted with a sprinkling of freckles and a soft, slightly too-wide mouth currently tight with temper.

Burning like fire, air returned to his lungs and he whispered, '*Frances*?'

As if receiving the correct cue, Time started again ... the only problem was that, for Max at least, it ran backwards.

* * *

Five years earlier ...

He might have refused the Earl and Countess of Grantham's invitation to Westlake Abbey had his family not combined to virtually thrust him through the door.

'Go!' said his mother. 'You've earned a holiday among people of your own age.'

'Go!' said Leo and Adam. 'We can manage without you for a fortnight.'

And, 'Go!' said sixteen-year-old Arabella, with a hug. 'Go – and bring me back a sister.'

But in the end, what made him accept was a letter from Simon Greville – youngest son of Lord and Lady Grantham and one of Max's closest friends.

Don't you dare make your excuses! Simon had written. At the end of the month, I'm sailing for Calcutta to take up a position with the East India Company. This is the last we're likely see of each other for years – so get yourself here!

No sooner had he arrived at Westlake Abbey than Simon dragged him out to the gardens where some of the other guests were enjoying the sunshine. And there, not ten minutes later and some fifteen feet away across the lawn with two other ladies, he saw Her.

He watched her while Simon bubbled with enthusiasm about his voyage to Calcutta.

Hair the colour of burnished chestnuts and a body curved in all the right places. He didn't know if she was beautiful. He only knew that something about her held him spellbound. She wasn't saying much – probably because one of her companions appeared to be saying a great deal. But the heart-shaped face was vivid with something Max couldn't name and which effectively held his gaze trapped. And then she tilted her head, a slow and enticingly wicked smile curling her lips and she said something that caused the talkative lady's shoulders to stiffen and the other girl to dissolve into startled, hastily suppressed laughter. And Max, unaware that he was grinning in response, cut across his friend's discourse to say, 'Simon ... who is she?'

'I knew you weren't listening,' grumbled Simon. Then, following Max's gaze, 'Oh lord. You don't mean Uxbridge's girl, do you? She may be a beauty but she's cold enough to give you frostbite – not to mention hanging out for a marquis, if she can catch one.'

'No, not her.' Belatedly, Max recognised the Earl of Uxbridge's raven-haired daughter. 'The girl in the lilac gown who is with her.'

Simon's brows rose and he shook his head mock-dolefully.

'You're out of luck there as well. That's Frances Pendleton ... and she's as good as betrothed to Archie Malpas.'

'Archie?' Max winced. They had known Lord Malpas since university and their shared opinion of him wasn't high. 'Unfortunate girl. Has he improved?'

'No. If the whispers are true, it's not only chambermaids and shop-girls now. He's got a taste for brothels – and not the better sort. Of course, Frances won't know any of that.'

'No – but surely her father does?'

'Hard to say. Pendleton doesn't spend much time in town these days. Then again, Archie's family is filthy-rich and he's two funerals away from a marquisate – so Sir Horace is probably delighted. Still ... I don't suppose you were planning to propose, were you?'

'Not exactly. I was thinking more of an introduction.'

'In that case, allow me.' Strolling towards the ladies, Simon added quietly, 'You'll like Frances. Personally, I've always thought her the pick of the bunch.'

Three pairs of feminine eyes turned as they approached. Only one pair smiled.

'Lady Constance, Mistress Beverley, Mistress Pendleton,' said Simon easily. 'Allow me to present Lord Brandon – newly-arrived and a very old friend of mine.'

'Not that old,' countered Max. He bowed, trying not to look directly at Her yet because he wasn't sure he'd be able to stop. 'A *pleasure, ladies. Although, Lady Constance and I have met before, I believe.'*

'Really?' The arctic blue gaze drifted over him. *'I do not recall it.'*

'L-Last year in London,' whispered Mistress Beverley. *'At the Haymarket?'*

Max nodded. *'Mr Foote's new play, wasn't it?'*

'One meets a great many people at the theatre,' said the earl's daughter dismissively. *'As for Mr Foote's play ... it was quite dreadful.'*

'Yet you remembered it, Connie,' remarked Mistress Pendleton. And offering her hand to Max, *'You were clearly not dreadful enough, Lord Brandon.'*

The instant his fingers touched hers, a bolt of something inexplicable shot through Max's body and he heard the girl's breath hitch, as if she'd felt it too. Staring into extraordinary lapis lazuli eyes, he managed a slightly unsteady 'Thank you', which was all but drowned in Simon's crack of laughter and her ladyship's irritable, 'Don't be ridiculous, Frances. And how many times must I tell you not to call me Connie?'

'I beg your pardon.' Mistress Pendleton managed to sound genuinely apologetic before immediately ruining the effect by adding cheerfully, *'My memory must be as unreliable as yours, Constance.'*

Her ladyship's colour rose; Mistress Beverley looked as if she'd swallowed a fly; Simon snorted and Max had to hide a grin.

'Mr Greville,' said Lady Constance glacially.

Simon started and eyed her warily. 'My lady?'

'Is not that the Earl of Derby over there with your father?'

'What? Oh – yes. I believe it is. Are you acquainted with him?'

'Sadly, no. But perhaps you will be good enough to remedy that.' She laid a hand on his arm, clearly confident that he would do her bidding. *'Lord Brandon ... you'll excuse us, I'm sure. Come, Prudence.'*

Mistress Beverley sent a faintly wild glance in Frances's direction then dutifully trailed after Lord Uxbridge's daughter.

Almost as one, Max and Frances turned to look at each other. Their eyes locked and neither spoke. Max still didn't know if she was beautiful. It was somehow irrelevant when that soft, pink mouth was addling his brain with thoughts he had no business having. What he did *know beyond a shadow of a doubt was that he wanted to count the faint scattering of freckles over her small nose and trace the curve of her eyebrows and determine whether or not the lashes fringing those gold-flecked, deep-blue eyes had been artfully darkened. Finally, clearing his throat and making a vague gesture towards his friend's retreating back, he said, 'Poor Simon.'*

Frances blinked, frowned as if trying to reclaim her thoughts, and then said, 'You might try sounding as if you meant it.'

'I do mean it,' protested Max. 'I know all about the penalties of being a son of the house, believe me. Every year my mother holds a ball and dragoons my brothers and me into dancing with any lady bereft of a partner – regardless of the fact we'd do it anyway.'

'Oh.' She wrinkled her nose. 'Duty dances, I suppose.'

'Sometimes. But often because although those girls may not be the most popular ones in the room, they're often the nicest.' And catching the faintly sardonic glint in her remarkable eyes, added innocently, 'That was the right answer, wasn't it?'

'It was – but you get no additional credit for knowing it.'

'I didn't expect to. But you can't blame a fellow for trying.'

From the tail of his eye, Max saw two gentlemen bearing down upon them and simultaneously realised that he wasn't ready to share Mistress Pendleton's company but didn't know how – on so slight an acquaintance – it could be avoided. Then, even as he debated the question, she altered the angle of her parasol and said brightly, 'If you've only just arrived you won't have seen the hermit's grotto. Would you like me to show you?'

'Very much.' Max offered his arm. A small, determined hand gripped the crook of his elbow and tugged. He obeyed its summons, suddenly feeling stupidly happy. 'I've never met a hermit.'

'And you won't meet one today.' She tilted her head to smile

at him. 'There isn't one.'

'Ah. He left? Moved to a better address, perhaps?'

'No.'

'Please don't tell me he died!'

She shook her head, laughter dancing in her eyes. 'Nothing so tragic. The truth is that there never was a hermit. It's just that it is the sort of place a hermit ought to live.'

'In that case, it's a shame there isn't one.' He considered the matter. 'I suppose there aren't many hermits about these days ... but you'd think there might be one who would be glad of a vacant grotto.'

'My thoughts exactly. Although,' she admitted regretfully, 'it isn't actually authentic. Simon's mother had it created a few years ago when the gardens were landscaped.'

'That is naturally a drawback,' agreed Max, eyes and voice both equally grave. 'But even so, I can't believe that a suitable hermit might not have been found. Perhaps Lady Grantham didn't advertise for one?'

'I'm sure she didn't. Rather remiss of her, really.'

'Perhaps.' The laughter he had seen in her eyes quivered in her voice. Wanting her to let it loose, he said, 'But we shouldn't judge her ladyship too harshly, you know. After all, where might she have placed such an advertisement? I don't suppose hermits take the *Morning Chronicle* or subscribe to the *Gentleman's Magazine. Do you?*'

She pressed her lips together and shook her head.

'And I refuse to believe that any *self-respecting hermit reads the scandal rags.*'

'N-No. I have to agree with you there.'

'There is, however, just one possible solution.' He stopped walking, swung to face her and said triumphantly, '*Vetusta Monumenta!*'

Her mouth quivered. 'And what might that be?'

'You don't know?'

'No. I think – I think you just m-made it up.'

'Made it up?' he echoed in mock affront. 'I? Certainly not! *Vetusta Monumenta is a serious and erudite periodical which* publishes illustrations of ancient buildings and archaic artifacts,' he said loftily. Then, ruining the effect, added, 'Fascinating stuff if one likes that kind of thing – and I'll wager that hermits do. Indeed, I wouldn't be at all surprised if they aren't among Vetusta's *regular contributors.*'

And that, finally, produced the effect he wanted. She looked directly into his eyes while laughter bubbled up in a delicious gurgle, creating a burst of euphoria in his chest.

She said unsteadily, 'You are so absurd!'

He grinned. 'So I've been told. Should I apologise?'

'Not for a m-minute!' Still giggling, Frances cast a brief glance over her shoulder and said, 'Oh good. We've shaken off Mr Woolrich.'

'Is that what we were doing?'

'Yes. He isn't remotely absurd – and quite dreadfully tenacious.'

'Well, that successfully punctures *my self-esteem,* doesn't it?' sighed Max ruefully. 'Worse still ... does it mean you aren't going to show me the artificial, hermitless grotto after all?'

'Knowing how much you're looking forward to it? I wouldn't be so cruel.' A hint of colour touched her cheeks and she avoided looking at him. 'As to your self-esteem ... you may regard it as being perfectly intact.'

Caught off-guard, he very nearly asked if that meant what he thought it might mean. But he stopped himself just in time and said, 'Thank you. I'm comforted.'

'Yes. I can imagine how worried you must have been.' She fell silent for a few moments as if debating something. Finally, on a renewed quiver of amusement, she said, 'Simon has told me all about you, you know.'

Max groaned. 'I sincerely hope he hasn't.'

'Well ... perhaps not *quite* everything. But enough, certainly.'

'Enough for what?'

She hesitated and then said simply, 'Why, enough for me to be sure that I would like you.'

CHAPTER THREE

'Enough for me to be sure that I would like you,' she had said.

Well, thought Max, looking into a face white with temper and eyes flashing sparks, *you certainly don't like me now – though I've no idea what I've done to merit it.*

Shock was still vibrating along every nerve. Shock ... and something else; something he was afraid to identify. But his priority now had to be getting her out of this room and away from their audience. Clearing his throat, he said expressionlessly, 'Forgive me. This is ... unexpected. If you will allow --'

'Forgive you?' she snapped. 'Right now, I'd like to *kill* you.'

'Frances – I don't know what you're talking about. But whatever it is, we should discuss it in private. So --'

'Why? Unlike you, I have nothing to be ashamed of.' Casting a glittering glance at Messrs. Balfour, Whitby and Royston, she said, 'If you're doing business with Lord Brandon, I suggest you be aware of his complete lack of consideration for --'

'That's enough.' Recovering at least part of his self-possession, Max took her arm in a firm grasp and propelled her towards the door. 'Hawkes will conduct you to my study. Wait there and I will join you in just a few moments.' And to his apparently dumbstruck butler, 'Hawkes! Now, if you please!'

'Yes, my lord. Of course. This way, madam.'

Slicing Max with a look of blistering contempt, she swept from the room, leaving him to pick up the pieces as best he could with the Rothwell officers. He said, 'Gentlemen, you'll have to forgive me. It seems I must deal with this immediately and can't predict how long it may take. Please continue your discussions with Mr Balfour. He has my full authority. Duncan ... ask Hawkes to send coffee and take over, will you?'

'Of course.' Both face and tone were grim. 'Go.'

He nodded and walked out, feeling both discomposed and helpless.

What the hell was this all about? Just for a moment, he wondered if it could have anything to do with Grey. But how could it? It had been five years, after all. Five years since he had last seen Frances Pendleton. Five years with nothing to connect them ... and little or nothing even before that. So why was she here now? Here, in his home. If there was trouble – trouble for which she somehow held him responsible, where were her menfolk? Where, he thought, was her father ... not to mention her bloody husband?

There were so many questions. Too many. For a moment, Max stood at the study door trying to regulate his breathing and find some semblance of calm. Then, accepting that he couldn't, he put his hand to the latch.

Inside the room, Frances stood motionless by the window, waiting and trying not to think. In that first moment ... the moment she'd seen him again ... the past had tried to suck her in, its pull so strong that she had feared she wouldn't be able to withstand it this time. He was there in front of her, within touching distance and looking every bit as severely handsome as he had when she'd first met him. Thick almost black hair, fathomless dark grey eyes and bones sculpted by a master hand. Temptation personified. But she had resisted both him and the lure of what had once been between them. After all, she'd had four years, six months and seventeen days in which to learn how.

Even so, when she heard the door open and then close behind him, it took her several seconds to find the courage to turn around ... and when she did, she looked anywhere except at his face.

Finally, Max said quietly, 'Frances ... why are you here?'
'Don't pretend. You know.'
'If I knew, I wouldn't be asking. You'll have to tell me.' He waited and when she didn't speak, said flatly, 'I can't play games. Not now and not with you. What is it you believe I have done?'

Frances finally forced herself to meet his eyes and was unprepared for the wave of anguish that washed over her.

You didn't come. Why? I waited and waited because you'd promised. I was so, so sure you would come. Why didn't you?

The words were so loud inside her head that for one horrible instant she was afraid she'd actually said them ... and even more afraid that, deeply as she'd buried it, the answer to that question mattered more than the thing which had brought her here. Stiffening her spine and summoning every scrap of both pride and courage, she said, 'Very well. You have lost my brother the only chance of suitable employment that has come his way in months.'

'*What?*' He couldn't believe he'd heard her correctly. 'How on earth could I do that? I haven't been near you or yours in five years.'

'You've been near my brother, God help him,' she said bitterly. 'Sir Rufus Pendleton – if you really need reminding. And please – *please* don't try convincing me that you didn't know who he was because you must have done. Unless, of course, you've erased me from your memory so completely that his name meant nothing?'

'No.' A small, wry smile twisted his mouth. 'I haven't done that.'

'Oh.' She swallowed, unsure why something in those words or perhaps the tone in which they were uttered threatened to overset her. 'Well, then. You can't have failed to know who Rufus was. But you didn't let the knowledge stop you, did you? And you were damned careful not to tell him that we – that you and I once knew each other.'

Max shoved a hand through his hair and stared at her uncomprehendingly.

'Frances … on my honour, I promise you that I've never met your brother.' She made a small contemptuous sound that infuriated him. He said frigidly, 'If my word isn't good enough for you, I'll swear it on the Bible if you like. *I have never met your brother.*'

For the first time, a hint of doubt crossed her face but then she shook her head, dismissing it. 'I thought you said you wouldn't play games?'

'I did and I'm not.'

'Then why not just *admit* it?' she demanded. 'You can't have forgotten already. You met him at the George in Stamford ten days ago. He was on his way to King's Lynn for an interview as Lord Cherwell's secretary. Does any of this sound familiar?'

'No. I wasn't --'

'You dined with him. You *befriended* him, damn you! You wouldn't have found it very difficult, of course. Rufus is barely out of university and still green as grass. He'd be flattered by being noticed by an older gentleman – one with some experience of the world.' Frances stopped, breathing rather hard. 'So he confided in you. He told you that Father had left nothing but debts. He told you he needed to take employment if our younger brother was to have any chance of completing his education. He told you how hard he'd found it even to be offered an interview. And all the while he was pouring his heart out, he matched you glass for glass – with the inevitable result.'

She stopped again, seemingly unable to continue.

Max hadn't known of her father's death. After that cataclysmic occasion five years ago, he'd never so much as opened the society pages with their listings of births, marriages and deaths. And no one had told him about Sir Horace Pendleton's demise because no one had any reason to suppose he might be interested. For the rest, her story was beginning to send ice sliding through his veins. Bizarre as it seemed, could her brother have fallen into Grey's clutches? If so, how the hell could that have happened? And why?

How could Grey have known I'd ever met Frances or guessed what no one else ever suspected? he wondered, returning to his earlier thought, *None of this makes sense.*

His head was awash with thoughts and questions; *too* many and completely jumbled. He could end this now, of course; could easily prove Frances wrong. But the longer she clung to her misconceptions, the deeper grew the hole that anger and hurt were carving in his chest ... and which made him perversely determined to see how far she would take it. So he said tonelessly, 'Since nothing you've said so far is particularly heinous, I'm assuming the real perfidy is still to come. Finish it.'

Frances looked at him with utter disdain. 'Do I really need to?'

'Unless you want me to guess.' Controlling himself was becoming difficult. If he wasn't very careful, he might start shouting. 'Very well. Your brother got drunk and either botched his interview or missed it completely. Am I close?'

'Of course you're close. Why are you still pretending? Rufus got drunk but not *quite* so drunk that he didn't remember he was to catch the Mail Coach at five the following morning. You told him not to worry about that because you were heading eastwards yourself and would be happy to take him up in your carriage – thus allowing him to rise at a civilised hour. Needless to say, Rufus was exceedingly grateful.' Her mouth curled in a derisive smile. 'He would have been even *more* grateful had you still been there in the morning – or even left orders for someone to wake him in time to catch the Mail. But you weren't ... and you didn't. Consequently, when Rufus presented himself at Cherwell Manor twenty-four hours later than he should have done, the earl wouldn't even receive him. He merely had his butler inform Rufus that clearly neither his reliability nor his organisational skills were of the level Lord Cherwell would expect of his secretary.'

Max stared at her and let a long, unpleasant pause develop. Finally, his voice dangerously low, he said, 'You actually believe this, don't you?'

'How can I *not* believe it?' Suddenly she wasn't quite so certain. Floundering a little, she said, 'You're Lord Brandon. There isn't another one, is there? So --'

'But you *know* me, Frances – or you did. You know me and yet you actually *believe* that I could do something as malicious as this – not only to your brother but to anyone.'

'Are you saying you didn't?'

'I said that some time ago, if you recall – but you refused to listen. And this is all circumstantial, isn't it? Every bit of it. You know only what your brother told you.'

'That and the loss of our grandfather's watch,' she shot back.

This apparent bolt from the blue all but rocked him on his heels. '*What?*'

'It isn't particularly valuable but Rufus treasured it. He was proud of it, too – which is why he took it out to show it off. Next morning, when he discovered he no longer had it he realised he must have left it downstairs when he retired for the night. But of course there was no sign of it – so the obvious c-conclusion --'

'Enough.' The volcano of temper that had been gradually building inside Max's chest finally erupted. His voice cold and sharp as a razor, he said, 'You would be wise to draw the line at accusing me of theft, Frances. I won't tolerate that from you any more than I would from a man. The only difference is that *you* won't find yourself facing me over a couple of pistols. However ... let us return to your brother – who is not merely green but imbecilic if he leaves treasured possessions lying about at a public inn and expects to have them returned to him. As for his naiveté in placing his trust in a perfect stranger ... that speaks for itself, don't you think?'

'Perhaps,' she admitted. 'I – I don't know! All I know is that it happened and --'

'Oh I don't doubt that it *happened*,' ground out Max. 'Just not quite as you think. Sir Rufus met a man who proceeded to make a fool of him. But that man was not I.' Aware that he was physically shaking, he folded his arms to disguise it. 'But you would rather believe that I tripped across your brother by accident and deliberately set out to ruin his future, wouldn't you?'

'You think I *wanted* to?'

'That is immaterial. The fact that you *did* makes very plain how low an opinion you have of me.' Turning, he wrenched open the door and, addressing the footman in the hall, said curtly, 'Ask Mr Balfour to join me here immediately.'

'Yes, my lord.'

Frances was beginning to feel sick. She said, 'Who is Mr Balfour?'

'He is my private secretary. He's been with me for eighteen months and lives here in the house. Amongst other things, he attends to most of my correspondence and keeps my diary.' A chilly, impersonal smile curled Max's mouth. 'Perhaps his word will carry more weight than mine.'

Silence, icily destructive, enveloped them again. No longer quite so sure about anything, Frances didn't dare speak ... and Max, furious and miserable, decided that he'd already protested his innocence once too often.

Duncan appeared in the doorway, felt the chill before he

even set foot in the room and said, 'You wanted me, Max?'

'Yes. Please list my recent whereabouts for this lady.'

He blinked. 'You've been here.'

'At Brandon Lacey?'

'Yes.'

'Since when?'

'Since just before Christmas when you came back after your sister's wedding.'

'So I was here ten days ago?'

'Yes.'

'Thank you.' He watched Frances clutch at a chair-back, looking slightly faint. 'Well? Nothing to say? Don't you want to argue the point?'

Wordlessly she shook her head. Max gave a tiny, harsh laugh.

Making the obvious assumption, Duncan muttered, 'Grey?'

'It would seem so – though I don't know how he did it. However – briefly – how are you getting on with Whitby and Royston?'

'It's encouraging. The company is well-managed and financially sound. But they won't put the figures in front of me without some assurances from you.'

'Give them. Pledge the investment they expected from Grey and hint that it might be more if the balance sheet warrants it. You'd also better make my apologies and let them know that it is you they need to impress.'

Duncan nodded and held Max's eyes, a hint of worry lurking in his own.

'Anything else?'

'No. We'll speak later.'

Still holding the chair in a death grip, Frances waited until the secretary had gone and then, her voice a mere thread, said, 'Who is Grey?'

If possible, the storm-grey eyes grew darker and even colder.

'Is that *really* the first thing you want to say to me at this point?'

'No.' She drew an unsteady breath. 'I – I'm sorry.'

'Yes. You should be.'

'I know. I don't ask you to forgive --'

'Good – because that is currently beyond me. You accused me of theft, Frances. You questioned my integrity and refused to accept my word of honour. Had we been total strangers, those things might have been – if not forgivable – at least understandable. Since we're not, they are completely unacceptable.'

'I know.' Shaking in every limb, she said, 'May I sit please?'

'Oh – by all means. Ready to discuss this reasonably now, are you?'

Staring down at her hands, she nodded wordlessly. Of course he was angry. He had every right to be. She hadn't asked – she'd accused. She hadn't even listened – or not to him. She'd let a different rage and misery take over ... as if being able to believe him guilty of one thing would ease the pain of another. She had been spectacularly wrong; and she had the terrible feeling that she'd known it, even as she had continued railing at him.

Max remained on his feet looking down on her. She looked drained and defeated ... and a voice at the back of his mind told him that, for the time being at least, he should put his anger aside. But it was *her*, damn it. It was Frances. She of all people should have known better, yet she'd found it feasible to think him some species of villain. And that was why he had to hold on to his wrath. If he didn't, the hurt would win.

To stop himself saying anything he shouldn't, he answered her original question.

'Grey is how we refer to a man who has been playing fast and loose with my name for some time now. He is the reason two officials of a steam company are currently in my library. He is also, quite possibly, the man your brother met in Stamford.'

Flinching, she glanced up at him then. 'You don't know who he is?'

'No.'

'Or – or why he is doing this?'

'Again, no. He has defrauded innkeepers and the like by having them send their bills to me – which suggests that, for reasons of his own, he wishes to cause me aggravation and embarrassment.'

Frances was beginning to understand, not only the hopelessness of her quest, but just how great an injustice she had done Max. She said, 'Don't you know anything at *all*?'

'Very little. He's virtually impossible to track because he's constantly on the move. I know what he looks like because he had the gall to come here in person and sell my brother a stolen horse and because, when they were shown his likeness, my visitors confirmed that he was the same man they had met.' Max paused briefly and then added, 'But your brother's case is somewhat different in that Grey can't have known there was any ... connection ... between you and me because, unless I'm very much mistaken, *no* one knew it.' Unable to keep his voice completely free of bitterness, he went on without giving her time to speak. 'Since I can't account for that, I don't know what to make of it. At present, the only explanation seems to be that Grey met your brother by chance and couldn't resist playing with him ... but I'm finding that hard to swallow.'

'I see.' Frances came slowly to her feet. This had been a disaster in every sense and it was probably irreparable ... but the very least she owed Max was a proper apology, so she lifted her chin and tried. 'I'm sorry. Truly, I am. I apologise for everything I said and – and everything I thought. Deep down, I sensed that it had to be wrong but ... well, I had nowhere else to turn. However, I've caused more than enough disruption to your day and should leave.' For the first time since she had arrived, she sent him a look that he recognised. 'Thank you for not showing me the door. Most gentlemen would have, I'm sure.'

Max's chest ached. Despite everything that had happened in the last half hour, he realised that he didn't want to watch her walk away. Finding a less abrasive tone, he said wearily, 'Sit down, Frances. I'll ring for tea and we'll see if there's anything I can do to help.'

'That's kind and more than I deserve,' she replied, pulling on her gloves. 'But there really isn't anything, is there? And if I start back this afternoon, there's a chance I'll get home late tomorrow.'

He frowned. There was something odd, if not actually wrong,

in this. Trying to pinpoint what it was, he said, 'How did you travel here?'

'In a hired carriage. I spent last night at the Red Bear in Knaresborough and --'

'Alone?'

She smoothed the gloves over her hands. 'Yes.'

'Without even the protection of a *maid*?'

'Yes. Scandalous, isn't it?'

That remark was so like the Frances he had known that he almost smiled. But it was also yet another thing that didn't make sense. Her father was dead and Rufus sounded like a broken reed. But she had a husband; a very *wealthy* husband who could well afford to take care of her family. So why did it appear that he wasn't? And that wasn't all. Max had never thought much of Lord Malpas ... but surely even *Archie* wouldn't let his wife travel around the country unaccompanied and in a hired carriage? Then again, why the hell wasn't it Archie who was here demanding explanations, rather than Frances? Max told himself he ought to ask. He wasn't sure why he hadn't already done so – except that, in spite of the hurt and desperately though he tried to ignore it, there was a tiny part of him that was too glad of her presence to want it to end.

He had addressed her throughout their meeting by her given name. This was mostly because he thought using her married title might choke him. But there was also the matter of his not being entirely sure what that title was. It had been five years. Archie might still be Viscount Malpas or, if his grandfather had died, he would now be the Earl of ... whatever title his father had held. Max, of course, had no idea. He didn't keep abreast of society news ... and on his infrequent visits to London it had been easy to avoid Archie and the crowd he ran with because, even at university, they had never been friends. Now, it occurred to him to wonder if something had happened to Archie – which would explain a good many of the things that were puzzling him.

He was still trying to find an acceptable way of asking when Frances said prosaically, 'I shall be quite all right, you know. I arrived here safely and see no reason why I shouldn't return the same way.'

'That may well be true. But --'

'I can manage without a maid and am well past the age of needing a chaperone.'

She moved towards the door, increasingly aware that if she didn't get away from him soon the past would become unavoidable. Already, it was crowding her mind with how it had been between them ... and everything she had felt both then and afterwards.

Frances was two steps from escape when Max stopped her with three words.

'Where is Archie?'

She froze and turned, staring blankly at him. 'Archie?'

'Yes. Archie. Lord Malpas or whatever his title is now. Surely he ought to be here instead of you – so why isn't he?'

Blankness became confusion. 'Because it's nothing to do with him.'

'*What*? Of course it's something to do with him!'

'No, it isn't. Why would it be? Rufus is *my* brother and--'

'Rufus could be your second-cousin, four times removed for all the difference it makes,' snapped Max irascibly. 'A gentleman – no, a *man* cares for his family. *All* of his family. And when problems arise, he shoulders them. He does *not* leave his wife to do it for him.'

The blood drained slowly from her face and, for a moment, he thought she was going to faint. Her voice a mere thread, she said, 'Wife? Oh.' And then, 'No.'

'No? What does that mean?'

She shook her head, seemingly incapable of speech.

Inside Max's chest, something gave a single, hard thud. Dragging in a painful breath, he said quietly, 'Frances ... why isn't your husband here?'

He waited, watching her seeming to grope for the words she needed. Finally she said raggedly, 'Because he isn't ... Archie isn't ... m-my husband.'

CHAPTER FOUR

For the second time that day, the floor shifted beneath Max's feet and the room blurred at the edges.

'*Archie isn't my husband.*' Had she really said that?

Unable to take in the enormity of it, he felt himself gaping at her. But finally, he managed to say, 'Not?'

'No.'

He had to remind himself to breathe. He also had to fight off the peculiar sensation that he was elsewhere and this wasn't really happening – because, clearly he wasn't and it was. Still struggling to find some sense of reality, he briefly and idiotically wondered if she and Archie had divorced. Then he realised that a divorce was something he couldn't have *failed* to know about. It would have been all over the newspapers – not merely confined to the society pages. So if Archie wasn't her husband, that must mean she hadn't married him ... except that he knew, none better, that she had.

Forcing the words past the rawness in his throat, he said, 'How can that be? I saw the notice of your wedding in the *Morning Chronicle*.'

Another silence yawned about them ... weighed down with foreboding.

Eventually, her heart heavy and cold in her chest, Frances said unevenly, 'If you saw that, then you must also have seen ...' She stopped.

'Seen *what*, for God's sake?'

She shut her eyes, unable to look at him ... unable to do anything but think, *He didn't know. Oh God - he didn't know,* over and over. Speaking was suddenly a Herculean task. But finally she whispered, 'The retraction.'

'Retraction?' he echoed, as if the word was in a language he didn't know.

'Yes. It was ... it appeared in the paper on the following day.'

He shook his head as if to clear it. 'I must be very slow ... because I don't understand what you're saying. Why --?'

And got no further as the door opened and his mother

breezed in, talking as she came.

'Max, dearest – there is wonderful news from Rockliffe! He writes that --' Louisa stopped, belatedly aware that she was interrupting. 'Oh. I'm so sorry. I had no idea you had company.' She smiled at Frances, glanced about the room and then looked back at her son. 'But why are you keeping this lady standing? And why have you not offered her tea? Really, Max, I thought I had brought you up to know better.'

Max didn't want tea. What he wanted was a stiff brandy. And what he really *needed* was for the refrain of *Five years. Five bloody years and I didn't know*, to stop filling his head. But he had somehow to hide the turmoil inside him from his mother, so he summoned something he hoped resembled a smile and said, 'And so you did, Mama. As it happens, the lady was on the point of leaving when it unexpectedly transpired that our ... business ... was not entirely concluded.'

'You are mistaken, my lord,' began Frances. 'It is *entirely* concluded and --'

'No, Frances.' cut in Max flatly. 'It is not – nor even close.' Seeing his mother's brows rise at his use of Frances's given name, he said smoothly, 'But allow me to introduce you to my mother. Mama – this is Mistress Pendleton. She is here on – on a matter concerning her brother.'

Frances sent Max a look of desperation and curtsied to his mother. 'Lady Brandon.'

Louisa smiled, reached out to take the girl's hands and said, 'I hope Max has been able to help, my dear. If he hasn't, I'm sure he will try. Have you come far to see him?'

'From Derbyshire, ma'am. Near Matlock. But truly, I have already taken up altogether too much of his lordship's time. And as I told him earlier, if I start back today I may hope to reach home tomorrow evening.'

'You won't do it,' said Max, not without a certain satisfaction. 'It's nearly two o'clock now and --' He stopped as Leo materialized in the doorway and said irritably, 'What?'

'The lady's driver wants to know if he's to wait or go back to Knaresborough.' Leo smiled engagingly at Frances. 'What should I tell him, ma'am?'

'To wait,' she replied. 'I shall be out --'

'I take it this isn't the carriage which brought you from Matlock?' interposed Max.

'No. The driver of that one wanted to rest the horses before making the return journey. So this morning I hired --'

'The one from the Red Bear,' he finished. 'Well, that makes it easy.' And turning, 'Leo – pay the fellow off and send him back.'

'*No!*' She almost shouted it. 'My lord, you take too much upon yourself --'

'Very possibly.'

'And how am I supposed to return to Knaresborough? My valise is --'

'I will drive you there myself. Later. Leo ... are you going?'

'Do not stir one *step*, sir! I am leaving this instant!'

'Good luck with that, ma'am. When my brother has the bit between his teeth, opposition is generally a waste of energy,' grinned Leo, still leaning against the door-frame. And then, 'What's it to be, Max? Are you going to let the lady go on her way?'

'Presently. So just get rid of the damned carriage, will you?'

'On your own head be it.' Leo shrugged and disappeared.

Throughout all this, Louisa had been looking from Max to Frances and back again with a confused mixture of suspicion and concern. Now she said, 'Enough, Max – and please moderate your language.'

'I beg your pardon, Mama.'

'Good. Now ... Mistress Pendleton. Do I understand that you journeyed from Derbyshire in a hired vehicle and put up at the Red Bear last night?' And when Frances nodded, 'May I take it that, along with your luggage, your maid is there?'

Frances coloured slightly and opened her mouth to speak but was forestalled by Max. The initially unwelcome arrival of his mother had produced a blinding moment of clarity. Without troubling to examine his reasons, he suddenly knew *exactly* what he wanted to do and also how to do it.

'Oh there's no maid, Mama. Frances doesn't need one, you

see. And she is *far* too old to require a chaperone.' He smiled innocently at Frances. 'That's right, isn't it?'

She pressed her lips together and said nothing while her eyes spoke volumes.

'Oh dear,' sighed Louisa. 'That really will not do, you know. Indeed, you were fortunate to get here safely. Anything might have happened. An accident to the carriage – footpads – *anything*. And Max is quite right. It is too late in the day to embark on a lengthy journey.'

'But --'

'However, the solution is quite simple,' she continued happily. 'We shall send to Knaresborough for your things, I will have a room prepared and you will stay here tonight as our guest.'

Frances could feel a scream building in her chest. She wanted to shout that she couldn't do this – that she needed to be alone, preferably locked in a dark closet – while she attempted to come to terms with the fact that Max hadn't known. And with the five dreary, achingly empty years that had been the result of it.

'My lady, that is extremely kind but --'

'Not at all. Since my daughter married, I have missed her company and so having yours for the evening will be a treat. Also, we can consider how best to get you safely home.' She turned to Max. 'When you have sent a groom to collect Mistress Pendleton's things, you may join us for tea in the drawing-room. Come, dear.'

Frances was swiftly concluding that Lady Brandon was an even more unstoppable force than her son. She was also becoming very tired of never being allowed to finish a sentence. Sending a baleful scowl in Max's direction, she trailed helplessly after his mother.

* * *

Having dispatched the groom and spent ten minutes signing papers with the Rothwell Company officers, Max raced to the drawing-room as fast as possible. It wasn't fast enough. By the time he got there, Leo was already lounging on a sofa with a cup of tea and Frances had apparently explained – mercifully without too much elaboration – that she and Max had met at the Westlake Abbey house-party in the summer of 1774. Max could tell by his brother's expression that Leo was going to have fun with this piece of information. What his mother thought was less evident except in one particular. She made it impossible for him to speak privately to Frances by sitting beside her all through tea and then accompanying her upstairs to a bedchamber.

The second the ladies left the room, Leo said lazily, 'Five years ago, Max? At a house-party lasting … *how* long?'

'A couple of weeks.'

'And now she's here asking your help for her brother? *Really*?'

'Really.' Deciding that distraction was necessary – not just for Leo but also from his own thoughts – Max took the easiest route. 'Rufus Pendleton was fooled into missing an important appointment by a fellow who used my name and was therefore probably our friend Grey – hence Frances's arrival here.'

He recognised the slip as soon as he had made it. So did Leo.

'Frances?' he queried. 'Just how well-acquainted *are* the pair of you?'

'Not nearly as well as you would like to think. Can you stop being provoking for a moment and focus on the real issue?'

'Which is what?'

'Weren't you listening? For reasons best known to himself, Grey enjoys annoying me and he has two methods of doing it. One is blackening my name with shopkeepers, innkeepers and my neighbours; the other is proving how close to home he can get with things like Mother's statue and that bloody horse. This is different. Why Pendleton … someone I've never met and with whom I have absolutely no connection, save that I once met his sister?' He stopped and drew a weary breath. 'If there's a link, I can't see it. But if it *is* Grey and he's trying to get my attention, he's damned well done it now.'

* * *

Upstairs in a comfortable, elegantly-furnished bedroom and blessedly alone at last, Frances lay in a scented bath, too tired and confused to stop the past intruding this time. She remembered the day in the garden at Westlake when she and Max had first met ... and then, inevitably, she remembered the one that had followed it.

* * *

She hadn't slept well. In fact, she'd tossed and turned throughout most of the night, grappling with knowledge that had burst upon her out of the blue and in the space of a single minute. Knowledge that was simultaneously both wonderful and terrifying.

When, almost a year ago, Papa had first told her that he and his old friend the Earl of Blandford were eager to unite the two families through the marriage of their children and that young Lord Malpas was agreeable to the notion, Frances hadn't minded. Or not very much, anyway. True, Archie wasn't very intelligent and he didn't have much of a sense of humour ... but he wasn't old or ill-looking and she saw nothing in him to dislike. So she had told herself she could do worse ... and that had worked perfectly well until yesterday. Yesterday when she'd met Max Brandon and fallen helplessly, ridiculously in love.

It wasn't merely a matter of extraordinary good looks; of thick, silky dark hair and beautiful storm-grey eyes; nor even the understated elegance, clothing perfect physical proportions. It was also a low, rich voice that slid over her like warm velvet; an invitingly teasing smile; and, more even than those things, his swift appreciation of the absurd. And suddenly the idea of marrying Archie Malpas was no longer palatable or even acceptable.

She had spent half the night dwelling on the hour she and Lord Brandon had spent together, marvelling at the way he had stolen her breath simply by looking at her and awakened her body just by taking her hand. And she spent the other half of it contemplating the reaction of her parents if she told them that she could no longer contemplate marriage with Lord Malpas. They were overjoyed that she'd be marrying a viscount; moreover, a very *rich viscount – and one who, on the death of his father and grandfather, would become the Marquis of Poole. They would be horrified if she refused the match without offering a good reason. And if she said that she was fathoms deep in love with a man she* had met for the first time mere hours ago, the results were likely to be anything but good.

But there was always hope, wasn't there? Archie hadn't arrived yet and wouldn't for at least a week. Frances didn't know what could happen in the space of a week ... but if the world could shift inside a mere moment then surely anything was possible?

She must have dozed a little because the next thing she knew, it was morning. It was too early to ring for her maid but she was too restless to linger in bed and when she threw open the window, a lovely day beckoned. It didn't need to ask twice. She scrambled haphazardly into her riding habit, tied her hair back in a ribbon and snatched up her hat.

In the stables, a new under-groom attempted to persuade her to let him accompany her, claiming that he'd lose his job if he let her ride alone.

'No you won't because I shall take the blame. Now ... saddle Pandora, if you please. I want to be away before anyone else comes down.'

Ten minutes later, she was flying across the fields enjoying the wind tugging at her hair, the exhilarating sense of freedom and the luxury of being alone. But when she reached the crest of the rise and reluctantly brought Pandora back to a canter, she heard the very last sound she wanted to hear. Hoofbeats, rapidly approaching.

No! she thought, gathering the reins ready to flee. *No, no, no! I don't want anyone. I don't want polite conversation. I don't want —*

Then she saw who it was ... and her heart threatened to leap into her throat.

Lord Brandon reined in a little way off, lifted one apologetic hand and said quickly, 'Forgive me. The stable-lad was anxious and I let him convince me to ...' He stopped, frowning. 'No. That's not entirely true. I didn't take much convincing to follow you – but I saw soon enough how unnecessary it was and could have changed my direction. So if you prefer to be alone, I'll go.'

'I – no.' Her lungs didn't seem to want to work properly. She hauled in a shallow breath and added, 'No. That is ... you need not. I – I would enjoy your company.'

'Thank you.' Smiling, he edged his horse closer to hers. 'You ride extremely well. In fact, the only female I know who might equal you is my little sister – but I'm probably biased since it was I who taught her.'

Although her pulse was still racing, Frances felt her nerves begin to settle. Casting him a mischievous glance, she said, 'You taught your sister to ride neck-or-nothing?'

'No. I taught her to ride with sufficient skill and confidence over ground she knew to be safe to be able to ride as fast as she chose. Isn't that what you were doing?'

'Yes. But you are the only man I've ever met who recognised it.' *What happened between us yesterday? she thought. If I asked, would you admit that you felt it too? For you did, didn't you? I was sure that you did.* But she said merely, 'Your sister is fortunate.'

He grinned suddenly. 'She knows and would agree with you.' Then, 'How unspeakably smug that sounds. I didn't mean it to. And now I suppose there's little chance of persuading you to dismount and walk with me.'

Frances felt her cheeks grow warm. 'Are you asking me to?'

'Yes – though I shouldn't, since we're alone and, having met me for the first time yesterday, you have no idea whether I can be trusted to behave as I ought.'

She stared at him thinking, *I know you. I feel as if I've always known you ... and we just hadn't met. But if she said that he'd probably think her mad,* so she smiled and said instead, 'I'll risk it. Are you going to help me down?'

Max blinked but wasted no time in dropping from the saddle and crossing to reach up to her. She put her hands on his shoulders and felt him grasp her waist as he slowly ... oh so very slowly ... lifted her down and set her feet on the ground. For far longer than was either necessary or proper they stood quite still, their eyes locked together, both seeming incapable of looking away. Frances saw answering knowledge in the unwavering grey gaze. She was aware of the pulse beating in his throat. She could feel his breath on her cheek, the warmth of his hands burning through gown and corset, the hard line of his shoulders beneath her fingers. Her breathing shortened, she swayed slightly towards him and ...

In one smooth movement, Max released her and stepped back offering his arm. Clearing his throat, he said, 'It appears we are to be blessed with another lovely day.'

'Of course. There is to be a picnic by the lake this afternoon so Lady Grantham will have put in a very firm order for sunshine.'

'And the weather always complies, does it?'

'Always. Everyone *complies* with her ladyship.'

'Ah. I'd best remember that.' He glanced down at her as they strolled slowly back in the direction of the house, the horses wandering behind them. 'Do you stay with the earl and countess a great deal?'

'Once or twice a year. There is a distant connection between our families, so Christmas is often spent here. And the summer house-party has become something of a tradition.' She looked back at him. 'This is the first time you've attended one, isn't it – though I can't believe it's the first time you've been invited.'

'No. The truth is that I generally avoid house-parties and plead the fact that August is a busy time at home, as my excuse. But Simon used his imminent departure as leverage, so I let him persuade me to come – if only for a few days.'

'Oh.' Frances swallowed a surge of disappointment. Keeping her gaze firmly away from his and her tone light, she said, 'Well, I expect he's happy to see you – for however short a time. And it's natural that you would rather be at home.'

He took so long to answer her that she thought he wasn't going to. But finally he said simply, 'Actually ... I suspect I've changed my mind about that. I think I might stay for the duration.' He slanted a smile at her. 'I don't suppose Simon would mind, do you?'

'No.' Hope blossomed. 'I'm sure he would be delighted.'

And then, so softly she barely heard it, 'Only *Simon*? That's disappointing.'

* * *

Suddenly aware that the water was growing cold, Frances

came reluctantly back to the present and climbed out of the tub to reach for a towel. She was going to have to face Max and his mother and brother over dinner so she supposed she'd better make some attempt to look presentable. Unfortunately, dressing didn't stop her mind turning.

Quite simply, it had never occurred to her that he might not know she hadn't married Archie. She'd assumed he *must* know – from her letters, if nothing else – and that therefore he would come for her. When he didn't ... when weeks, then months went by without a word ... she'd forced herself to accept that he had changed; that he had fallen out of love as easily as he'd fallen into it. Unable to bear the hurt, she had tried to hate him because she had not been able to do the same thing herself. Then she tried to hate him for being the cause of her burning her bridges and dooming herself to lifelong spinsterhood. And finally she tried hating herself for her own terminal stupidity in ever loving him at all.

She'd often tortured herself by imagining him married to someone else. Apparently, he wasn't – though that did not mean he wasn't betrothed or didn't have an interest elsewhere. However it was, he seemed determined to get to the bottom of what had happened five years ago ... and he would have two questions. Why had there been a wedding announcement if there had been no wedding? And why *hadn't* there been a wedding – since there had most certainly been a formal betrothal? Well, thought Frances sadly, she would have no difficulty answering either of those. Equally, she had two questions of her own – though she would probably ask only how he had managed to miss the retraction notice, printed the very next day. There wasn't, after all, a great deal of point in asking the only thing that really mattered. *If you had seen it ... if you had known I wasn't married ... would you have come?*

Frances thought that *What if ... ?* had to be the saddest and most useless question in the history of the world because, no matter what the answer was, the result was always the same. The inescapable fact was that Max hadn't known and he hadn't come. And now it was five years too late. She wasn't the person she had been then ... and she doubted if he was either.

It occurred to her that she was so bound up in things that might have been that she was forgetting the matter which had brought her to Brandon Lacey. Rufus – without both employment and grandfather's watch. The knowledge made her feel sick. Until three years ago when Father had died, none of them – not even Mama – had known of the debts and the parcels of land which had either been sold or mortgaged. They were why, Frances had finally realised, Papa had been so eager to see her married to Archie's money. She'd often wondered if – had she known – she might have acted differently. But she hadn't known. Gentlemen, she thought sardonically, were scrupulous about shielding their womenfolk from these unpleasant little details, leaving them to find out when they themselves were beyond either reach or censure. She tried *not* to think that her refusal to marry Archie might have been responsible for Papa setting his horse at a wall he'd known perfectly well had a steep ditch on the other side of it. It was enough that Mama blamed her. But since Papa's death, Mama had become a ghost who rarely left her room, even for meals and who spent her days lying on a chaise, a book or an embroidery frame idle in her lap; and an angry, complaining, demanding ghost at that.

A tap at the door heralded a maid who curtsied and said she'd been sent by her ladyship to see if Mistress Pendleton needed anything.

Frances shook her head. 'Thank you – but no. As you can see, I am quite ready.'

The girl cast a dubious glance at the out-moded russet taffeta gown but merely said hesitantly, 'Not to be impertinent, Miss ... but there's an hour till dinner, if you'd like me to do something prettier with your hair.'

The best part of an hour with only the maid for company sounded a better prospect than the drawing-room with Max and his family. Frances nodded and sat down before the mirror.

* * *

Lady Brandon entered the drawing-room to find her sons and Mr Balfour in apparently deep discussion. Smiling but in a tone that brooked no argument, Louisa told Leo and Duncan to remove themselves elsewhere. Then, the instant the door closed behind them, she said, 'And now, Max, I would like to understand the precise nature of your relationship with our unexpected guest.'

'I thought she had already explained it.'

'Oh, she did.' Louisa ticked facts off on her fingers. 'You met at the Westlake house-party, where you spent some time together. There has been no communication between you since then. But when your name came up in connection with an unspecified matter concerning her brother, she thought you might have information that would be useful.' She fixed him with an acute gaze. 'All of this may be true. But none of it explains why she came here in person rather than writing ... or why you feel entitled to use her given name ... or why you are drinking brandy before dinner. Perhaps you'd like to clarify *those* things.'

I wouldn't, thought Max, draining his glass. But knowing he had to tell her something, said dryly, 'Very well. There was ... an attraction between us, with the result that we spent more time together than was probably wise, given that she was already promised to Viscount Malpas – a long-standing arrangement that both families wanted. The betrothal was formally announced at the Westlake ball the evening before I came home.' He paused, contemplating his glass and wishing it wasn't empty. 'Six weeks after that, the notice of their wedding appeared in the *Morning Chronicle*. Today I learned that the wedding never took place – though I've no idea *why* it didn't or how the newspaper managed to make such an error. As to why Frances came here ... her brother appears to have been the victim of a malicious practical joke. Suspecting that I was either a fellow sufferer or complicit in it, she wanted to find out which. And before you ask,' he finished a shade irritably, 'I'm neither. I know nothing of the matter and have no idea how my name came into it.'

Louisa considered this in silence ... knowing that, in essence it was probably true but aware that Max's account had left a lot of things out – most notably, she thought, his feelings for Frances Pendleton. The two weeks he had spent at Westlake Abbey were engraved on her mind because he had been unlike himself when he returned; uncommunicative, withdrawn and edgy. This uncharacteristic mood had lasted for several weeks ... after which he had disappeared for a fortnight, ostensibly to investigate replacement equipment for the weaving sheds and to meet a new supplier of dyes. He'd come back pale, drawn and looking generally unhealthy, claiming to have been laid low for a few days with a slight fever. Since Max had never suffered a day's illness in his life, Louisa hadn't believed a word of it; and now, she was beginning to suspect what the truth behind those weeks might actually have been.

Keeping her thoughts to herself, she said musingly, 'It all sounds very odd. Of course, one can't help wondering what happened to prevent the wedding ... but doubtless you are more concerned about her brother and what any of it may have to do with you.'

'Which is why I need to speak to Frances,' agreed Max, hoping his mother would take the hint and stop asking questions. 'I don't know exactly when her father died but it seems he left his family financially embarrassed and her brother in need of gainful employment which, as yet, he has failed to secure. It may be that I can help with that ... but first, I need more information.'

'Of course.' Louisa nodded and rose from her chair. 'It is all very unfortunate. The poor girl must be at her wits' end with worry. But really, Max ... travelling all this way alone? What can she have been thinking?'

'She was clutching at straws, Mama. But you need not worry. She won't be travelling back the way she came – even if I have to drive her home myself.'

CHAPTER FIVE

Dinner was both less awkward and less nerve-racking than Frances had expected it to be. Lady Brandon set the tone with the usual well-mannered small talk; condolences on the death of her father, enquiries about the health of her mother and reminiscences regarding Lord and Lady Grantham – with whom Louisa had some slight acquaintance. The gentlemen discussed the meeting with the Rothwell officers – most of which Max had missed thanks to Frances. Mr Balfour described Secretary Royston as a canny gentleman and Leo volunteered to accompany Max if and when he decided to visit the foundry in Leeds. From time to time, Frances sensed Max's gaze resting on her but took care not to meet it. It was alarming to discover that she was no less attuned to him now than she had been five years ago ... and tempting to wonder if it was the same for him.

At some point towards the end of the meal, Lady Brandon said, 'Good heavens – I almost forgot the letter from Rockliffe! He says that Adeline has been delivered of a healthy boy. Both are doing well and the baby is to be named Charles Louis. Isn't that good news? Rockliffe is clearly delighted – though no less besotted with little Vanessa.'

'I doubt if Rock is as delighted as his brother,' remarked Max with a smile. 'I've never met a man so eager to stop being a duke's heir as Nicholas Wynstanton.'

Louisa turned to Frances, saying, 'You must forgive us, Mistress Pendleton. The Duke of Rockliffe is a distant – a *very* distant – connection of ours. But we were guests in his London home last November in the weeks surrounding Arabella's wedding.'

Frances nodded. 'I believe I saw the notice of it in the newspaper. She married the gentleman they are calling the Virtuoso Earl, did she not?'

Her ladyship's reply was all but drowned by Leo's crack of laughter and Max muttering, 'God – I'll bet Julian just *loves* that.'

'Very possibly. But he *is* a virtuoso and he *is* an earl – so it's no more than the truth, is it?' retorted his mother, rising from the table. 'Max ... if you and Mistress Pendleton have things to discuss, the library might be best. Leo and Duncan ... you may join me for tea in the drawing-room.'

'Now?' asked Leo, startled.

'Now,' agreed Louisa firmly. And she herded them from the room.

Left looking across the table at Frances, Max came slowly to his feet.

'Mother has spoken. In this house, that carries the weight of a royal decree ... so the library it is. Shall we?'

It was the moment she had dreaded and was still hoping to avoid.

'Surely there can be nothing left to say? I came on a fool's errand and --'

'Stop.' Both face and voice suddenly hard, he stalked round the table to grasp her elbow and draw her to her feet. 'Just stop, Frances. After the bombshell you threw at me earlier, do you honestly think I can let this rest? I *loved* you, for God's sake. I loved you and believed that you loved me ... but everything suddenly fell apart and I didn't know why. For five bloody years I've thought you married – only to learn today that you weren't. So come to the library where we can be sure of some privacy and let us clear up this unholy muddle.'

* * *

Max fell in love so hard and fast it left him dizzy. And yet it did not seem in the least odd. On the contrary, it was as natural and effortless as breathing. As if every day of his adult life had been leading to the moment when he would lay eyes on Frances Pendleton and just know, deep inside, that she was the woman he had been waiting for; the one who would complete him. He shook his head over that thought, laughing a little. A week ago, if someone had asked him, he'd have said he was entirely complete, thank you very much – and marriage could wait a few years yet. Now everything was different. The air was crisper, the colours brighter, every sound clearer; and all because of her.

He refused to worry about Simon's warning.

She's more or less betrothed to Archie Malpas.

That couldn't be right. Or if it was, it couldn't be immutable. Frances might not belong to him yet ... but Max had a bone-deep conviction that she would. From the first moment, there had been a connection between them; a current of something so strong it was almost tangible and which, as yet, neither of them quite knew how to handle. And a joyous, vibrant girl like Frances most certainly did not belong with Archie Malpas – who, aside from being one of the dullest men on the planet, had a reputation for being unable to keep his breeches fastened. So Max told himself that 'more or less' wasn't definite ... and merely meant that, for the time being, it was necessary to be mindful of appearances.

And so it began. Days of stealing precious time together ... sometimes by design, like their early morning rides ... and sometimes by accident, as if some strange gravitational pull was at work. Every day brought snatched moments of magic. Every evening was one of excruciating care throughout dinner and the entertainments that followed it, so that no one would remark on their growing closeness. There was an instant rapport between them. They talked of anything and everything. They teased each other and laughed at the silliest of jokes. Occasionally in company, they sought each other's eye when something struck them as foolish or funny. But there were two things they did not *do. Aside from when Max helped her down from her horse, they did not touch. And they never mentioned Archie ... finding it easy, since he wasn't there, to relegate him to the shadows.*

And then, as had been inevitable from the beginning, everything changed.

It was late afternoon. While most of the guests went to their rooms to rest before dressing for the evening, they had formed the habit of meeting briefly in the copse by the lake. But on this particular day, Frances was late and Max was growing increasingly tense. At best, the short time which was all they could have would be even shorter. At worst, she might have been prevented from coming at all.

The relief when he heard running footsteps was so acute he strode forward to meet her ... which was how she came to run, quite literally, right into his arms.

He didn't stop to think. With her body against his and every sense overflowing with her, there was nothing except instinct. His arms closed about her, his mouth found hers ... and oh, the sheer rightness and sweet, exultant bliss of it; then the massive strength of will it took not to feast but to merely brush her lips in a light, teasing way that was almost a question.

But when Frances put her arms about his neck, restraint became impossible. He gathered her close and closer still, one arm about her waist and the other at her nape. He groaned her name and kissed her again, differently. This time it wasn't a question. It was all heat and hunger and, more than either of those, a wave of emotion more powerful than anything he'd ever experienced. And Frances responded with answering fire ... sighing into his mouth, her fingers sliding against his throat and through his hair.

It took him several moments to hear the faint voice of reason at the back of his mind and several more to heed it. But finally and very reluctantly, he released her, stepping back to create a little space between them. Her breathing was as uneven as his and he suspected that the expression in her eyes mirrored the one in his own. Then she reached out to touch his cheek and she smiled; a sweet, radiant smile that made his heart stutter.

Catching her fingers in his, he said huskily, 'I love you. There ought to be better words for something as huge as this but these are the only ones I know. I love you.'

Her smile trembled and her eyes grew luminous. 'They're beautiful words, Max.'

'Yes.' He swallowed hard. 'I shouldn't ask but --'

'And you need not. It – it's the same for me. Of course it is.'

His hand tightened on hers. 'I'm not alone, then?'

She shook her head. 'I've loved you since that very first moment.'

'I, too.' Euphoria filled him, making him feel as if he was floating. Drawing her back into his arms, he whispered, 'You should know that this is new to me. Not only knowing beyond all doubt the instant I saw you ... but love itself.' He smiled suddenly and added, 'I'm saying I don't make a habit of it – in case you

were wondering.'

Frances rewarded him with a tiny gurgle of laughter and kissed his jaw.

'I wasn't. This moment is too perfect to spoil with foolish thoughts.'

And that was when one not-so-foolish thought touched Max's mind, like the snake sliding into Paradise. Once more setting her away from him, he said gently, *'But there is something that can't be ignored, isn't there? Perhaps we ought to speak of that.'*

She didn't pretend not to understand and he watched her eyes clouding.

'I – yes. I suppose we should.'

He waited and, when she didn't continue, said, *'Simon told me that you are 'more or less betrothed' to Lord Malpas. Is that true?'*

'Yes.' The word was no more than a breath.

He nodded, feeling himself come back to earth.

'What does that mean exactly?'

'There has been an ... understanding ... for over a year,' she said reluctantly. *'Archie's father and mine have been friends since they were at school and they decided to unite their families through marriage. Mama says it's also to do with linking two very old and distinguished bloodlines – but that's probably because she disdains any title that is less than two hundred years old. At any rate, when it was suggested, Archie had no objections and, though I was scarcely enthusiastic, I made none either.'*

Not needing to wonder what Lady Pendleton would think of his own title – conferred on his grandfather and a mere sixty years old – Max returned to the thing he most needed to know and which she still hadn't told him.

'So is there a formal betrothal or not?'

'No. Contracts haven't been drawn up yet and there's been no announcement.'

'So it isn't fully binding as yet?'

'No.'

'Do you want it to be? Do you want to marry Archie?' Somehow, he managed to keep the urgency out of his voice. *'If*

you do, please tell me now. This – this thing that has grown between us was just about acceptable while we weren't going beyond simple companionship. But today has changed that. If you are going to marry Archie, my behaviour becomes dishonourable. And though stepping aside will likely kill me, I have to do it.' He paused and hauled in a steadying breath. 'So ... I need to know what you want.'

She stared at him, her eyes wide and dark. 'You. I want you.'

The world rocked around him and his heart was beating so hard he wondered if she could hear it. 'You're sure? Archie may be boring as hell but he's rich and heir to --'

'I'm sure. I don't care what he's heir to. I don't want to marry him. I never did. And I'm quite, quite sure about that.'

'Thank God.' He released the breath he'd been holding, took her hands in his and sank down on one knee before he lost his courage. 'Then will you please marry me instead? I know it's sudden. I know your parents would prefer you to marry Archie – of course they would. But I love you, Frances – more than I can express. And ... well, do you think you might consider taking me instead?'

Tears sparkled on her lashes, making her smile sunshine through rain.

'Yes, Max. Oh yes.' She tugged at his hands. 'I'll marry you. I will.'

He rose to wrap her close, his cheek pressed against her hair and so full of emotion he thought he might burst with it. 'Thank you. I'll make you happy – I promise.'

'I know you will.'

Silence and peace settled around them. But finally Max said slowly, 'You have to tell your parents. I realise that persuading them to listen won't be easy ... but until you put an end to any possibility of marriage to Archie, my hands are tied. I can't ask for you while you're still promised to another man – however loosely. You see that, don't you?'

'Yes.' She smiled at him and reached up to smooth back his hair. 'Yes, of course. I'll tell them. But I suppose I shouldn't say anything about us until they've accepted it.'

'No,' he agreed a shade grimly, 'you shouldn't. And since I can't pretend I'm comfortable with that, the sooner you're free of Archie, the better.'

* * *

Sensing something powerful and barely repressed in him, Frances did not try to pull away. But when the library door closed behind them, she turned saying, 'We can talk, if that is what you want – but there is little point, since it won't change anything.'

'You think I don't need to know why, despite everything, you let them announce your betrothal to Archie Malpas? Or why – for five years and without a word to the contrary – I've believed you married to him? Oh – and let us not forget the wedding announcement of a wedding that didn't happen. For God's sake, Frances ... do I not deserve *some* kind of explanation?' He stopped, breathing rather hard. And then making a visible effort to regain his self-control, said, 'Forgive me. But I don't think you have any idea just how completely you've swept the ground from beneath my feet.'

'You think I'm any less shocked than you?' she retorted. 'I thought you knew. Everyone else did – *everyone*. It never crossed my mind that – that you might not. How should it?'

For the first time, a truly terrible thought occurred to Max. He wondered why it had taken so long. *Did you think I would come? Did you wait for me?* But he didn't ask ... didn't dare ask. Her answer might unbalance him completely. So instead he tested the water with a different but equally pertinent question.

'Frances ... why didn't you answer any of my letters?'

For a moment, she simply stared at him, her lower lip clenched between her teeth. Then she sank rather suddenly into the nearest chair and bent her head over her hands. Max noticed that they weren't steady. Finally she said unevenly, 'I never ... received any letters.'

Frowning, he took a couple of slow steps towards her. He had sent so many he'd lost count. 'None at *all*?'

'No. I never knew you had written. I supposed that you hadn't.' She looked up. 'Of course, that is what they wanted me to believe. I should have guessed but – but I didn't. As week after week went by with no word, I thought … I just thought …'

'That I had forgotten you?'

'Yes.' She hauled in a shuddering breath. 'Doubtless you didn't receive mine either.'

'No.' For the first time, he began to get some inkling of the campaign her family had waged to see her married to Lord Malpas. 'Did you write very many?'

'Dozens. My maid took them to be posted. I trusted her. She'd always been loyal and I believed she still was. It never occurred to me that she might be taking her orders from Mama instead.' She gave a tiny, bitter laugh. 'Looking back, it's so easy to understand. All Mama probably had to do was threaten her with dismissal.'

Max sat down facing her. As calmly as he could, he said, 'It seems they worked very hard at keeping us apart. When did they find out?'

'About us? I'm not sure that they did – or not then. They probably guessed that – that there *was* someone. But I doubt if they knew it was you until …'

She stopped, leaving Max to say grimly, 'Until you returned home from Westlake and my letters started arriving. Yes. We'll come to what happened after that in a moment. First, I'd like to hear why you went through with the damned betrothal after promising me that you wouldn't.'

'I tried to stop it. You know that.'

'I know some of it. After you promised to marry me, you told your parents that you didn't want to marry Archie. They didn't listen. Five days later, when Archie finally turned up you told him the same thing – and with the same result. Yet without your consent, both families agreed to announce the betrothal at the ball on that last evening. That was the last conversation you and I had because, for the remaining two days, you were so closely watched that we were unable to exchange a single word in private.' He paused and then said, 'What happened during those days?'

'More of the same,' replied Frances wearily. 'Papa's answer to the problem was to avoid both me and a conversation he didn't want to have. Mama listened ... or at least, she pretended to. She even seemed sympathetic. But nothing changed and time was running out. So instead of saying I didn't *want* to marry Archie, I started saying that I *wouldn't*. And that was when Mama made it impossible for me to stir a step without her knowing.'

Max nodded. 'I thought that perhaps your parents had guessed.'

Frances shook her head. 'No. But I'd planned to tell them once everyone had accepted that I meant what I said about Archie.'

'Which they never did. The betrothal was announced as planned and you stood there between your father and Archie, looking calm and composed and without making a single objection. Why?'

Frances's mouth turned dry and she looked away from him. He wasn't going to believe her – and why should he? If she could have explained at the time, perhaps ... but he had left Westlake that same night and she had neither seen nor had any communication with him since then. Telling him the truth now was going to sound like an excuse – and not a very plausible one at that. But since avoiding his eyes wasn't going to make it any better, she turned back to him and said, 'By the evening of the ball, I was desperate. So with only an hour or so left, I tried one last time with Mama. I repeated everything I'd said before – everything I could think of except that I was in l-love with you.'

She paused. He waited and, when she showed no sign of resuming, said gently, 'And?'

'And she seemed to be listening. I truly thought she was.' Frances could hear her voice growing flatter with every word. 'She patted my hand and told me not to worry. She would speak to Papa and everything would be sorted out. Meanwhile, I should stop agitating myself and take a glass of wine. It would calm me, she said.'

An unpleasant presentiment stirred in Max's chest. Once again, he waited.

Finally she said, 'I don't know what she put in it but whatever it was certainly did the trick. It turned me into a docile little doll for just as long as they needed to make the announcement. I don't remember it at all. I recall the crippling headache that followed it, though. It lasted almost two days. But by the time I felt better, you had gone.'

Bile rose in his throat. He said, 'God, Frances ... I'm so sorry.'

'Why? You couldn't have known. We went home immediately afterwards and the wedding was set for six weeks later. That was when I started writing to you ... and planning how to stop them forcing me into marriage the way they had forced me into betrothal. Fortunately, I had the sense not to put any of that in my letters, even though I didn't know they were ending up in Mama's hands rather than yours. I also stopped saying I wouldn't marry Archie. However, they must have suspected something because Papa put the wedding announcement in the newspaper early – so that it would appear on the day of the ceremony instead of the day after. He thought that if the world believed Archie and I had married, I'd have no choice but to make it true.' Something not quite a smile touched her mouth. 'He miscalculated. It was the last straw and I decided I'd *die* sooner than give way.'

All through dinner and without really being conscious of it, Max had registered the changes the last five years had wrought in the girl he had known. She was thinner; the bones of her face more clearly defined, making the lovely gold-flecked eyes seem larger. But the real changes came from inside. Gone was the ready laughter; gone also the bright glow of joy and hope. It was as if, he thought, all the light had been sucked out of her.

How had that happened? he wondered. *Did I have something to do with it? Or was it the result of the pressures your family put on you ... of learning your mother wasn't to be trusted ... and finally the money worries that followed the death of your father? God. I hope it was those things. Because if I'm responsible for any part of it ... if you were even* half *as destroyed as I was during those first months ... it would have been better if we'd never met at all and you'd simply married Archie.*

'What did you do?' he asked.

'I let them dress me for my wedding. I smiled at everyone

and behaved exactly as they wanted me to behave.' Having already decided that this was as much of the truth as he needed to have, Frances looked him in the eye and proceeded to lie. 'When everyone except Papa had left for the church, I locked myself in my room and barricaded the door. By the time they finally broke in, I'd cut my wedding dress to ribbons and Archie was apparently yelling that he wouldn't have me if I was the last woman on earth.' She shrugged slightly. 'There wasn't much anyone could do after that.'

'No. I don't imagine your parents took defeat well.'

'They didn't. Papa was apoplectic. In the end, I believe it was Lord Blandford who sent the retraction notice to the newspaper.' She eyed him coolly. 'How come you didn't see it?'

It was Max's turn to withhold a large part of the truth. He couldn't share that shameful fortnight in York with anyone – least of all her.

'I stopped looking at the society pages the day after I read the announcement of your wedding. Naturally, it never occurred to me that it might not be true.' He hesitated and then added tonelessly, 'That was when I stopped writing to you. But you ... were you still ...?'

'Yes.' She looked away across the room. 'But I don't suppose you received those letters either.'

'No.' The sudden surge of hot anger in his chest threatened to choke him. He thought, *If I ever lay eyes on your bloody mother, I'll probably kill her. One letter – just one – and it could all have been different.* And then, *You waited, didn't you? I know you did. But I don't think I can bear to hear you say it.*

For a long moment, neither of them spoke.

Then she said abruptly, 'I thought you'd be married by now.'

'That makes two of us, then,' he muttered bitterly.

Colour crept across her cheekbones and she rose abruptly to her feet.

'If there's nothing else, I'll return to the --'

'No. I'm sorry. That wasn't ... helpful,' interrupted Max jerkily. 'Please sit down again. We haven't discussed your brother's situation.'

'Is there anything to discuss? Rufus's problems are not of your making so --'

'No. They are not. But if the man he met in Stamford is the man who has been plaguing me, there is a connection that must be worth exploring. Also, I imagine you came here to demand I find Rufus employment, did you not? So please ... sit.'

With unconcealed reluctance, Frances sank back into her chair. She muttered, 'Have you *always* been this annoying?'

For the first time that day, he felt a spurt of genuine amusement.

'No. I've spent the last five years working on it.' Without warning, he bathed her in a brief, familiar smile. 'Why are you so eager to get away from me?'

Don't! thought Frances, everything inside her melting. *Don't smile like that and don't be kind. I can't bear it.*

'Isn't it obvious? I shouldn't have come. I *certainly* shouldn't have burst in on you like a mad woman, hurling accusations instead of simply *asking*. I've infuriated you and embarrassed myself and --'

'Let it go. I have.'

'Have you? So easily?'

'I didn't say it was easy. But nourishing one's anger is a waste of time and energy. Do you want me to find out if any of my acquaintances are seeking a secretary or not?'

She nodded helplessly. 'I – yes. That is very good of you.'

'It is, isn't it? Positively noble, in fact.' And when her only response was to look away from him, he said softly, 'Come on, Frances. Laugh at me. Tell me I'm a pompous, self-satisfied ass. Just don't sit there being grateful. This is *me*, remember?'

Yes. Of course I remember. I wish I didn't, was her unbidden thought. But she said stiffly, 'It has been a long time. People change.' And looking at him, 'You should have let me go on my way, Max. There is nothing between us now ... and I hold by what I said. It was wrong of me to come here.'

Was it? thought Max. *Or was the mistake waiting so long to do it? Why did you? Come to that, why did I? Did you ever wonder how our story would have turned out if I'd stormed down the middle of the Grantham's ballroom and carried you off? I thought of it. More than thought of it, if the truth be known.*

He said slowly, 'You're saying the clock can't be turned back? I know it. But I can't be sorry you came – if only because I suspect we have both been beset by unanswered questions all these years. At least now we know.'

'Yes,' agreed Frances dryly, getting to her feet again. 'So we do.'

CHAPTER SIX

Frances appeared at the breakfast table looking pale and heavy-eyed.

Max sympathised. He hadn't slept very much himself. He wondered if she had been kept awake by the same sort of things that had disturbed his own rest. Echoes, to begin with, of her words to him in the library.

It has been a long time.
People change.
There is nothing between us now.

He couldn't argue with the truth of the first two statements. But the third one? *Could* there ever be nothing between them? The notion left him off-balance and uneasy so he pushed it to the back of his mind. This turned out not to have been such a good idea because it made room for something he *really* didn't want to think about.

Understandably, if mistakenly, she had believed he must know that she wasn't married and had expected him to go to her. Of course she had. Knowing how she must have hoped and waited made Max feel sick. Worse still were the questions that raised. How *long* had she waited? How long had she *hoped*? When had she finally given up on him? And what had she thought then? That he was fickle and she, easily forgettable? Or that it had all been lies and he had never loved her at all?

At that point, he'd given up trying to sleep. Getting out of bed, he'd hauled on a robe and gone to stare into the darkness outside the window. His mind was still reeling from the discovery that she'd jilted Archie on what should have been their wedding day. That must have taken a great deal of both planning and courage. It also told him that she had meant what she'd said about repudiating the betrothal publicly if either family had tried to announce it at that thrice-damned ball.

Inevitably, this led him to ponder what she'd told him about that night and to damn himself for not realising that something wasn't right. He'd never once seen her face wiped of all animation and expression the way it had been then. He should have known something was wrong. Why the hell hadn't he? Had he been blind to everything but his own emotional knife-edge? The deep-seated fear that he might have to stand there and watch while he lost her because there was nothing he could do to stop it?

* * *

By the evening of the ball, Max hadn't had any opportunity to speak privately to Frances for two days and he was becoming increasingly frantic. It didn't bode well. If she had succeeded in making either her parents or Archie call off the betrothal, she wouldn't be so hedged about with chaperones that he couldn't get near her. Each hour that passed brought the ball closer and closer and his every instinct was screaming that the Pendletons and the Blandfords had joined forces and intended to announce the betrothal regardless of all Frances's persuasions or denials. And if that happened, she would be left with only two choices; yield to the pressure or refuse to be coerced, loudly and firmly before everyone.

The last time they had spoken, she had vowed she wouldn't let them force her.

'If I have to shout it out to the entire ballroom,' she had said, 'I'll do it.'

He hadn't doubted that she had meant it - although it was no small thing for a gently-bred girl to do. He'd said grimly, 'Let's pray that it doesn't come to that. Because if it does, I can't do anything – will have no right *to do anything - until you've publicly repudiated Archie.'*

'I know. But afterwards ... after it's done, you'll come to me?'
'In a heartbeat, love. I promise.'

The next forty-eight hours were the longest and most miserable ones of his life. Either Lady Pendleton or one of the other married ladies remained glued to Frances's side and he could do nothing but watch her in mounting frustration.

He could understand her parents' determination to see her married to an indecently wealthy man who would one day be a marquis. Lord Blandford's desire for the match was less easy to explain unless he was becoming concerned about his son's burgeoning reputation as a lecher. And as for Archie himself ... try as he would, Max couldn't fathom why any man could conceivably want to marry a girl who had told him to his face that she *didn't want* him.

By the evening of the ball, he had prepared as best he could for the worst possible scenario. He'd had his valet pack his bags and load them on the chaise. Then he'd ordered his coachman to be ready to leave at a moment's notice. If all else failed, he decided that he would storm through the Grantham's ballroom and announce to one and all that Frances would be marrying him. If necessary, he'd simply pick her up and carry her off. All he needed was some small sign from her. The merest gesture or glance would suffice.

He dressed carefully. A black brocade coat over a silver-embroidered silk vest. It seemed important though he wasn't sure why. And all the time, his heart was heavy with dread. They would try to take Frances away from him. He knew they would. He didn't know if he was going to be able to stop them. And the possibility that he might not *be able to was making it difficult to breathe.*

The ballroom was a blaze of colour and light. Max spotted Lord and Lady Blandford as soon as he walked in and a few minutes later he saw Archie lounging in the doorway of the card room with a couple of his cronies. Of Frances and her parents, there was no sign at all. Max would have liked to find that encouraging ... but something told him it wasn't. Simon Greville emerged at his side and teased him about something or other. Max responded without knowing what he said and was grateful when Lady Grantham summoned Simon to do his duty by the wallflowers.

And finally, just as the supper dance was beginning, Frances walked into the room, flanked by her parents. They took up a position near the orchestra's dais and were immediately joined by Lord and Lady Blandford ... and Archie. Minutes later, Lord Grantham also joined the group. Everything indicated that an announcement was about to be made. Too far away to see Frances's expression and something coiling unpleasantly in his stomach, Max started to edge closer. Her face was angled away from him. He wished she would turn. He *needed* her to turn so that she would see him. The urge to stride right up to her was overwhelming but he forced himself to resist it. She had said she wouldn't let this happen. She had *promised*. He had no choice but to wait for her to speak ... and it was bloody torture.

The music stopped, the dance ended and Lord Grantham's major-domo prayed silence.

Oh Christ, *thought Max*. They're going to do it. They're really going to do it. Look up, Frances. Look around. Find me. Look at me. Please, for God's sake, *look* at me.

For a seemingly endless moment, she didn't. She just remained, perfectly still, her hand tucked into her father's arm. Lord Grantham started addressing the assembled guests. His old friends Sir Horace and Lord Blandford, he said, had kindly given him the privilege of announcing that their families were to be united through marriage.

Max stopped listening, everything in him communicating silently with Frances.

Speak up, love. You must speak up now or it will be too late.

For an instant, it seemed that she had heard him. Her chin lifted a fraction and she turned very slightly in his direction ... just enough for him to see her expression and feel as if he had been punched in the stomach.

She looked serene, composed ... and utterly blank. Her gaze passed over his without a vestige of recognition. For a second, sheer disbelief deprived him of breath ... swiftly followed by a sensation of drowning. He thought, *She isn't going to do it. She's changed her mind. She's going to let it happen and I can't stop her. Why? Why*, Frances?

Wearing his usual inane smile, Archie stepped forward and reached for her hand. Passively, Frances allowed him to take it ... and Max suddenly realised that he couldn't bear to watch any more. He had to get out of there before he was sick.

He made it through the balcony doors and down into the garden. And then he vomited into the shrubbery.

* * *

He had thought that had been the worst of it but he'd been wrong. He had gone home and written letter after letter, pleading with her not to throw away what they felt for each other. She had not replied. And six weeks later, when he'd seen the notice of her wedding, it had been as if his chest had been sliced open with a blade. He couldn't think, couldn't function, could not – absolutely *could* not – be with his family. So he'd manufactured an excuse, ridden to York and taken a room in a part of the city where he could be sure of not meeting anyone he knew. Then he'd proceeded to drink himself into oblivion. He hadn't washed or shaved. He'd barely eaten. He simply drank until he passed out and then, waking up to find the animal still clawing at his insides, reached for the next bottle. He had spent ten days sodden with drink and might have spent ten more the same way had he not woken up one morning in a filthy alley, his purse and watch gone. This finally told him that, unless he was looking for an early grave, it was time to pull back from the brink while he still could.

He was responsible for Brandon Lacey and every man, woman and child who lived on it – not least, his own family. His father had been dead for five years and his mother still mourned him. Arabella was seventeen and due to make her curtsy to society next season; Leo was insisting on studying art in Italy instead of completing his degree at Cambridge ; and Adam was desperate to perfect his swordsmanship in the Paris academy reputed to be Europe's finest. Tending the land and its tenants was his own job; and wallowing in self-pity wasn't going to change the past or make him feel any better. It was time get a grip on himself and remember who he was.

It took four days to mend a little of the damage done by the previous ten; but at the end of them, he went home and picked up the broken pieces of his life. It was clear to him that both Mama and Belle had seen something was wrong. He was grateful to them for knowing him well enough not to ask.

It had been nearly a year before the pain eased. A *year* ... and *he* had both a loving family and enough work to occupy every waking moment. Frances had neither of those things. If she *had* hoped and waited, he couldn't begin to imagine how the hell she had coped with the disillusionment.

If he'd known the truth – if he'd had even the merest suspicion – he wouldn't have wasted a second in going to her. But he hadn't known ... and now she was here, telling him that it was too late. *People change. There is nothing between us now.* He didn't know which saddened him most ... the fact that she believed this to be true or the possibility that it actually *was*.

He looked at her across the table, watching her push food around instead of eating it. Leo was busy heaping his plate from the dishes on the sideboard; Duncan would join them when the day's post had arrived and been sorted into personal and business; and Mama always breakfasted in her rooms. This, then, was the nearest thing to privacy that they would have.

He said, 'Are you still determined to return home today?'

'Yes. There's nothing to be achieved by delaying.'

'Very well. Give me an hour. I'll have my valet pack a bag while Mr Balfour and I deal with any necessary matters and then we'll leave.'

'You don't need to do that,' she protested. 'I can easily hire --'

'Humour me. Quite aside from wishing to ensure you get back safely, I should meet your brother before recommending him for a position.'

'Oh. I see. Yes, of course.'

I also have a few things to say to your mother, thought Max. *But it's best you don't know about that yet.*

Frances went back to the absorbing task of cutting bacon into tiny pieces while she thought despairingly, *Why can't you just let me go? I'd got over you. I had. But this is going to bring everything back ... and I'm not sure I can bear it a second time.*

Leo sat down before a laden plate and said, 'What shall I do about Persephone's foal, Max? Weston and Lawley both want him and are trying to outbid each other.'

'Say no to both of them. We'll keep him for Belle's birthday,' replied Max absently. And then, as Duncan came in, 'Anything urgent?'

'Not especially. A handful of bills, a very belated payment

from Prestwicks and the report you asked for on the Langthorpe coal mine.' Mr Balfour handed over four letters. 'But one of these is odd.'

Max glanced through them. One from Adam, one from Arabella, one from Sebastian Audley ... and one addressed merely to Lord Brandon of Brandon Lacey and written in a hand he didn't recognise. Frowning slightly, he tossed the other three aside and broke the seal. Then he froze.

My dear Max, he read.

Forgive the familiar address ... but really, I am beginning to feel that I know you so well.

I do hope Lady Brandon is enjoying her sculpture. Sadly, Lady Ripley – or perhaps her husband? – was less than delighted. Such a shame.

Perhaps you are wondering why I am writing to you ... or then again, perhaps not.

I feel confident that, by now, you have been trying to find me and become frustrated by your lack of success. Doubtless the fair Frances's unexpected arrival will have you re-doubling your efforts. How did that feel, by the way? A mixed pleasure, I imagine.

But I should come to the point – and it is this. We shall *meet, Max, but at a time and place of my choosing. Meanwhile, here – should you wish to play – is my opening gambit. Sir Rufus Pendleton's watch may be recovered from the Castle Inn at Brough two nights from now. Will you come, I wonder?*

Yours in anticipation,

The signature was a pair of initials, so heavily convoluted as to be illegible.

Max threw down the letter and was out of his chair in one lithe movement.

'Who brought the mail today?'

Duncan's brows rose. 'Alfred from the Red Bear, as usual. Why?'

'Because *that* one,' he snapped, pointing at it, 'didn't arrive on the Mail Coach. Addressed like that, it can't have done. I'll lay money it was handed to Alfred this morning.' He drew an unsteady breath. 'He's here. Grey. He's somewhere nearby.'

'He's written to you?' Leo looked up from his breakfast. 'Saying what?'

'Later. I need you take Grey's likeness and show it to Alfred. Show it to *anyone* who may know something.'

'You want me to go to Knaresborough? *Now*?' Leo gestured to his plate. 'Can't it wait?'

'No. This is urgent – so for God's sake, just *move*, will you?'

Sighing, Leo picked up a sausage and pushed his chair back. On his way to the door, he said, 'You should know I don't intend to let you forget this.'

'Noted. Now go.' Max reached for Grey's letter and tossed it to Mr Balfour. Then, looking at Frances, he said, 'He knows you're here.'

'What?' She stared at him. 'He can't. How *can* he?'

'I've no idea. But he's offering to return your grandfather's watch if I go obediently galloping off to parts unknown. Which,' he added sourly, 'I probably will.'

She looked from him to the secretary and back again. 'May *I* see the letter?'

'Oh – by all means.'

Handing it to her, Duncan eyed Max thoughtfully.

'Arrogant, isn't he? Almost deliberately so, in fact.'

'In case I'm not already sufficiently annoyed? Yes. I noticed that. However ... where exactly *is* Brough?'

'In the North Pennines.'

'Half-way to *Scotland*? Wonderful.'

'A two day journey, I would think – which means leaving this morning if you're thinking of keeping this appointment. Are you?'

'Yes.' Scowling balefully, Max dropped back into his chair. 'He's unlikely to be there, of course. He says Pendleton's watch *may be recovered* from this inn. He doesn't say he'll return it in person. My guess is that his new game will be luring me into playing grandmother's footsteps with him. And he knows I'll do it because there's no other choice.'

'Yes, there is,' replied Duncan calmly. 'You could send me instead.'

Max shook his head. 'You think he'll let you catch up with him? He won't. It's me he wants. And *I* want the chance to ask a few questions, either side of a little satisfying violence. So check the distance to Brough and find me the best route. Then we can come up with an excuse for Mother – since I'd still rather not worry her with Grey's misdoings.'

As the door closed behind Mr Balfour, Max turned back to Frances and said, 'I'm sorry. If, as seems likely, I need to leave immediately, I'll have to make different arrangements for getting you home. The best thing might be --'

'Wait.' She smoothed the letter out and sat frowning at it. Ten minutes ago, two days in his company on the journey home had seemed unendurable. Now the possibility of a very different journey was opening up ... and it didn't seem unendurable at all. It beckoned and seemed almost ... desirable. Instead of allowing herself to contemplate exactly why that was, she began working out how best to convince Max of it and, looking up at him, said flatly, 'This changes things.'

'Obviously. But I can still get you home.'

'So you said. And you think I'd *go*?'

Max eyed her uneasily. 'Yes. Why wouldn't you? Half an hour ago you couldn't wait to get away from here.'

'Half an hour ago, I never expected to see Grandpapa's watch again – let alone have the chance to give a piece of my mind to the mischief-making fellow who stole it.' She stood up, colour burning in her cheeks. 'I'm not going home, Max. I'm coming with you.'

'*What*?' he snapped. Then, 'Oh no. Not a chance. It's impossible.'

'I don't see why. It need only take a few days and --'

'I have no idea *how* long it may take. Didn't you hear what I said to Duncan? Grey isn't going to make this easy. He won't be at the first destination – or even, quite possibly, at the second one. Unless I can out-guess him, he's likely to have me running around over the whole of northern England – so I am not, absolutely *not*, taking you with me. And don't – do *not* say you'll be happy to turn homewards as soon as the watch is in your hands. If I wouldn't permit you to travel alone from here, I certainly won't send you off on your own from God knows where.' Max drew a steadying breath and tried to silence the sly voice of temptation in his head; the voice that whispered, *She said there is nothing between you now. You aren't sure if that is true – either from her perspective or your own. If you want to find out, you need time ... and she's offering it.* The notion both tempted and alarmed, making him wish it hadn't occurred to him. Pushing it aside, he said, 'You want your brother's watch and you shall have it. I give you my word.'

'I also,' she insisted doggedly, 'have a few things to say to Grey.'

'And having a fair idea of what they are, I promise to make your feelings plain.'

'With your fists. Yes. I gathered that much and wouldn't dream of stopping you.' Frances faced him with a calm she didn't entirely feel. 'However, I'd as soon fight my own battles, if you don't mind. I've been doing it for a while and have become quite good at it.'

'I'll have to take your word for that because I am not taking you with me. No – listen to me. I want to travel fast and light. I will be driving myself. I will not even be taking my valet. So I am *certainly* not taking you and the maid necessary to preserve your reputation.'

'*What* reputation?' she demanded. 'I haven't had one worth saving since I left Archie at the altar, gaping like a cod.' And stopped, abruptly and belatedly aware of what she had said. Hauling in a slightly ragged breath, she hurried onwards. 'The proprieties don't matter. And no one will know --'

'*I'll* know. And *you* are taking a lot for granted.' Max eyed her narrowly over folded arms, shock still vibrating through his chest. 'In a moment you can explain why what you just said differs significantly from what you told me last night. But first I'm afraid you must simply accept that *I* am going after Grey and *you* are going home. And that is quite final.'

Frances stared back mutinously while she scoured her mind for a bargaining chip. Then Mr Balfour re-entered the room and unwittingly supplied her with one.

Casting a brief but shrewd glance from one to the other of them, Duncan said, 'Brough is about seventy miles away, so you need to set off soon or you may not get there in time. Head for Richmond. It's the mid-point and Great North Road virtually all the way. You should be able to get further directions from there.' He paused and added wryly, 'If Grey lures you on beyond Brough, you may find yourself taking the Stainmore Pass across the Pennines. But at least at this time of year you won't be up to your knees in snow.'

Max swallowed a curse and swung away to address the footman in the hall.

'Have the stables ready my curricle and tell Burrell pack a valise — everything I'll need for a week but nothing formal. He won't be coming with me.'

'He'll cry,' murmured Duncan with a grin. And when the door closed again, 'What are we going to tell her ladyship?'

Max groaned. 'No idea. I'm open to suggestions.'

And that, Frances immediately realised, was her chance.

Tilting her head and summoning a small, decidedly wicked smile, she said, 'From what you said earlier, I gather that Lady Brandon doesn't know about Grey.'

'She does not.' Max remembered that particular smile better than he wanted to but now wasn't the time to let it sway him. He was already having enough trouble standing firm when every minute brought him closer and closer to giving way. 'And unless you are eager to find out how poorly I respond to blackmail, you will not threaten tell her.'

Frances tutted reprovingly.

'What a nasty, suspicious mind you have, my lord.'

He inclined his head and said genially, 'I do, don't I? I wonder why that is? However ... do go on. We are all ears.'

'I was merely about to observe that her ladyship believes you will be escorting me back to Derbyshire today,' she shrugged. 'All you need to do, is let her *continue* believing it.'

Leaning on a chair-back and letting his head drop forward, Max made a long-suffering sound that was half sigh, half groan.

Taking another long, hard look at him, Duncan said thoughtfully, 'She's right, Max. It would certainly account for your absence and be no more untrue than any other excuse we might dream up.'

'True as that is, it's not why she suggested it.' Max lifted his head, his mouth curling in an acid-edged smile. 'She wants me to take her with me.'

Duncan blinked. 'To find Grey, you mean?'

'Yes.'

'Oh.' For an instant, he appeared to consider this and then he said, 'In that case, why did you order the curricle?'

Max stared at him. 'Because it's the fastest way of getting there, obviously.'

'That's as maybe. But you can't drive long distances in an open vehicle with a lady. You need the carriage – and Miller on the box.'

Her eyes suddenly luminous, Frances made a tiny inarticulate sound and clenched one hand hard over the other. Max looked as if he'd been pole-axed. He said, 'Have you run mad, Duncan? She *can't* come with me. It's out of the question.'

'Why?'

'Oh – for God's sake! Do I really need to spell it out? She ought to be accompanied by a maid. But if I take one of ours I'll have to tell Mother where I'm going and why – which I don't want to do. As for Frances, travelling alone with me will ruin her.'

'It might if this was July or August and folk were either heading back to their estates or to some house-party or other,' agreed Duncan reasonably. 'But it's April and in any case, Grey is unlikely to choose the more popular posting-inns. I doubt you'd meet a soul you know.'

'*Thank* you, Mr Balfour,' smiled Frances. 'That's what *I* said.'

'And it's no less nonsensical coming out of his mouth than it was coming out of yours,' said Max irascibly. 'If this is your idea of a joke, Duncan --'

'It isn't. Think about it. If Mistress Pendleton doesn't go with you, we have to supply her with a suitable escort back to Derbyshire – and it can't be Leo because one or other of you ought to be here. We also have to find an urgent reason for you suddenly being called away at short notice and at such an inconvenient time. Personally – and bearing in mind that Lady Brandon isn't easy to deceive – I can't think of anything remotely credible. Can you?'

For a long moment, Max subjected his secretary to a fulminating stare. Finally, he ground out, 'No. Unfortunately, I can't.'

'So?' asked Frances, unable to remain silent any longer.

Silent and frowning, Max took his time thinking it over. Finally, on an explosion of breath, he said, 'All right. Much against my better judgement and purely because I don't have the time to waste continuing to debate the issue, you can come. We'll leave in half an hour.' Stalking out into the hall and seeing his butler, he said, 'Hawkes ... send new orders to the stables. I shall require the travelling chaise and Miller should prepare for a journey of some days.'

'Certainly, my lord. And your previous orders to Mr Burrell?'

'Remain unchanged. Please also have Mistress Pendleton's valise brought down and show her to her ladyship's rooms to make her farewells.' He turned to Frances. 'You may tell Mama that I'll be up myself presently but don't let her keep you talking. I won't wait.'

She awarded him a triumphant smile and was out through the door almost before he had finished speaking. The instant she had gone, Max rounded on Duncan, saying, 'What the hell has got into you? You know as well as I do what a bad idea this is.'

'Actually, I don't. I think it's something you need to do.'

'What on earth gives you that idea?'

'The way the air fairly crackles between you is a bit of a clue,' returned Duncan sardonically. 'And from the moment she stormed in here yesterday, it was obvious that the two of you have unresolved business.'

'Which perhaps is better left that way.'

'Do you really expect me to believe that? Admittedly, I don't know the lady – but I *do* know you and leaving things unfinished isn't your style at all.' He paused, subjecting Max to intense scrutiny. 'Convince me that there isn't some part of you that is glad to see her ... the same part that doesn't want to lose her again just yet. Well?'

There was another lengthy silence before Max stalked away to the window and, as expressionlessly as he was able, said, 'Five years ago, there was something between us. She says it no longer exists. If she's right – and after so long she probably is – being thrown into each other's company now is unlikely to be helpful.'

'But you want it, don't you?' asked Duncan gently. 'Enough to take the risk.'

'Yes. Yes, I want it enough for that.'

* * *

Max was about to hand Frances into the carriage when Leo rode into the courtyard. Dropping from the saddle, he said, 'If you were about to go haring off to parts unknown without waiting for my report, that's the last time I sacrifice my breakfast to do you a favour.'

'I'm sure you found a sympathetic female to feed you. Did you learn anything?'

'Yes. A stranger gave Alfred a letter to deliver. Alfred and three other townsfolk confirmed that the stranger was the man whose likeness I showed them. This same stranger quit Knaresborough at a little after eight this morning. He was on horseback and heading towards the Great North Road. Betty Pine and Sally Ruddock are still sighing over his charm and nice manners.'

'More fool them,' grunted Max. 'Anything else?'

'Isn't that enough?' Leo turned a wounded gaze upon Frances. 'I try my very best, you know – but some people are never satisfied. They think nothing of sending me to run their errands on an empty stomach. They don't tell me why. They never thank me or say 'well done'. My feelings are simply trampled upon. And you would not *believe* ...'

Max eyed his brother with resignation. He had seen variations on this performance countless times and had to admit that it was a bloody good one. It would be wasted onstage of course. But played for the benefit of one susceptible lady, the soulful, periwinkle eyes and vulnerable-seeming mouth rarely failed to have their effect. However, time being of the essence, Max was just about to cut it short when he saw that, far from wanting to pat Leo's hand, Frances was struggling not to laugh. He waited, watched her lose the battle ... and remembered how *he* had once had the ability to coax that deliciously husky ripple of amusement from her.

She said, unsteadily, 'Oh dear. Clearly, you are very ill-used, Mr Brandon.'

'I am,' he agreed, looking bitterly hurt. '*Very* ill-used. And I must say that it is cruel of you to laugh at the afflicted, ma'am. I am cut to the bone.'

'No you're not. You're perfectly atrocious,' corrected Frances. 'But I daresay that many young ladies are taken in.'

'It never fails,' said Leo with a complacent grin.

'It just did,' pointed out Max. Then, pulling his brother into a brief hug, 'I have to go, Leo. I hope not to be away more than a week – less if I'm lucky – but I've no way of knowing for certain. Duncan will explain everything so make sure you speak with him before you see Mama.'

'That suggests that you're not merely going to Matlock,' murmured Leo, his expression suddenly deadly serious. 'You'll take care, won't you?'

'Yes, little brother. You can count on it.'

CHAPTER SEVEN

It did not take long for Frances to start questioning the wisdom of her impulsive decision. Having done the gentlemanly thing of taking the backward-facing seat, Max said nothing for the first half-mile. He merely contemplated her with a speculative air that she found increasingly unnerving. But finally he murmured, 'So ... here we are.'

She decided that, for the time being at least, saying as little as possible was safest.

'Yes.'

'Happy with getting your own way, are you?'

'Very.'

He nodded. 'Why?'

She blinked. 'Why am I happy?'

'No. Why were you so determined to accompany me on this insane quest?'

'I've already told you that.'

'You told me *something*,' he agreed. 'A lot of stuff about wanting to confront Grey and fighting your own battles. Was all that true?'

'Of course. I wouldn't have said it otherwise.'

He lifted one faintly satiric brow. 'Forgive me. I had wondered if perhaps you doubted my ability to retrieve your brother's watch and return it to you.'

'That's nonsense! You know it wasn't that.'

'Frances ... to be honest, I no longer know where the solid ground is. After the things you said last night in the library, the fact that you're currently here with me instead of running home to Matlock is beyond my understanding.'

'I don't see why,' she retorted. 'However, if you are suggesting that I had an ulterior motive for coming with you, it makes me wonder if perhaps *you* had one of your own for letting me.' She managed a coolly enquiring smile. 'Did you?'

Of course I had an ulterior bloody motive, thought Max moodily. *I wish I didn't – or that I had at least managed to resist it instead of putting myself in a situation which I should have fought tooth and nail to avoid.*

'No. I simply took the line of least resistance. If I hadn't, we'd still be in the breakfast-parlour, arguing about it.' He let the silence linger for a short time and then said abruptly, 'I can predict only one thing about the next few days – and that is that very little will work in my favour. If we're very lucky, we'll find Grey waiting at Brough. But I'm not depending on that because he is fond of tricks and surprises. *My* only advantage is that he isn't aware that I know what he looks like. Speaking of which, so should you.' He reached into the slender document case at his side, withdrew a sheet of paper and handed it to her. 'It's an accurate likeness – so take a good look at it. Not that it will be any use unless he shows himself.'

Accepting the change of subject with gratitude, Frances studied the charcoal portrait carefully. Then, glancing up, she said, 'Did Mr Brandon draw this?'

Surprise touched the dark eyes. 'Yes. How did you know that?'

'You told me what a talented artist he was. You hoped that one day he'd decide he wanted to take his drawing seriously. You were very proud of him.'

'Was I? Yes. I suppose I was – still am, come to that. I'm amazed you remember.'

I remember everything you ever told me, she thought. But, handing the portrait back to him, said merely, 'I didn't until you showed me this. But Grey's tricks and surprises ... do you mean things like selling Mr Brandon the stolen horse?'

'And telling the horse's owner where to find it,' finished Max grimly. 'Yes. Grey delivered the horse himself and took the opportunity to snoop around close to the house – thus discovering the empty stone plinth in the centre of the walled garden. So he sent Mama a piece of sculpture. She was delighted with it and, assuming it was a gift from me, thanked me profusely. Since I couldn't tell her the truth, you may imagine how that felt.'

'Horribly awkward, I should think.'

'That is certainly one way of putting it.' Leaning his head against the squabs, he gazed through the window. 'Eventually, the bill for the statue arrived. That was when I learned that the piece my mother had received was one of two.'

'Oh. And you didn't know where the other sculpture was?'

'No. I found out a couple of days later when a distant neighbour called on me and, by way of greeting, attempted to knock my head from my shoulders for sending his new wife the gift of an obscene statue. There might have been a funny side to that if Lord Ripley hadn't also come close to calling me out.' Max paused and looked back at her. 'My next visitors were two gentlemen from an iron-foundry to which I had apparently pledged an investment. And that, of course, was when you walked in and attacked me. No.' This as she would have spoken, 'You don't need to apologise again and I've something more important to say. If you're wondering why I've been keeping the entire situation from my mother, it is this. Though I have no idea why, Grey is targeting me personally. Worse still is the fact that he appears to know a great deal about me and again, I've no idea how or where he can have acquired his information. Understandably, my mother would find all of this disturbing. She would worry – about me to begin with and then, later, she'd start to fret in case Grey was also interfering with my sister's life. So Mama would write to Belle and then *Belle* would worry. I can't let any of that happen.'

'No. Of course you can't.' Frances looked down at her hands. 'I know you don't require any further apology but I'm truly sorry to have added to the burden you're already carrying. If only I'd written to you instead of descending like the wrath of God --'

'You weren't to know. As to the burden, it's mine to carry and I've broad enough shoulders.'

'Yes,' she said and managed not to add, *I've noticed.*

They did not talk for quite a long time after that, both of them pretending greater interest in the passing scenery than in each other. But after they passed a second toll, seemingly little distance from the first, Frances said curiously, 'Are there a lot of turnpikes on the Great North Road?'

'I can't speak for it beyond Darlington – but yes. There are quite a few along this stretch. The three trustees who own sections of it don't stop at merely keeping the road in good repair. They also like to make a little money for themselves. Putting the gates closer together and adding a shilling or two to the toll achieves that.'

'Do *all* the trustees do that?' asked Frances, a little shocked.

'By no means. But when a system is open to abuse, some men are bound to take advantage of it.' Max smiled at her. 'We'll be turning off the north road at Catterick Bridge – after which it's only a few more miles. You'll like Richmond. It's a pretty place overlooking the river and still possessing a castle. Not that you'll get much time to explore it. Tomorrow morning, we set out for Brough – about which I know next to nothing. The only thing I imagine we can be sure of is that the roads taking us there won't be nearly as good as this one. But at least the weather looks set to remain dry and that is something for which to be grateful.'

He had his coachman draw up at an inn near Leeming for the noon-day meal and in order to rest the horses while he and Frances stretched their legs. Then they set off again, once more in silence but less uncomfortably so than before.

As they were leaving the Great North Road, Max recalled something that had occurred to him earlier and said, 'When you left home, how long did you anticipate being away?'

'Four or five days.'

'And packed only as much as you thought you might need.'

'Yes.' Frances had already started to worry about clothes and how she was going to manage for possibly as much as another week.

'Might I ask how many gowns you have with you other than the one you are wearing?'

'One.' She shrugged. 'It's of no consequence.'

'If that's true you must be unique among women,' said Max with mordant humour. 'However, Richmond is a market-town. We may be able to add to your wardrobe there.'

All her muscles tensed. 'No we can't. I don't have sufficient funds.'

'Then it is fortunate that I do, isn't it?'

She gaped at him incredulously.

'I can't let you buy me clothes! It – that would be highly improper.'

His brows soared.

'More improper than travelling alone with an unmarried man who is not a relative?' he asked pleasantly. 'More scandalous even than staying overnight with him at a public inn? *Really?*'

'I thought we agreed that didn't matter as long as nobody knew.'

'*I* didn't agree anything of the sort. You and Duncan came up with that one between you ... and, that being so, it's a bit late for maidenly scruples, don't you think? The simple fact is that you are going to need more clothing than you have with you. I can hopefully remedy that. This is merely a matter of practicality – not the first step on the slippery slope to ruin.' He paused, a caustic note entering his voice. 'Then again, did you not assure me that you hadn't a shred of reputation left to you?'

Frances refused to answer this because she knew exactly where it would lead. She pressed her lips together and gazed out of the window, hoping he would be satisfied with having the last word.

Inevitably, of course, he wasn't. With an appearance of laziness she did not believe for a minute, he said, 'Of the two versions you've given me of *How I Avoided Marrying Archie* ... which one is true?'

'The second one,' she sighed, still preferring the view through the window to risking a glance at Max's face. 'What I told you last night was what I originally *planned* to do – not what I actually did when the day came.'

'And you didn't tell the truth when I first asked because ...?'

'Because it's much, much worse.'

He looked faintly baffled. 'It is?'

'Yes. If I'd stuck with my plan and barricaded myself in my room, Papa would have been forced to make an excuse – that I was ill or had unexpectedly gone insane. If he'd done it quickly enough it would have spared Archie some embarrassment and lessened the inevitable scandal. In time, it might even have been forgotten.'

She stopped and Max waited. Then, when she didn't continue, he said, 'So what made you change your mind?'

'On the night before the wedding, Rufus told me that Papa had put the announcement in the newspaper a day early – and *why* he had. More to the point, Archie knew it too – and he didn't merely *condone* it. He laughed. He actually thought it was *funny!* A really good joke – coercing me to marry *him,* when I'd told him in words of one syllable that I loved someone else. And that was when I realised that he didn't deserve to be spared anything. Why *should* I make it easy for him? He wouldn't do as much for me, after all. Why *not* let the world see him for the idiot he was? At least, I'd finally be free of him. So that's what I did.'

This, thought Max, didn't sound at all like the girl he had known. The girl who had spent time chatting with a pair of elderly spinsters whilst helping wind their wool or sort their embroidery silks. The girl who had listened to an old gentleman's tales of his youth when, he assured her, he'd been the very devil of a fellow … and then, rapping his knuckles with her fan, informing him that he didn't appear to have changed a bit. And the girl who had always been unfailingly kind to the little dab of a poor relation that Constance Hartley had dragged around in her wake. *That* girl hadn't a malicious bone in her body. She was all sunshine and sweetness, threaded through with an irrepressible sense of humour.

He said slowly, 'Did you go through with it?'

'Oh yes. Every last bit.' Her brows rose. 'Why? Don't you think me capable?'

'I don't know *what* I think. But if you can bear to talk about it, I'd like to hear what really happened.'

* * *

Still simmering with rage behind a docile smile, Frances had taken her place in the carriage with her father. She'd let him help her from it outside the church and waited patiently while her attendants straightened the train of her blue silk brocade bridal gown and fussed with the flowers she would carry. Her face began to ache from the effort of keeping her smile in place. Then the moment came for her to make her entrance … and walk slowly down the aisle on Papa's arm.

At the end of it stood a robed and mitred cleric.

Of course, thought Frances. *Allowing his son to be married by anything less than a bishop would be below Lord Blandford's dignity, wouldn't it?*

She reached the place where Archie waited, all unsuspecting. He turned his head and winked at her.

Idiot, she thought coldly. *And I was an even bigger one for ever imagining I could spend the rest of my life with you. But not any more.*

The service began and Frances paid close attention. She couldn't afford to miss her cue. That would ruin everything.

It seemed a long time coming. But eventually the bishop stopped rambling about the holy sacrament of matrimony and got around to asking if anyone could show any just cause why she and Archie might not lawfully be joined together. Frances had considered using this part herself, then discarded the idea. As expected, no one else said anything either, so after a brief pause, the cleric asked the same question of the bridal pair. Once again, she let it pass – aware that, beside her, Archie was tugging at his cravat.

I hope it's strangling you, she thought. *By the time I've finished, you'll wish it had. And we'll see if you feel like laughing then.*

'Wilt thou have this woman to thy lawful wedded wife ...' intoned the bishop.

Nearly there, thought Frances, *her nerves starting to vibrate. They'll try to stop me. I can't let them. I* won't *let them.*

'I will,' mumbled Archie.

'Wilt thou have this man to thy wedded husband, to live together after God's holy ordinance ... wilt thou obey him, serve him, love, honour and keep him ... forsaking all other ... as long as ye both shall live?'

Frances looked the bishop in the eye and let a pause develop. Then, quietly but distinctly, she said, 'No. I will not.'

Time seemed to freeze while the bishop absorbed what she had said. His gaze acute but his voice kind, he murmured, 'Bridal nerves, my child? Let us try again. Wilt thou--?'

'No.' This time she spoke a little louder. 'I will not. I have never, as everyone concerned is fully aware, consented to this. Indeed, I have repeatedly refused – despite being coerced, bullied and even drugged. But no more.'

From behind in the congregation came a collective gasp of shock, followed by a susurration of whispering. Frances was aware of her father taking a step towards her, then stopping in receipt of a hard look from the bishop. At the same moment, Archie finally grasped what was happening and said, 'Look here, Frances – you don't mean this nonsense. Daresay you're just feeling a bit vapourish and --'

Frances silenced him by shoving her bouquet at him with all the strength she could muster and sending him staggering back with a sort of strangled grunt.

'I am not vapourish, you feeble excuse for a man. I will not marry you today or tomorrow or ever. In fact, I would sooner die an old maid. Is that clear enough for you?'

Then, gathering up her skirts and transfixing her father with a look of freezing contempt, she stalked rapidly down the aisle wearing an expression that defied anyone to get in her way. Half-way to the door, she started running. She thought she heard a scattering of discreet applause. She definitely heard a lady say, 'Well done. If you don't want him, nobody should make you.'

By the time Frances reached the porch, her heart was hammering in her chest. There had been no way of planning anything beyond escaping from the church – though she knew that eventually she would have no option but to go home to Dover Street. She had a little money inside her sleeve. If she was lucky, she might find a hackney carriage. If not ... well, the most important thing was to get out of sight before anyone caught her.

She reached the porticoed entrance and checked briefly. At the foot of the steps a dark-haired, severely elegant gentleman was just descending from his carriage; a belated wedding-guest ... and one, moreover, who Mama had only invited under duress. Then, in the second she hesitated, he looked up and, seeming to take in the situation at a glance, held out his hand to her saying coolly, 'My carriage is at your disposal, if you wish it – but I suggest you hurry.'

He was probably the last man in the world from whom she would ever have expected help. Now, needing no other urging, she fled down to grasp his hand.

'Thank you. I – oh, thank you.'

'It is my pleasure.' Bundling her into the vehicle with more haste than grace, he glanced over his shoulder and added, 'Crouch down. They are coming. My coachman will drive you around until you are ready to tell him where you wish to go. You hear me, Cox?'

'Yes, my lord.'

'Then go. Quickly.'

And without further ado, he sauntered up the steps into the path of the would-be pursuers.

* * *

All the time she had been speaking, Max had watched the play of emotions on her face as she re-lived that day. Now, recalling her unexpected saviour, she was smiling.

'Someone you knew?' he asked lightly.

She shook her head. 'Only by sight. It was Lord Kilburn.'

Kilburn? Max pondered the name, wondering why it seemed familiar. Then the answer came to him and he said, 'The gentleman who is now the Earl of Sherbourne?'

'Yes. Of course, he hadn't originally been invited. However, his grandfather, the earl, *had* been but wasn't well enough to make the journey and said that his heir would represent him. So Mama was forced – very unwillingly – to send the viscount a card.'

'A fact of which his lordship was doubtless aware?'

'Yes, I imagine so. Later, I wondered if that played some part in his readiness to help. At any rate, he didn't ask a single question. He just behaved as if assisting runaway brides was an everyday occurrence. He was quite wonderful.'

Max felt a stirring of something annoyingly akin to jealousy. Ignoring it, he said, 'Sherbourne married my cousin a few months ago. He struck me as a bit of an iceberg … but perhaps I judged him too soon.' He paused. 'I take it that you eventually went home?'

'Yes.' Frances lifted one shoulder in a token shrug. 'There was nowhere else *to* go. With the exception of Archie, everyone from both families was still there – and most of them were still shouting. When they saw me they stopped long enough for Mama to tell me that my bridges were well and truly burned. I was as ruined as it was possible for any woman to be, she said. Not only would *Archie* not marry me – no *other* gentleman ever would either.' She paused and then added dryly, 'I didn't need to be told that. I knew before I did it that there would be no going back afterwards.'

There was a long silence, filled only by the rumble of the wheels.

Finally Max said, 'Was it worth it?'

'If you mean have I ever regretted it ... no. I haven't. Life may not have been very enjoyable since that day but years of living with Archie would have been infinitely worse.'

Once again, the questions he hadn't yet had the courage to ask surfaced. Once again, he held them back. Sooner or later, he would voice them ... but not now. Not while the air between them throbbed with a tension that was almost tangible. And not until he was ready to answer her questions as honestly as he hoped she would answer his. So instead, he said quietly, 'I'm sorry you were left with no other way out. I don't suppose your parents ever quite forgave you for it.'

'No.' She turned to stare through the window and concentrated on keeping her tone cool and lightly ironic. 'Mama had a great deal to say and was happy to go on saying it – her main complaint being that I'd deprived her of the opportunity to boast about her daughter, the future marchioness. Papa, on the other hand, could scarcely bear to *look* at me, let alone speak. It wasn't until after his death that I understood he'd been counting on my marriage to Archie solving his financial difficulties.' She paused and then added consideringly, 'Mama hadn't known about the debts either. I think learning that the London house had to be sold hit her worse than losing Papa. After that, she took to her rooms and lived on spite. Everything that comes out of her mouth is either angry or rude.'

Max had no idea what he could possibly say that might be helpful. Piece by piece, since she had walked back into his life twenty-four hours ago, everything he had thought he'd known had been proved to be wrong ... and it gave him a disconcerting sense of becoming gradually unravelled. It occurred to him that Frances must be feeling similarly confused; that perhaps she wasn't nearly as composed and unaffected as she wanted him to believe. In fact, he was *sure* she wasn't. She was trying to hold back a potential maelstrom of emotion that she didn't know how to deal with. Just as he was.

The carriage rattled into Richmond at a little after four in the afternoon and drew up at the King's Head in the market place. Before opening the door and getting out, Max said, 'I'm known here so you'll have to be a distant cousin I'm escorting to stay with friends in the north. Agreed?'

'Yes.'

'Good. Then let us find out if they can accommodate us.'

The innkeeper was delighted to welcome Lord Brandon again and pleased to offer his two best bedchambers, a private parlour and a chambermaid who would be happy to wait on his lordship's cousin, if required.

'Thank you,' said Max. 'What my cousin actually needs just at present is a modiste or seamstress – the bulk of her luggage having been sent on ahead and our journey having been unexpectedly delayed. Where might we find one?'

'Well now, there's Mistress Sutton on the far side of square. She sews for most all the ladies round about. Or for quality ready-made, you'll want Maggie Thompson in Castle Street. I'm sure either one'd be happy to call on your lordship here if I send a lad over.'

'No. After spending hours cooped up in the carriage, a stroll in the fresh air is just what we need – don't you think so, Araminta?'

'Oh yes, Cousin!' Frances clasped ecstatic hands and fixed him with a lash-fluttering gaze of shy worship. 'A walk about the town would be delightful. It looks a charming place and I'm sure I glimpsed a castle. I love castles above all things. Do not you?'

His mouth quivering slightly, Max said repressively, 'I can take them or leave them.'

'But do you not find them excessively romantic, Cousin? And what stories they could tell if only their stones could speak! One has only to *enter* a castle to feel its aura. Do you not think so?'

'No. If you wish to make some purchases, shall we go?'

'Oh – yes. Yes, I do. This is wonderfully good of you, Cousin – I know how unfortunate and tiresome it all is when you had hoped to discharge your duty speedily and --'

With a long-suffering glance for the benefit of the innkeeper, Max hauled her outside still talking. Then, grinning at her, he said, 'What exactly was that little display all about?'

'I was being an Araminta,' she replied as though he shouldn't have needed to ask. 'Any female unfortunate enough to be called that probably feels impelled to live up to it. Was it *really* the best you could think of?'

'Well, it's better than Fanny – which was the first thing that sprang to mind. Luckily, I recalled your views on that in time to save myself from bodily harm.'

Frances shook her head and eyeing him satirically, said, 'And you doubted your ability to defend yourself?'

'No. But I couldn't take the risk.' He waited until she glanced enquiringly up at him and then said, 'You threatened me with emasculation.'

The effect of his words was even better than he could have hoped. She emitted a strangled choke and half-tripped over something he suspected wasn't there but which gave him the excuse to draw her arm through his. She immediately pulled it free and, fixing him with an outraged blue stare, stammered, 'I did n-no such thing!'

'You did. You said that if I ever called you Fanny, you would remove certain significant parts of my anatomy. What's that if not --?'

'I don't believe we ever had any such conversation! But if we *did*, I'd have meant your – your fingernails – or some such thing.'

Deciding to capitalise on the fact that he had shocked her out of her iron-held composure, he gave her a pitying smile and said patiently, 'Frances ... there isn't a man alive who would interpret the removal of a *significant* body part to mean fingernails.'

She could feel herself turning steadily scarlet.

'I was nineteen, for heaven's sake! I wouldn't even have *known* – let alone made reference to – to --' She stopped, unable to continue.

'To a gentleman's most treasured assets?' he said helpfully. 'Well, perhaps not ... young girls being kept in the state of total ignorance that they are. However, you imply that you're more knowledgeable now. How did that come about?'

Frances opened her mouth, closed it again and then, just when she was on the verge of another protest, caught sight of the errant gleam in his eyes. She took a long, steadying breath and hissed, 'Stop this minute. You are being deliberately atrocious!'

He grinned at her. 'You said the same thing to Leo. Perhaps it runs in the family.'

'That seems all too likely,' she grumbled. And then, under her breath, 'Treasured assets, indeed.'

Max re-possessed her arm and, when she didn't object, said, 'It was the most polite term I could think of. Would 'family jewels' have been better?'

Her involuntary gurgle of laughter set off a small explosion of pleasure inside Max's chest. He thought, *Yes. That's my girl.*

'No – it's worse. And there is nothing *remotely* polite about this conversation.'

'I know. But at least it has lightened the mood.' He hesitated, smiling down at her. 'Frances ... do you think we might shut Grey and everything that happened before this moment in a box and leave it there? Just for today? Speaking for myself, I would enjoy a few hours of nothing more complicated than becoming re-acquainted. What do you think?'

Frances looked up at him, understanding why he was asking and also the dangers of it. But she was no more proof against his smile or the sincerity in his voice than she had ever been; and the temptation to enjoy again the easier-than-breathing rapport they'd once shared was too great to resist.

'Yes,' she said softly. 'Yes, Max. We can do that.'

CHAPTER EIGHT

Upon learning the very reasonable nature of Mistress Thompson's prices and calculating that, with careful management, she could find the money for them once she got home, Frances agreed to allow Max to buy two simple but becoming gowns requiring only a slight degree of alteration.

Not bothering to apprise her of his intentions, Max simply used the time it took for her to change back into her own clothes for a brief, private exchange with the dressmaker. Then he swept Frances off to the castle and its view over the river while chatting easily about Richmond – the prosperity of which, evident in numerous elegant new houses, was founded largely on wool and also, more recently, on lead mining.

When they returned to the King's Head an hour before dinner, Frances discovered that her new gowns had been delivered; and not *only* the gowns. Along with them was a chemise, a petticoat, a night rail and two pairs of stockings. Half relieved and half mutinous, she changed into the new cream-sprigged blue tiffany and went downstairs to set Lord Brandon straight on a few things.

Max, who had been expecting it, did not give her the chance. Throwing up one hand in a gesture of surrender, he said, 'Yes. I know I exceeded what was agreed upon. But it's done now so there is no point in arguing about it. Furthermore, if we're never anywhere for more than a night, you can't depend on having your underthings laundered.'

'You aren't supposed to know about a lady's underthings – let alone *talk* of them.'

'I know they must exist,' he retorted. And with a lift of one teasing brow, 'Unless … and this is a concept I *really* ought not to be contemplating … you aren't wearing a stitch under that rather fetching gown?'

Frances sighed. 'This is the second wholly inappropriate topic of conversation you've begun today. I am in dread of what tomorrow may bring.'

'Oh – tomorrow you can trust me to behave.' He smiled

engagingly and handed her a glass of wine. 'In truth, I'm only *mis*behaving now in order to stop you scolding me for indulging in wanton extravagance. However ... may I, without impropriety, observe that it really *is* a very pretty gown? Almost, though not quite, the same blue as your eyes.'

The words and the tone in which they were uttered unfurled a coil of warmth in her chest. She couldn't remember the last time anyone had complimented her. What she *did* remember all too clearly were the things Max had once said to her. That her eyes were the most beautiful he had ever seen – the tiny flecks of gold amongst the blue like a sprinkling of stardust; that her freckles enchanted him and that one day he was going to enjoy counting them; that her hair had the lustre of –

Stop, she admonished herself sternly. *You agreed to shut the past away for a little while – and that means* all *of it. Goodness knows, this setting is intimate enough with the light fading and candles already lit. My bedchamber is just through there ... and though the door to Max's room is in the hall, the room itself is on the other side of that wall. I hadn't bargained for such – such proximity. So letting my wits wander isn't an option.*

It was perhaps fortunate that a tap at the door heralded the arrival of their dinner. When the table was set, she took the chair Max pulled out for her and accepted a slice of chicken and ham pie. Then, watching him serve himself, she sipped her wine and tried to think of some innocuous topic of conversation. Finally, in lieu of something better, she said, 'Since your sister is married to the Virtuoso Earl, I imagine you have probably heard him play. Is he as brilliant as the newspapers say?'

'I'm afraid the finer points of musical technique are wasted on me,' replied Max dryly, 'and some of the stuff Julian plays makes my teeth ache. But yes ... there's no denying his brilliance at the keyboard. The rest of the time, you wouldn't think him capable of even walking on to a concert platform in front of a couple of hundred people, let alone playing for them.' He grinned and, when she looked enquiringly at him, said 'He's shy and awkward and uncertain – and he can usually be relied upon to say *exactly* the wrong thing. But when he sits down at a harpsichord, he becomes a different person – confident and relaxed, without a nerve in his body. The transformation is remarkable.'

Frances eyed him thoughtfully, 'Do you like him?'

'*Everyone* likes him – which ought to be annoying but somehow isn't.' He shrugged. 'The earldom, along with its failing estate, dropped on him out of the blue. He didn't want it and still won't use the title if he can avoid it. There's also the small matter of three illegitimate children. But the only thing which really matters to me is that Julian loves Belle and makes her happy. So even if he irritated the hell out of me – which, fortunately, he doesn't – I'd put it aside for her sake.'

'Did you just say,' she asked weakly, 'that he has three illegitimate children?'

'Yes. But they're not his. He inherited them – and gave them a home.' Max looked up from his plate. 'But it's your turn to do the talking. Tell me how you spend your days.'

She reached for another spoonful of green beans, apparently not noticing those already on her plate. 'There's nothing very interesting to tell.'

'I might disagree. Try me.'

'Well, I oversee the running of the house ... but that is hardly taxing. Planning the week's meals with Cook, keeping the linen in good repair and making sure that expenditure stays on the right side of income – which is more than Mama ever managed to do. And I confer with the estate steward on various matters, though I have little knowledge of what ought to be done and --'

'Wait a moment. Doesn't your brother do that? The property is his now, after all.'

'Yes. But when Papa died, Rufus was still at university so it was left for me to deal with and somehow it has continued that way.' Catching the expression in his eyes, Frances hurried on, unhappily aware that she was babbling. 'In the summer, I do a little gardening. Most of it goes untended now but I enjoy planting things and taking care of the roses. And when the weather is fine, I walk a great deal. The local countryside is quite beautiful, you know.'

'I'm afraid I'm not familiar with Derbyshire.' Reflecting that

Rufus needed a kick up the backside, Max returned his attention to his plate and continued trying to watch her without appearing to do so. He noticed that so far she hadn't mentioned riding even though she had always loved it. He wondered if that was because, like the London house, the stables had also been sold and suspected that it probably was. So, instead of asking, he said casually, 'What about friends and local society?'

'Mama's friends used to call but most of them gradually stopped coming when, as often as not, she failed to receive them.' A faintly acidic smile dawned. 'As for the younger ladies ... they weren't allowed to call in case jilting one's husband-to-be at the altar was catching.'

Max was beginning to lose his appetite.

'So ... few visitors and therefore, I am guessing, few invitations either.'

'Yes.' In fact, she did not receive *any* invitations but wanted to avoid admitting it. Finding a more positive tone, she said, 'There are my brothers, of course. William has still one more year at Eton and is desperate to study mathematics at Cambridge. Rufus, you already know about. Luckily, he never wanted to be an idle young gentleman about town so he's happy to take employment. I suspect his ambitions, such as they are, may be political ... but he says nothing of it.'

Because he knows he's unlikely to have any opportunity of achieving them, thought Max. *And you don't ask because you know it, too. God. What the hell did your father spend his money on? Come to that – what kind of mess is your estate in? Is the land not paying for itself at* all? *From the little I know so far, it's beginning to sound damnably like the problems Julian was drowning in.*

Obviously feeling that the silence had lingered long enough to feel uncomfortable, Frances pushed her plate aside and, contemplating the bowl of apple charlotte, said, 'Where is *your* other brother at present? Or does he not live with you at Brandon Lacey?'

'He does ... but Adam is mad about swords and swordsmanship. When he's at home, he spends half his time either practicing or wielding a hammer down at the forge, trying to make the ultimate blade. Right now, however, he's visiting a friend's fencing academy in Paris.' Correctly interpreting the expression on her face, he pushed both the pudding and its accompanying jug of cream towards her. 'Are you going to have some of this – or are you content to merely look at it?'

'I was enjoying the anticipation,' she replied, taking a generous portion and proceeding to drown it in cream. 'And when he has finished studying ... what then?'

'Good question. I haven't the remotest idea and suspect that he hasn't either.' Watching her dip her spoon into the cream and slowly taste it, almost sighing with pleasure, Max promptly forgot what he had been about to say. His body tightened in response to a number of inappropriate thoughts that he did his best to banish. Clearing his throat, he said stupidly, 'Adam? Yes. He might become a blacksmith or an armourer ... or hire himself out as a bodyguard or private assassin.'

'I take it the last one was a joke?' asked Frances, savouring another mouthful of cream.

'The assassin? Yes. One would hope so.' He took refuge in his wine-glass so he needn't look at her. 'On the other hand ... when was the last time you saw a man walking around with a sword at his hip? And I don't mean a pretty dress sword of the kind some gentlemen wear in the evening. I mean the sort used for serious fighting.'

'Never, I think. You are saying that your brother does?'

'All the time. As you may imagine, people look at him sideways and tend to step out of his path.' He managed a grin. 'I'd worry about that if Adam was in the least bloodthirsty – but he's not. With him, it's all theory and the pursuit of perfection.'

Frances eyed him thoughtfully for a moment. Then, turning back to her pudding, 'So the responsibilities of Brandon Lacey fall solely to you?'

'It's no sacrifice. My days are rewarding and not without challenge. I know every family whose livelihood depends on my land or various holdings and I enjoy working alongside them when I have the opportunity. But I'm not tethered to the estate. I visit

London a couple of times a year ... though rarely for more than two or three weeks at a time. Catching up with friends is always pleasant, but there is a limit to the amount of time I'll spend lounging at my club or sitting at a card table.'

'Perhaps you're too accustomed to being active.'

'That's part of it,' he agreed. 'But I also find the constraints of polite society stifling. The code of gentlemanly conduct is one thing. Rules about things which – for no good reason I can see – one must absolutely *not* do, are quite another.'

'Be grateful you're not female,' muttered Frances. 'Compared to us, you gentlemen can get away with more or less anything.'

'You sound like Belle. Remind me some time to tell you how she met Julian. However ... for now, I must ask you to forgive me.' Max pushed back his chair and stood up. 'After Duncan's gloomy words, I want to hear what the men drinking in the tap-room can tell me about the Stainmore Pass. If we're likely to encounter any problems, it would be helpful to have advance warning.'

'I thought Mr Balfour said that it would be all right at this time of year?'

'He did. Let's hope the locals share his opinion.'

* * *

Fully aware that his coachman, Joe Miller, would already have asked all the right questions, Max did not need to spend time in the tap-room. What he *had* needed was an excuse to leave the parlour ... because he wasn't sure how much longer he could endure the torture of watching Frances lick cream from a spoon.

After a tankard of home-brewed with Miller and some other cheerful company, he went upstairs and prepared for bed resolutely thinking of anything other than the lady sleeping two rooms away. This lasted until his head hit the pillow ... after which he was finally forced to acknowledge a basic truth which had been growing inside him all day.

He wanted Frances Pendleton now as much as he had wanted her five years ago – and more than he had ever wanted any other woman, either before or since. Since this was quite bad enough he absolutely refused to consider whether or not it might be more than that. He remembered all too clearly how he had felt before;

the dizzying, completely overwhelming love ... the heart full of hope ... the eviscerating pain. He did not want any of it again. And unless he was much mistaken, neither did she. Lust – even constant, unsatisfied lust – was perfectly controllable if one chose to make it so. His only difficulty might be in making sure she never suspected. There had been moments throughout the day when it had been plain to him that the connection between them still existed. Even though Frances was busy not letting herself feel anything, he knew exactly what she was repressing and when she was withholding some part of the truth. And that being so, it was entirely likely that she could read him just as easily.

Max turned over, thumping the pillow and berating himself yet again for not standing firm and refusing to let her come with him. He had known it was reckless, dangerous and downright stupid – but he had done it anyway. Now, they both had to live with the consequences for as long as it took Grey to show his face.

God willing, sooner rather later, thought Max irritably. *Otherwise, I may well be lured into doing something terminally stupid.*

* * *

Max seemingly having breakfasted early and elsewhere, Frances did not see him until they were boarding the carriage. As it rolled away from the King's Head, she said, 'Did you learn anything useful last night?'

'I was assured that we would have no difficulty reaching Brough – though the road is reputedly poor in places. But the first part of our route lies along the old Roman road towards Bowes and passes, or so I'm told, the site of ancient forts. Stainmore summit is some six miles further on.'

'The Romans were *here*? So far north?'

'They went further than this. Hadrian's Wall is still some considerable distance away. But before that was built, they threw a defensive line across northern England here and the signs of it are still visible in places. At Bowes and Brough, castles were built where the forts had been ... though they're apparently in ruins now. I imagine they either fell into disrepair or were slighted after the civil wars.' Max grimaced slightly. 'Knaresborough Castle is a prime example of the latter. It survived the wars only to be largely destroyed by Act of Parliament. I don't know what my ancestors made of that ... but it isn't hard to guess.'

'You think they would have disapproved?'

'My great-great-grandmother certainly would. She wasn't merely a beauty but also a woman of strong convictions. She and my great-great-grandfather enjoyed a long and very happy marriage – though it can't have started out that way.'

'Why not?'

'Because Venetia was the daughter of a knight and a dyed-in-the-wool Royalist. Gabriel, though the son of Sir Robert Brandon, had been born on the wrong side of the blanket and was a colonel in the New Model Army. A more unlikely pairing is hard to imagine.' He paused and, seeing the interest in her face, said, 'Do you want the story?'

'Yes, please. It sounds intriguing.'

'It's ... complex.' He hesitated as if considering where to start. 'We know that Gabriel's birth pre-dates Sir Robert's marriage by more than a year. We *think* his mother was the Countess of Gillingham ... already married but not, for some reason, in a position to pass the child off as that of her husband. At any rate, though Gabriel was acknowledged as Robert's son, he was reared by a foster-family – with whose descendants we still retain close ties. In due course, Robert and his wife also had a son – Ellis. Time passed and both boys grew up. Gabriel became a soldier and went to fight abroad. Ellis held some position at court and, by the time civil war came, he was engaged to marry one of the queen's ladies-in-waiting.' Max raised one brow, smiling a little. 'Venetia Clifford.'

'Your great-great-grandmother?'

'The very one. But before we get to the bit that I'm sure interests you most, I'd better explain how war and politics affected what happened next. Robert Brandon supported the Parliament; and when Gabriel returned to England, he took a command in Parliament's army. Ellis, by contrast, took the King's side, as did Venetia's family.'

'So what happened to Ellis? Did he die?'

'No. Robert disinherited him in Gabriel's favour.'

Frances stared at him. 'Why? Because of *politics*?'

'Not only that. From what we can tell, Ellis was an unreliable spendthrift and, in the wake of the war, Brandon Lacey was already failing. Robert apparently thought that Gabriel would make a better job of mending matters.' Max grinned suddenly. 'A further complication was that, at some point in the past, Robert had taken the Clifford lands into his own possession to save them from sequestration. It was meant to be a temporary arrangement but both Robert and Venetia's father died before it was terminated – which meant that Gabriel inherited Ford Edge as well as Brandon Lacey.' Another smile and a sideways glance. 'Are you still following?'

'Just about. So what did Gabriel do?'

'Swore, probably. His knowledge of estate management and his desire to learn would have been non-existent. But Robert's will offered a solution to one part of the problem. It stated that Ford Edge would revert to the Cliffords ... if, and *only* if, Venetia married Gabriel instead of Ellis.'

Frances emitted a sound that was half laugh, half groan.

'Oh dear. I can imagine her response to that.'

'So can I. But, however unwillingly, they *did* marry.'

'And lived happily ever after?'

'Oddly enough, yes – though probably not immediately. But I've read the letters they wrote to each other when they were apart and there is no doubt they were deeply and passionately in love.'

'I'm glad. With so many things dividing them, their marriage could have been unbearable for both of them.' She looked through the window, smiling a little sadly. 'It's comforting to know they found their happy ending.'

'Unlike us, you mean?' asked Max gently.

'Unlike many, many couples, I think.' And immediately returning to the story, '*Did* Gabriel rescue the estate?'

'Yes. He set up a system of co-operation with the tenants which, in his day, would have been considered revolutionary and is unusual even now. By the time he died, Brandon Lacey was flourishing and its tenants were more prosperous than those on neighbouring estates. We still use Gabriel's methods today and they continue to benefit everyone.'

'He sounds a remarkable man,' observed Frances.

'Yes. I believe that he was.'

'And what of Ellis? Do you know what became of him?'

'No. According to Robert's will, he inherited a manor in Oxfordshire ... but I've never been there. And if that branch of the family still exists, we've had no contact with it since Gabriel's time.'

'In one sense, that is a pity.' She thought for a moment. 'But in another, perhaps not?'

'No,' agreed Max dryly. 'Perhaps not.'

* * *

Max agreed to stop briefly at Bowes so that Frances could walk through the castle ruins, then they set off again to climb up and up through the emptiness of the Stainmore Pass. It wasn't difficult to imagine that winter frequently found it blocked with snow; but today, as Frances remarked, the rolling hills lying beneath sunshine and scudding clouds had a certain picturesque – if lonely – charm. Max replied that neither of them would find it in the least charming if the carriage were to lose a wheel.

They arrived in Brough at around five o'clock and drew up at the only coaching inn which, fortuitously, was the one where they might or might not encounter Grey.

'Are you still convinced that he won't be here?' asked Frances, as Max led her inside to bespeak rooms. 'Surely, there's *some* chance --'

'Very little,' came the slightly grim reply. 'However, we can but hope.'

The landlord of the Castle Inn was pleased to offer Lord Brandon two comfortable bedchambers but was unable to provide a private parlour.

'It being a rare day when Quality comes to stay, there's no call for such, m'lord,' he explained. 'But likely thou'll find the coffee-room pleasant enough – it opening on to the garden, as it does. Or if the young lady prefers, we can serve her dinner above-stairs.'

'There's no need for that,' said Frances quickly. 'The coffee-room will do very well – will it not, Cousin?'

'Indeed,' said Max. And, to the landlord, 'I was expecting to find a letter or perhaps a small package waiting here. Has anything been left for me?'

'Why no, m'lord – or I'd have given it to thee straight. But now thou's mentioned it, I'll keep an eye out. Is it just the one night thou'll be staying wi' us?'

'Probably – though, as yet, my plans are uncertain. In the meantime, having been travelling for two days, my cousin and I would greatly appreciate baths. Is that possible?'

'Certainly, m'lord. The young lady first, mebbe?'

'Thank you.' Max smiled at Frances. 'Do not hurry on my account, Araminta.'

'You are too good,' she sighed soulfully. 'You never utter a *word* of complaint about how much trouble I am putting you to or how much more quickly you could travel were I not with you. And I *so* enjoyed the castle earlier today ... *such* a romantic spot. I vow I could have been happy to spend the entire *day* there!'

'So you said. Several times. But now you must excuse me. I need a brief word with Miller. Enjoy your bath.'

Miller was rubbing down the horses and giving a stable-boy orders about precisely what fodder he required when he caught sight of Max in the doorway.

'Jump to it, lad. Here's his lordship come to check on his cattle and you're still standing about like a great lummox. What are you waiting for?'

'Nowt.' The boy took off at a run.

Grinning, Max strolled forward saying, 'Stop terrifying the help, Joe.'

'Does 'em no harm to be kept on their toes,' returned Miller. And then, 'What can I do for you, my lord?'

'The man whose likeness I showed you ought to turn up here at some point today. I take it you'd recognise him?'

'Aye, my lord. I mind how clever Mr Leo is with his drawing. If I see the fellow, I'll know him right enough. But what do you want me to do? Lay hold on him – or send you word?'

'Send word,' said Max crisply, 'but don't let him out of your sight until I get there. However, I doubt we'll be that lucky. Since it doesn't seem that he's already been and gone, I suspect he'll use a go-between. But if he doesn't ... and if he risks a visit to the tap-room, you're more likely to spot him than I am.'

Frowning, Miller said bluntly, 'Forgive me asking, my lord – but does this fellow wish you harm?'

'Yes, though not physically, I believe. He is playing ducks and drakes with my good name. Do you recall the incident with Sir Desmond Appleby's horse?'

'Aye. That was him, was it?'

'It was. One of many such little jokes. He has also involved Mistress Pendleton's family – which is the only reason she is travelling with me in what I am fully aware is an extremely improper fashion. I'm counting on your discretion regarding that, Joe.'

'And can rely on it, sir.'

'I know.' Max thought for a moment. 'I was intent on keeping the whole matter from Lady Brandon but not bringing a groom to assist you may have been taking caution a step too far. If the journey looks likely to continue – and it might – what would you think about hiring someone on a temporary basis?'

'Probably wouldn't hurt,' shrugged Miller. 'But there's nobody here as'd be any use. From what I've seen so far, they're all as dozy as sheep.'

'Ah. *Now*, Joe. They're dozy as sheep *now*. But by tomorrow morning you'll have them hopping about like rabbits.'

Miller laughed.

'Maybe so, my lord. Maybe so. I'll have to see what I can do.'

* * *

Knowing that the inn could not heat water for two baths simultaneously, Frances bathed with swift efficiency in order not to keep Max waiting for his turn. When the water had been removed, she dressed in the same blue dimity she had worn on the previous evening, pinned up her hair and then, rather than wait in her room, wandered downstairs to find the garden.

It was larger than she had expected and mostly planted with fruit trees and raspberry canes. But the air was still warm and dusk was falling slowly, so she sauntered around, enjoying the first of the apple blossom before finding a low dry-stone wall to sit upon. Then she contemplated the story Max had told her about his great-great-grandparents – and his evident pride and pleasure in the telling of it. It occurred to her that her own family history went back much further – the Pendleton knighthood having been granted by Richard the Lionheart after the Third Crusade. But although her father had been proud of holding such an ancient title, she had never heard him talk about his forebears with the affectionate understanding with which Max spoke of his.

Voices at the outer gate caused her to glance to where two people stood in the shade of an ancient beech tree. One looked like a maid from the inn. The other, a shabbily-dressed man with sun-bronzed skin, appeared to be handing her a coin. Losing interest, Frances restored her attention to small pink flowers pushing obstinately between the cracks in the flagstones beneath her feet. Wondering what they were, she was just about to pick one when a strange prickle of awareness touched the back of her neck, causing her to look around. The shabby man was still there and apparently staring at her, a small smile bracketing his mouth; then in the second she saw him, he was gone. Frances's heart gave a single, hard thud and she shot to her feet, her mind whirling.

That had been him – Grey. Hadn't it? She was sure – almost sure that it had been. One more glimpse was all she needed. Without stopping to think, she flew across the garden and out into the narrow lane beside the inn. It was deserted. Not a soul in either direction. Where could he have gone so quickly? She wasted a handful of seconds on indecision ... and then pelted back inside the inn, colliding with a chambermaid.

'Which is Lord Brandon's room?' she demanded. 'Quickly – which is it?'

'The end of the hall, opposite side to yours, Miss. But his lordship is --'

Frances didn't wait to hear the rest. She shot up the stairs and along the passageway to hammer on Max's door – which, since someone hadn't latched it properly, promptly swung inwards to reveal his lordship, arising from his bath.

Frances froze, brain and body both equally paralysed. She had a swift, breath-stopping view of broad shoulders, a flat back tapering to a lean waist and long, powerful legs; of a lightly-tanned torso ... paler, well-shaped buttocks ...and smooth skin glistening with moisture. Her mouth dried, her pulse thudded and, for a few moments, her wits completely deserted her. Then, coming abruptly to her senses and making a strangled choking sound, she spun round, pressing her hands over her eyes.

'I'm s-sorry,' she stammered. 'I didn't – I w-wouldn't have – but the door w-wasn't --'

Behind her, his colour slightly high and grateful that he'd been half-turned away from her so she couldn't have seen quite *everything*, Max stepped from the bath and reached nonchalantly for a towel to wrap around his hips. He said, 'I'm moderately decent now, if you want to turn around.'

'I don't. I *can't*.' She left her hands where they were – for all the good it did, since the picture of that sleekly-muscled body was engraved on her brain. Burning with embarrassment, she moaned, 'I want to die.'

The humour of the situation dawned forcibly on Max. He said, 'A bit extreme ... and *not* a reaction I'm accustomed to. However ... do you think you might tell me where the fire is?'

That cut through her desire to sink through the floor. Still with her back to him, she cautiously let her hands slide from her face. 'Not a fire – Grey.'

'*What?*' Amusement fled and, snatching up another towel, Max began rapidly drying himself. 'Where?'

'Outside the garden a few minutes ago. I tried to follow him but he disappeared.'

Ignoring the fact that his hair was still dripping, Max started hauling on clothes.

'Go back – find out if Miller saw him. I'll be with you shortly. *Hurry!*'

Frances fled, glad to escape. She found Miller and swiftly

discovered he hadn't seen the man she described. He did however say, 'This was the fellow in Mr Leo's drawing, was it?'

'Yes. I'm sorry. I wasn't sure if – if you knew about that.'

Miller grunted an assent. 'Where's his lordship?'

'He's coming,' she began, just as Max tore into the yard, minus either coat or cravat.

'Anything?' he demanded of the coachman.

'No, my lord. There's been no one in the stables but me since you left.'

Max swung round on Frances. 'And you saw him where?'

'At the gate between the garden and the lane.'

'Show me. Joe – take a look around the village. If he doesn't know he was recognised, he may still be here.'

Fifteen unsuccessful minutes later, Max led Frances back inside the inn, muttering, 'Damn. I was really hoping to spare us a good deal of trouble by laying hands on him today. As it is, we're going to have to wait --'

'My lord!' The innkeeper bustled up, beaming and holding out a small rectangular parcel. 'Good news, my lord – I reckon this must be the package you was expecting.'

'Almost certainly, I should think.' Max sounded more resigned than delighted. 'Who brought it – and when?'

'Not half an hour since. A foreign-looking gent left it with my girl Meggie.'

'I see. I'd like to speak with Meggie, if I may.'

'Of course, my lord. I'll fetch her for thee.'

'Thank you.' Waiting until the fellow had gone, Max slit the seal on the parcel and opened it. As expected, a gentleman's pocket-watch tumbled into his palm. He handed it to Frances saying, 'Your brother's, I presume?'

Still incapable of meeting his eyes, she nodded, her fingers closing around the watch.

'Well, I suppose that's something.' He unfolded the accompanying letter and scanned its contents. Then he said flatly, 'When I catch up with Grey, I'm going to kill him.'

'What does it say?' asked Frances.

He passed it to her. 'See for yourself. Meanwhile, I hope somebody here can tell me where the hell Kirkoswald is.'

CHAPTER NINE

The Inside the tap-room of the Castle Inn, the debate on the location of Kirkoswald had lasted most of the evening. It was to the east, somewhere on Hunderthwaite Moor; it was west, near Wickerstack; it was north, miles the other side of the Wall. The only thing everyone could agree upon was that none of them had ever been there. But eventually someone came up with the idea of consulting the doctor – an educated, well-travelled gentleman who everyone respected as the font of all knowledge. And much to Max's relief, the doctor had not proved a disappointment.

'It lies in the Eden Valley, some six or seven miles north of Penrith,' he had announced after taking a moment or two to think about it. 'Your lordship should continue along the Roman Road past Appleby-in-Westmorland as far as the turning for Langwathby. From there, if memory serves, the road follows the course of the Eden and crosses the river just below Kirkoswald.' He paused, frowning. 'There is an inn ... but its name eludes me.'

'The Black Bull,' supplied Max dourly. Then, 'How far, do you think?'

'Between twenty-five and thirty miles? No more than that, I'm sure – and most of it on a good straight road. All being well, your lordship might do it in four hours.'

His lordship had shaken the doctor's hand and instructed the innkeeper to give everyone a drink on his account. Then he'd sent a maid to inform Frances that she must be ready to leave by seven the following morning and, having told Miller the same thing, added tersely, 'If we can get to the next destination early enough, I might have a fighting chance of catching up with Grey. Otherwise, we're likely to end up in bloody Scotland.'

* * *

Frances did not sleep well. She'd avoided Max during the evening by dining in her room on the feeble excuse of being tired. But every time she closed her eyes, she saw mental images of smooth, wet, lightly-golden skin overlaying the muscles of shoulders, arms and ... other parts of him. These, she thought crossly, were vivid enough to keep any female awake. They also put ideas in her head and sensations in her body that she really didn't want. By the time she walked outside to the carriage, she still did not know how she was going to face him without turning scarlet with mortification.

They left Brough exactly on time and resumed their journey north-west along the Roman Road. With other things on his mind, Max did not immediately notice that Frances was unusually silent and seemingly intent on not meeting his eyes. Since the reason for this wasn't difficult to guess – and since he found both yesterday's incident and her reaction to it more than a little amusing – it lightened what had otherwise been a mood of brooding impatience. And eventually, when the most he could charm out of her were monosyllabic replies, he said, 'I don't know why you're so embarrassed. *I* was the one caught at a – a disadvantage.'

The note of laughter in his voice wasn't calculated to make Frances feel any better and she shot him a brief, darkling glance.

'Try imagining how you would feel if our positions had been reversed.'

This – or variations upon it – was not an idea Max needed putting into his head. The thought of having Frances naked had been his constant companion five years ago and had occurred more often than he cared to admit during the last two days.

He said nothing for a full minute while his eyes lingered on her. Finally, he said slowly, 'I don't think you'd find my imaginings helpful.'

As soon as the next words left her mouth, she regretted them. 'Why not?'

'Because I wouldn't have closed my eyes.'

Everything inside her lurched as if the carriage had bounced over a bump in the road. She felt the beginnings of another epic blush and pressed her lips together to prevent herself saying anything stupid.

Max grinned unrepentantly. 'What did you expect? That I'd pretend I wouldn't have looked and thoroughly enjoyed looking? Quite aside from the fact that no man would pass up an opportunity like that, you'd have known it for a lie the instant I said it.' He paused briefly, then added, 'And I *certainly* wouldn't have wounded your self-esteem by saying I wanted to die.'

'I didn't mean it that way,' burst out Frances hotly. 'You *know* I didn't! How could I when you're so – so --'

'Yes?' he prompted, eyes brimming with wicked laughter. 'I'm so what?'

'So perfectly well aware of – of your own attractions.'

'That may be true,' he admitted, with a shameless grin, 'but I'd much rather *you* were aware of them.' And then, when she glared at him apparently lost for words, 'Forget yesterday, Frances. It was merely one of life's little mishaps. And if *I* don't want to hide in a cupboard because you saw me in the buff, there's no reason why *you* should either. So can we please put it behind us and address the matter in hand?'

She nodded and, clearing her throat, strove for her normal tone.

'I – I presume this early start is because you have a plan?'

'Yes. I am hoping, even with a couple of brief stops to rest the horses, to reach Kirkoswald by one o'clock. I'm further hoping to get there before Grey leaves and thus cut this waste of time shorter than it might otherwise be. And to that end, we will halt a little way out of the town in order to let Joe – who, so far as I'm aware, Grey will not recognise – go ahead to reconnoitre.'

Frances risked a wary glance at him and, seeing that he looked as serious as he sounded, said, 'Grey gives the appearance of knowing this part of the country rather well. Do you think his home may be around here?'

'I've no idea and don't dare speculate. The man is a wild card which means anything is possible. But the only way to end his game swiftly is for me to out-guess or out-pace him. And that is what today is about.'

They paused at Appleby-in-Westmorland and again in a tiny village just after they left the Roman Road. A little way outside Kirkoswald, Miller drew the carriage down a farm track and into the shelter of trees. Then he set off on foot to hunt for Grey. Frances spent the time watching Max growing increasingly impatient and checking his watch every five minutes. Half an hour later, Miller jogged back ... and answered the unspoken question with a shake of his head.

'Damn,' muttered Max. 'He's already gone?'

'Rode off about an hour afore I got there,' said the coachman, fishing in his pocket and handing over the now familiar letter. 'I spun the landlord at the Black Bull a tale and he finally let me have this.'

Max tore it open.

My dear Max, it read

I see that the delightful Frances is travelling with you. Doubtless her company is making your journey a good deal more enjoyable than it might have been otherwise – so much so that I feel sure you would not wish it to end too soon. I have shaken the dust of Kirkoswald from my feet and departed for Gilsland. Do feel free to join me there.

Yours, in anticipation,

And the same indecipherable initials as before.

'I *am* going to kill him,' growled Max. 'Slowly.'

'I'll watch,' said Frances. 'But first, we'd better find out where Gilsland is, don't you think?'

'More significantly,' said Max, looking at Miller, 'how *far* it is.'

The coachman nodded in unspoken understanding. Then, 'There's a church. Maybe the vicar, d'you think?'

'Worth a try. Let's go.'

The Reverend Baggott eyed Lord Brandon doubtfully.

'Gilsland, sir? Are you quite sure? It is little more than a hamlet, you know.'

'I didn't – but obviously you do. Where is it?'

'It is one of numerous settlements built along the great Roman Wall.'

'Christ,' muttered Max. And in response to a look of sharp reproof, 'I beg your pardon, Reverend. My temper has been sorely tried recently. So ... Hadrian's Wall, you say. How far and how do I get there?'

'You continue on the road you came in on as far as Brampton and then turn north-east along the Wall. I would estimate it to be a distance of some twenty miles.'

Max shot a glance at Miller, received a decisive nod and quickly pressed a couple of guineas into the vicar's hand. 'My thanks – and something for the church roof, sir.'

Wasting no time, both men strode back to where Frances waited beside the carriage while an ostler from the Black Bull watered the horses.

'You think we can do it?' asked Max.

'I reckon so. The horses have had best part of an hour's rest here. They'll be good for the distance if we take it easy.'

With a nod, Max handed Frances back inside the carriage. She said, 'Are we not stopping here?'

'No. It's twenty miles to Gilsland. We can be there before dark.'

Frances leaned her head back against the squabs and thought about it. Finally she said, 'He won't be there. He'll know you won't waste time here – that you'll give chase.'

'Not necessarily. For all Grey knows to the contrary, we might not have left Brough until mid-morning – or we might have met with an accident along the road. Since he departed Kirkoswald an hour before we arrived here, he can't know where we are right now. And sooner or later, the luck must favour us rather than him.' He smiled at her, albeit a shade grimly. 'Let us hope that this is that moment.'

'He didn't tell you which inn to go to.'

'No. But since the vicar described the place as a hamlet, I doubt there will be any choice in the matter.' Max refrained from voicing his private concern that whatever accommodation they found there might well be inadequate – in which case he was likely to be spending the night on a bench in the tap-room. 'Cheer up. You're going to see Hadrian's Wall. And in the meantime we can decide how we want to murder Grey.'

By the time they arrived in Brampton, Frances had a stiff neck and was aching in every muscle. When they stopped to rest the horses and take a belated meal, she would have given anything not to get back in the carriage and found it a struggle not to say so since it would merely give Max the opportunity to point out that she was only there at her own insistence. So she ate half a bowl of thick soup and a slice of bread still warm from the oven. Meanwhile, the innkeeper laughed when he heard their destination but directed them to take the road to Lanercost Priory, after which they could simply follow the Wall.

'You're tired, aren't you?' asked Max quietly when they were on the road again. 'It's all right to admit it, you know. So am I. And Joe must be more exhausted than either of us.'

'I don't know how he manages to drive for so many hours at a stretch.'

'He comes of good Yorkshire stock; tough, loyal and discreet. He's been at Brandon Lacey since we were both fifteen and as boys, we did everything together.'

'You trust him.' It was not a question.

'With my life. And to a degree just at the moment, with yours, too.' He glanced through the window. 'Look. That must be the priory.'

Lanercost was constructed of rough, local stone and appeared to be composed of a number of buildings fused into a whole. Many parts of it lacked a roof but the nave of the church showed signs of relatively recent repair which suggested that it was still used for parish services. Frances stared up at it feeling oddly sad.

'Do you want to stop?' asked Max. 'It can't be far now – so we can if you wish it.'

She shook her head. 'No. It seems … forlorn. Lonely.'

His brows rose slightly. 'Do you think so?'

'Don't you?'

'No. I was thinking that there might be a hermit.'

Caught unawares, laughter flared in her face and escaped in a warm, delighted ripple.

Feeling as if a hole had been punched in his chest, Max stopped breathing … a single truth hammering through his brain.

And there it is … the answer I was seeking which has actually been staring me in the face all the time. How could I have thought, even for a second, that I didn't know? Why did I doubt? Why did I question? I love you. I've always loved you … through every day, every hour since we first met … even through those five empty, wasted years. Why did it take me so long to understand that the love we had for each other was strong enough to survive anything? For it was, wasn't it? And the only question that truly matters is whether you understand that too. For I don't believe I am alone in this. You and I were always destined for each other.

Her expression still vivid with laughter, Frances said, 'You still haven't found one then?'

'No. And I've searched Knaresborough Forest from end to end. Of course, no hermit who values his privacy would move into Mother Shipton's cave since everyone knows the old beldame's shade still lives there. But there are plenty of other suitable grottos – all inexplicably vacant. I've been forced to conclude that hermiting is a dying profession.'

She was laughing again before he had finished speaking.

'There's no such word as hermiting.'

'Of course there is. I just said it.'

'Yes – but you made it up.'

He grinned at her. 'And you can do better, I suppose.'

'I could hardly do worse. No one could.'

'Go on, then.'

Frances suddenly realised they were in the midst of exactly the sort of nonsensical bickering that had left them helpless with laughter five years ago. He had never let her win at this game. And right now, with the old familiar and wholly irresistible gleam in his eyes, productive thought was impossible, so she said experimentally, 'Anchoriting?'

'How, exactly, is that better than hermiting?'

'It isn't. But it's no worse either.'

'That's a typically female argument. And I beg to differ.'

'Of course you do. It's the typically *masculine* response.'

Refusing to laugh, Max shook his head.

'Anchoriting sounds like someone who writes on anchors – though I can't imagine why anybody would. You're at sea. Admit it.'

Yes, she thought, *I am. Far out at sea and drowning*. But she said, 'I admit nothing – save for curiosity about Mother Shipton. Who was she?'

'You've never heard of Knaresborough's famous prophetess and her petrifying well? Shame on you!'

'There's a petrifying well at Matlock Bath,' retorted Frances, 'so you needn't sound so superior. But perhaps all you know about your prophetess is her name.'

'If that is a challenge, you've lost it,' said Max calmly. 'Ursula Southill – better known as Mother Shipton – lived about two hundred years ago in the forest of Knaresborough, near what we call the Dropping Well. She was reputedly born in a cave and so horrendously ugly that people thought her father had been the devil. After she died, her numerous prophesies were published, foretelling all manner of bizarre wonders the future has in store – none of which have so far come to pass.'

'Such as what?'

'Carriages without horses and men flying – presumably in some sort of machine, since I don't imagine we'll all start sprouting wings. But she's best known for predicting that the world will end in 1881. Whether or not this turns out to be true isn't likely to bother us or even our children … but it will give the superstitious a very anxious time in 1880.'

'Spare a moment's sympathy for your grandchildren,' advised Frances dryly. Then, 'Oh – we've reached the Wall.'

He looked through the window at the imperfect but continuous rough stone barrier, much of what they could see built to a height of some four feet.

'So we have. A remarkable achievement, isn't it? And even more remarkable that more of it hasn't been carted away for use elsewhere.'

'People *do* that?' she asked, faintly shocked.

'Yes. The northerners are a canny, practical lot. When a cottage needs repairing or an extra room is required to house the eight children, it's easier and cheaper to take stones that somebody else has kindly already quarried for you. Antiquity means little – and the Wall serves no useful function, after all. I'd even lay money on some of it being used to build that priory we passed a little while back.'

'No useful function? How can that be? It's the border to

Scotland, isn't it?'

'No, thank God. That is still a fair way further north. To the best of my recollection, Hadrian built his wall to mark the edge of the Roman Empire under his reign. And that, I regret to say, is the sum total of my knowledge.' Turning back from the window, he said, 'Even more regrettably, we appear to have reached Gilsland ... and I don't see an inn.'

Letting down the window, he called for the coachman to pull up and then, hopping down said, 'Any sign of an inn from up there, Joe?'

'No. Nowt but cottages ... and a fellow mending a fence. Best ask him, I reckon.'

Leaning out of the carriage, Frances watched the villager reply to Max's question by pointing further down the road. She hoped this was a positive omen. She didn't think she could bear the thought of travelling any further today.

Max returned, saying, 'Down there and off to the right, Joe. It's a place called the Shaws – which, good, bad or indifferent will have to do since the only alternative is five miles on to Haltwhistle.'

Settling back into his seat, he smiled faintly and said, 'Relieved? So am I. Supper and bed for you, I think. Joe and I can track down Grey – assuming he's still in the vicinity.'

The Shaws was a small place but spotlessly clean. They were greeted with a surprised smile by a woman clearly interrupted in the middle of baking and who told them, in an accent verging on incomprehensible, that she did indeed have two rooms – though they might not be what the lady was used to.

Frances smiled back and said, 'Don't worry about that, ma'am. My cousin and I have been travelling all day and I'm so tired, I believe I could sleep on a table-top.'

'Away, lass – we can do better than that, I hope. Come along in and sit while the kettle boils. I'll have tea ready in no time.' She dropped a quick curtsy to Max and added, 'I'm Jenny Shaw, sir and my girl, Lissy'll make up the bedchambers straight. Your driver'll find stabling round at back and there's a room above where he can sleep.'

As Max escorted her inside, Frances murmured, 'She's said nothing of another guest, has she? And I think she would have if there had been one.'

'If Grey sticks to the usual pattern, he'll merely pass through. We'll see.'

When Mistress Shaw returned bearing tea and warm, fragrant scones, Max said, 'I half-expected to find a letter awaiting me here. It would be addressed to Lord Brandon.'

'*Lord* is it?' This won Max another and deeper curtsy. 'My word! 'Tis a red-letter day for Shaws when titled folk come to stay. Whatever brings you to Gilsland, my lord?'

'A small matter of business, merely. I take it that there's been no letter?'

'None. There's been nobody else by all day.'

'Then it's possible the man bringing it has yet to arrive. If and when he does, I would appreciate being informed of it.' Max bathed Mistress Shaw in his most charming smile. 'I am extremely eager to meet him, you see ... but thus far, he has proved somewhat shy.'

Shy? Frances choked over her tea.

Fortunately, still melting under his lordship's smile, Jenny Shaw didn't notice. She said, 'I'll have my folk keep an eye out, m'lord. If he comes, you'll know of it directly.'

He bowed slightly. 'Thank you, ma'am. That would be most helpful.'

The bow completed Jenny's enslavement. Murmuring something about bedchambers, she curtsied yet again and withdrew.

Frances eyed Max meditatively. 'That was completely unscrupulous.'

He grinned at her. 'I know. But it worked, didn't it? If Grey shows up, I wouldn't be surprised if she locks him in the cellar.'

'Nor would I.' She took a bite of scone. 'Still ... the fact that he hasn't already been and gone is good, isn't it?'

The grin was replaced by a faint frown.

'It ... might be. But he had a head start on us and was travelling on horseback. Although it's possible he was delayed for some reason, it's equally possible that he isn't sticking to the usual pattern. And if that is the case, there's no predicting what he may be planning. The only thing I think we may be certain of is that this place isn't our final destination. But then, I never expected it to be.'

CHAPTER TEN

At Max's request, Miller joined them for supper. This was taken in a parlour cluttered with more brightly-coloured ornaments and knick-knacks than Frances had ever seen in one place. Staring at them, she managed not to giggle while Mistress Shaw served a steaming hot-pot and fresh bread but lost the battle when, as soon as she left, Max muttered, 'Don't move, Joe. There's a shelf full of nasty-looking dogs just behind your head.'

'And another of simpering shepherdesses b-behind yours,' added Frances. 'Pity the poor person who has to dust them all!'

'The pity is that she hasn't managed to drop a few.' Max took a bite of hotpot and gave an appreciative groan. 'But Mistress Shaw can certainly cook. This is the best meal we've had since we left home.'

'D'you reckon Grey's going to show up?' asked Miller, after a while. 'There's scant places round here for him to lurk wi'out being seen – and strangers get noticed.'

'True. As for Grey, I don't know. But my instinct is that he won't abandon the game before it comes to some sort of point. And the only thing making this jaunt worthwhile is the prospect of finally getting my hands on him.'

Miller glanced up from his plate. 'Do I get a turn?'

'Not this time, Joe.' A half-grin formed. 'You can hold my coat.'

'Ah. Reckon there won't be too much left of him after that, then.'

They were part-way through enormous helpings of plum crumble when they heard the sound of loud male voices, punctuated by Mistress Shaw's infuriated tones. Then the door burst open on a pair of grim-faced individuals carrying small batons which identified them as constables. Max and Miller came abruptly to their feet, causing both dogs and shepherdesses to rattle ominously while, from the doorway, Mistress Shaw snapped, 'I tried to stop 'em, my lord, but the great loobies pushed me out the way – and in my own house!'

One of the intruders said placatingly, 'Now see here, Jenny --'

'Don't you Jenny me, Harry Carter. You should be ashamed to be disturbing decent folk at table.'

'But we've been sent official-like, with proper orders and--'

'I don't care if the *King* sent you! Ye've no right --'

'We has *every* right,' growled the other man, 'so stow your gab, woman.' He stared across the room and, stabbing a finger in Max's direction, said, 'Be you the fellow calling hisself Baron Brandon?'

'I *am* Lord Brandon,' replied Max, becoming every inch the haughty aristocrat despite the uneasy suspicion that was taking shape in his mind. 'What of it?'

'Ye've to come along wi' us. There's been information laid agin ye.'

Miller clenched his fists. Suddenly anxious, Frances opened her mouth to speak ... then, seeing the almost imperceptible shake of Max's head, stopped.

'What information? And laid by whom?' he demanded coldly.

'Ye'll be told that by the magistrate --'

'I'll be told *now*, if you expect me to take a step from here. Well?'

The constable scowled and advanced a step.

'Resisting arrest's a serious offence. Ye'll be in more trouble than now if'n --'

'I am not resisting arrest,' replied Max, in the tone of one addressing an imbecile. 'I am asking for information – as I am perfectly entitled to do. Now answer my questions.'

'Might as well tell him, Matt,' said Carter. 'No point making it harder than needs be. And the sooner this is done, the sooner thou and me'll get home.'

'Sense at last,' remarked Max. 'Now ... of what am I accused?'

'For a start, calling yoursen a lord when I'll bet you ain't one – 'cos what'd a titled gent want in a place like this?'

'Don't be a bigger fool than you can help, Matt Johnson,' scoffed Mistress Shaw. 'Don't you know Quality when you sees it?'

'But mostly,' continued Johnson through his teeth, 'because

there's complaints out agin ye for piking off wi'out paying at The Bell in Longtown and The Feathers in Brampton. That's theft, that is. And there's charges to answer.'

'Are there indeed?' His mind busy with what he suspected were very few alternatives, Max eyed Johnson over derisively folded arms. 'You will find them impossible to prove.'

'Why?' asked Carter, clearly less sure of his ground than his colleague.

'Because, since I have never visited the aforementioned establishments, no one at either will able to identify me. Someone has played you for fools, gentlemen. And that being so, I would strongly advise you to consult with your superiors before proceeding further with this farrago -- '

'Oh no – we'll have none of that!' said Johnson, reaching out to grasp Max's arm.

Fists still clenched and slightly raised, Miller instantly stepped towards them – only to hesitate when Max said softly, 'Don't, Joe.'

'You heard him,' spat Johnson. 'Back down.'

'Get your grubby hands off his lordship, then,' retorted Miller.

'I'd do that, if I were you,' murmured Max. 'You'd be unwise to risk damaging any of Mistress Shaw's charming ornaments.'

'Start summat in my parlour,' threatened Mistress Shaw, 'and I'll see thee barred in every tavern from Carlisle to Hexham, Matthew Johnson. Don't think I won't!'

Johnson's hand dropped away but he said doggedly, 'Up to you to come quietly, then in't it? Because, lord or no, I'll not let you slope off. Harry and me was ordered to bring you in – and that's what we'll do. You can save yon excuses for magistrate.'

Seeing little help for it, Max shrugged and capitulated. 'Very well. If nothing else will satisfy you – by all means, let us visit the magistrate.'

No longer able to stay out of it, Frances said, 'No! Max – you can't!'

'Why not? This can all be cleared up very easily – and the alternative is to spend the entire night arguing with this precious pair.' He gave her what he hoped was a reassuring smile and turned to Miller. 'Stay here, Joe – and don't do anything rash. It won't help if we're *both* arrested.'

'But my lord --'

'*No.* You know as well as I how this happened. I doubt Grey will show his face ... but if he does, you can vent your anger on him.' And to the constables, in a tone that brooked no argument, 'You will apologise to Mistress Shaw for the intrusion, then wait in the hall while I fetch my hat. What you will *not* do, if you are wise, is speak to me again.'

* * *

While the constables took Max away with them, Frances and Miller remained staring helplessly at each other in wordless consternation. Then Jenny Shaw ran back into the parlour, saying breathlessly, 'They've gone off Haltwhistle way.'

'Yes.' There was a lead weight of fear in Frances's throat. 'That's what they said.'

'But that isn't right, Mistress! His lordship thinks to see magistrate – but Sir George don't live in Haltwhistle. He lives over to Thirlwall. If'n that daft lump Johnson is driving to Haltwhistle, it's to put his lordship in lock-up till morning.'

'*What*? Over my dead body, he will.' Already heading for the door, Miller said, 'Stay here, Miss. I'll hitch the horses and get after them.'

'No – wait!' Trying to think past the welter of emotions, Frances said, 'They won't give him up to you, Mr Miller – and fighting will make it all worse. It would be better if ... yes. We should go to the magistrate. *Both* of us. He might not receive you but I can probably make him see me.' She looked at Jenny. 'He's Sir George ...?'

'Caxton. Sir George Caxton of Thirlwall Manor. But it's a tricky road out there wi' darkness falling and he'll likely not receive you neither at this time o' day.' She stopped and then said slowly, 'You'll have to take Lissy. She knows the road and, in her Sunday bonnet and cloak, she'll pass for your maid. I'd come mysen 'cept Sir George'd know me. I'll fetch her while the horses are put to and you get your things.'

She bustled away, leaving Miller looking thunderous but

indecisive.

'She's right,' said Frances, heading for the door. 'I'll be out in five minutes.'

Upstairs, she went first into Max's bedchamber in search of the document case and, finding it, withdrew both Grey's likeness and the letter that had awaited them at Brough. Fortunately, it was less irritatingly chatty than the one from Kirkoswald which, she supposed, was still in Max's pocket. Then, not wasting time tidying her hair, she grabbed her cloak and ran back down the stairs.

Lissy, brimming with excited self-importance, beamed at her from the tiny hall.

'Ma says as I'm to be a pretend lady's maid, ma'am!'

'I'm sure you'll do it beautifully.' Frances flashed a grateful smile at the girl's mother. 'I'm sorry for the trouble and I – well, I *thank* you.'

'No need for thanks, lass.' Jenny patted her hand. 'Just fetch the bonny lad home. I'll have a toddy waiting.'

Without needing to be asked, Lissy clambered up beside Miller to show him the way. Inside the carriage, Frances concentrated on working out first how to make Sir George receive her and then, how to make him release Max from whatever dingy hole they had put him in. Her biggest problem, she realised, was going to be making the magistrate take her seriously.

Thirlwall Manor was a modest house, standing in splendid isolation. Miller brought the carriage to a halt outside the main door and helped Lissy down from the box. While letting the steps down for Frances, he said, 'D'you reckon we'd get away with saying you're his lordship's wife?'

'I don't know. I thought of it ... but Max won't know so he might --'

'Give the game away? No. He's smarter than that. And even if he weren't, by then you'll have got your way. Let's do it.'

Miller rapped on the door, waited for a moment and then knocked more forcefully. It opened a few inches and a servant peered around it. 'Yes?'

'Lady Brandon to see Sir George on pressing business.'

'Tell her to come back tomorrow. Sir George is at dinner and can't be disturbed.'

'That's for him to say, not you. And if he's any sort of gentleman, he won't thank you for keeping her ladyship standing on the steps – so open the door.'

Grudgingly but cowed by Miller's authoritative tone, the butler gave in. With Lissy at her heels, Frances sailed inside and, stripping off her gloves, said, 'Inform Sir George that Lady Brandon desires a few minutes of his time on a matter of some urgency. I will wait ... though not, I think, in the hall.'

Having once given way, the butler yielded to the inevitable and led Frances into a small parlour. 'Please be seated, your ladyship. I will inform Sir George that you are here – although, as I said, he is at dinner and has guests this evening.'

'And as *I* said,' returned Frances coolly, 'I will wait.'

He made a small bow and left. Seeing a clock on the mantelpiece, Frances made a mental note of the time. Lissy, meanwhile, turned in a circle examining the room in wide-eyed admiration.

'My stars! I never saw anywhere so grand as this. I wish Ma was here to see it. Sir George must be terrible rich.'

Amused despite herself, Frances agreed that yes, indeed he must be. Then she went back to marshalling the words she would need if and when Sir George deigned to see her.

Ten minutes ticked by. The butler returned with an offer of tea. Frances thanked him and refused. By the time a further fifteen minutes had elapsed, impatience and worry about Max was corroding the edges of her mind. And then, finally, the door opened on the burly figure of the magistrate.

Casting a brief glance at Lissy, standing demurely in the corner, he said bluntly, 'Well, ma'am, you've dragged me away --'

'My lady,' interrupted Frances glacially. 'You should, more properly, address me as my lady. Did your man not inform you of my rank?'

'He did – but you'll have to pardon me having my doubts. There's a fellow calling himself Lord Brandon locked up for diddling innkeepers. Unless you're married to somebody else --'

'No. The man your underlings arrested earlier this evening is indeed my husband. And there is no question of his identity. He is Baron Brandon of Brandon Lacey in Yorkshire. He is known by all the best families in the North Riding and related to half of them. He is also a distant connection of the Duke of Rockliffe. What I can assure you he is *not*,' finished Frances flatly, 'is either an imposter or a thief.'

'So you say – but I don't know who the devil you are, do I? So what makes you suppose I'll take your word on all this?'

'You took the word of whoever brought you these fictitious charges, did you not? And I very much doubt you knew who the devil *he* was either.'

A dull flush mantled Sir George's cheeks. 'He gave me a signed deposition with chapter and verse in it. I saw no reason to disbelieve him.'

'You met him yourself?'

'Yes.'

'Good.' Frances handed him Leo's drawing. 'Was this the man?'

The magistrate frowned at the likeness in stunned silence for a moment. Then, looking at Frances with a faint glimmer of uncertainty, he said, 'Yes. Who is he? And why do you have this?'

'He is a thief and a fraudster, sir. We do not know his name – only that he often misuses that of my husband. We have been pursuing him for some days. He knows this – hence the false accusation designed to impede our progress.' Since she appeared to have Sir George's whole attention, she pressed her advantage. 'As his lordship told your constables, he has never visited the inns he has supposedly cheated, so no one there will recognise him. It would be no surprise at all, however, if they were to recognise *this* man.'

'Maybe so – but I'd have to send somebody to Brampton to verify that. And there'll be no catching up with him now. He said he was heading over the border to Canonbie … though, if what you've been telling me is true, he probably isn't.'

On the contrary, thought Frances. *He counted on you telling us that.*

Reclaiming Leo's drawing, she handed over the letter in order to settle the matter once and for all. 'If you require additional proof, here is a sample of his handwriting which you may compare with his statement. Or perhaps you already recognise it and don't need to?'

Sir George shuffled uneasily. 'It looks ... similar.'

'Similar? I'd guess it is *identical*,' she said aridly. 'Really, sir – your fellows ought to have listened when my husband told them that they had been deceived and should lay the matter in front of you before proceeding further. Instead, they have hauled him off to Haltwhistle, thus compounding the original mistake and making you responsible for incarcerating a peer of the realm like a common felon. I am sure I don't need to tell you that my husband will not take kindly to such treatment.'

He scowled. 'Don't think to threaten me, my lady.'

'I'm not. I am merely pointing out the realities of the situation. You were over-hasty in taking the word of a man you did not know and it has resulted in a very regrettable mistake. Can you *really* not see that letting it continue any longer than necessary will only make things worse?'

The magistrate huffed an impatient breath.

'I know what you want. But if you think I'm leaving my guests to drive over to Haltwhistle at this time of night --'

'And there is no need for you to do so ... if the man in charge of the lock-up can read?' Frances held back a sigh of relief which might prove premature. 'You need merely write a note instructing him to release Lord Brandon – and I will take it there myself.' She smiled suddenly. 'A brief note, Sir George ... and you can rejoin your guests.'

He took so long to reply that she began to think he wasn't going to. But finally he snapped, 'Very well. If that's what it takes to be rid of you. Wait here.'

When the door closed behind him, Frances sank into the nearest chair queasy with nerves. From her place in the corner, Lissy said admiringly, 'You're a bold one, Miss. I'll bet the old curmudgeon's never had a lass stand up to him like that afore.'

'Possibly not,' replied Frances weakly. 'Thank God he finally listened.'

'Oh he did that alright, Miss. Gave him a right telling off and no mistake.'

Sir George stalked back into the room and held out an unsealed missive.

'Read it,' he ordered.

Lord Brandon is innocent of the charges laid against him and should be released without delay or argument. Tell Johnson and Carter to bring me their explanations first thing in the morning.

Frances looked up from the magistrate's bold and perfectly legible signature.

'Thank you, sir. I am obliged to you.'

'Yes. Well ... see to it that your husband is too.'

* * *

Max had spent an extremely unpleasant few hours. It was not until they drew up outside a building that was very clearly *not* the magistrate's residence that he had realised where Johnson had brought him – and by then it was too late to do anything about it. Using his fists against two constables and the fellow in charge of the lock-up wasn't going to achieve anything other than earning himself a few bruises and ruining his coat. He'd tried remonstrating, of course, but with little hope of being attended to. And after Johnson and Carter left and he'd been locked in a small, filthy cell reeking of urine, he offered the jailer a bribe ... but the man refused it on the score of preferring to keep his job. So all that was left for Max to do thereafter was lean against a wall, grimly and impotently furious, and wonder how long he would be kept here before someone recognised the error of their ways.

Time crawled by at a snail's pace. Dusk faded into dark and he was left in the pitch black until someone at a nearby house lit an outside lantern and a glimmer of light crept through the narrow grating above his head. It wasn't much but he was grateful for it. If there were rats here – and there probably were – he'd prefer to be able to see them before they climbed on his boots.

He was just, for perhaps the twentieth time, wondering what

the hour was when he heard the sound of someone hammering on the outer door. Max straightened and moved away from the wall. He thought, *I hope to God that's you disobeying my order, Joe – otherwise it's going to be a very long night.*

There was a good deal of incomprehensible grumbling, followed by the screech of the bolts being drawn back. Then Miller's blessed tones saying clearly, 'The magistrate reckons you can read – so read *that* and be quick about it.'

A pause ... followed by a mumbled response.

'I know what it says,' snapped Miller. 'The magistrate orders you to release his lordship right now. So bloody jump to it.'

The door between Max's cell and the outer office swung open and the jailer ambled over, fumbling with his keys. He muttered, 'Seems there's been some mistake, m'lord.'

'I am only too aware of that fact.'

'But the mistake weren't mine.'

'So? Just unlock the damned door. I'd like to leave here tonight, if possible.'

'Aye. I daresay that little wife o' yourn's been right worried --'

'*Wife?*' echoed Max, as the lock sprang open. And immediately covering his presumably misplaced incredulity, 'I told her to remain at the inn. She's *here*?'

'Aye, m'lord. Out in the --'

But Max didn't wait.

And neither, the instant he appeared in the doorway, did Frances. She flew across to cast herself against his chest, whispering rapidly, 'I'm your wife.'

Since up to this point, he'd had a hell of an evening, Max decided he was entitled to enjoy himself. His arms closed about her; he murmured, 'It's all right, my darling. I'm fine.' And then he captured her mouth in a long, luxurious kiss of the kind a man was entitled to have from his wife. Startled, Frances gasped and clung. He had kissed her before and she'd thought she remembered how it had been. She discovered the reality of it far outstripped her hazy recollections ... and her only thought was that she didn't want it to stop.

Max might *not* have stopped had he not heard Miller telling the jailer to put his eyes back in his head. Very, very reluctantly, he released Frances's mouth but continued to hold the rest of her. Meeting Miller's eyes over her head, he said, 'Let's go, Joe. I'll express my thanks later.'

'No need to express 'em at all. You didn't think we was going to leave you here all night, did you? And it was your lady wife did most of the work.'

Max smiled down into Frances's eyes. 'Then I'll thank you, as well.'

She blushed and shook her head. However, before she could speak, the jailer said hopefully, 'I'll take that guinea now, m'lord – if it's still on offer.'

'It isn't.' Max swept Frances out into the street, then stopped looking enquiringly at Lissy, still perched on the box.

She beamed at him. 'I went with Miss to the magistrate like a real lady's maid so it was all proper. And I'm to show Mr Miller the road home.'

'You've clearly been a great help.' And, aware that the jailer was lurking in the doorway behind him, he tossed a guinea up to the girl. 'Thank you.'

'Ooh – thank *you*, m'lord. Not as I needed paying. I've never had so much fun!'

'I'm glad someone has,' he murmured, helping Frances into the carriage. 'Though I'll admit my own evening has improved tremendously in the last few minutes.'

'I don't know how you can take all this so calmly,' she said as Miller set the horses in motion. 'If I'd spent hours locked in a filthy cell, I'd want to hit someone.'

'So do I. But the person I want to hit isn't within reach right now.' Since she hadn't noticed that her fingers were still folded in his, he left them there. 'Now ... tell me how you got me out.'

'I told the magistrate that I was your w-wife so he'd listen to me. And since nobody knows us here and we're not staying, I didn't think it would matter so very much or --'

'It doesn't matter in the slightest,' said Max. And promptly startled himself by thinking instinctively, *It doesn't matter because, if you'll let me, I've every intention of making it true.* For a second, the breath left him. Then he said carefully, 'What happened then?'

'I told him the same things you told the constables earlier. Then I showed him Grey's picture and the letter you received at Brough – oh.' She stopped, looking even guiltier. 'I'm sorry. I had to get those from your bedchamber.'

'That doesn't matter either. Go on.'

'There isn't much else. It helped that he had guests and was desperate to be rid of me. When I could see him starting to believe me, I pointed out that he'd made a big mistake which would become even bigger if he didn't order your release. So he did.'

'And for which I am exceedingly grateful.'

She shook her head. 'You need not be. Neither Mr Miller nor I could bear the thought of leaving you there all night. Was it very horrible?'

'It wasn't pleasant.' He drew the line at describing the smell and found himself hoping he hadn't brought it with him. 'One more score to settle with Grey when I finally catch up with him.'

'He told Sir George he was going to Canonbie,' blurted Frances. 'I think it's in Scotland.'

Yesterday, Max would have found this extremely annoying. Today, he suddenly no longer minded very much how long their journey lasted since it was providing opportunities he would not otherwise get. So he shrugged and said, 'Ah well ... I'm told Scotland is lovely at this time of year. So let us hope that the weather holds.'

CHAPTER ELEVEN

Although the next day began well with the information that Canonbie lay less than thirty miles away, Max was to regret having tempted fate by mentioning the weather. By the time they reached Brampton an intermittent drizzle had set in and was bringing a distinct chill to the air. Frances sat huddled in her cloak, looking tired and seeming disinclined for conversation. Then, as they were crossing to the other side of the Wall, she said abruptly, 'Grey doesn't seem to have a problem with money, does he?'

'No. But perhaps he's sending his accommodation bills to Brandon Lacy – speaking of which, I must write to Duncan. I ought to let him know that we're still chasing a phantom and that I have no idea how much longer I'll be away ... because in a couple of days' time, if not sooner, he's going to find himself fielding questions from my mother.'

'So will Rufus,' agreed Frances gloomily. 'The note I sent from Richmond was deliberately vague. I didn't hint that I'd no intention of going home once I'd recovered his watch but he probably assumed that I would. *Now* I suppose I'd better tell him the truth.'

'Does that include the fact that you are travelling unchaperoned with me?'

'No!' She stared him, appalled. 'If I tell him *that* and Mama bullies it out of him, she'll jump to stupid conclusions about what has been going on between us and absolutely refuse to accept that nothing *is*.'

Max refrained from pointing out that something had very definitely been going on between them last night. However, he couldn't resist raising faintly enquiring eyebrows and saw, by the hint of colour rising behind those charming freckles, that she was remembering it too. Smiling inwardly, he remained silent – knowing that she wouldn't be able to.

'That was just pretence,' she muttered. 'We had to act as if we were married.'

I wasn't pretending, thought Max. *And I don't believe you were, either.* But he said lazily, 'And we were doubtless very convincing.'

The flush deepened. 'Of course. That was the point, wasn't it?'

Not to me. But he didn't say it and instead changed the subject.

'You said you showed the magistrate one of Grey's letters. Did you see the statement?'

'No. Since he obviously recognised the writing, I didn't ask. Should I have done?'

'It might have been helpful to know what name he signed. Or then again, not.' Leaning back, he let his gaze drift through the window, on the other side of which the rain appeared to be getting heavier. 'My main concern – aside from the obvious question of how long he intends to keep this up – is how he is managing to keep track of us so accurately. And I see only two explanations for that. Either he is always much nearer than we think; or he is paying someone to follow us while he remains ahead. I wish we knew which.'

They halted for food and to rest the horses at a small inn some miles short of Longtown but did not linger as long as Max might have done had the rain not become unrelenting. Back in the carriage, he said, 'You look tired, Frances. We've another dozen miles to go and the rain will slow us down. Why don't you try to sleep for a little while?'

'I can't. Every bump jolts me awake.'

'Does it? Then let's see if we can do something about that. Move over.'

She blinked at him. 'What?'

'Slide over to your left.' He waited until she had done so and then crossed to sit beside her, wedging himself into the corner and putting an arm about her to draw her to his side. When her head was resting on his shoulder, he said prosaically, 'Thanks to me being hauled off to gaol last night, you didn't get much rest. This is me making it up to you. Now shut your eyes and sleep.'

Although she obediently closed her eyes, Frances wasn't at all sure she would be able to sleep. Max's proximity made her remember things she had spent a long time working hard to forget. Worse still, the scent of his skin brought last night's kiss back with startling clarity and wakened things in her body that were best left undisturbed. She told herself that the sensible thing was to make some excuse and move away. But he was so warm ... and it was so comfortable being held securely in the curve of his arm. She decided it couldn't do any harm to enjoy it a little longer.

She awoke some considerable time later to the realisation that her cheek was pillowed on Max's thigh and his hand gently stroking her hair. Feeling awkward, untidy and embarrassed, she struggled upright saying, 'I'm so sorry. How long have I been lying on you like that? You should have woken me.'

'Why? It was no trouble. In fact, I rather enjoyed it.'

Frances ignored the little pulse of pleasure his words provoked and pushed ineffectually at her hair. 'Where are we?'

'Scotland. We crossed the border a mile or so back – though, with no bagpipes waiting to welcome us, it was a little hard to be sure. And according to the last milestone, Canonbie is the next town.' Smiling, he pulled out his watch and added, 'It's not quite four o'clock. How does a bath and a nap before dinner sound?'

'Blissful,' she admitted. 'Nearly every bit of me aches. And I must look a fright.'

'No.' *Your eyes are sleepy and your hair is coming down. You look as if you've just woken up – which, indeed, you have – though unfortunately not next to me in bed. And though I've more sense than to say any of this aloud, bits of me are aching as well.* Choosing his words carefully, he said, 'You don't look a fright. Merely ... delightfully disarranged.'

This produced a tiny choke of laughter. 'Disarranged? How flattering.'

'Actually,' he murmured, 'it *was* a compliment. Ladies are always intent on looking immaculate when, in fact, a little dishevelment can be extremely appealing.'

* * *

The Cross Keys, Canonbie's coaching inn, lay in the centre of the small town and was a very welcome sight after hours of driving through the rain. The fire blazing cheerfully in the coffee room was even more welcome and Frances sat gratefully beside it while Max bespoke rooms and asked the usual question. Presently, he joined her and put a cup of chocolate in her hands while he scanned the now familiar letter. Finally, he said, 'Selkirk next ... for a scenic tour of the borders.'

'Is that all he says?' she asked, warming her hands around the cup.

'By no means.' He passed the letter to her. 'A man of many merry words is Grey, all of them designed to show us how clever he is.'

My dear Max, she read

Did you succeed in talking your way out of trouble – or did you spend the night less pleasantly than you had hoped? I make no apologies, by the way. You did not play by the rules yesterday so I had no alternative but to put you in check. I suggest you remember that in future. Your next move takes you to the The Grapes in Selkirk. The road there passes through some pretty country. Perhaps this time I may feel inclined to linger. Who knows?

Yours in anticipation,

Frances looked up. 'He's treating this as a game of chess?'
'Yes.'
'With us as his pawns?'
'Again, yes.' He grinned suddenly. 'You sound thoroughly insulted.'

'I *am* thoroughly insulted. Aren't you?'

He shook his head. 'Grey wants to annoy me. I prefer not to let him. And it's much better to concentrate on turning the tables.'

'I daresay – but when?'

'Soon? Eventually? I don't know.' Max took the letter from her and read it again. 'He says the road passes through some pretty country – which suggests that he knows it. Perhaps you were right about this area being home to him. If so, it gives him numerous advantages regarding help and information on our progress.'

'But doesn't help us at all,' sighed Frances.

'Quite the reverse.' Max paused, eyeing her thoughtfully. Then deciding to test the water, 'I said I wouldn't let you travel alone and I won't. But if you've had enough of rattling around the countryside and want to go home, I can make enquiries about hiring a carriage and outriders for you – possibly even a maid. Shall I?'

'No.' The word left her mouth before it had passed through her brain but she immediately knew it was the right answer. No matter how exhausting or uncomfortable or potentially risky these days with him were, they were too precious to be needlessly given up. 'No. I don't want to go home. I want to see this through to the end. Checkmate, to put it in Grey's terms.' She gave a tiny, reckless laugh. 'I want to see you knock seven bells out of him. You will, won't you?'

'That is the general idea, yes – though one doesn't generally do that kind of thing in front of a lady. Then again, there's also the question of why he's doing this and what he thinks to achieve by it ... so brute force may have to wait a little while.'

'Pity,' said Frances.

* * *

Eager to be rid of any residual aroma of *Eau de Haltwhistle Lock-up*, Max ordered a bath and, beginning to seriously miss his valet, sent two shirts to be laundered and his boots downstairs for polishing. Vests and cravats were not yet a problem, though they might soon become so, but his coats were starting to gather a well-worn look. Although Max never gave much thought to his appearance when out and about around his estate, he was fastidious about his apparel the rest of the time; and sitting down to dine in tired-looking pewter velvet wasn't what he was used to.

Discovering that Frances had not yet come downstairs, he asked the landlord a few questions before sauntering outside for a breath of air. The rain appeared to have stopped. Hoping it wouldn't start again overnight, he visited the stables to check on the horses and discovered Miller there on the same errand.

'They're fine, my lord. I ordered a hot bran mash after the drenching they had and they've taken no hurt. Should be well enough for tomorrow.'

'Good. And you? Suitable accommodation and a good meal, I hope?'

'Aye.' Miller grinned. 'I've no complaints.'

'Ah. Found a pretty face already, have you?'

'Might've. Do you want me to keep an eye out for Grey?'

Max shook his head. 'He's already been and gone. Our next port of call is Selkirk ... forty miles on the same, reputably reasonable road. It doesn't sound too strenuous. But it will be our fifth day of travel – so it's time I took a stint on the box myself, don't you think?'

The coachman laughed. 'I've been wondering when you'd get around to it.'

Max walked back inside in time to see Frances descending the last few stairs. Clad in the second of the gowns they had bought in Richmond – a cream and green striped polonaise which set off the rich chestnut of her hair – the sight of her caused something to squeeze at his heart. It also re-awakened his awareness of his own slight shabbiness.

Bathed, rested and feeling fully restored, Frances didn't see any fault in his lordship's apparel. She only saw the faint smile, the long, dark hair neatly tied and the perfectly-sculpted bones. Despite trying not to, she also remembered what lay beneath the scarlet and silver silk vest and felt herself flush.

Really, she told herself sternly, *I have to stop doing that before he realises.*

'We'll be dining in the coffee room,' he said, offering his arm. And when she took it, 'Is your bedchamber comfortable?'

'Yes, thank you.' Frances hesitated. Not for the first time, it occurred to her that this journey must be proving expensive. 'I didn't think ... when I insisted on coming with you, I didn't spare a thought for the additional costs it would entail. I ought --'

'Stop,' said Max pleasantly. 'The expense is by no means huge and I have sufficient funds with me. There is nothing that need concern you.'

'But --'

'No.' He handed her into a seat at a table by the window, sat down facing her and said, 'You look charming. I think that gown suits you even better than the blue one.'

'So do I,' she admitted. Then, 'Have you found out about tomorrow.'

'I have.' He repeated what he'd told Miller and added, 'Apparently the road passes through Langholm and Hawick – both of them larger towns than this one. If there is anything you need, one or other of them may be able to provide it.'

Repressing a shudder at the thought of what she already owed him, she said quickly, 'I don't require anything. The clothes we bought in Richmond are more than adequate.'

He sighed. 'You're doing it again, aren't you? Worrying about money. I really wish you wouldn't. We are promised freshly-caught trout, followed by venison and, after last night, it would be pleasant to simply enjoy it.' Smiling, he reached for the surprisingly good claret he had been offered earlier. 'And while we wait, perhaps you'll take a glass of wine with me?'

'Thank you.' Frances searched for a new topic of conversation and, finding it, said, 'I have written to Rufus, telling him that I won't be home for some time but that I have Grandpapa's watch safe. Does the Mail Coach come through here?'

'It does – and will collect your letter, along with mine to Duncan. Hopefully, that will set both families' minds at rest for a few days more.' The smile became grin. 'Duncan will be envying us if the trail takes us near Jedburgh. His home is there and he hasn't been back in nearly a year – not, I hasten to add, because I keep him chained to his desk but because he thinks I can't manage without him.'

Conversation paused briefly as a maid arrived with portions of trout in lemon sauce.

Picking up her knife, Frances said, 'And *can* you? Manage without him, I mean?'

Swallowing a morsel of fish, Max thought about it for a moment and then said wryly, 'Truthfully? I managed perfectly well before and was used to doing so. *Now*, having come to rely on Duncan's particular brand of efficiency, I suspect it may be a different story. Also, of course, he's become a friend ... half of the time, I even forget his father is an earl.'

'*Is* he?' Frances's brows rose. 'And yet Mr Balfour has taken employment?'

'He's the youngest of four brothers – exactly like Simon Greville, in fact.' Max frowned into his glass. 'News of his death didn't reach me until quite recently. My odd little habit of not reading the society pages again. An obscure Indian fever, wasn't it?'

'Yes. Lady Grantham wrote to Mama. She was devastated. Towards the end of last year, one of Simon's colleagues from the East India Company finally arrived at Westlake with his things ... but that can't have been much comfort.' She managed a small smile. 'Apparently, Simon was good at starting letters but hopeless at finishing them. Her ladyship said there were a great number of half-written ones among his belongings.'

'I suppose that explains why I only ever heard from him once, just after he arrived.'

'Yes. Since the ones he never sent were mostly about his work for the Company and English society in Calcutta, Lady Grantham saw little point in sending them on so long after his death – and probably preferred to keep them herself.' Frances took a sip of wine, hesitated briefly and then said, 'Did you ever tell Simon about us?'

Max blinked. 'Of course not. Why would you ask that?'

'Because I didn't say anything to him, either. But I think he knew.'

'He can't have done. At least, I can't imagine *how*. What makes you suppose it?'

'When we were leaving Westlake ... it would have been three days after the betrothal ball ... Simon insisted on escorting me to the carriage. And when no one was paying attention, he whispered, *Don't marry Archie, Frannie. Marry someone who loves you. Someone like Max, maybe.*'

For a long moment, Max stared at her. Finally, he said, 'I don't know how he knew. I didn't think he was that perceptive.'

'Neither did I,' she replied. 'Clearly, we both underestimated him. But he wouldn't have said anything to anyone else, would he?'

'No. I'm sure he wouldn't. And as things turned out, it would have made little difference if he had. Except ...' He stopped, examining a sudden thought. 'I suppose, if he *did* know of our attachment ... and if he'd heard you hadn't married Archie, he might have written to me, asking whether or not I intended to take advantage of the fact – and actually posted the letter. In which case, I wouldn't have been left in ignorance for five years.'

Both of them fell silent as the maid returned to replace the trout with portions of venison in golden pastry and bowls of vegetables. As soon as they were alone again, Frances said, 'Why *don't* you read the society pages?'

Max's pulse gave a hard thud. He concentrated on serving her with fluffy potatoes and buttered peas while he decided whether to say that the doings of society didn't interest him ... or whether to be honest. In the end, because he had no right to expect it from her if he didn't offer it himself, honesty won and he said flatly, 'The last time I did so was the day I saw the announcement of your wedding – after which I spent the best part of a fortnight seeking oblivion at the bottom of a bottle. Suspecting that reading about the birth of your children might have a similar effect, I decided not to risk it.' He met the shock in her eyes and shrugged. 'I'm sorry. I realise it's not pretty – but you did ask. You are also the only person who knows about it. At least I had that much sense.'

Frances sucked in a breath. 'I'm sorry, Max. I'm so sorry.'

'Don't be. It wasn't your fault. If anyone was to blame, it was your parents and, as we have repeatedly agreed, it was all a long time ago and water under numerous bridges.' He summoned a smile and turned back to his plate. 'Try the venison ... it's extremely good.'

* * *

In the dark hours of the night, Max half-regretted telling her the truth and tried to decide whether it had been wise or not. On the whole, he supposed it probably had been. He hoped, before the end of their bizarre adventure, that she would stop trying to guard her heart against him ... and to that end, learning that his pain had been no less than hers could surely only be helpful.

It wasn't hard to understand why she was putting a wall between herself and whatever feelings she might have for him. While he had spent five years believing her married, she had spent those same years believing that he had abandoned her and presumably wondering *why* he had. And then there was her thrice-blasted mother who had probably told her over and over again that no gentleman would ever want to marry a girl famous for leaving a man from a prominent family stranded at the altar. It was utter nonsense, of course; or if it wasn't, the man who let that influence him was an idiot. But Frances wouldn't see it like that. And if one was repeatedly told the same thing, one eventually accepted it as fact.

Max hoped that when he asked her to marry him, she would question neither his sincerity nor his motives but instinctively recognise that his proposal was as heartfelt now as it had been the first time he had made it. He reasoned that time was on his side. Even if they found Grey at Selkirk, it would still take days to travel home; days during which he could gradually erode her defences to the point where all that mattered was that she loved him as much as he loved her.

If that didn't happen, his other options were limited. He refused to consider taking advantage of their current circumstances in order to seduce her – not because she might not let him or because it wasn't the act of a gentleman but because, when he took Frances to bed, he didn't want guilt or regret lying in wait afterwards. But that aside, there wasn't much else he'd baulk at in order not to lose her for a second time. And if all else failed and his only choice was dragging her to the altar ... well, he'd damned well do it and deal with the consequences later. There were advantages, after all, of being in Scotland.

* * *

In her room on the opposite side of the hall, Frances found it impossible to stop his words ringing through her head.

I spent the best part of a fortnight seeking oblivion at the bottom of a bottle.

She wanted to think he hadn't meant that literally but suspected that he had. Max was a strong, rational confident man ... so if the notice of her marriage had reduced him to drinking himself insensible for days on end, it spoke of unendurable suffering. And while that had been happening – despite everything that had passed between them and everything she knew of him – she had been thinking him fickle and shallow.

She pressed the heels of her hands over her eyes. Crying never helped and there was certainly no point in it now, so long after the event. But knowing she had been the cause – albeit unwittingly – of pain like that felt like a knife in her heart.

You are also the only person who knows about it. At least I had that much sense.

From everything he had said and the little she had seen, he and his brothers were extremely close and yet he hadn't turned to them for companionship and comfort. Why not? Because he hadn't been capable of talking about it ... or didn't want anyone to witness what he considered a weakness? However it was, if no one knew about the drinking it meant that he had gone off to lick his wounds alone.

For a few craven moments, she wished he hadn't told her ... and then was ashamed of herself. If he could bring himself to speak of something he'd told no one else, then she could bear to hear it. But why *had* he told her? She was fairly certain that he hadn't originally intended to or he would have done it five days ago. So what had changed?

She loosed a small unsteady breath. Stupid question. *Everything* had changed. They spent hours every day in each other's company ... and they talked on a myriad of different topics just as they always had. Even laughter had been returned to them. She had never expected to find that again, so had not thought to look for it. Yet Max had known, hadn't he? Or if not known, at least guessed that the key was not beyond their reach. And shared laughter, thought Frances, was every bit as dangerously seductive as kindness and kisses.

Thinking of the kisses was a mistake so she thought of his kindness instead. The clothes he'd insisted on buying for her in

Richmond because he had guessed she would need them; ordering her bath before his own so she would not have to wait; holding her in warm, steady arms and offering his body as a pillow when he saw she was on the verge of exhaustion. He could not know how long it had been since anyone had shown any consideration for either her convenience or her comfort ... or how his every small act of kindness made her weak with longing. But she knew she should not read too much into it. Max *was* kind. It was as much a part of him as the beautiful storm-grey eyes or his physical perfection. More than that, he looked after those in his care – and just now, as he saw it, he was responsible for her. That's all it was. Nothing more. It couldn't be.

It couldn't be because Frances knew that Mama was right. She was unmarriageable; not because she'd jilted Archie but because all she had to recommend her was good lineage – which didn't outweigh her disadvantages. Her dowry had gone to settle Papa's debts; the land earned scarcely anything; and then there was her family. Mama's incessant spite; the cost of sending William to university; and Rufus's lack of backbone. The man who would knowingly take all that on, assuming such a one existed, was either a besotted idiot or had more money than he knew what to do with.

Marriage, therefore, was not an option. But surely Fate hadn't thrown her in Max's way for no reason at all. *Surely*, Frances thought mutinously, *I might be allowed just a tiny, brief taste of what might have been? Is that really too much to ask?*

It need not last. She wouldn't expect it to. But now, in these days while they were together in places where no one knew them and free of all the usual constraints ... could she not experience the thing she would never otherwise know in the arms of the only man she had ever wanted? It wasn't as though she had anything to lose, after all.

Frances sighed. It could never happen. Even if she found a way to ask and gave written assurances that whatever happened between them would end without either recrimination or expectation on her part, Max wouldn't do it. Even if he wanted her – and she thought that perhaps he did – he wouldn't take a gently-bred girl to bed outside marriage. He'd be shocked by the mere suggestion.

She could imagine the conversation. He would be excruciatingly kind; he'd say that she didn't really mean it; he'd tell her that he was flattered and extremely tempted but she must see that it was quite impossible. One day, he'd say, she would be grateful he had refused her offer. And by the time he had finished speaking she would be ready to die of humiliation and feel that walking back to Matlock would be preferable to facing him across the carriage for even one more minute.

CHAPTER TWELVE

The morning dawned breezy but dry. Max told Miller to make a brief stop at Langholm.

'It's only six or seven miles but I'm told it's the only place of any size between here and Hawick. So we'll give Frances a chance to look at the shops ... and I'll take the reins for the next stretch.' He raised one seemingly innocent brow. 'Feel free to ride inside if you wish, Joe.'

In two, not entirely polite words, the coachman declined this generous offer.

Max laughed.

Taking his usual seat opposite Frances, he said, 'I hope you slept well?'

She hadn't. 'Very well indeed. And you?'

He hadn't either. 'Like a log. For a small place like Canonbie, the inn was surprisingly good. Let us hope we'll be similarly fortunate in Selkirk.'

'Let us also hope that, this time, Grey stays to chat.'

Max nodded his agreement but thought, *Do you* really *hope that, sweetheart? Much though I want to meet the fellow, I'm no longer in any particular hurry to do it*. He said, 'Ah yes. Well, that goes without saying, doesn't it?'

Thinking she detected something in his voice that should not have been there, Frances shot him a sharp glance – only to look quickly away when she realised that he was watching her. She gazed through the window as Canonbie fell away behind them and said colourlessly, 'Of course.'

Max let silence linger while he considered his next words. If she was avoiding his eyes – and clearly she was – it was because she was uneasy about what he had told her the previous evening. But since he didn't think raising the subject again would be helpful, he said, 'We'll be stopping in Langholm if you've changed your mind about needing to buy anything.'

'As it happens, I have. I broke my comb this morning and also seem to have lost a great number of hairpins.'

'Well, I daresay you'll be able to replace those.' He sent her a lazy smile and added, 'Though, personally, I wouldn't mind if you lost *all* your hairpins. Every last one.'

Frances cast him a look of amused exasperation.

'And go about with my hair hanging down my back? I'd look ridiculous.'

'That's a matter of opinion.' The smile lingered. 'You have very pretty hair.'

Unsure whether he was teasing or flirting but concluding that it didn't matter, she smiled serenely back and said, 'Thank you, my lord. So do you.'

Startled into laughter, he said, '*Pretty?* No. I most certainly do not!'

'Another matter of opinion.' And without stopping to think, she added flippantly, 'Here's an idea. I'll wear my hair loose when you do the same.'

For an instant, Max couldn't believe she had said it and was perfectly sure she hadn't meant it seriously. But since it was too good an opportunity to miss, he decided to call her bluff. 'That sounds fair. Now?'

She blinked. 'What?'

'I accept the challenge. Do you want to do it now?'

Frances hesitated. Then, aware that he expected her to back down so he could laugh at her cowardice, she held out her hand and said recklessly, 'Why not? Your ribbon for my hairpins.'

Shrugging, he released his hair from its queue and shook it loose.

The sight of all that thick, silky dark hair falling about his face and on to his shoulders promptly scattered Frances's wits. Seeing it and feeling inordinately pleased with himself, Max used the opportunity to murmur, 'You *do* recall that we're stopping in Langholm?'

She hadn't but, not wanting to admit it, said, loftily, 'Of course.'

'Liar,' he grinned. Continuing to hold the ribbon out of her reach, he extended his other hand, saying simply, 'Pins.'

Frances huffed and gave in. For every hairpin she dropped in Max's waiting palm, another long curl fell free. Without the aid of a mirror, she had to find them by touch. It seemed to take forever. One glimpse of the expression in Max's eyes brought the blood to her cheeks and made her careful not to look at him again.

When the last pin was gone and she was running her fingers through the gleaming, elbow-length mass, he took a moment to picture how it might look against her bare skin. Then he said huskily, 'I don't suppose you'd let me do that?'

Her pulse stuttered. This wasn't the Max of five years ago and she didn't know how to respond to him. 'No.'

'Ah. Pity.' He handed her his ribbon. 'I'll have to content myself with looking, then. Fortunately, that won't be any hardship.'

Frances wound the ribbon around her fingers.

'You should stop flirting before I begin taking you seriously.'

'You mean you're not already doing so? Damn. I used to be better than that.'

He sounded so cheerfully unconcerned that she couldn't help laughing.

Smiling, Max said, 'That's better ... and just in time, since we appear to have arrived at Langholm where, fortunately, we won't meet a soul we know.'

Accepting his hand to descend from the carriage, Frances muttered, 'I think I shall put up the hood of my cloak.'

'Do that and be prepared to pay a forfeit,' he retorted swiftly. 'We had a deal. And if I'm going to walk about looking disreputable, you can do it looking --'

'Like a – a courtesan?'

'Not at all. Courtesans never venture abroad in anything but the latest fashion and with their hair professionally styled. No one will ever mistake *you* for one of them.'

'Oh. Thank you so much,' said Frances, torn between laughter and a desire to hit him. 'So if I don't look like a loose woman – what *were* you going to say?'

'That you look beautiful. Like a painting I once saw of Aphrodite – only she was wearing rather fewer clothes.' He grinned suddenly. 'Don't look so shocked. You did ask. Now ... go and buy your hairpins. The lady shopkeepers will be falling over themselves to supply you and probably offering you a mirror so you can use them. But of course, you won't.'

'I won't?'

Max shook his head. 'As my siblings will tell you, I can dream up truly *awful* forfeits.'

Having taken a moment to watch her walk away, he sauntered round to the front of the carriage where Joe was feeding pieces of apple to the horses. The coachman took one look at him and gave a snort of laughter.

'I know,' sighed Max. And then, 'But look over there and tell me it isn't worth it.'

Miller caught sight of Frances, hovering outside a shop window with a torrent of chestnut waves cascading down her back. He gave a low whistle of appreciation but said, 'I hope you know what you're doing.'

'I know what I'm *trying* to do. For the rest … well, we'll see.'

A slow smile dawned. 'Still planning to join me on the box instead of staying inside to enjoy the view, are you?'

'Yes. I wouldn't wish to make myself too obvious.'

'No. Terrible mistake that'd be – and after you've been so subtle, an' all.'

'Joe.' Max looked him in the eye. 'Shut up, will you?'

'Aye, my lord. Reckon that might be best all round.'

Frances returned some ten minutes later in possession of both hairpins and comb but flushed and with her hair tied at her nape using Max's ribbon. Seeing the budding hilarity in his face, she pulled the ribbon away and said flatly, 'Do not say a word. The woman in that shop plainly doesn't know as much about courtesans as you do because she told me to tidy myself before people took me for a harlot. And since, aside from the pins, I needed a new comb, I had to do *something*.'

He laughed and found that her expression of outrage made it rather hard to stop. Finally he managed to say meekly, 'May I have my ribbon back while I'm driving?'

'No.'

'Please?'

'No. You can sit up there and let the ladies of the town ogle you.'

'You think they'll want to?'

'Only if they've got a pulse,' she muttered.

And clambered unceremoniously back into the carriage leaving him laughing again.

While she made use of her new comb, Frances watched the scenery unfold. As it had done since Longtown on the previous day, the road continued to follow the course of the river. But on either side, the landscape grew progressively hillier. It was wild and empty save for occasional flocks of sheep, placidly cropping the sparse grass and sometimes slowing the progress of the carriage by invading the road. Frances thought it peaceful and strangely beautiful but shuddered to think what it might be like in winter.

They stopped again to water the horses and eat some bread and cheese at a tiny tavern in Teviothead but although Max let his gaze dwell appreciatively on her untrammelled hair he chose not to rejoin her in the carriage but resumed his seat beside Miller. Feeling unaccountably aggrieved, Frances spent the next half hour confining her hair in a thick plait to lie over one shoulder and tied it off with Max's ribbon. Then, just before they reached Hawick, the carriage drew to a halt and Max finally relinquished the reins to Miller, saying, 'Find a decent inn, Joe. We'll take a break here. According to the last stone, it's only another nine miles to Selkirk so, even with an hour's stop, we should be there by five.'

Jumping down from the box, he climbed inside the carriage and, seeing the plait, said, 'Ah. Aphrodite has become a Celtic priestess. I like it.'

He was windblown and untidier than she had ever seen him. He also looked as if he had been thoroughly enjoying himself and had come back to her years younger. Something unfurled inside her chest. Repressing it, she said, 'No forfeits, then?'

'No. We're approaching Hawick and will be staying for a while. That being so, I'd better not walk around looking like a gypsy. May I borrow your comb?'

Frances gave it to him and watched while he dragged it

briskly through the thick, dark locks, instantly taming them. Then, as she had known he would, he held out his hand, saying, 'And my ribbon, if you please.'

She shook her head, unable to repress a smile. 'I need it.'

'As do I.' Max pulled her hairpins from his pocket and dropped them in her lap. 'You can do something with those, I'm sure. I, on the other hand, can't. So ... the ribbon, please.'

'No.'

His eyes locked with hers, he stroked the length of her braid with lazy fingers.

'It is mine, you know. I didn't give it to you.'

'Yes. But as a gentleman, you will let me keep it a little longer.'

Reaching the end of the plait, he tugged gently. 'Sure about that, are you?'

'Of course,' said Frances, even though she wasn't.

'So you aren't, by any chance, daring me?'

'No. I'm merely relying on your unfailing courtesy and – *oh*!' This as he tweaked the ribbon away, forcing her to grab the end of the plait before it unravelled. 'That was cheating!'

'No. Merely reclaiming my own property.' He gathered his hair into a queue, calmly re-tied it and, with a grin, said, 'You should have expected it.'

'What I *expected*,' she grumbled, raising her hands to wind the braid around her head, 'was for you to argue longer. And a second or two of warning.'

'I'm not *that* stupid.' Seeing what she was trying to do, he picked up a hairpin and said, 'You appear to need more hands. Shall I?'

'Only if you promise to help not hinder.'

'You have my word.' Sliding across to sit beside her, he began deftly inserting pins where they seemed likely to be most useful. For a time, he worked in silence, taking pleasure in the subtle scent of her skin and the silky feel of her hair beneath his fingers. But when he thought the heavy mass was reasonably secure, he said, 'Take your hands away. I think it will hold while you finish it yourself.'

Frances did as he suggested and cautiously turned her head this way and that. Sounding surprised, she said, 'It feels fine. How does it look?'

Returning to his own seat, Max considered her.

'To a woman, neat and suitably demure.' He watched her resolutely resisting the temptation to ask the obvious question and added, 'To a man ... something rather different and which is probably best not admitted.' He glanced through the window where the emptiness of the fells was giving way to a straggling street. 'We appear to have arrived.'

Crossing the river, Miller drove through to the centre of the town and pulled up outside a large coaching inn. It was market day and the place was busy with stalls selling everything from cabbages to canaries. Frances looked around, her face bright with interest and, seeing it, Max said, 'Shall we take a stroll around?'

'May we? I haven't visited a market like this for months.'

He offered her his arm. 'Then let's find out what it has to offer. Joe – we'll see you back here in an hour.'

It soon became plain to Frances that Max's idea of looking around involved numerous foolish purchases. In no time at all, she had a posy of primroses in one hand and a several lengths of gaudy ribbon in the other.

'Just so you don't need to steal mine again,' he explained, his eyes already moving on to the next stall.

A yard of lace joined the ribbons. Next and in rapid succession, came a straw bonnet trimmed with big, yellow roses, a tartan shawl and a box of sweetmeats. Max put the bonnet on her head, cast the shawl around her shoulders ... and declared that she looked extremely fetching.

Struggling with laughter, Frances said, 'Enough! You can't buy something from every trader here.'

'Why not? Look – gingerbread. We should definitely have some of that. It's Joe's favourite. Ah – and honeycomb. *Everyone* likes honeycomb, don't they?'

'If you buy that, *you* can carry it. It's sticky and will ooze and ...'

She stopped, giving up when it was clear he was going to buy it anyway. When, however, she saw him gazing admiringly at a large cage occupied by a malevolent-looking parrot, she decided that he really must be stopped.

'No. Absolutely not. I'm not sharing the carriage with that bird.'

'It won't be much trouble ... and I always wanted a parrot. I wonder if it talks?'

He bade the bird a good-day, then tried telling it what a handsome fellow it was. The parrot gave him a dirty look and turned its back.

'It doesn't like you,' observed Frances, trying unsuccessfully to haul him away.

'It will when it knows me better,' he argued. 'People always do. And being stuck in a cage all day would put anyone in a bad mood. I feel sorry for it. Don't you?'

'Not especially,' she began – and stopped abruptly as, from the other side of the market-place came shouts and sounds of pursuit, followed by pushing as people tried to get out of the way.

Intent on preventing Frances from being jostled, Max did not immediately look for the cause of the disturbance. Then Miller came surging past them and, without checking his stride, said, 'Grey. Nearly had him.' Then he was racing on in the wake of his quarry.

Max froze briefly, torn between joining in the chase or staying with Frances.

'Go,' she said, giving him a shove. 'I'll find you back at the carriage. *Go!*'

Shrugging and simultaneously depositing the honeycomb into her already laden hands, Max took off at a run. Frances watched him winnowing his way through the crowd in Miller's wake and then looked down at the honeycomb which hadn't yet seeped through the paper it was wrapped in but soon would. Spotting a small girl sitting on a nearby doorstep, she walked over and offered it to her.

The child accepted it with a beaming smile while, from behind Frances a hopeful voice said, 'Forgive me, Missus – but will the gentleman be wanting Sylvester, do you think?'

'Sylvester?' she asked blankly, her mind busy with visions of what might happen if Max managed to catch Grey. Then, turning, 'Oh. The parrot. No. I'm sorry, but --'

'Only four guineas, ma'am – and I'd throw in the cage.'

Reflecting that one could scarcely take the wretched bird *without* the cage, Frances shook her head. 'Very generous of you, I'm sure – but the answer is still no.'

'Three guineas, then,' wheedled the parrot-seller, following her as she began to move away. 'And that's cutting my own throat, it is. 'Vester's as fine a bird as you'll find.'

'I'm sure. But the gentleman will be definitely *not* be buying him. Good day to you.'

While Frances was extricating herself from the parrot-seller, Max had left the crowded market-place behind him and could see Joe some way ahead, leaning on his knees while he tried to get his breath back.

'Which way?' asked Max.

Miller pointed. 'Down ... towards the river.'

'I'll take this turning – you take the next one.'

Max took off again and Miller heaved himself upright muttering, 'Bloody hell.'

They met on the riverside and searched it in both directions but saw no sign of Grey.

Max said, 'Hardly surprising. I'll wager he's doubled back towards the market-place. It's easier to hide in a crowd. Come on. You go that way – I'll go this.'

After a good deal more running and still without a glimpse of their quarry, they found each other again. By now Max was breathing nearly as hard as Joe and could feel himself sweating. He said, 'Damn it. Are you *sure* it was him?'

'Yes. I was just going into the King's Head when I saw him on t'other side of street. I only realised it was him because he stood there staring. Then the cheeky bugger smiled and tipped his hat.'

Sighing, Max withdrew Leo's drawing from inside his coat.

'I wish I'd had the forethought to bring more copies of this with me. However ... take a turn about the market and ask around. Someone must have seen him. I'll show this,' he waved the sketch, 'and see if anybody recognises it.'

Not far from the bird-seller's stall, a small girl sat on a doorstep sucking a piece of honeycomb, her face and fingers liberally smeared with stickiness. Since she was no more than half a dozen steps from where he had left Frances, Max had a fair idea how the child had come by the treat. She looked roughly the same age as Ellie, the youngest of Julian's orphans. Knowing it was a long shot but thinking anything worth a try, he dropped on his haunches before her and, with a smile, said, 'Did the lady in the straw hat give you that?'

The girl licked the honeycomb and nodded.

'And have you been here all the time?'

Another nod, another lick.

Max held up Leo's picture, sensibly keeping it out of reach of sticky fingers.

'Did you see this man while you were sitting here?'

She looked at the drawing, head slightly tilted and wearing an expression of intense concentration. Then she licked the honeycomb again, swallowed and said, 'He bought tablet.'

'Did he?' Max felt a resurgence of hope. Having no idea what tablet was, he said, 'Where did he buy it?'

'From Mistress Baird.' She pointed. 'Over there.'

He glanced across to the far side of the market to where a comely woman was busy packing up her wares. Fishing a shilling from his pocket, he dropped it in the child's lap. 'Clever girl. Well done.'

Mistress Baird took one glance at Grey's likeness and continued with her work, saying, 'Aye. Last customer of the day, he was.'

'How long ago was that?'

'Not so long. Maybe ten minutes?' She waved a hand towards the other end of town. 'He went that way.'

Max thought quickly. He and Joe had been combing the lower part of town and the riverside for probably half an hour. And while they'd been doing that, Grey had sauntered back through the market and done a bit of shopping. Suppressing a curse, he smiled pleasantly at Mistress Baird and held up a florin.

'Will this purchase some tablet?'

She laughed. 'Bless you, sir – how much of it do you want? 'Tis only a sweet.'

'One packet, then – and please keep the change as thanks for your help.'

Leaving the lady smiling, Max looked around for Miller and, eventually spotting him, beckoned him over, saying, 'Back to the carriage, Joe. I suspect we've lost him.' And, having repeated what he had learned, 'If there's another inn down that way, I'll wager he's collected his horse and left town by now.'

'We'll maybe get another chance at him in Selkirk.'

'Perhaps. It depends if he has yet to go there or has already been. For now, I just want to know that Mistress Pendleton got back to the carriage without mishap.'

Joe slanted an amused glance at him. 'Mistress Pendleton now, is it? And the two of you playing games and cosy as kittens wi' one another.'

'*Kittens?*' echoed Max, revolted. Then, differently, 'As to the games ... there's a point to them.'

'Aye, my lord. Reckon I knew that.'

They found Frances sitting on the steps of the carriage, eating an apple. She had discarded the tartan shawl but was still wearing the straw hat. Taking one look at them, she said calmly, 'You didn't catch him, did you?'

'What makes you think that?' asked Max.

'I don't see any signs of a fight. Did you even get a *glimpse* of him?'

'No. We just did a lot of pointless running. He'll be long gone by now ... and we should get back on the road ourselves.'

Frances tossed her apple-core away and let him help her into the carriage.

Max took the seat facing her and said accusingly, 'You gave the honeycomb away.'

'I did. I also refused Sylvester on your behalf.'

He blinked. 'Sylvester?'

'Three guineas including the cage.' Frances grinned. 'I knew you wouldn't pass up a bargain like that – so I did it for you. And who in their right mind would call a parrot *Sylvester*, for heaven's sake?'

* * *

The carriage trundled into Selkirk – lying on Ettrick Water and another typically neat border town – and pulled up at The Grapes, a relatively modern, comfortable-looking building on the main street.

'Thank God,' breathed Max, as one of the inn's servants brought their baggage inside. 'There may be some chance of a private parlour. Find somewhere comfortable to sit and order coffee, please. I'll engage rooms and discover whether Grey has been here yet or has still to show up. On this occasion, I'm rather hoping the former. After my exertions in Hawick, I really, *really* want a bath.' He stopped, turned back and, pulling something from his pocket, held it out to her, grinning. 'I nearly forgot. A replacement for the honeycomb. It's called tablet. Don't eat it all before I get back.'

Frances sampled the tablet and found that a little went a long way. Setting it aside, she sipped her coffee and, when Max returned, said, 'Don't worry. I saved you some.'

He sat down. 'Thank you. How is it?'

'If you like very sweet things, it's excellent.' She poured a cup of coffee and handed it to him. 'Well? What news?'

'Bedchambers, a private parlour and a bath within the hour.'

'And Grey?'

'Been and gone a bare hour since and having left a much brisker note than usual.'

'Perhaps he's getting bored,' suggested Frances.

'After today? I doubt it. However, our next destination is Coldstream. The landlord says it's just under thirty miles and recommends we pause at Kelso to admire the ruined abbey.' He flashed a smile at her. 'Since we might as well enjoy ourselves, I plan to conduct a thorough hermit search. If you can suspend your cynicism, you're welcome to join me.'

'I suppose I'd better,' she sighed, setting her cup down and getting to her feet. 'I'll never hear the last of it if you see a hermit and I don't.'

'That's the spirit,' applauded Max. 'And apparently there are other similar ruins in the vicinity – all of them destroyed by the wicked English. Only think! If we're really lucky, we may get to visit all of them.'

* * *

Grateful to be clean again, Max joined Frances in the private parlour just before dinner and found her once more wearing the green gown, with her hair becomingly if simply arranged. Glancing up at him from the book in her hands, she said, 'There is a walk which takes in all the ruined abbeys you spoke of. It's only sixty-five miles.'

'Only? And people actually *do* that?'

'Aside from the man who wrote the book? Not very many, I would think.' Closing the book and setting it aside, she said, 'It's probably a silly question ... but how long do you suppose Grey will keep this up?'

'I can't begin to guess. I imagine it depends on whether or not he has chosen the place where we are to finally meet. At present, we are moving further and further north-eastwards into Scotland – though I believe we're still some considerable distance from the Highlands.' The sound of rain pattering against the window caught his attention and he said, 'Let us hope that stops before morning.'

'You're a fair-weather hermit-hunter?' She tutted gently. 'How disappointing. I thought you were made of sterner stuff.'

He grinned at her. 'Darling, you can see what I'm made of any time. You need only ask – though I thought you'd had ample opportunity at Brough.'

Darling? thought Frances, feeling her heart twist. *Don't. Don't start showering me with empty endearments. I can't bear it.*

But she said severely, 'Stop putting me to the blush. You've been doing it all day. And although I know perfectly well you only do it out of devilment, you ought --'

'Do I?' he interrupted, his tone light but his eyes watchful. 'What makes you so sure?' *Perhaps I mean it – though admittedly not the reference to Brough. That was said out of fun and aimed* mostly at myself. But what else have I said that I didn't mean?'

'All that nonsense about Aphrodite and Celtic priestesses and – and so on,' she mumbled. 'You can't have meant any of that.'

'Can't I, Frances?' The dark grey eyes were suddenly very serious indeed. 'I seem to recall saying those things – or ones very like them – to you five years ago and you are no less lovely in my eyes now than you were then. So why should I *not* mean them?'

This time her heart splintered into fragments. She had thought insincerity painful but this was a hundred times worse. She opened her mouth, then closed it again, realising that even if she had known what to say, the words would not get past the constriction in her throat. So she merely stared mutely at him, too anguished to even think of looking away.

Max read her expression but wasn't sure how his words had caused it. Fortunately, two maids bearing dinner stopped him risking another blunder. And by the time, the table was set and they were alone again, the moment had passed. On the surface, Frances appeared to have regained her usual composure and so – for the time being, at least – he decided it was best to let the matter lie.

Pulling out a chair for her while glancing at their meal, he murmured, 'Ah. *This* will be interesting.'

'Will it?' she asked, more for something to say than because she cared. 'Why?'

Max shook his head, grinned and set about serving them both with something from each of the dishes. Frances looked dubiously at a moist, granular-looking mixture she didn't recognise but which at least offered a safe topic of conversation. 'What is this?'

'This?' Max ate some of it. 'It's haggis. A Scottish delicacy, I believe. Have you never had it?'

'I've never even heard of it. What exactly *is* a haggis?'

Max had never eaten haggis either but he knew what it was. If she had phrased her question differently, he might have been able to resist temptation. But she hadn't … so he didn't try.

'A haggis is a small animal which, for some inexplicable reason, lives and breeds nowhere but Scotland – thus making it a regional speciality.'

She glanced up, looking interested. 'Really? Have you ever seen one?'

'No – but that's not surprising since I've previously never been north of Carlisle.'

'But we could see one around here?'

'We *might*, I suppose. Though I recall Duncan telling me that they are very shy creatures. And apparently haggis-hunting is limited to certain times of the year because there are few herds and those there are tend to be small.' Max kept his attention on his plate and continued eating. 'Since you're so curious, why don't you try some?'

'It – it just looks *odd*.' She poked doubtfully at the haggis with her fork. 'Why is it all minced up like this?'

'I believe this is the traditional way of serving it. Just taste it, Frances – preferably before it goes cold. You'll probably like it.'

Frances shrugged and put a small, cautious forkful into her mouth. Then, looking surprised, she ate a larger amount and finally said, 'It does taste better than it looks.'

'Told you,' murmured Max, glancing briefly at her before once more veiling his eyes.

Frances ate a little more and sampled the peppery mashed swede that accompanied it. Then she said, 'Do you know what a haggis looks like?'

'No.' He stopped and cleared his throat. 'No ... I don't recall Duncan ever describing them. Why do you ask?'

'Because it would be nice to be able to recognise one if we happened to see it.' She smiled across at him. 'Spotting a haggis would make up for not finding any hermits, don't you think?'

He made an odd sound and managed to say, 'Now you mention it ... yes. I suppose it would. But if – if they lurk about in the heather, I doubt we have much --'

He broke off as a tap at the door was followed by the maid bearing two small glasses of amber liquid. 'Beg pardon, m'lord,' she said, 'but I forgot the wee dram that's supposed to go along wi' the haggis.'

'Dram?' asked Frances.

'Whisky,' replied Max. And to the girl, 'Distilled locally, is it?'

'Och no. There's no making good malt hereabouts. 'Tis all done further north where the water is fit. But yon dram comes from Murdo Maclivet's still over at Pitlochry. Ye'll no be disappointed.'

She turned to leave but stopped when Frances set down her fork and swivelled to look at her saying, 'Wait a moment, please.'

'Yes'm?'

'Don't,' said Max, in a slightly strangled voice.

'Don't what?' asked Frances impatiently, without bothering to turn her head.

'Just ... don't,' he managed.

With no idea what he was talking about and deciding to simply ignore him, she smiled at the maid and said, 'Have you ever seen a haggis? His lordship has explained that they're small and shy but unfortunately he's never actually *seen* one and I'm curious to know what they look like.'

For perhaps three seconds, the maid looked mildly dumbstruck. Then, seeing that behind Frances's back, Max had dropped his head in his hands, his shoulders shaking, she nodded several times and said, 'Och aye, Mistress. And his lordship has the right of it. Forbye, ye have to get up gey early to catch a sight of the wee, timorous beasties. Brown they are, wi' four legs and not much bigger than a hare. But we Scots ... well, we ken their ways well enough – though we dinna share the secret wi' the Sassenachs.'

Max made a peculiar choking sound and, when Frances glanced around at him, gasped, 'The whisky. Went down the wrong way.'

'Mind ye tak more care, m'lord,' advised the maid. And with a quick grin and a shake of her head, made good her escape.

Frances turned back to the table, looked at Max's flushed face ... and then watched, baffled, as he finally dissolved into gales of helpless laughter.

She stared at him. 'What is so funny?'

'Th-that girl. She – she's even better at it than – than --' He laid down his fork and pushed his chair back in order to drop his brow on his wrists, his shoulders shaking uncontrollably. 'I'm s-sorry. I'm t-truly sorry – but I c-couldn't help myself. Promise you won't hit me.'

'Why should I want to?' His laughter was so infectious, she found herself smiling in response. 'What are you apologising for?'

'The h-haggis,' he sobbed. 'It isn't – it's not – n-not quite what I said. Or what *she* s-said either.'

Frances also laid down her fork, her eyes narrowing slightly. 'In what way?'

'It isn't a shy S-Scottish animal. It – it's …' He stopped, hauled in a steadying breath and went on, still hiccupping faintly. 'It isn't an animal at all as s-such. It's minced sheep intestines m-mixed with oatmeal, all boiled together in a sort of skin.' He looked up at her, his face vivid with laughter. 'I'm sorry. When you asked what *a* haggis was, I just couldn't help myself.'

There was a long silence. Finally she asked ominously, 'You made it all up? All that about small herds and restrictions on hunting and – well, all of it?'

'I'm afraid so.'

'And you let me make an idiot of myself asking the maid?'

'I t-tried to stop you.'

'And that makes it all right, does it?'

'Perhaps not. But the way she joined in …' He stopped, struggling to contain another paroxysm. 'I'm sorry. Truly, I am. Forgive me?'

This time the silence was even longer. Then, just when he had given up expecting it, Frances also began laughing but said, 'Max Brandon – that it the worst, positively the *worst* stupid story you've ever told me. And no, I won't forgive you. I'll just wait for a chance to get even.'

CHAPTER THIRTEEN

At around the time Max and Frances were leaving Selkirk for Coldstream, Mr Balfour was handing Leo the letter Max had sent from Canonbie.

Leo read it and then, on an incredulous laugh, 'He's in Scotland? And where *is* Selkirk, for God's sake?'

'In the borders, not far from my own home. I've a map somewhere,' responded Duncan, sifting through large rolls of parchment. 'Yes. Here.'

Making space on the desk, he unrolled the map and weighted the corners. Then, pointing, 'Jedburgh is there ... and here's Selkirk, between Roxburgh and Dumfries.'

'Bloody hell,' breathed Leo. 'At this rate, he's going to end up at John o'Groats.'

'Let's hope not – or he'll be gone a month or more.' Straightening his back, Duncan said, 'Max knew it might be a trek. It's one of the reasons he didn't want to take Mistress Pendleton with him. But he can't have bargained for this.'

'No. On the other hand, if his feelings for the lady are what we suspect they may be, I don't suppose he's finding it too much of a chore.'

'Possibly not. But if this goes on, how are we going to --'

He stopped abruptly as the door opened upon the last person either he or Leo wanted to see at that precise moment. Trying to look casual about it, Duncan sauntered around the desk to shield the map with his body and managed both a smile and a bow.

'Good morning, my lady. How may I help you?'

Having cornered both the secretary and her youngest son, Louisa Brandon came directly to the point. She said, 'You may tell me where Max is. And please don't use Mistress Pendleton as an excuse. If Max had merely taken her home to Derbyshire, he would have been back by now – instead of which he has been absent for six days. So ... where is he, Duncan?'

Having little choice in the matter, Mr Balfour delivered the answer he'd prepared some time ago but which was now looking a trifle thin.

'I'm not entirely sure … but before he left, he said something about a colliery for sale in Pontefract which he might look at on his way back. And I imagine he may also take the opportunity to visit the Rothwell Steam Company as he passes through Leeds.'

Her ladyship's blue eyes regarded him steadily for a long, uncomfortable moment. Then she said coolly, 'Well done. Now tell me where he *really* is.'

'I'm afraid I can't be any more accurate than that. But I'm sure he'll be back soon.'

'If you don't know where he is, you can't be sure of anything.' Louisa drew an impatient breath and brandished not one but two letters at him. 'We were not expecting Elizabeth and Lord Sherbourne and the children until the middle of May – but that has changed because Julian has accepted another, earlier engagement in France. Consequently, they will all arrive a fortnight sooner than originally planned … in other words, roughly a week from now. And I would really like to rely on Max being here.'

'Ah,' said Duncan uneasily.

'Quite,' she agreed. And waited.

'He won't stay away unnecessarily,' offered Leo, also manoeuvring himself in front of the tell-tale map. 'You know he never leaves the estate for more than a few days except at the really quiet times of the year. And --'

'Stop,' said his mother firmly. 'Just stop – both of you. I am not entirely stupid. I am aware that there is something more than Max is willing to admit between himself and Frances Pendleton. I am also aware that there has been something going on for weeks that he and the two of you don't want me to know about … something which is connected to whatever you are trying, not very subtly, to hide on the desk.' She fixed both gentlemen with a gimlet stare. 'It is time to stop prevaricating. I do not need protection. I *do* need to know where my son is and exactly what he is up to.'

Duncan and Leo exchanged rueful glances.

'She's got a point, you know,' observed Leo. 'What's more, if things carry on as they are, we're going to have to tell her eventually – regardless of what Max said.'

Mr Balfour sighed and reluctantly capitulated.

'Very well, my lady. Max is in Scotland.'

Her ladyship stared at him incredulously. '*Scotland*?'

'Yes. Two days ago, he was in a small town just north of the border and yesterday he expected to reach Selkirk. As for today, I have no idea. He may be travelling onwards … or he may have completed his business and be heading back.'

Louisa considered this, frowning a little. 'Is not Selkirk near your home?'

'Yes.' Stepping away from the desk to reveal the map, he said, 'There is Fernieholme and Selkirk is here, less than twenty miles away.'

'I see. Or no, perhaps I don't. Since it appears that the one place Max has *not* been to is Matlock – where is Frances?'

Not wanting to be the one to break this piece of news, Duncan glanced at Leo and, as he might have expected, got no help whatsoever.

'Don't look at me,' said Leo. 'You're the one who helped talk him into it so --'

'I did no such thing! It was Mistress Pendleton herself who did that.'

'That's not what you said after they left. You said --'

'What I may or may not have said is beside the point. And --'

'And is not what interests me at this moment,' cut in Louisa. '*Where is Frances*?'

Duncan shut his eyes briefly and then, opening them again, 'She's with Max.'

Her ladyship sat down slowly on the nearest chair.

'Oh dear. I was beginning to suspect as much. Her idea or Max's?'

'Hers. She was quite … determined.'

'Why?'

'I'm sorry, my lady – but Max made his wishes on that subject very clear.'

'Max,' remarked Leo somewhat unnecessarily, 'isn't here.'

'I know that,' snapped Mr Balfour. 'And since you are his

brother rather than his employee, I suggest that *you* tell her ladyship what she wants to know. I have work awaiting me in the study. Excuse me.'

Leo watched the door close behind him and groaned. 'Oh. Damn.'

Under normal circumstances, Louisa might have reproved him for cursing. Instead and in a tone against which all her children knew it was unwise to argue, she said, 'Sit down, Leo.' And when he had done so, 'Now ... how bad is it?'

He shoved a hand through his hair, not at all sure where to start. Deciding to temporise, he said, 'I wouldn't call it *bad* so much as annoying and peculiar.'

'And what would Max call it?'

'To begin with? Irritating. In fact, until the business with Sir Desmond's horse, he took it pretty well. But after that, there was the statue and Lord Ripley riding over to take a swing at him – which naturally made Max take it more seriously. However, he didn't really start wanting *blood* until he found out that Frances – Mistress Pendleton – had somehow got dragged into it.' He stopped and, reading his mother's expression, added, 'But perhaps I'd better start at the beginning?'

'Yes,' agreed Louisa stonily. 'I think perhaps you had.'

* * *

The rain having fortunately ceased overnight, the journey to Coldstream began under fitful sunshine. Watching the hills rolling by outside the carriage window, Frances thought about the previous evening. *You are no less lovely in my eyes now than you were then*, he had said ... and she'd wanted to cry. Ten minutes later, he'd had her laughing until her sides ached.

She still caught herself on the verge of giggling over the haggis tale. Max had always had a way of making the most absurd thing sound eminently reasonable and keeping his expression perfectly serious while he did it. And when he collapsed into helpless laughter afterwards, it was impossible to be angry with him because this frivolous side to an otherwise serious man, whose life was dedicated to fulfilling his responsibilities to the best of his ability, was both a surprise and a delight.

She had no difficulty believing that he couldn't resist an opportunity to tease ... but she knew he had also been seeking to take her mind off what he'd said earlier. That *may* have been because he'd said more than he meant ... but she didn't think so. It was much more likely he had done it to re-establish the ease between them and make her feel comfortable again. Given the vulnerability of her position while they travelled together like this, he was careful never to give her cause to think he might take advantage. He flirted, yes – and in a more risqué fashion than he had five years ago – but not for a second had she ever wondered if words might lead to action. She wished they would.

Watching her without seeming to do so, Max saw the moments when her mouth quivered on the edge of a smile and, suspecting that he knew why, felt a sense of deep satisfaction. She was forgetting her determination to be cautious with him and soon, if he was lucky, he might be able to bring his intentions into the open.

Since the previous day, something about Coldstream had nagged at the back of his mind but refused to come into focus. It wasn't, he was sure, anything to do with the old and prestigious regiment which shared its name. It was something else ... something more recent. He cudgelled his brain for a time and then, with a mental shrug, gave up. After all, whatever it was couldn't be of any great significance.

At St Boswells, some nine miles from Selkirk, Miller halted the coach at the first of the ruined abbeys and called down, 'Want to stop here, my lord?'

'Do you?' Max asked Frances. 'After last night, I have some fences to mend – so today your wish is my command.'

'I'll bear that in mind,' she replied absently, gazing out at the stark remains of a towering wall which had once held a lovely window and a separate building the book had told her was the Chapter House. 'But no. This is Dryburgh Abbey, I read about it last night. And impressive as it is, I believe there is more to see at Kelso – so we'll save our hermit-hunting until then, I think.'

'As you wish.' He called the necessary order out to Miller. 'Just how much of that book did you read?'

'Enough. I took it to bed with me to finish the chapter on the abbeys.'

Max had a sudden mental image of her sitting in bed, reading and clad in nothing but that torrent of hair. Swallowing hard, he banished it and said, 'And what else did you learn?'

'That most of the abbeys were ruined during the reign of Henry the Eighth on account of the King's determination to kidnap the small Queen of Scots as a bride for his son, Edward.' She laughed. 'The book calls it the Rough Wooing.'

'*Very* rough – judging by the level of destruction it caused. It's as well that it happened a couple of centuries ago or the Scots would be taking pot-shots at us.'

'They don't need to do that. They have their revenge feeding us haggis.'

He grinned. 'Don't pretend. I know you enjoyed it.'

'Awful as it sounds, I enjoyed it more while I thought it a timid little animal than when you told me it was made of sheep intestines.'

'Speaking for myself, I don't generally relish the idea of eating intestines of *any* variety.' Max looked out of the window. 'We appear to have found another river to follow. I don't recall Duncan ever mentioning that his homeland was so very … wet.'

They arrived at Kelso around noon and found a small tavern close to the abbey where the horses could be watered and rested while they fortified themselves with bread, ham and home-made pickle.

'Will you join us, Joe?' asked Max, as they were about to set off for the ruins.

'Thank you, my lord – but the tavern-keeper says the fishing here in the Tweed is some of the best in Scotland and he's offered me rod and line.' The merest hint of a knowing smile crossed the craggy features. 'Pity you can't join me. But I reckon there'll be other compensations.'

Max glanced from the coachman to the river and back again.

'Watch your step, won't you? It would be a shame if you got a ducking.'

And walked away, leaving his old friend laughing.

A moderate breeze had picked up causing Frances to wrap herself in the tartan shawl and knot it about her waist as the countrywomen did.

'A bonny Scots lass today, I see,' remarked Max. 'Trying to conceal the fact that you're a Sassenach, are you?'

'I think one of us should,' she agreed. 'You look too lordly-English for words.'

'In *this* coat? My valet would have a fit. Not that he hasn't seen me look worse, you understand – but never outside the estate.' A fleeting grin. 'I believe he finds me something of a trial.'

'I doubt he's alone in that.'

'Minx,' said Max, lacing his fingers companionably through hers.

For a few moments, they stood looking silently up at the soaring remains of what had once been a large tower.

'The abbey was founded in 1128 during the reign of King David,' announced Frances, in the tones of one about to impart a lecture. 'The monks were Benedictine, of some sort. And this is the West Tower. Originally, it was one of a pair and the body of the Abbey church lay between the two of them.'

Max look around, trying to visualise it. He murmured, 'I'd never have guessed. *What* a good job you memorised the book.'

'Isn't it?'

Entering through an archway, they found themselves completely alone in an open space dotted with old graves. Frances said, 'I'm not sure when my book was written but it said that people are still buried here – mostly the Dukes of Roxburgh, I think.'

'Well, it wouldn't do to let the peasants in, would it? This may be a ruin – but it's a *noble* ruin.'

'Does that mean you think a hermit unlikely?'

'A *little* unlikely, perhaps – but not entirely so.' He looked down at her, marvelling as he always did at the tiny flecks of gold in the blue of her eyes and enjoying the fact that the freckles, which six days ago seemed to have grown very faint, were now reappearing. He had wanted to count them, he remembered. He still did. 'And one should never lose hope.'

Turning away from his scrutiny to examine a lichen-encrusted gravestone, Frances said, 'And when you find your hermit – assuming you ever do – what will you say to him?'

'I shall engage him in a deeply philosophical discussion.'

Amused by his solemn tone, she said, 'About what exactly?'

'About why, as soon as a man chooses to eschew society in favour of solitude, society immediately feels impelled to seek him out for a chat.'

She laughed. 'Well, I'm sure he'll have numerous things to say about *that*.'

'Yes,' said Max, sounding pleased with himself. 'I think so, too.'

'The most obvious one being *Go away*?' she suggested. And without giving him chance to reply, she towed him across the grass towards an intact and shady cloister. 'As good a place as any to look for a hermit, don't you think?'

What Max thought was that it was an exceptionally good place to steal a kiss ... but then he'd thought the same about the carriage, the gateway and the graveyard. And that was just during the last half hour. The trouble was that she looked so happy and enthusiastic and so very, very like the Frances he'd tumbled headlong into love with that keeping to the guidelines he'd set himself was becoming increasingly difficult.

They didn't find a hermit – which was no surprise to either of them.

Strolling back through the graveyard, Frances said, 'It's lovely here, isn't it?'

'Yes,' agreed Max, thinking less of their surroundings than the girl on his arm. 'Yes, it is.'

'Thank you for allowing a delay so I could see it. I know all you really want is to get on with finding Grey.'

No, he thought. *All I really want is to wrap my arms about you and keep you there. In many respects – aside from having unwittingly done me the favour of bringing you and I together again – Grey has almost become an irrelevance. I want to find him, yes. But only so I can put an end to his games and take you home with me.*

But he said merely, 'You don't need to thank me. It was my pleasure.'

Back in the carriage and once more on the road, Frances said, 'How far is it?'

'Eight or nine miles, I think. There will be plenty of time to take a bath if you wish.'

She agreed that she did and then said, 'You've given up expecting to find Grey waiting there, haven't you?'

'Yes. But what I'm mostly hoping for – and sooner rather than later – are two nights in the same place with a day of rest in between. You need it ... and I need my shirts properly laundered and pressed. What was done to them at Canonbie was an atrocity.'

She smiled but knowing why he really wanted a rest, said, 'You need not worry about me, you know.'

'I am not worrying, precisely.' Max shifted his position, grimacing slightly. 'But I'd be sorry to think your posterior is suffering as badly as mine is from hours on the road.'

Although she wanted to laugh, Frances said, 'Lord Brandon – I'm shocked!'

He directed a sideways glance at her. 'You don't *look* shocked.'

'Well, I am. Did your Mama not teach you that a gentleman should never under any circumstances refer to a lady's p-posterior?'

'I don't recall. But at least she taught me to call it a posterior and not a --'

'Stop!' She put her hands over her ears.

'You don't know what I was going to say.'

'No – but I can guess.'

'Really?' He grinned. 'Now *I'm* shocked.'

They were little more than a mile from their destination when Max finally captured the thing that had been teasing his mind all day. The river they had been following since Kelso was the Tweed. The town of Coldstream lay on one side of it ... and on the other, was England. Max couldn't believe it had taken him so long to remember that because, until Gretna Green had eclipsed it,

Coldstream had been the destination of choice for eloping couples.

Max wondered if Frances was aware that Scottish law permitted couples to marry wherever and whenever they chose or that virtually anyone could perform a civil ceremony. He suspected that she might not be. He, on the other hand, had been thinking about it more and more frequently ever since they had crossed the border.

Now, however, Coldstream was the closest they had been to England for some time and there was a distinct possibility that Grey's trail was going to lead them south. In one sense, Max supposed that would be a good thing. In another ... well, he'd cross that bridge when he came to it. Literally.

The town, which was not particularly large, was composed of mostly narrow streets and the Crown Inn, when they found it, was a good deal less grand than its name suggested. Max eyed it dubiously and prayed there were no fleas.

Inside, however, the place looked reasonably clean and the landlord welcomed them effusively. Unfortunately, he then proceeded to put both feet in his mouth.

'Two rooms, m'lord?' he asked, looking surprised. And then, smiling, 'Ye'll not have visited the Marriage House yet, then.'

'No,' said Max repressively. 'In fact, we --'

And simultaneously, 'Marriage house?' asked Frances.

The landlord glanced from one to the other of them and said, 'Mebbe I spoke out of turn, m'lord. 'Tis just old Murdoch at the turnpike still gets young couples coming for the hand-fasting and afterwards they take a room here to make it legal, if ye follow ma meaning.'

Max did. Frances didn't and seeing her about to ask for an explanation, he said, 'You are mistaken. We merely require rooms for the night and stabling for the horses. My cousin also requires a bath. I take it none of this will present a problem?'

'Not at all, m'lord. If ye'll take a seat in the parlour, I'll have Mollie bring tea while the rooms are made ready.'

Max nodded. 'One other thing. Perhaps you have a letter for me? It would be addressed to Lord Brandon.'

Although the landlord had been addressing Max as 'my lord' since he'd first laid eyes on him it was clear from his reaction that he hadn't realised that his new guest was indeed titled. Bowing deeply, he said, 'Why, yes! A fellow delivered it this morning. Mollie will fetch it for ye.'

'Thank you.' To prevent further conversation, Max shepherded Frances firmly into the small parlour murmuring, 'If Grey was here this morning, there's little point in hoping he'll show his face again today.'

'No. I suppose not. What is this Marriage House the innkeeper was talking about? And why did he seem to think we'd been there?'

'He made an assumption.'

'I know that. But what *was* it?'

Max sighed. 'You know about couples running off to be married at Gretna Green?'

'Of course,' she said. And then, 'Good heavens! He thinks you and I are *eloping*? But why? Why on earth would he assume that?'

'Because before a new toll road made Gretna easier and quicker to reach, many of those runaway couples came to Coldstream instead – and clearly some still do. Here, Scotland and England are only separated by the width of the River Tweed. And the toll-keeper at the bridge has performed so many weddings that the turnpike lodge is now known as the Marriage House.'

Frances shook her head, laughing a little.

'Tollgates as well as blacksmiths' shops? Where else, I wonder?'

'Since the bridge here was only built a decade or so ago, probably in the ferry-man's hut,' shrugged Max. 'But couples who flee to Scotland do it because English law doesn't permit them to marry – so I suppose that, if the choice is Scotland or giving each other up, the wedding venue is largely immaterial. However, I take it that the notion doesn't appeal. You don't find it romantic?'

'A frantic dash for the border with an enraged father in hot pursuit? No. I don't see the romance in that.' She paused, remembering all the fuss and bother surrounding her non-wedding to Archie and decided that perhaps a border ceremony might have its advantages after all. 'But the landlord called it hand-fasting – which, to me, sounds more like a betrothal than a wedding.'

'Hand-fasting is what some Scots call a civil ceremony.'

'So what did he mean about the couples coming here to make it legal?'

Max rather thought that, in a moment or two, she would realise that she had missed a very obvious point. Amusement stirred and, preparing to enjoy himself, he said, 'Well, there's one thing on which Scottish and English law agree ... and that is that *no* marriage is binding until it's been consummated.'

'Oh,' said Frances, wanting to kick herself for her stupidity. 'Of course.'

'So after the ceremony at the Marriage House,' he continued helpfully, 'and hopefully before the enraged father arrives, the couple come somewhere like this to --'

'Yes,' she said rapidly, feeling her cheeks heat. 'Thank you. You needn't elaborate.'

Max had no intention of elaborating. A bit of naughty innuendo was allowable; anything more was not. Also, although it wouldn't put any ideas into his head that weren't already there, it would definitely make them more graphic. However, there was no harm in letting her think he might be willing to supply the kind of details no gentleman ever would and of which unmarried girls were always kept in ignorance, so he said enticingly, 'Sure about that, are you?'

'I'm positive.'

'Only, if you're really set on understanding all the various ramifications, I can probably help by furnishing a few additional --'

'*No!* I – I understand everything perfectly.'

A wicked smile curled his mouth and he thought, *I very much doubt that, my darling. But if I have my way, you will.* But said only, 'Excellent. Ah ... here is the tea. And another of Grey's annoyingly jolly epistles.'

While Max broke the seal and read the letter, Frances busied herself with the tea tray and willed her blush to die down. She knew he'd never intended to describe what men and women did in the bedroom – that he was merely teasing. Unfortunately, the idea of learning about it first-hand and from him wouldn't quite go away.

Max, meanwhile, was deciding whether he was irritated or relieved.

My dear Max, Grey had written

I found Coldstream something of a disappointment – as, I suspect, will you. But did not someone say that it is better to travel hopefully than to arrive? I am sure they did. I am also sure that your charming companion insisted on exploring the ruins at Kelso when you passed by them. Ladies always enjoy the picturesque, do they not? There is more of the same to be found at Jedburgh. And so our travels take us first there and then back to Hawick – of which I have some happy memories. Perhaps your own memories are less fond and you did not enjoy the exercise. But perhaps Hawick is our Fate. Perhaps this time, you will find me.

Yours in anticipation,

'What does he say?' asked Frances, handing Max a cup of tea.

'Too much, as usual.' As before, he noted the existence of local knowledge. 'We are returning to Hawick, for God's sake – because from here the road lies through Jedburgh and he thinks you would like to visit another ruined abbey.'

'Oh.' She tried not to sound pleased. 'When you told me how close we are to the border, I thought we might be returning to England.'

'So did I – but apparently not.' Like her, Max was also careful not to betray the fact that, as far as he was concerned, the prospect of further excursions through Scotland was not completely bad news. 'I'll admit to some slight concerns about visiting Jedburgh. Duncan's home, Fernieholme Castle, is near there. Quite *how* near, I don't know – never having been there. But I am acquainted with most of his family members and would prefer not to be seen by any of them. In particular, I don't want any of them seeing you and me together.'

'No. That would be awkward.'

'That's one way of putting it,' he agreed dryly. 'Another is that the fat would be in the fire as far as your reputation is concerned.'

Frances kept her back very straight and her tone perfectly level.

'You would feel obliged to marry me. I wouldn't let you, of course … but it would be best to avoid the eventuality at all.'

I wouldn't feel obliged, you idiot girl, thought Max. *I've every intention of marrying you. I just don't want you thinking I'm doing it to preserve your good name. And as to what you will or will not let me do … we'll see about that.*

But he nodded, set his cup aside and said, 'Yes. I think we can agree on that.'

CHAPTER FOURTEEN

Max was awoken shortly after midnight by the sound of rain lashing against the window. He didn't bother getting out of bed to look. It would either stop or it wouldn't. The roads would either be passable or not. There was no point in concerning himself about it now. He had wished for Frances to have a day of rest and it seemed possible that wish might be granted. He would have preferred, however, that that day could have been spent in some other town and at some other inn. His bed was clean but not remotely comfortable and last evening's dinner of boiled mutton had been barely edible. So he sighed, turned over and drifted back to sleep without wondering what the morrow might bring.

What it brought was a continuation of the deluge. Before joining Frances for breakfast, Max went directly to the taproom and sought out his coachman.

Miller didn't wait for the obvious. He said, 'You don't need me to tell you. There'll be no going anywhere today – or maybe even tomorrow, neither.'

'No,' agreed Max. 'It was to have been back to Hawick, by the way – about the same distance we came yesterday but on a different road. However, if we can't travel, the chances are that Grey may not be able to either and, in most senses, the delay is welcome.'

'The horses be glad of it, at any rate – and the stabling isn't bad here.'

'That's something, I suppose – because the rest of this place isn't up to much.'

'You never used to be finicky.'

'And I'm not finicky now. I'd just prefer a bed that wasn't a foot too short and a half-way decent bottle of wine with my dinner.'

'Take ale instead like the common folk,' recommended Miller, with a grin. Then, 'I reckon I'll spend an hour washing the mud off the carriage. It'll likely be as bad as ever again when we *are* able to travel but at least it won't be three layers thick.'

Finding Frances about to sit down at the breakfast table, he bade her good morning and added, 'You will not be surprised to hear that we are to get that day of rest I spoke of – which only goes to prove that one should be careful what one wishes for.'

'You'd rather we were able to press on?'

'No. I'd rather we were spending the day at an inn that offered a private parlour for your use – but there's little choice in that. I won't risk us being stranded in the middle of nowhere or the carriage sliding off the road or one of the horses suffering an injury. And I'm *certainly* not going to let Joe spend the day getting soaked to the skin. So here we stay.'

Frances handed him a cup of coffee, saying serenely, 'The private parlour doesn't matter. With the weather as it is, this room is likely to be private enough. But surely the real problem is that we won't get to Hawick by this evening ... and if Grey had planned on meeting you there, he may not wait.'

'Unless the downpour is confining itself to Coldstream, I doubt Grey will be going anywhere himself today. And if he doesn't wait, so be it. We are not dancing to his tune in weather like this.'

The maid, Mollie, came in bearing enormous, steaming bowls of porridge, deposited them on the table and turned to go.

'Wait,' said Max. He peered down into the greyish, lumpy mess and then across at Frances, who was watching him and, for some reason that escaped him, looking as if she wanted to giggle. 'Did you order this?'

'No.'

'Do you want it?'

'Not really.'

'Good. Neither do I.' He eyed the maid with pleasant implacability and said, 'Neither the lady nor I ordered this. Please remove it.'

Mollie hovered uncertainly. 'Ye'll no be trying the porridge then?'

'Porridge? Is that what it is?'

Frances made a small choking sound.

'Aye, m'lord. Made wi' the very best oatmeal.'

'Really? I'll have to take your word for that. But no. We will not be trying the porridge. So take it away and bring toast, butter and whatever preserve you have. If whoever does the cooking could manage to scramble some eggs, that would also be welcome.'

Dolefully, Mollie picked up the bowls and trudged out.

As soon as she had gone, Frances gave way to laughter, saying, 'That was wicked of you. As if you didn't know perfectly well what it was.'

'I know what *porridge* is. When it's well-made, I have even been known to enjoy it. But that looked like … well, I'd sooner not consider what it looked like.'

Over the rim of her cup, Frances eyed Max thoughtfully. She had seen him in a variety of different moods both five years ago and during the course of the past week … but she didn't think she had ever seen him grow irritable over a triviality or complain about the service he received. She had certainly never seen him wearing an expression that verged on sulky and which made her want to pat his hand and tell him that nobody would make him eat the nasty porridge.

Realising this might not go down well, she said reasonably, 'Since you clearly don't like this inn, is there nowhere else we could stay?'

'I've no idea. I doubt the landlord here will recommend anywhere and neither I nor Joe are tramping around in the rain on the off-chance.'

'No. Of course not.' She smiled encouragingly at him. 'So we'll just have to make the best of it, won't we? And it's only for one more night.'

'God willing,' muttered Max. Then, with a sigh and a half-smile, 'My apologies. I'm grumbling, aren't I?'

'Just a little.'

'The truth is that I woke up countless times through the night – first because of the rain and on numerous other occasions because the bed seems to have been made for a midget. When you add to that last night's dinner and a breakfast of something that looked as if it should be used to plaster walls, I am led to an uncanny suspicion.'

'Which is what?'

'That this inn is unused to catering for overnight guests because the only ones who ever come here are eloping couples – and few of those ever stay long.'

The blue eyes widened. 'But they would have to, wouldn't they? In order to – to legalise their union.'

Her choice of words rekindled Max's sense of humour. 'Not necessarily. There's no law that says consummation has to happen at night or even under the cover of darkness.'

'Oh. No. Of course not.'

Struggling not to laugh, he watched her trying to imagine this. Then, deciding to help her out, added, 'In truth, so long as the innkeeper will tell anyone who asks that the newly-wedded pair shared a bedchamber – however briefly – the wise bridegroom will leave the whole consummation thing for a more conducive occasion. A young lady only gets one wedding-night, after all, and she deserves to have it take place somewhere more romantic than this.'

His matter-of-fact tone made the whole subject sound much less outrageous than Frances knew it was. It also made her want to ask where *he* would want to spend the first night of his marriage. Sense prevailed, however and she said nothing, merely sipping her coffee until Mollie re-appeared with buttered toast, a pot of apple jelly and a dish of scrambled eggs.

Max waited until the maid had left them again and then, lifting a couple of bits of the egg on a spoon, let them fall from some six inches above his plate. They bounced.

* * *

The rain continued throughout the morning, sometimes easing to a heavy drizzle before turning heavy again. Max stared grimly through the window and then, in an attempt to take his mind off it, asked the innkeeper for a pack of cards and taught Frances to play whist. A second consultation with Miller at around noon resulted in both men concluding that, if the deluge didn't stop soon, they weren't going to be going anywhere tomorrow either – and was responsible for Max reversing his earlier decision.

'If we're going to be trapped in Coldstream for another day, I refuse to spend it in this bloody place. The rain has lessened again so I'll go out and see what alternatives there are.'

'I could do that, my lord,' offered Miller.

'No, Joe. It's my turn to get wet. And I need something to do.'

Having snatched up his cloak and hat, Max put his head round the coffee-room door to tell Frances where he was going, only to find that she wasn't there. Since he didn't expect to be away long, he turned on his heel and went out.

Frances returned to the coffee-room with stockings which needed darning. This wasn't her favourite occupation or one she was even very good at but she couldn't find anything to read and the stockings had to be made to last, so she sighed, sat down and set to work. The job wasn't made either easier or quicker by the thickness of the only yarn Mollie could find but Frances persevered and had almost finished when the clatter of hooves in the yard made her look up.

Horses; more than one but no sound of carriage wheels – which meant that the new arrivals would be soaked through and wanting to get dry. Frances rose and began swiftly gathering up her things. Male voices in the hall called for an ostler and the landlord. English voices. Clutching her sewing, Frances hesitated, unsure what to do. Whoever these men were, it would be best if they didn't see her – but she couldn't get from this room to the stairs without crossing the hall. On the other hand, a quick flight was better than being found here. She headed for the door and was just about to reach for the latch when it swung open, sending her stumbling back.

'Beg pardon, ma'am,' said the first gentleman automatically.

'Not at all,' murmured Frances. 'Please excuse me.'

He stepped aside. His companion didn't. He subjected Frances to a long, head to toe scrutiny and smiled. Then he strolled forward saying, 'No need to rush off, my dear. We don't mind sharing the fire with a pretty young lady – do we, Jack?'

Tossing his hat down on the hearth-stone and starting to

unfasten his greatcoat, Jack said, 'Speaking for myself, I merely want to get out of this sodden coat.'

Also shrugging off his coat, the other man remained standing full-square in front of the door. 'Fearful weather, ain't it, ma'am? We've only ridden a matter of ten miles or so and, as you can see, we're drenched.'

'Then by all means, sit down and get dry. I am leaving.'

He still did not move. 'What's the hurry? I've asked the innkeeper to bring a rum punch. It'd be a pleasure to share it with you – ah. We should introduce ourselves. My friend here is Mr Holden and as for myself ...' He bowed. 'Viscount Ellwood, at your service. And you are?'

'Leaving,' she repeated crisply. 'Please step aside, sir.'

He winked at her. 'Come to Coldstream for the hand-fasting and waiting for your lucky bridegroom? But there's no harm in enjoying a bit of company in the meantime, is there?'

Beginning to wonder where Max was, Frances stared the viscount in the eye and said frigidly, 'I require no company and you are under a misapprehension. So step aside --'

'What? You mean there's no lucky fellow? A pretty girl like you? That's a shame, damn me if it's not. So why not sit down and let us console you, darling?'

'I can't think of anything I'd like less. Now – get out of my way before I am forced to shout for someone to remove you.'

Ellwood laughed. 'Spirited little thing, ain't she, Jack?'

'Oh for God's sake,' said his friend wearily. 'If she wants to go, let her. I should have thought you'd had enough female company at Thorne's this last week.'

'Don't be a spoilsport, Jack. You know I can't resist a redhead.' He reached out towards Frances's hair, then lurched sideways as the door opened again, hitting him in the back.

'Begging your pardon, sir,' said Miller, not sounding at all sorry. 'Didn't know you were standing there.' And to Frances, 'Is there any problem here, ma'am?'

'There won't be when Lord Ellwood moves out of my way.'

Having already swung to face the intruder, the viscount said, 'Who the hell are you?'

'Somebody with better manners than you,' retorted Miller. 'Now – let her pass.'

Ellwood's brows rose. He turned back to Frances and laughed.

'Good God! If you're looking for a tumble, you can do better than him, surely? Say the word and I'll oblige you myself.'

'Mind your mouth,' growled Miller. 'You're addressing a lady.'

'Alone at an inn like this?' came the sneering reply. 'She's no lady.'

'She's not alone, either.' Fists clenched, the coachman advanced on the viscount causing him to take a step back. 'Go upstairs and lock your door, Mistress. I'll deal with this.'

'Deal with what, Joe?' asked Max silkily from the doorway.

There were several seconds of absolute silence. Then, without turning around, Miller said, 'Just clearing up a misunderstanding, my lord.'

'Excellent.' Max sauntered into the room, smiled at Frances and said, 'Have either of these ... gentlemen ... laid a hand on you or insulted you in any way?'

'Now see here!' blustered Ellwood. 'I don't care for your tone, sir!'

'When I actually address you – which so far I haven't – I suspect you'll care for it much less,' drawled Max. And then, 'Frances?'

Although she was very glad to see him, she decided that it would be best to defuse the situation before anyone hit anyone else. 'No harm was done.'

'That isn't what I asked but I suppose it's answer enough. Now please do as Joe suggested and go. You might also pack. We are leaving this sorry place.'

'Max --'

'No. Go, please.'

Reluctantly, Frances did as he asked and, as she left the room, heard Mr Holden say placatingly, 'Look, sir – neither of us touched the lady, nor would we have done. As for Ellwood here, he just can't help flirting a bit. He don't mean --'

'Shut up!' snarled the viscount.

'Is that what it looked like to you, Joe?' asked Max gently. 'A bit of flirting?'

'No. *He*,' Miller jabbed a finger in Ellwood's direction, 'wouldn't let her leave the room when she asked him. And he talked to her as if she was some sort of doxy.'

'Did he?' And to the viscount, 'Did you?'

Ellwood opened his mouth on a heated reply then closed it again when he saw that the mild tone did not match the look in those dark grey eyes.

'No,' he said tersely.

'There!' said Mr Holden with spurious good cheer. 'All a misunderstanding, as your man here said. My friend is a gentleman, after all and would never --'

'Will you *shut up*!' spat Ellwood again. 'I don't need you apologising for me. I --'

'No,' agreed Max, coming a couple of steps closer. 'You need to do that yourself. And now would be a very good time for it.'

'You can't talk to me like this! I'll have you know that I'm a viscount and --'

'Good for you. It's a pity you're not also gentleman enough not to accost and insult a lady just because you happen to find her alone.' The tone was now a good deal less gentle and liberally laced with derision. 'I will have your apology, you know ... either here or outside in the yard. Which is it to be?'

In the seconds Ellwood hesitated, Mr Holden muttered, 'Just apologise and be done with it, will you? You were at fault and you know it.'

Casting his friend a filthy look but seeing no help for it, the viscount ground out, 'Oh very well. I did no harm and meant none. But if I gave any offence to the lady, I am sorry for it. There. Will that do for you?'

'Sadly, no,' replied Max. 'But this will.'

And drawing back his fist, poleaxed Lord Ellwood with a single, crashing blow to the jaw. Then, flexing his hand and turning to Miller, 'Get your things together and put the horses to, Joe. We're crossing a couple of miles into England for the night.'

* * *

On the mercifully short drive to Cornhill-on-Tweed, Frances's gaze rested thoughtfully on the slightly reddened knuckles of Max's right hand. Finally she said, 'You hit him, didn't you?'

'Yes. He's an ass.'

'I know. But if he had apologised --'

'He didn't mean it. Perhaps next time, he will. Better yet, perhaps in future he'll think twice about inflicting his company on a lady who clearly doesn't want it.' Clearing the condensation from the window with his sleeve, Max said, 'We're about to cross the Tweed. And look – there's the Marriage House.' He grinned to hide the fact that he wasn't being nearly as flippant as he wanted to sound. 'Shall I ask Joe to pull up so we can drop in and be hand-fasted?'

Feeling something lurch behind her ribs, Frances shook her head. 'Not today.'

'No?'

'No. It's still raining ... and don't they say *Happy the bride the sun shines on*?'

'The French don't. They say a wet knot is a tight knot. But the choice is yours.'

* * *

The Heaton Arms, recommended by the vicar's wife, proved to be a sprawling building from the previous century with oak beams, big welcoming fireplaces and several well-appointed bedchambers. Grateful to see a bed of generous proportions, Max sent shirts to be laundered, coats to be brushed and sighed over the state of his boots. Really, he thought, when he finally got home again, Burrell was going to have his work cut out.

While waiting for a bath to be brought up, he leaned against the window embrasure and stared moodily out across the sodden fields. It was rare for him to lose his temper – indeed he couldn't recall the last time he had done so. But from the moment he'd walked into that little scenario at the Crown, he had been seething. And afterwards, when Joe had told him what the bastard had actually *said* to Frances ... and that when he'd entered the coffee-room he'd thought Ellwood had been about to *touch* her ... Max's temper had boiled over. He'd hidden it, of course. But he wished more than ever that he'd forced the issue and hauled the bloody viscount outside for a thorough pasting. That, at least, might have made him feel better.

And then there was Frances herself. They had spent the whole of the last week together but she was clearly still not ready to trust what the future offered. He thought she loved him; he was *sure* she did – or as sure as a man could be without hearing the words – yet she continued to hold him at a distance.

Perhaps it had been a mistake to hide behind levity in the carriage. Or perhaps the mistake had been suggesting they visit the Marriage House at all. But oh … if she'd responded differently … if she had laughed and said, 'Why not?' … he'd have been on his knees in a heartbeat and whisking her into the toll lodge before she could draw breath. Her cool composure and trite little answer, however, had been a brick wall that left him, powerless and frustrated, on the wrong side of it.

Max wondered if it was time to start pushing her a little. He had chosen to be patient … to let the days of constant companionship show Frances what words, particularly if spoken too soon, might not. But perhaps he had been *too* patient. He couldn't believe she had no idea of his feelings; God knew he had let them show over and over again. But he supposed it was possible that she hadn't also recognised his intentions. Perhaps it was time to give her some sort of clue.

* * *

Having unpacked her few belongings, Frances returned to the private parlour which lay between their bedchambers and, like Max, stood looking through the window. The rain had turned heavy again and, even if it stopped completely in the next hour or two, the roads would be seas of mud tomorrow. The mile between the English side of the bridge over the Tweed and this village had been accomplished with difficulty and taken far longer than it should have done – all of which made Frances glad that Max had removed them from the vicinity of Lord Ellwood and to a more comfortable inn.

She tried not to think of their conversation in the carriage but ended up dwelling on it with brooding intensity. First, there had been the small, visceral thrill she'd felt when Max had admitted having punched the viscount. She ought not to be glad of it or enjoy knowing he had done it because of her or still feel the glow of warmth it had created ... but the simple truth was that she felt all those things.

It was getting harder and harder to hide her heart from him. A dozen times a day, he said or did something that left her overflowing with love for him and weak with longing. As for what he'd said in the carriage ... that had nearly undone her.

We could drop in and be hand-fasted. What do you think?

Instantly rising unbidden to her lips were the words, *Can we? Please?*

She didn't know how she had managed to hold them back and also manage to answer the question as flippantly as it had been asked. Only then something had changed in both Max's eyes and his voice and she had been left feeling that her answer had been wrong – though she didn't see how it could have been. He had been joking, hadn't he? Except that didn't explain why, after his brief response, the rest of the journey had been passed in silence ... or why she sensed that he had withdrawn from her, disappointed.

The possibility that he might actually have meant it caused her heart to constrict. If he had ... if there was the remotest chance that he had, she needed to tell him the truth without delay.

I love you. I've always loved you. But if we'd married five years ago, you would now have my family hanging around your neck like a millstone. That you don't, is the only good thing to come out of what happened – because I was no more eligible then than I am now. The only difference was that then *I didn't know how matters stood. Now I do. So even if you were to ask, I would refuse because I won't lay my burdens on you.*

From the other side of his bedchamber door, she heard sounds that told her he was taking a bath. This, inevitably, led her thoughts back to Brough and the image of what she had seen there that remained indelibly stamped on her mind's eye. Her body reacted as it always did when she remembered the all-too-brief glimpse which was all she'd allowed herself.

Frances whirled away from the window and fled back to her bedchamber where those sounds from his room could no longer torment her. Then she thought, *Enough. This is stupid. I don't know if marriage is on his mind or not so there's no point in worrying about it. But if – if he wants me, even just a little bit ... perhaps I can tempt him to act upon it. That can't be so very wrong, can it? I wouldn't ask anything more of him. I just want ... oh God, I just want to know what it's like to lie in his arms and to have something of him to remember in the years ahead. This is the only chance I'll ever get ... so the very next time he makes one of his outrageous remarks, I'm going to take him up on it. And if I end up humiliating myself to no good purpose because his honour gets in the way, so be it.*

CHAPTER FIFTEEN

Having time on his hands before dinner was due to be served, Max spent half an hour in the tap-room with his coachman.

Miller took one look at him and said, 'Fine as five-pence tonight, my lord. Your courting clothes, are they?'

Max sighed and signaled for the pot-boy to bring ale.

'Do you know, Joe ... there are times when you walk a very fine line.' Then, when Miller merely grinned, he said, 'Does the stabling meet your standards?'

'Aye. As good as I've ever seen at an inn. Our boys think they're in clover – which is just as well, being as we're going to be here at least another day.'

'Yes. I suspected as much when we took some of the bends sideways on our way here.'

'Could turn into a problem, I reckon.'

'Perhaps,' agreed Max. And thought, *But it may also solve another one*. The ale arrived and he tossed a coin to the pot-boy. 'As far as Grey is concerned, I'm holding on to the hope that he is also tied by the weather and therefore realises that we must be, too. If that is the case, the game will remain in abeyance until we reach Hawick.'

Miller nodded and took a swallow of ale. And then, deciding to voice what was uppermost in his mind, said, 'I don't know how you stopped yourself battering that lecherous bastard earlier. You must've wanted to.'

Max gave a hard laugh. 'Somewhat.'

Miller had suspected as much. When his lordship spoke in that soft, seldom-used voice, it always ended badly for somebody. He said, 'So why didn't you?'

'I told myself he wasn't worth skinned knuckles and a soaking. But if I'd known then what you told me later, I wouldn't have risked an apoplexy restraining myself.'

'Ah well. It's an ill wind, as they say. The lassies are always telling us not to fight – but they like it well enough when we do it over them.' He slanted a grin at Max. 'You have told her, haven't you?'

'And risk giving the impression of having enjoyed myself?'

'You didn't, then. I'd call that a wasted opportunity.'

'It might have been ... but fortunately she guessed.' Max thought back to the fleeting expression that had crossed Frances's face. 'I didn't notice her disapproving.'

'No. You wouldn't.' Miller decided to chance one last and exceedingly risky question. 'How much longer are you going to leave it before you ask her?'

Max pushed his half-empty tankard across the table and stood up.

'Ask her what?' he said.

* * *

When he returned to the parlour, he found Frances sitting by the window with a book. She was wearing the blue Richmond gown which he liked partly because it intensified the colour of her eyes but mostly because it had a lower décolletage than the green polonaise. She glanced up when he entered the room and then seemed to freeze for an instant.

Lifting one brow, he said, 'Is something wrong?'

'No.' She swallowed, trying – as she so often had to – not to let his looks steal her wits. The black brocade coat with its deep cuffs and the purple embroidered vest worn beneath it – neither of which she had seen before – turned him into the epitome of saturnine male beauty. 'You look far too elegant for a dinner up here with me.'

'You think so? But perhaps it was you I hoped to impress.'

She tilted her head and, mindful of the vow she'd made to herself a bare half-hour ago, let her gaze stray over him. 'You succeeded. Very well, as it happens.'

Max blinked, startled and mildly suspicious. 'Thank you.'

'You look surprised.'

'I believe I am.' He gestured to the book. 'Please tell me that isn't another erudite tome on the history of the Scottish borders and the depredations of the marauding English.'

'No. It's a very bad novel. I've only read three chapters and the heroine has swooned in every one of them.'

'You disapprove of swooning females?'

'I disapprove of this one. She's an absolute ninny. And I've never seen anyone faint from shock. I suppose a girl might *pretend* to do it in the hope of being clasped to some manly bosom ... but usually it's because her maid has laced her too tightly.'

Max laughed. 'That certainly puts a different complexion on it. However, I take it that you've never swooned into some lucky gentleman's arms?'

'Certainly not. Aside from the fact that I would feel immensely silly, I'd also worry that he might not catch me.'

'More fool him if he didn't.'

An idea slid half-formed into Frances's mind and her heart lurched. Could she do it? Would it work if she did? Or would he simply laugh?

With what she hoped was a careless shrug, she said, 'Perhaps. But timing must be crucial, mustn't it? A mere second could make the difference between success and ending in a heap on the floor.'

'Perhaps they practice it,' he shrugged.

'The girls who pretend? Yes. I suppose they might ... but with whom?' She cast him a speculative glance. 'I assume no lady has ever attracted *your* attention that way?'

'You assume correctly.' He lifted one brow. 'Are you suggesting we try it?'

Her pulse was hammering madly. She hoped he couldn't tell.

'I hadn't actually thought of it ... but why not?' With a tiny laugh and before she could talk herself out of it, Frances stood up. 'Now?'

Surprised for the second time but not bothering to consider what her motives might be since the advantages were all on his side, he said, 'By all means. Am I supposed to notice that you are about to faint – or should I be taken by surprise?'

'The latter, probably.' She hesitated, knowing all too well the kind of devilment he was capable of. 'You *are* going to catch me, aren't you?'

'Oh ye of little faith. Do you really think I'd drop you deliberately?'

'Yes. And don't pretend you're not considering it.'

'I'm not,' he protested, managing to look aggrieved. 'But if you don't trust me --'

'I do,' she said swiftly. And without any warning at all swayed away rather than towards him and slowly began to crumple.

Max's arm was around her in an instant, holding her against his shoulder. Frances let her head fall back and kept her eyes shut, partly in the hope that he would kiss her but mostly because, if he was laughing, she preferred not to know.

Her body soft and pliant in his arms, Max looked down at her face ... at the long, sepia eyelashes and lips slightly parted as if in invitation; an invitation he wasn't going to be able to resist if he held her like this much longer. Then the suspicion he'd felt earlier re-surfaced and solidified because this was the point where she ought to be laughing and pushing him away. He wondered what she thought she was doing and concluded that he ought to find out. He also decided that if, as he suspected, she *wanted* him to kiss her he'd damned well do it at a time of his own choosing – which wouldn't be when their dinner was likely to arrive at any minute.

Sweeping her up, he carried her across the room and deposited her, none too gently on the sofa, saying, 'Very convincing ... but you can come round now. Or do you want me to singe some feathers?'

The blue eyes flew wide and she sat up, frowning.

'You're doing it all wrong. You're supposed to be more ... solicitous.'

'My apologies for being unfamiliar with the proper protocol.' Max folded his arms and looked quizzically down on her. 'And now, Frances ... what are you up to?'

'What do you mean?' Disappointment, confusion and a small measure of guilt were at war inside her. Why on earth did he have to choose *now* to be well-behaved? 'I'm not up to anything. Why should you suppose I was?'

'Well, let's think, shall we? During the course of the last week, you have never once flirted with me or even come close. You have also side-stepped or laughed at any such attempt on my part. But now, suddenly, here you are all but asking me to kiss you.'

'I was doing no such thing!'

'Oh I think you were. That whole scenario was --'

'Your idea – not mine,' she cut in quickly.

He regarded her silently for a few moments. Then, sighing, 'I can't argue with that, I suppose. But your usual habit is to ignore my more inappropriate suggestions. So naturally I'm wondering what has changed.'

'Nothing, so far as I can see. You didn't *have* to kiss me – and you didn't.'

'Ah. That rankles, does it?'

'Not in the least.' She rose and shook out her skirts. 'You're making far too much of it.'

'Perhaps. But allow me to point out that not kissing you and not *wanting* to kiss you are two entirely different things.' He smiled and then, hearing a knock at the door, added, 'You might want to bear that in mind. And while you do, here is dinner.'

Still smarting over her failure, Frances expected sitting at table with him to be fraught with pitfalls. Max, however, seemed determined to make sure that it wasn't by being at his most urbane and avoiding the merest hint of innuendo. They ate tiny fish tartlets, then medallions of lamb in a rich sauce and, by the time they arrived at glazed pears in port and Frances was drinking her second glass of wine, she decided that he had put the matter from his mind and wouldn't ask any more awkward questions.

No sooner had the maids cleared the table, however, than he said thoughtfully, 'There is a conversation we should have … and one which is long overdue.'

'Is there?' she asked warily.

'You must know there is. We touched on it the day we set out from Brandon Lacey but didn't pursue it. *Then*, I was content to let the matter lie because I wasn't quite ready to discuss it and assumed you wouldn't be either. But now, for various reasons, I think we need to address it.' Max fell silent, frowning into the ruby brightness of his glass. 'You know as well as I do that we shouldn't be travelling together like this. And the responsibility for that, which belongs to both of us, raises a question which I believe needs to be answered.'

'What question?'

'Why – knowing it was wrong in a hundred ways and also potentially calamitous – did we do it anyway?' He looked across at her, his eyes serious and intent. 'And please don't bring Grey into it. He is the cause of the journey, yes. But he isn't the reason you demanded to accompany me or the reason I allowed it. I think – I hope – that those reasons were similar. But I can't *know* until we are honest with each other.'

She shook her head. 'I haven't the faintest idea what you mean.'

'Don't, Frances.' His voice suddenly sounded weary. 'We can't carry on skirting around this issue forever. It would help if you went first but since I don't think you will --'

'I don't see why we need to have this conversation at all.' Frances feigned interest in cutting up her pear. 'What difference can it possibly make?'

'A great deal.' Max drew a long breath and loosed it. 'Let's start with something I think we can agree upon. Five years ago, we fell in love in the space of an afternoon but circumstances allowed us very little time together. True?'

'Yes.'

'And when you came to Brandon Lacey – setting aside my shock and your anger – I don't believe either of us knew what we felt or even how we *should* feel. Yes?'

'Yes.'

His next pause was a long one as he sought for the right words. Finally he said, 'When the shock wore off, I understood *one* thing very clearly. Seemingly random events had brought us together again and given us a second chance, should we choose to take it. I would never have suggested that you make this journey with me and you know all the reasons for that. But I *did* want time ... time to get to know you again and time to discover what, if anything, still lay between us. So when you insisted on coming with me, I ... didn't resist nearly as strenuously as I ought to have done.' He smiled, albeit crookedly. 'And I don't regret it, even though I know I should.'

Frances continued to stare down at the pear, now reduced to a mangled mess on the plate. After a long moment, she whispered, 'I don't regret it either.'

'I'm glad.' The smile grew and lingered. 'So ... now I've admitted the real reason I allowed you to come with me, do you think you could tell me why you wanted to?'

She swallowed hard. 'I suddenly realised that I wasn't ready to go home. And ... and I wanted the same thing you did. Time. Just a little more time ... with you.'

Max's heart gave a single, hard thud. He said huskily, 'Thank you. That is what I'd hoped you might say. And now, of course, I'm hoping that these days we've shared have led both of us to the same conclusion.'

For the first time, Frances raised her eyes to his, knowing that the moment of truth was upon her and recognising that, since it must come sooner or later, there was no point in avoiding it. 'Which is what, do you think?'

'That, despite five years apart, nothing between us is fundamentally changed.' He watched her turn away just a fraction too late to hide her expression. Keeping his tone level, he said, 'I see that you don't agree with me.'

'N-not entirely.' Not ready to explain why this was so and suddenly terrified of what he might say next, she blurted out the first thing that might serve as a distraction. 'But you were right earlier. I *did* hope you might kiss me and I was sorry that you didn't.'

Something wasn't right but he had no idea what it was. In the hope that simple truth would mend it, he said, 'I wanted to, Frances. You have no idea how much.'

'Then why didn't you?'

'Because if I had, I'd have wanted a great deal more.'

Silence lapped the edges of the room while Frances tried to quell the surge of heat and hunger those few words created. Eventually, when she was able to think again, two notions became inextricably tangled in her head. First, that Max deserved better than to be tempted or tricked into breaking his own code of honour; and second, that if she was going to be completely honest about anything it might as well be this. So harnessing every ounce of courage she possessed, she said softly, 'And you could have had it. You can *still* have it. If you wish.'

If he wished? God! For a second or two, Max struggled to breathe. Did she know what she was saying? And if she did ... why did every instinct warn him to be cautious?

'You'll have to forgive me. I'm clearly being very slow-witted ... but are you saying that you would like me to make love to you?'

'Yes.' The word *please* hovered but she didn't say it.

This time his chair and the floor beneath it seemed to melt away, leaving him feeling curiously suspended. 'And you – you're sure about that, are you?'

'Yes.' Colour flamed in her cheeks but she held his gaze. 'So will you?'

For a few crucial moments, his brain seemed to shut down while his body reacted with immediate and ill-timed inevitability. But finally he managed to say, 'I don't think you have any idea how very tempting that offer is; and in the general way I'm all for cutting directly to the point. But this is ...' He stopped, shifting in his seat and trying, so far without much success, to think. 'Actually, I'm not sure *what* this is – aside from being a bolt from the blue.'

'I'm sorry. I didn't mean to – to shock you.'

'I don't think shock quite covers it,' he replied, dryly. 'However ... what mostly occurs to me is that you appear to be bypassing a couple of rather important points.'

Frances knew that and wanted to continue bypassing them. But suspecting he might not let her, she said lightly, 'Perhaps it would be best to forget that I said it.'

'That might be difficult.' Max drew a long, faintly hysterical breath. 'Did you ... when you made this suggestion, did you honestly think I'd snap it up without further ado? That I'd say something along the lines of "*That's a terrific idea, darling. Let's get to it!*"?'

'No. Of course not.' Frances did not think it was possible to feel more embarrassed. 'You – that's absurd.'

'I'm relieved to hear it – because this is *us,* we're talking about, Frances. You and me. We *know* each other. And I'd be somewhat unhappy if you thought me so shallow I'd go skipping off to bed with you without a second's reflection.'

'I never thought any such thing. I --'

'Good. Then let's take a couple of steps back.' Max had never envisaged saying the things he wanted to say in circumstances like these but, after the bombshell she'd hurled at his feet, it didn't seem that she had left him with much alternative. So he took a moment to assemble the words and then said simply, 'When I said that – for me, at least – nothing between us has changed, I meant it. Five years ago, I loved you and wanted to marry you. I love you now and still want the same thing ... so I'll ask again. Will you marry me?'

Her throat closed painfully. She couldn't speak, couldn't even swallow. It wasn't only that she hadn't expected the question. It was the knowledge that Max was not, as he might have been, responding reflexively to her bald proposition of a moment ago. He had thought about this and been waiting to say it. The knowledge fractured something inside her. He was offering his heart ... open, unprotected and hers for the taking ... and after what she had said earlier, he expected her to accept it. Of course he did. What else *could* he think?

Watching the expressions chasing each other across her face, Max waited. But eventually, when she still did not answer, he said quietly, 'It's a straightforward question, love. Yes or no will do.'

'I – I know. I'm sorry. I just wasn't – I hadn't expected you to ask.'

'I hadn't expected you to ask me to make love to you. But here we are.'

She shook her head. 'No. I meant ... not after what happened before.'

'What happened before was neither your fault nor mine but still wasted five years of both our lives. Are we to let it ruin the rest of them?' Reaching across the table, he took her hands in his and gently squeezed them. 'Earlier today when I suggested visiting the Marriage House, I wasn't joking. If you'd said yes, this conversation wouldn't be necessary. Since you didn't ... let's try a different question. Do you want me, Frances?'

Well, she could hardly deny that. 'I – yes.'

'So you'll marry me?'

'I don't know. That is ... I'm not sure.'

Max released her hands and sat back, a frown lurking behind his eyes.

'I appear to be missing something. I thought you wanted to go to bed with me?'

'Yes.' He was driving her into a corner and she didn't know how to stop it. 'I do.'

'But you're less enthusiastic about the idea of marriage.' He waited and when she said nothing, 'If there is logic in that, I can't see it – unless you have some idea of trying out the goods before committing yourself?'

It took a moment for his meaning to reach her. When it did, she stared at him, horrified and said, '*No!* That isn't it, at all. How could you *think* it?'

'Given that you'd rather be my mistress than my wife – what else *am* I to think?' Max could feel anger mingling with the hurt and drew a long, steadying breath in order to control it. 'All right. Enlighten me. *Why* don't you want to marry me?'

'It isn't a matter of what I want. It's a matter of what is *right*. For you, I mean.'

'And what might that be?'

'Not me.' Frances twisted her hands together in her lap and said despairingly, 'You don't know what it would be like. The estate is failing badly. Despite selling everything we could and using the whole of what should have been my dowry, we are constantly hovering on the brink of debt. *I* wouldn't expect you to mend any of that – but my family would. Mama is a nightmare. She's rude and impossible to satisfy. William talks of nothing but Cambridge. And Rufus is ... well, I doubt anyone will ever employ him.' She hauled in a ragged breath and added, 'Nearly all these problems existed five years ago – I just didn't know about them. Now I do. And if you married me, you'd be getting a liability.'

Max's anger evaporated, along with most of his hurt.

'None of this comes as a huge surprise, love. I'd already gathered most of it. And as to whether or not I'm prepared to take it on ... surely that is my decision to make.'

She shook her head. 'No. It isn't. I can't let you. I just *can't*.'

'And that's your last word, is it?'

'Yes. I'm sorry.'

'Not as sorry as I am.' Pushing back his chair, he rose to look down at her with an expression she couldn't interpret. 'You'll sleep with me but you won't marry me ... and I won't take you to bed outside wedlock. That puts us at an impasse, wouldn't you say? Upon which note, I think the best course is to bid you goodnight.'

And with a small formal bow, he left her.

CHAPTER SIXTEEN

Max stared up into the dark and contemplated the evening's unexpected developments. Oddly enough, he didn't feel despondent. True ... Frances hadn't accepted his proposal; but when he went back over their conversation, he realised that she hadn't actually refused it either. Although she was apparently determined to let her circumstances stand in their way, she had apparently been incapable of framing the word 'no'; so she'd temporised and hidden behind uncertainty. Max found that encouraging.

Of course, neither had she said she loved him – or not in so many words. But the truth of that was implicit in two things. A girl like Frances didn't offer a man her body unless he already had her heart ... and her ridiculous desire to sacrifice herself rather than encumber him with her disaster of a family said the same thing. There was no doubt in Max's mind that she loved him and wanted him, exactly as he loved and wanted her. And that being so, it was time to formulate a strategy.

The first thing to do was to convince her that her family's rotting property need not be an issue. Max might not have as much money as Archie bloody Malpas but he was by no means poor and there was little he didn't know about estate-husbandry. If Ben Garrett had been able to put Julian's property on the road to recovery inside six months, the same could be done with the Pendleton lands. And if Ben didn't fancy the job, Max would damned well do it himself. Also, if Rufus Pendleton needed employment and wasn't either lazy or incapable of learning, he ought to be taking on the stewardship of his own land. The younger boy wanted Cambridge and Max could provide that – on the firm understanding that he did something useful with his life afterwards. As for Lady Pendleton ... after her treatment of Frances, Max wasn't disposed to do anything for her at all.

With the practicalities covered, he turned his mind to Frances. There were the obvious tactics. He could tease and provoke and make her laugh ... startle her with an unexpected compliment and make her blush with no more than a sensual glance. But he'd been doing those things for a week and, though they hadn't been ineffective, neither had they produced the required result ... which meant it was time for stronger measures.

She wanted to go to bed with him and though he had no intention of taking her there, he could – without letting things go too far – show her a little of what her refusal to marry him was costing her. Of course, it would cost him something as well, Max thought ruefully. But if a little acute discomfort was the price of getting what he wanted, he was more than willing to pay it.

Finally, he could propose to her again and more persuasively than he'd done this evening. He could instruct Joe to halt at the Marriage House when they crossed back into Scotland and suggest, with utter seriousness this time, going inside. Rolling over on to his side, he wondered if they would be spending another day here. It seemed likely even though the rain had eased to a trickle. He didn't mind the delay. He could put the time to good use and the problem of Grey would wait. As he slid towards sleep, he wondered what Frances was thinking right now ... and hoped it was mostly second thoughts.

* * *

Frances wasn't thinking anything with any clarity. He'd said he loved her and offered her marriage ... and oh, how *badly* she'd wanted to say yes. If she had, she might even now be lying in his arms, the apparent ease with which he had refused her, forgotten. But she hadn't said yes, had she? And unless she did, he would go on refusing. He had made that plain enough and she didn't know how to persuade him otherwise.

He had said the decision of whether or not to take on her burdens was his to make. If that was so, why couldn't he see that, equally, the choice of what to do with her body was hers? She wasn't an ignorant girl of nineteen any more. She was twenty-four years old and she knew her own mind. He meant well, of course. She knew that. And it wasn't merely obstinacy that prevented him taking what she offered. It was that solid vein of gentlemanly honour – which, admirable as it might be, was proving a damnable nuisance right now.

With hindsight, she supposed that she might have been a bit

too blunt; that blurting out what she wanted of him without working up to it gradually might not have been the best idea. But Max could and would ignore subtlety. He'd simply let it float over his head. And she didn't have time for it, anyway. She had already wasted a week – and Grey couldn't play this idiotic game of his much longer. It was turning into a farce, as it was. She had hoped the weather might force them to spend another day here. But if the rain stopped and Mr Miller pronounced the roads fit for travel, they would be off to Hawick in the morning – and, for all she knew, that might be journey's end.

She wondered if Max was still angry with her. She also wondered how she was going to face him over breakfast and whether he would re-open this evening's discussion. Would he propose to her again? She hoped not. It had been difficult enough not to say yes the first time and, as it turned out, completely impossible to say no. Refusing the only thing she had ever wanted ... the only *man* she had ever wanted... had been almost impossibly hard. And the quickly suppressed hurt she had glimpsed in his eyes had carved a hole in her chest. How she'd stopped herself saying that she would love him to the edges of her life, she didn't know.

Only one thing was crystal clear. If she wanted Max to put this evening behind them, she would have to do the same herself and give up any hope of the physical intimacy she so badly wanted. The only alternative was to give up her scruples and marry him ... then pray that he didn't end up wishing she hadn't.

* * *

Frances awoke to find that the rain had indeed stopped and a weak sun was peeping out behind the clouds. She also found – when she reluctantly emerged from her room – that she need not have worried about facing Max over breakfast. The maid who served it informed her that his lordship had risen early, broken his fast in the coffee room and gone out on horseback to investigate the state of the roads.

In one sense, this was a relief. In another, the next two hours allowed ample time to imagine Max's every potentially embarrassing remark or question with the result that by the time he finally strolled in, her nerves were in shreds. He, on the other hand, looked damp, windswept ... and thoroughly relaxed.

Frances said awkwardly, 'Good morning. I take it we're not leaving for Hawick today?'

'No. The roads are mudslides and we would almost certainly get stuck somewhere.' Max tossed his hat and gloves on the table and pretended not to notice the way her hands held each other in a death grip. 'However, the landlord believes we can rely on the weather remaining dry – at least for today – so we should be able to travel tomorrow.'

'Oh. Good. And what of Grey?'

'Who knows? If he's been stuck at Hawick while we've been stuck here – and if he has any sense at all – he'll bring the game to a close by waiting for us.'

'Yes. It's time, isn't it?'

'I think so.' He dropped into a chair, crossed one long leg over the other and gave her a pleasant smile. 'I won't deny that it's been fun ... but I believe I've seen enough of the Scottish borders. Haven't you?'

'Yes. Of course.'

'No longer eager to explore Jedburgh Abbey, then?'

Frances was beginning to find his innocuous tone suspicious. She said, 'No. And as I recall, you didn't want to stop in Jedburgh in case we were seen together by someone who might recognise you.'

'Ah yes. Thank you for reminding me.'

Silence fell. Making no attempt to break it, Max let it linger and watched Frances begin to fidget. Finally, unable to stand it any longer, she said, 'Are you annoyed with me?'

'*Annoyed*?' he echoed. 'No. Not at all. Why would you suppose I might be?'

'You *know* why.'

'No. I really don't. Enlighten me.'

Certain that he was being deliberately difficult, she muttered, 'Because of last night.'

The dark grey eyes widened and then filled with unexpected laughter.

'Perish the thought. I can't take offence at that. Indeed, I doubt there's a fellow alive who wouldn't thoroughly enjoy learning that a pretty woman was lusting after his body.'

Turning rapidly scarlet, she stuttered, 'How – that's not – I *wasn't*.'

Max began laughing in earnest.

'No? But how else am I supposed to interpret an invitation to bed you? And trust me – I'd be more than happy to do so. In fact, I deserve a medal for refusing.' He paused, letting the hilarity fade from both face and voice. 'But you know my terms. Speaking of which, the offer is still open and will remain so – in case you were wondering.'

'I wasn't.'

'Really? Think the matter is cut, dried and neatly tucked away, do you?'

'Not exactly. But I explained all the reasons why we shouldn't marry and --'

'You handed me a fistful of *excuses*, not one of which has any substance. If you're interested, I'll gladly tell you why that is.'

Although his tone remained consistently pleasant, there was no longer even a hint of humour in it. Without understanding why, Frances suddenly felt oddly guilty. She said haltingly, 'Yes. Please do.'

'Well, then. I'm perfectly prepared to give your family some practical help – but only if your brother shoulders his responsibilities. Proper stewardship can mend many of the problems on his estate – though I won't know precisely what needs to be done until I've seen it for myself. Then, if Rufus is willing to learn, I can send someone to educate and work with him.' Max chose not to mention that if, as he suspected, an injection of capital would be necessary, he would provide that as well. Instead, he added, 'It won't work overnight, of course. But results should start to show in six months to a year. So … what do you say?'

Frances stared at him as if trying to make sense of the words. Finally, she managed to say, 'Thank you. That would help immeasurably. And it – it's generous of you to offer.'

'Not especially. And it won't succeed if Rufus doesn't work at it. Will he?'

'Yes. I believe he would.'

Max nodded and decided to take a gamble.

'Very well, then. Let us agree that – regardless of whether or not you marry me – I will supply the help necessary to turn the estate around. Do we have a deal?'

Frances could feel tears pricking at her eyes. She said huskily, 'That wouldn't be fair.'

He gave her a sudden dazzling smile.

'Don't let that worry you. You think *I'll* be playing fair? I won't. I intend to win, you see – by whatever means.' He watched her eyes widen with doubt and, on a note of laughter, added, 'And whether that is a threat or a promise, I leave you to decide.'

'It – I'd call it more of a warning.'

'Yes. *Wasn't* it noble of me to issue it?' He stood up, stretched and said, 'I need to write to Duncan again to apprise him of our progress – or rather the lack of it. It's nearly the end of April and Mama is expecting a houseful of guests to arrive in the next week or two. I, of course, am supposed to be there to greet them.' He glanced down on her and, appearing to recall something, said, 'One of those guests is your friend Lord Sherbourne. He's bringing Lizzie to visit her parents and also conveying Julian's orphans to Brandon Lacey while Belle accompanies Julian on a concert tour abroad.' He grinned briefly. 'I don't envy Sherbourne travelling with three children. Then again, I'll be the one responsible for them once he deposits them with us. However ... no peace for the wicked, as they say.'

Frances couldn't help smiling back. 'Are they a trial?'

'No. Considering their abysmal start in life, they're surprisingly well-adjusted. But these few weeks may be difficult for them. They adore Julian and this will be the first time he's been away from them for more than a day or two. Still ... doubtless Ellie will stick like a burr to Mama and Belle's been teaching the boys to ride, so I can continue with that. I don't foresee it being too difficult to keep them occupied. And now I'd better set about writing that letter.' He hesitated briefly. 'If you want to warn Rufus of the good fortune about to befall him, do so by all means. Having given you my word, I won't take it back.'

I know you won't, thought Frances, watching him saunter towards his bedchamber. And then, *On the other hand, I can't help wondering what your notion of not playing fair entails – and whether I might actually enjoy it.*

* * *

Having written his letter, Max left their rooms on the pretext of speaking to Miller – though his real reason was leaving Frances alone to absorb, not only what he'd said, but what it meant. He had other plans in mind for the evening ... plans which could prove unnecessary if she began to understand that, since he wasn't going to let anything stand in his way, she might as well give in without further argument.

Whilst winning another guinea from Max at cribbage, Joe said, 'The rain's kept off all day and looks set fair for the night. The roads won't be wonderful tomorrow but they ought to be just about passable if we take it easy.'

'Let's hope so,' agreed Max. 'If the visitors get to Brandon Lacey before I do, Mama will blister my ears. On the dubious likelihood that we'll catch up with Grey at Hawick ... how long do you think it will take us to get back?'

'Five days at the very least, I reckon – and that's assuming the weather don't turn against us.' The coachman glanced up. 'And longer yet if you've to take Miss Frances back to Derbyshire.'

Max shook his head. 'I'm going home first, so she'll have to come with me. I'm fairly sure that, by now, Mama will have wheedled the whole story out of either Duncan or Leo – which means that walking in with Frances on my arm won't come as any great surprise.'

'Maybe not,' agreed Joe. And grinning, 'But I reckon her ladyship'll do more than ring a peal over you. You'll likely be in scalding water up to your neck.'

'Probably. But there's no need for you to sound so damned cheerful about it.'

* * *

Frances used Max's absence to wash her hair and think about what he had said. That he would offer his help left her stunned, grateful and feeling as if a great weight had been lifted from her shoulders; that he should do it without attaching conditions made her so weak with love for him that she had almost thrown herself into his arms and promised him anything he wanted. At the time, she wasn't sure why she hadn't. Max had made everything sound so easy that she had been overcome with a dizzying sense of lightness and possibility. She had thought, *I can say yes. I really can. I can tell him I love him – will always love him – and we could be married tomorrow if that is what he wants.*

But she hadn't said it ... and later, reality brought her back to earth with a bump.

It wouldn't end with Max sending someone to begin bringing the estate back to profitability and teaching Rufus how to keep it there, would it? Money would be needed as well and he would supply that too. And finally, there was Mama ... with her complaints, her criticisms and her monumental selfishness; Mama, who could have turned the Garden of Eden into a desert and who would gradually do the same to Frances's marriage.

Whilst drying her hair in front of the fire, Frances wondered how to make Max understand the scope of that particular problem but could think of nothing she could say that he wouldn't simply brush aside as irrelevant. He was so determined ... so confident that nothing of importance stood in their way. She did not think he had spared a thought for how her circumstances would affect, not only him, but also his family. And if he guessed how close she was to weakening ... how he had undermined her defences to the point where she was incapable of constructing any logical, convincing argument ... he'd whisk her off to the Marriage House without further discussion.

Inevitably, her hair was no more cooperative than her brain and refused to stay up even with the aid of every hairpin she had. After struggling for half an hour, she gave up and tied it back in a garish yellow ribbon Max had bought for her in Hawick. She wouldn't be leaving their rooms, after all. And it wasn't as if he hadn't seen her hair loose before.

* * *

When Max walked in, that tumble of lightly-curling chestnut hair was the first thing he saw and, for a second, it halted him mid-stride. When he'd seen it loose that day at Langholme he'd wanted nothing more than to gather it in his hands and let his fingers travel through it. He hadn't, of course. Aside from helping to pin up her braid, he hadn't even touched it. This evening, however, he promised himself that he would.

Hoping she hadn't noticed his slight hesitation, he smiled and said meditatively, 'I see we are to be informal tonight. Does it mean that I can dispense with my cravat?'

She shrugged, feeling mildly uncertain. 'If you wish.'

'Then I will.' He paused and added hopefully, '*Just* the cravat?'

Something in his voice sent a spiral of heat through her.

'You have something else in mind?'

'I have numerous things in mind ... but I fear they would embarrass you.'

His voice teased. The glint in his eyes spoke of something else entirely. Feeling her breath catch, Frances said, 'You don't usually let that stop you.'

'True.' He grinned at her. 'Perhaps I'll get around to it later. But for now, I had best make myself presentable – assuming that the hot water I asked for has arrived?'

'They brought it a little while ago.'

'Excellent.' He turned to go and then, looking back, gestured towards the book lying beside her. 'Is the heroine still swooning?'

She hadn't read a single page but she nodded, glad to be on firmer ground.

'And screaming and wailing whilst depending on the equally tedious hero to save her. Personally, I think she'd do better to stick with the villain. He may be evil – but at least he isn't stupid.'

'Nothing wrong with a bit of wickedness,' returned Max, over his shoulder as he left the room. 'In my experience, it's usually rather enjoyable.'

Frances watched the bedchamber door close behind him and

reminded herself to breathe. If the brief conversation they had just had was any indication, she suspected that she had better keep her wits about her during the rest of the evening.

While he washed and shaved, Max reviewed a number of possible alternatives and eventually came to the conclusion that his best chance of success lay in taking her by surprise. This, he reflected, wouldn't be difficult. He had already set her slightly off-balance. He smiled to himself and reached for his coat, thinking, *Yes. This should do the trick.*

Frances had expected him to re-appear without a cravat. It hadn't occurred to her that he might also discard his embroidered vest and wear the black brocade coat over a shirt of fine, white lawn, worn open at the neck. Her gaze was immediately and helplessly riveted by the bare skin of his throat. It took several moments for her to realise that he was watching her stare at him … and that the expression in his eyes was both amused and knowing. Finally, clearing her throat, she said, 'I think that you have quite surpassed me in the informality stakes.'

'It's easier for men,' he shrugged. 'I can shed a garment or two without revealing very much at all. You can't. If you removed the over-dress of that gown, you'd be left in your corset and petticoats … which I wouldn't mind in the least but which would doubtless leave you feeling indecent.'

Aware that he was trying to shock her and determined not to let him, Frances said, 'I wouldn't just *feel* indecent – I'd *look* it, too.'

'Not really. You wouldn't show much more than in a slightly daring ball gown.'

'The operative word there being *daring*. And no.' Catching the speculative gleam in his eyes, 'I am *not* going to prove it.'

'Spoilsport. I imagine you look particularly fetching in a pretty corset.'

'Go on imagining it, then.'

'I believe I will.' Smiling, Max shut his eyes and said, 'What colour is it?'

Frances narrowly avoided choking. 'Whatever colour your imagination wants it to be.'

'Pink, then. Pink with black ribbons and --'

She slammed both palms against his chest. 'Stop this instant!'

'Ow!' He opened his eyes. 'That was just becoming enjoyable.'

Frances couldn't help laughing. As severely as she was able, she said, 'You are truly outrageous, you know. Do you behave this way with all the ladies of your acquaintance?'

His expression became abruptly serious and, taking one of her hands, he lifted it to his lips. 'No. Only with you, love. Only ever with you.'

And as easily as that, left her heart wide open with love for him ... and unaware that everything she felt was written clearly on her face.

Satisfied with his progress thus far, Max put aside risqué innuendo for a time. Over an extremely good salmon terrine, followed by slices of chicken in a tarragon sauce, he let Frances direct the conversation and found himself answering questions about his sister and their cousin.

'There was a lot of gossip about Lord Sherbourne – Kilburn as he was then – five years ago,' said Frances when the earl's name cropped up. 'People said he'd killed a man in a duel and had spent a year in France to escape justice. I never quite believed it myself but most others seemed to. Mama certainly did. It was why she didn't want to invite him to the wedding.'

'No one said anything of it in my hearing while I was in London,' replied Max slowly, 'though they must all have heard the same rumours you did. Most pertinently, perhaps, is that the Duke of Rockliffe would have known about it ... and since I can't imagine him inviting a murderer into his home, I doubt that's what Sherbourne is.'

'Well, he was very kind to me at a time when I needed it so naturally I'm prejudiced in his favour. I've often wished I'd had the chance to thank him properly.'

'You'll have it when we get back to Brandon Lacey.'

Frances looked away, not wanting him to read her expression. 'Perhaps.'

Sighing inwardly, Max recognised that she was still retreating.

Well, he thought. *Let's see if I can't change that.*

Watched her toying, without a great deal of interest, with a fruit tartlet, he said, 'Are you going to eat that or merely destroy it?'

She laid down her spoon and pushed the plate away. 'It needs cream.'

This was perfectly true. The reason there wasn't any was that Max had told the maid not to serve it. He hadn't forgotten Richmond and didn't want a repeat of that particular torture ... especially tonight when raging lust so early in the evening would seriously disrupt his plans for later.

'Perhaps they forgot it,' he said innocently. 'But if you have finished, why not take your wine over to the sofa and I'll ring for them to clear the table?'

Frances nodded and did as he suggested. Throughout the meal, she had spent quite a lot of time trying not to look at his throat and, instead, had found her attention riveted by his strong, capable hands. Now, she watched him leaning negligently against the mantelpiece and looking so sinfully beautiful she couldn't drag her eyes away from him. And when the maid finally withdrew with the last of the dishes and he discarded his coat before coming to sit beside her, it took her several seconds to find her brain.

Smiling lazily beneath slightly raised brows and angling his body towards her, Max murmured, 'Say it, why don't you?'

'Say what?' asked Frances, all her senses awash with his nearness.

'What you were thinking just now.'

Struggling to focus, she said, 'And you know what that was, I suppose?'

'Yes. I believe so. You were thinking that I am too gorgeous for words; you were wishing that, however well-intentioned, I'd stop behaving like someone's maiden aunt; and you were hoping I'd kiss you.'

She swallowed. 'I ... may have been thinking *one* of those things.'

'Only one?'

'Well ... perhaps two.'

'That's disappointing.' The dark grey eyes travelled to her mouth and lingered there. 'So you *don't* think I'm utterly gorgeous?'

Laughter stirred. 'As you're well aware, I think you're impossible.'

'Oh.' Lifting one hand, he trailed the back of his curved fingers over her cheek. 'I could try not to be. I could also admit that my current thoughts aren't at all aunt-like.'

Her pulse stuttered. 'That sounds as if ... as if you're asking permission.'

For a moment, he appeared to consider this. 'My mistake, then. I wasn't.'

And he gathered her smoothly into his arms.

The instant his mouth touched hers, Frances was back under the trees at Westlake when he'd kissed her for the first time. *Then* he had merely brushed her lips with his before placing a trail of butterfly kisses along her cheek and jaw. And when he'd finally returned to her mouth, he'd encouraged her to open it by running the tip of his tongue along her upper lip. Now he did not need to teach her that again. She remembered it all. And remembering, instantly offered what they both wanted.

Max remembered that day too – but differently. It was the day she'd promised to marry him so of course he hadn't been able to resist kissing her. But *then* she'd been a girl of nineteen and, with the shadow of her projected betrothal to Archie Malpas looming over them, she hadn't been indisputably his. So he had been ... circumspect. He'd kissed her languorously and sweetly and with only a hint of the passion burning like wildfire inside him. He hadn't let his hands go anywhere they shouldn't and he'd been careful to conceal the evidence of how badly he wanted her. Things were different now. And although she hadn't yet agreed to marry him, Max was confident that she would because it was inconceivable that either of them could ever belong to anyone else. They were destined to be together and she fitted perfectly in his arms because it was where she belonged. So now, although he kept the first kiss light, he also allowed one hand to find the curve of her waist while the other drew the ribbon from her hair so he could slide his fingers into the cool, heavy mass.

Any intentions he might have had about not rushing her evaporated when her mouth opened beneath his, inviting him in to a world of warmth and sweetness. The pleasure was so great that he almost groaned. He felt her hands charting the muscles of his arms and shoulders … her fingers travelling on to explore his throat, before gliding into his hair … and her body pressing close, then closer. And far sooner than he had anticipated, he had to start reminding himself what this was supposed to achieve. He'd leave circumspection behind him, yes; he would also reveal some, though not all, of the maelstrom of passion that drove him; but what he wanted from this was for her to discover her own fires and the secrets of her body that ignited them.

His fingers trailed a gossamer path along the neckline of her gown. She sighed into his mouth, then scorched his jaw with kisses. Choosing his moment with care, he said, 'Frances … do you love me?'

'Yes. Yes. You know I do.'

'Perhaps.' His fingertips dipped inside her décolletage, then withdrew. 'But it would mean a great deal to me if you could say it.'

Her body singing a song of anticipation, she said raggedly, 'I love you. I've always, always loved you. Don't stop.'

He had no intention of stopping – at least, not yet.

'And I love you … truly, hopelessly, eternally.' The bodice of the ready-made Richmond gown fastened at the front with a series of small hooks. Distracting her with a long, hungry kiss, he made short work of unfastening them … and then lost the ability to breathe as he raised his head and looked down on delicate, creamy shoulders and the exquisite curves revealed by her corset. 'You're so beautiful … and I want you more than I can say.'

'I want you, too.'

The words ended on a strangled gasp as he slid the straps of her chemise away and deftly freed her breasts from their prison so that his fingers could explore this new and wildly tempting territory. At his first touch, Frances gave a startled, shuddering moan and her arms tightened about him. Keeping a stranglehold on his self-control, Max kissed her again and then, long moments later, adjusted his position so that his mouth could follow the trail blazed by his hands. A swirl of his tongue had her clutching his hair and sobbing his name, followed by something that sounded like please.

'Please what, love?'

She shook her head helplessly, unable to find the words. 'Just ... please.'

Max knew what she wanted. He wanted the same thing and his anatomy was playing merry hell with him as a result. He said unevenly, 'Marry me.'

Her reply was to arch up into his palm while her fingers found their way inside his shirt. The breath hissed through his teeth and, though his hands resumed their caresses, he lifted his head to look into her face.

'Would you like,' he murmured huskily, 'to complete this in bed.'

Her breathing became even more fractured. 'Yes. Oh yes.'

He smiled and used a thumb and forefinger to good effect. 'Promise to marry me and we can.'

Yet again, she said nothing. But finally, dilated, passion-glazed eyes opened on his and she said, 'That isn't f-fair.'

'I know. But you can't say I didn't warn you.' Somehow – and God alone knew how he did it – Max managed a smile whilst simultaneously sliding his palm over and around her breast. 'You promised to marry me once before. Promise again now ... and let me take you to bed.' And when she still hesitated, 'You want me to, don't you?'

'Yes.'

'Well, then?'

Frances shut her eyes. 'I don't ... I shouldn't ... you have to let me think.'

Just for a second, he remained absolutely still. Then, abruptly releasing her, he was up and away across the room, snatching up his coat and shrugging it on as he went. 'By all means. I'd hoped we had disposed of the baggage you've been clinging to – but clearly not. Or perhaps I've been over-estimating the strength of my appeal?'

She sat up, clutching her gown to her and feeling suddenly cold. For a second, she stared at his back as he leaned against the mantel with his back to her. His hands were braced against the dark beam and his knuckles glowed white. 'You know it isn't that.'

'Actually, I'm not sure I know anything at all.' The rustle of her skirt told him that she was on her feet and about to approach him. That, since his body was still in turmoil, was the last thing he needed. Turning, he said, 'There is no need to come any closer. However ... if I haven't made myself sufficiently plain, I'll say it one last time. It's marriage or nothing, Frances. And if it's to be nothing, you are the one who will have to say so.'

Upon which, he swung away to towards his bedchamber.

CHAPTER SEVENTEEN

Frances watched him go, everything inside her a twisting mass of confusion and misery. It came to her suddenly that he was as tired as she was of fighting the same up-hill battle.

If it's to be nothing, you are the one who will have to say so.

That was clearly an ultimatum – and he couldn't be blamed for issuing it. He had laid his heart at her feet and, to all intents and purposes, she had trodden on it. Or that, she supposed, was how it must look to him. How could he believe she loved him if she continually pushed him away? He couldn't, could he? She was hurting him ... and the knowledge seared her insides, making her want to cry. Her reasons might be well-meant but they weren't worth a single instant of pain for Max. She couldn't bear it.

If it's to be nothing, you are the one who will have to say so.

The truth, she realised, was very simple. It couldn't be nothing. It couldn't *ever* be nothing because the cord that bound them was unbreakable and she didn't know how she could ever have supposed that it wasn't.

Fastening the hooks on her bodice with clumsy haste as she went, she crossed to his door and knocked. 'Max? Come back – please.'

On the other side of the door, Max had thrown his coat at a chair and was already regretting those final words. He was perfectly well aware that they'd had more to do with his physical discomfort than any loss of patience with Frances. He would not use sex as a way of forcing her into marriage any more than he'd use any other means of coercion or compromise. He wanted her to agree to be his wife freely because the only thing that mattered to her was spending the rest of her life with him. Well, walking away and leaving her thinking he was angry at not getting his own way was no way to achieve that, was it?

Drawing a long, bracing breath, he turned around to go back and froze when he heard her voice. He hadn't expected her to call him back – had no idea why she would. So he turned and opened the door, immediately taking in the anxiety in her eyes, coupled with the fact that she'd made a spectacularly bad job of re-hooking her gown. The latter went some way to restoring his equilibrium ... but before he could speak, she said rapidly, 'If you're sure – completely sure it's what you want, I'll g-give you the promise you asked for. But first, can I ... will you let me try to explain?'

'Yes. In a moment.' Reaching out, he set about putting her gown to rights. 'I can't pay proper attention while you're all lopsided. I'm likely to laugh at an inopportune moment – and we wouldn't want that, would we?'

Though she continued to search his face, some of her anxiety faded.

'I'm just relieved that you think you *can* laugh,' she mumbled. And then, 'I'm sorry.'

'So am I. I spoke more sharply than I intended through no fault of yours.' Reaching the last hook, he stepped back and added, 'I was using my last means of persuasion – but you had the right to say no. You will always have it. I hope you know that?'

'Yes.' Her voice cracked on the word. 'Your sense of honour again.'

'A nuisance, isn't it?' he asked with a smile, as he led her back towards the sofa. Then, when she was seated, 'Now ... what did you want to say to me?'

Frances gripped her hands together and looked him in the eye.

'It's about what you called the – the baggage I've been clinging to.'

'Yes. I suspected it might be.' He took the chair facing her. 'Let's hear it, then.'

'Your idea about Rufus learning to manage the estate is brilliant and your offer to help him do it is more than generous. That alone is more than enough. But if we marry, I don't think it would stop there. I think money would be needed as well and that you would supply that too. If you told me about it at all – which I doubt you would – you'd call it a loan.   But I suspect you might not ever ask for it to be repaid.'

'If that's what is worrying you, we'll have a clause insisting on repayment inserted into the marriage contract,' he promised. 'Next?'

'William. He's seventeen and we had to let his tutor go a year ago. But Mr Moss said his education wouldn't suffer because his grasp of higher mathematics would probably already outstrip that of most other first-year university students. I hoped that, if Will waited another year, the estate might be able to pay for Cambridge. Does that sound possible?'

Max had to laugh. 'No, love. It's likely to take two years rather than one. And if your little brother is a mathematical prodigy, the sooner he completes his studies, the better.'

'Yes. That's what I thought you'd say.' Frances spread her hands and eyed him sadly. 'You can see how the expense of having me as your wife is already adding up?'

'Not to more than it is worth to me or even more than I can afford. What else?'

She shut her eyes for a moment and prepared to reveal the worst of it.

'Mama. Once you open your purse for one thing, she'll expect you to open it for everything else. She won't be polite about it and she won't take no for an answer. She'll --'

'Stop,' said Max calmly. 'How feeble do you think I am? I don't mind helping your brothers or setting your family land on the road to recovery. But your mother's past transgressions make her a vastly different matter.'

'How can I make you see?' asked Frances worriedly. 'She'll find ways of – of interfering between you and me. She'll buy things and have the bills sent to you – just as Grey has been doing. I wouldn't even put it past her to turn up uninvited at Brandon Lacey and expect to be made welcome.' She stared at him. 'Why are you laughing?'

'Because I'd like to see her try.'

'Marry me and you probably will. You don't know her, Max.'

'She doesn't know me either ... and neither do you if you think I'd permit her to do any of those things. No. Just listen.' This as she opened her mouth to speak. 'Don't run away with the idea that I'm so bloody honourable I'm incapable of giving short shrift to anyone or anything that threatens me or mine. I'm not. And I can safely guarantee that, after her first conversation with me – to which, by the way, I'm looking forward immensely – your witch of a mother won't want to come within a mile of me ever again.'

The blue eyes widened. 'She won't?'

'No, love. She won't. And in the unlikely event that I require reinforcements, I'll set my own mother on her. That should send her scuttling for the hills.'

'Your mama is lovely,' said Frances wistfully. 'But she must want what is best for you and she … well, she isn't going to think that is me.'

'God,' said Max, shoving a hand through his hair. 'Are we never going to be done with this? All Mama wants for any of her children is that we be happy. Most mothers would have taken one look at Julian Langham with his impoverished estate, his wreck of a house, his three illegitimate children and his complete lack of social graces and been appalled. *My* mother saw the man my sister had fallen in love with – and who loved her back in equal measure – and took him to her bosom.' He smiled and took her hands. 'Now … can we please stop this? You've explained, I've listened and none of it makes any difference at all.'

'I want to say yes,' she blurted. 'I want to marry you so badly it feels as if something is clawing holes inside me. But I'm afraid you'll regret it. And that would hurt much worse.'

By way of answer, Max pulled her across to sit on his lap. Then, putting his arms about her, he said, 'Listen to me. You're busily trying to protect me from the depredations of your family. So busy that you don't seem to have considered the other side of the coin.'

'Which is what?'

'If it's my well-being that concerns you, you're worrying about the wrong things. I can afford to help your family and I can deal with your mother. What I *can't* do is to face more years like the last five. There was no one for me before you and I met and there has been no one since. That isn't going to change. If you feel the same … if my future happiness is what you truly want …

you will put aside all these other irrelevancies and say, *Yes, Max – I'll marry you.*'

Tears stung her eyes and she laid her cheek against his.

'Then yes, Max,' she whispered. 'I'll marry you.'

'*Thank you*,' he breathed. And threading his hand through her hair so he could tip her head back, he proceeded to kiss her until neither of them could breathe. After a while and still holding her close, he said, 'Promise?'

'Yes.'

'When?'

'Tomorrow, if you like.'

'Mm. In the toll-lodge?' He thought about it. 'No. I'd like you to have a wedding you can enjoy remembering. And though the so-called Marriage House *may* be romantic ... I suspect you'll like a wee Scottish kirk in Hawick much better.'

'I'll enjoy remembering my wedding to you no matter where it's held.' She smoothed back a lock of his hair and tried to absorb the fact that this beautiful, incredible man would be hers to touch for the rest of her days. Daringly but with no intention other than that of testing her new powers, she said, 'Now I've promised to marry you ... are you going to take me to bed?'

'Ah.' He smiled ruefully. 'I did say that, didn't I?'

'You did.' She smiled back. 'But now you're realising that you'd rather do things in the proper order.'

'Yes. I am, rather. After all, having waited five years, another day or so isn't going to kill me. Would that be all right?'

'Better than all right. It's perfect.'

'Then we're agreed, love.' He settled her head on his shoulder and kissed her brow. 'We'll marry tomorrow.'

* * *

On the following morning, Joe Miller took one look at Max's face and, grinning broadly, said, 'Will we be making a stop at the Marriage House?'

Laughing, Max said, 'No. But you can congratulate me, if you like.'

'I do that, my lord – I truly do.' Miller grasped his hand. 'And I wish you both happy. Miss Frances is a lovely young lady – and one with her head screwed on right. I was beginning to think she'd got more sense than to have you ... but I reckoned as you'd wear her down in the end.'

'I'm glad I've justified your faith in me,' retorted Max dryly. And then, 'We're hoping to tie the knot in Hawick, Joe ... and I'll need you to stand witness for us.'

'It'll be my honour, sir. You know that. But her ladyship's going to be disappointed.'

'In which she won't be alone. I know that. But I'll worry about it later.'

Frances accepted the coachman's good wishes with a becoming blush and a smile. Max handed her into the carriage, jumped in after her and immediately swept her into his arms.

Some minutes later, he murmured, 'Good morning.'

She shook her head a little. 'You said that earlier, over breakfast.'

'And now I've said it again – properly. I'm starting as I mean to go on, you see.' He settled her comfortably in the curve of his arm. 'Are you still happy to wait till Hawick?'

'If you are.'

'Yes – though I suspect Joe is disappointed we won't be making use of the Marriage House.' He paused. 'Our families will also doubtless feel cheated. How would you feel about a church blessing – or even a second wedding? One with flowers and bells and a pretty new gown?'

'I expect I'd enjoy it.' She reached up to touch his cheek. 'But, with or without the trimmings, I'll marry you as many times as you like.'

'Good. That's what we'll do, then. Planning it will help pass the long ride home.' Grinning, he murmured, 'That ... and other things.'

They re-crossed the Tweed to re-join the post road towards Kelso, where they could turn south-west in the direction of Jedburgh. It was a slow ride. In some places, the road had dried out reasonably well but in others, where the ground sloped to a dip, the mud was still inches thick. It was nearly two o'clock before they reached Bonjedward and Miller brought the carriage to a halt outside a tiny village inn.

Jumping down from the box, he opened the door of the carriage, saying, 'This'd be a good time to rest the horses, my lord. If you're wanting to see the abbey at Jedburgh, the head groom back in Coldstream said we'd have to turn off here for a mile or so, then come back on ourselves.' He turned and pointed. 'Hawick's that way.'

'Then I don't think we have any choice,' said Max reluctantly, as he helped Frances from the carriage. 'If we had made better time, a detour might have been possible. But progress has been slow and I doubt it's likely to improve. Also, if something should go wrong, we could be stranded in the middle of nowhere and that isn't a risk I want to --'

'Stop.' Frances interrupted him firmly. 'Stop apologising. Of *course* we must press on. It's the only sensible choice if we're to be sure of getting to Hawick today. And if I'm to choose between a wedding and another hermitless abbey, I'll take the wedding, thank you.'

'Good choice,' he said, sweeping her towards the inn. '*Very* good choice. So, with that in mind, let's find something to keep your strength up.'

* * *

They were a mere three miles outside Hawick when the wisdom their decision not to pause at Jedburgh was proved right. Drawing the horses to a standstill, Miller jumped down and set about examining the harness.

'What is it?' asked Max, emerging at his side.

'I think we've got a crack in one of the poles,' came the grim reply. 'Reckon I heard it go just now when we was going over that rough bit ... but this'n seems all right.' He swung round to check the other side and muttered, 'Yes. There it is. Bugger.'

'A crack or a break?'

'Crack. It might hold if I can strengthen it with summat and we take it right slow.' He looked across at Max. 'I'm sorry, my lord. It was fine this morning. I check every bit of the tack before --'

'Don't be an ass, Joe. I know you do. This is a damned

nuisance but it can't be helped. Now ... we need a splint and something to bind it with. Any ideas?'

They eventually settled for narrow and reasonably straight branches cut from the trees beside the road and tied them on tight with strips of leather purloined from the spare set of reins Miller kept under his seat.

'Well,' said Max, shrugging back into his coat, 'that's the best we can do – so let's just hope it lasts. If we can get to Hawick, you should be able to get it replaced.'

Back in the carriage beside Frances, he took her hand in his and said ruefully, 'And that, having wasted the best part of an hour, is starting to make a wedding today look unlikely.'

She squeezed his fingers. 'Then we'll marry tomorrow. I can wait that long.'

'I suppose I can too. But that doesn't mean I like it.'

* * *

They drew up outside the King's Head at around half-past five. Miller announced that he'd go in search of someone who could replace the pole as soon as he had seen to the horses. Max bespoke rooms, asked the usual question and returned to Frances saying, 'There's no letter.'

'Oh.' She frowned a little. 'What does that mean, do you think?'

'I don't know. The landlord says the weather here has been as bad as it was in Coldstream and several parties had to extend their stay – which suggests that Grey wouldn't have left before today. There are several other inns in the town so I suppose he could be staying at one of those. It's also possible that he's been waiting for us to arrive before delivering an onward clue. If that's the case, there is a chance he means it to end here. And if he doesn't and we're to continue retracing our steps, I hope to God it will be in the direction of home. But for now, the only thing we can do is to wait and see ... and I suppose I'd better --'

He stopped as the innkeeper rushed up, smiling broadly.

'My lord! You asked about a letter – and an express rider has just arrived with this!'

Max took the proffered letter, glanced at the superscription and immediately looked up. He said, 'Is the fellow who brought this still here?'

'Yes, my lord. He's taking ale in the tap.'

'Don't disturb him – but ask him to wait.' And to Frances as he broke the seal, 'It's from Duncan. I wrote from Coldstream, saying we would be stuck there for one day, if not two – so he obviously hoped there was a chance of catching me here.'

She said nothing, watching him read. Finally, he looked up, sighed and said, 'Blast.'

'What is it?'

'See for yourself,' he replied, handing it to her. 'I'll have to reply. Excuse me, will you?'

Frances nodded and looked down at the letter.

Mr Balfour had stuck, very briefly to the point.

Max,

We had to tell her ladyship the truth some days ago. Lord and Lady Sherbourne arrived today and the truth has been shared with them also. The tenants are asking where you are – as are the Chalfont children. You need to get back here. But if you can't, at least give us more information than your current whereabouts – such as how much longer you intend to continue with this wild goose chase.

Duncan

P.S. *Grey's earlier activities appear to have ceased. There has been nothing further since you left.*

Frances re-folded the letter and absently followed a maid upstairs to her room, reflecting that Mr Balfour sounded frayed. She sympathised with him. From her own point of view, the news that Ralph Sherbourne had been admitted to the secret was disturbing. During the short time she had been at Brandon Lacey, Frances had seen nothing to suggest that Louisa Brandon knew about her scandalous flight from the altar. But Lord Sherbourne knew – so the conversation that these two might have was therefore one which Frances preferred not to imagine.

She was still very carefully *not* imagining it when Max walked in and, reading her expression without difficulty, said, 'What is it? Worrying about what Sherbourne might say to Mama?'

'Wondering more than worrying,' she replied, leaning into him. 'I *think* he's probably too discreet to say anything at all. But it's suddenly occurred to me that perhaps he doesn't need to. Perhaps, although she said nothing of it, Lady Brandon already knows about it.'

'I think that all too probable – though she didn't mention it to me either. But like most ladies she devours the society pages, so I doubt she missed your spectacular appearance in them. But her choosing to raise the matter with Sherbourne is much less likely. As you've seen, she can keep her own counsel and often prefers to do so.' He gave her a hug, dropped a kiss on her hair and added, 'It's of no consequence, Frances. None. And we have more important matters to think of – such as our wedding.'

She smiled at him. 'Tomorrow?'

'Tomorrow. I'm going out now to attempt to arrange matters suitably – and, since I don't know how long that will take, I've ordered dinner for a little later than usual.' Max saw no need to mention that he wasn't only looking for a kirk and a minister. Bells and the perfect wedding gown might be beyond him ... but flowers, hopefully, were not. 'If I'm delayed for any reason, I'll send a message and I've asked Joe to report his progress in getting the carriage repaired.'

'And Grey?' she asked.

'Should a letter arrive, it will doubtless be brought to you. Open it, by all means.' He tilted up her chin in order to enjoy a long and very thorough kiss. Then, releasing her, he said, 'And now I'm going – before I forget what I'm supposed to be doing.'

After he left, Frances decided that the green polonaise was the best choice for her wedding and sent it downstairs to be pressed. An hour passed, during which she washed, changed her gown and tidied her hair. In due course, the maidservant reappeared with her refreshed polonaise, along with a message from Mr Miller saying that the carriage was being repaired in a workshop a couple of streets away and that he would remain with it until the job had been completed. Nothing, however, arrived from Grey.

When she heard a clock somewhere chiming seven, Frances

started to wonder how much longer Max would be ... and whether he had found a pretty church ... and when she would become accustomed to the idea that, despite everything, she was actually going to be his wife after all.

A tap at the door heralded the return of the maidservant, this time accompanied by an older woman wearing the unrelieved black of mourning.

'Beg pardon, ma'am,' said the maid, 'but Mistress Craig says she has word for you from his lordship so I brought her up. I hope I did right.'

'Yes, of course.' Frances smiled at Mistress Craig. 'What is the message?'

With the merest hint of a curtsy, the woman said, 'He asked me to bring you to the Green Man over by Gretal Bar. He's to meet you there, ma'am.'

'Gretal Bar? Where is that?'

'Not far off. Ten minutes' walk, maybe. No more.'

'It's up the end of the High Street, then off towards the river on the edge of town,' supplied the maidservant, with something resembling a sniff.

'If you'd rather not venture out, ma'am,' said Mistress Craig, as if she didn't care either way, 'I'll go and tell his lordship. He didn't say why he wanted you to go there but --'

'No,' said Frances decisively. It was still light and would be for at least another hour ... and Max *had* said he might send a message. 'I'll come. Wait while I get my cloak.'

On the short walk across the town, Frances attempted to make conversation but received no encouragement. Though Mistress Craig could not be called rude, she was very definitely a woman of few words ... and the only fact to be gleaned from her was that she had been asked to deliver a message and show Frances the way. And that, it seemed, was the total sum of her interest.

The Green Man was a small tavern in a poor state of repair but otherwise little different to the various inns Frances had seen throughout their travels through the borders. Shrugging inwardly, she stepped towards the entrance only to have her guide unlock her jaws on a whole sentence.

'Not that way, ma'am. The tap-room's no place for a lady like you. I told his lordship I'd take you in the back way to the parlour. It's just through this gate here.'

Frances's brows rose slightly. 'Does this establishment belong to you?'

'To my family, ma'am. Yes. Here we are.'

Finding herself shown into a shabby but scrupulously clean parlour, Frances felt a prickle of unease. Firstly, it seemed a very odd place for Max to ask her to meet him ... and secondly, he wasn't there. Had it not been for the fact that the maid at the King's Head knew exactly where she was, unease might have become alarm. As it was, mentally castigating herself for not asking more questions, she said, coolly, 'Well, Lord Brandon is clearly not here, is he? So I'll allow him five minutes grace and then return to the inn.'

'As you wish, ma'am. Would you like tea?'

'No, thank you. I'm unlikely to be here long enough to drink it.'

'Very well, then. I'll leave you to wait.'

And she went out, closing the door softly behind her.

Frances looked through the small-paned window into the tiny garden. The more she thought about it, the more peculiar this all seemed. Frowning, she tapped her fingers against the sill and decided that she would *not* wait. Turning on her heel, she took two steps towards the door only to stop dead as it opened.

A smile of welcome and relief swept over her face and then froze.

It wasn't Max. Of *course*, it wasn't Max.

It was Leo's sketch made flesh.

Tanned skin and neatly-tied brown hair, streaked with blond – both suggesting he had spent time somewhere sunnier than Scotland. A wide, mobile mouth and level brows, beneath which eyes the colour of brandy held the merest hint of a smile ... even that slight bump in an otherwise straight nose. Leo had captured this man's every feature with uncanny accuracy.

Frances's stomach was lurching unpleasantly but her voice,

when she spoke, held exactly the right note of acidulous sweetness.

'Why – Mr Grey,' she said. 'Emerging from the shadows at last? Max *will* be pleased.'

CHAPTER EIGHTEEN

By the time three heavily laden carriages arrived at Brandon Lacey one of the occupants could feel his sangfroid beginning to evaporate.

The first few days, reflected Ralph Sherbourne, had been tiring but otherwise enjoyable. With Elizabeth's maid and his valet following in a separate carriage, it had been no hardship having his wife's sole companionship for hours on end. The time had been passed in easy conversation or, sometimes, in even more pleasurable activities ... resulting in the book he had slipped into his pocket before leaving London remaining unopened. Then they had stopped at Chalfont to collect Langham's three children and everything had changed ... after which the only thing he could find to be grateful for was that they weren't *also* being accompanied by an extremely ugly little dog answering to the unlikely name of Figgy.

To be fair, the older boy had been no trouble. But little Ellie – tearful from having said goodbye to Arabella and Julian – had clung to her Aunt Lizzie. This, inevitably, put an end to any prospect of Ralph spending time alone with his wife and the inconvenience hadn't ended there. At some point during the afternoon of the first day, Ellie had grown tired and, releasing Elizabeth's hand for the first time, climbed on to his own lap where she had promptly fallen asleep. Ralph could only assume that his astonishment at suddenly finding his arms full of a six-year-old had been responsible for the peal of laughter Elizabeth had had to stifle with her hand.

On the second day away from Chalfont, an existing problem of which he had so far been unaware, forced itself upon his attention when it escalated. At the noon-day stop, Frayne – who had been riding in the third carriage with the boys – revealed that they'd been forced to stop three times on the previous day due to young Master Rob suffering from motion sickness. This had been unfortunate, but manageable. Today, however, they had already stopped four times since breakfast and, on the last occasion, a fraction too late. According to Master Tom, this was because Rob had insisted on eating bacon and eggs – which he knew perfectly well he wasn't allowed when they were travelling. At this point, Ralph had cast his eyes to heaven and wondered why no one had informed either Elizabeth or himself of that fact … but one glance at Rob's woebegone and distinctly green-tinged face was sufficient to make him withhold comment.

After that, the journey had turned into the sort of parlour game where everyone constantly changed places. Elizabeth maintained that it was unfair to make Annie and Frayne shoulder the whole burden and had volunteered to care for Rob herself. This, Ralph had flatly forbidden. Instead, since the weather was fine, he instructed his coachman to take Master Rob up beside him every other hour in the hope that fresh air might prove a cure. And since Ellie remained with Elizabeth, he decreed that during the times when Rob was outside on the box, Annie and Frayne should get some rest while he entertained Master Tom in the third carriage.

This, since Frayne had packed a travelling chess-set and already begun teaching the boy to play, turned out to be less of an ordeal than Ralph had expected – though the incessant questions about things glimpsed through the carriage window grew a trifle wearisome. And the whole journey was becoming a severe test for other reasons entirely since Ellie didn't even relinquish her hold on Aunt Lizzie at night – meaning that Ralph had perforce to sleep in a separate chamber, a state of affairs he neither liked nor was accustomed to. The sight of Brandon Lacey, therefore, was immensely welcome in a number of ways.

* * *

Alerted to the arrival of her guests, Lady Brandon was outside waiting to greet them before everyone had climbed down from their respective carriages.

'Lizzie, my dear!' She folded Elizabeth in a warm embrace. 'Are you completely exhausted?'

'Not quite *completely*,' smiled Elizabeth, 'but something approaching it. We have been travelling close to a week, you know.'

'And it has felt,' murmured Sherbourne, bowing over Louisa's hand, 'like twice that. How do you do, ma'am? It is a great pleasure to see you again.'

'The pleasure is all ours, my lord. Welcome to Brandon --'

'Aunt Louisa!' Ellie catapulted against her ladyship's skirts. 'We've come such a long way and I thought we'd never get here. And Rob was sick again – in the carriage, this time – so Sir Ralph made him ride outside and --'

'Hush, darling!' laughed Louisa. 'You can tell me everything later. But for now, let's get everyone inside. Annie ... the green suite has been prepared for Lord and Lady Sherbourne and the nursery suite for the children. You'll remember where both of those are, I'm sure, and can show his lordship's valet the way. And while Hawkes has the luggage brought in, we can all have tea.' She sent a twinkling smile in the direction of the boys and added, 'Cook has been busy making what Arabella assures me are all your favourite things. And your Uncle Leo will doubtless join us as soon as he's told you've arrived – because they're all *his* favourite things as well.'

Leo strolled in just as his mother got everyone seated in the parlour with tea and cakes.

'Cousin Lizzie!' he said, dropping a kiss on Elizabeth's cheek. 'Beautiful as ever, I see – and terrifyingly elegant into the bargain.'

'Cousin Leo,' she replied. 'Still the biggest flatterer in the whole of Yorkshire?'

'Nothing of the sort.' He offered his hand to Ralph. 'How do you do, my lord?'

'Better now the journey is behind us.'

Leo grinned. 'I can imagine. The infantry been a trial, have they?'

Ralph became aware that three pairs of eyes were watching him anxiously. Repressing a sigh, he said, 'Not ... intentionally. And I seem to have survived the experience.'

Hiding an odd little smile, Elizabeth reached for another lemon cake. She said, 'More than survived it. You did rather well, I thought. What do you think, Tom?'

The boy coloured a little and muttered, 'His lordship was – was very patient with us all. And sending Rob ride on the box was a brilliant idea.'

'I wish everyone would stop making it sound like a punishment,' complained Ralph. And to Rob, 'Is that how it felt?'

'No, sir,' came the prompt response. 'It was famous fun. And I wasn't sick *once*.'

Leo held Ralph's gaze and said merely, 'Ah. My sympathies.'

'Thank you.'

Feeling that she had been quiet long enough, Ellie tugged at Louisa's hand and said, 'Where is Uncle Max?'

Louisa and Leo exchanged glances. Louisa said, 'He had to go away for a little while, darling, but we expect him back very soon. Leo ... ring for Sarah, please. I daresay the children would like to see their rooms.'

'You'll like them,' promised Leo, pulling the bell. 'They're the rooms *we* all had when we were your ages – and all our stuff is still there for you to play with. And out in the stables, aside from horses, ponies and a goat, there's a new litter of kittens.'

'And here is Sarah,' interposed Louisa with relief, as a smiling, rosy-cheeked maid appeared in the doorway. 'She will be looking after you while you're here. So go with her now and get acquainted ... and you can join us downstairs a little later.'

Seeing Ellie about to demur, Elizabeth said quickly, 'I'll be up presently to see how you're getting on. Tom?'

He nodded and hauling his sister to her feet, said, 'Come on, pest. It'll be fun.'

When the children had left the room and the door closed behind them, Leo looked at his mother and said cryptically, 'You may as well tell them. Judging by the letter that came yesterday, Max isn't going to be back any time soon.'

Ralph sat back, sipping his tea. Elizabeth said, 'Is there some problem?'

Sighing, Louisa said, 'After a fashion. Max is currently in Scotland. Coldstream, to be precise – or that's where he was when he last wrote. He is ...' She stopped, unsure how much to say and quite how to say it. 'He is attempting to catch up with a person who has been at some pains to annoy him and it is taking rather longer than he anticipated.'

'Dear me,' drawled Ralph idly. 'That all sounds very ... intriguing. I take it that Lord Brandon is not in any physical danger?'

'No. Well, not so far, anyway,' responded Leo with a shrug. 'It's Grey – the fellow he's chasing – who'll need protection when Max catches up with him.'

'How long has he been gone?' asked Elizabeth.

'Nine days as of today. According to his last letter, heavy rain kept him trapped in Coldstream for two days – though, all being well, he expected to be heading back to Hawick today,' said Louisa gloomily. 'But that's not the worst of it.'

'No?' asked Ralph.

'No.' She sighed again. 'He isn't alone – and hasn't been since the day he left here. He has a young lady with him.'

'My goodness!' said Elizabeth. 'How on earth did that happen?'

'She got caught up in the same idiotic business that was affecting Max,' grinned Leo. 'So she demanded he take her with him on the quest.'

'And he agreed?' murmured Ralph. 'How very ... singular ... of him.'

'That's one way of putting it. The trouble is, Max can't ever have imagined it would take this long or that the pair of them would end up touring the Scottish borders. As best I can recall, they've taken in the sights at Brough, Gilsland, Canonbie, Selkirk, Kelso and Hawick – to which, as Mama said, they're about to retrace their steps from Coldstream.' Leo paused and gave a short laugh. 'By now, either Max is ripe for murder – or he and Frances are having too much fun to care.'

'Frances?' queried Elizabeth. And then, 'Or shouldn't we ask?'

'Since Max is quite likely to have her with him when he finally gets home, you're going to find out anyway,' replied Louisa with mild exasperation. 'It's Frances Pendleton.'

An odd expression lit Lord Sherbourne's tawny-green eyes. He said, 'Daughter of the late Sir Horace Pendleton?'

'Yes. Are you acquainted with her?'

'I met her once. But it was some considerable time ago.'

'Max's case exactly,' nodded Louisa. 'He met Mistress Pendleton at one of the Grantham's house-parties five years since but had no further contact with her until she arrived here, seeking his help on behalf of her brother. Or that's what she said.' She stood up. 'Lord knows what will come of it, of course – but it's pointless speculating on why Max has apparently taken leave of his senses. Meanwhile, I'm keeping you talking when you must both be exhausted. If you've finished your tea, I'll have Hawkes show you to your rooms. We'll dine a little later this evening so there's no need to hurry down. And *I* will see to the children, Lizzie. You've done quite enough and have earned a rest.'

* * *

Upstairs in their room and finally alone, Ralph wasted no time in pulling Elizabeth into his arms for a long, leisurely kiss. Then, against her hair, he murmured, 'I've missed you.'

'And I you.' She laid a palm against his cheek and smiled up at him. 'It seemed very odd waking beside a child instead of cuddled up to you.'

At home, Ralph rarely spent a night in his own bed. This had surprised Elizabeth at first – her understanding of fashionable marriages being that husbands visited their wives beds, before returning to their own. But then, bit by bit, a lot of things about Ralph had surprised her … not least the fact that, within a week of their marriage and probably without realising it, he had let her see how deeply he treasured even the smallest gesture of affection.

Wicked lights dancing in his eyes, he said, 'I shall enjoy making it up to you.'

'I'm glad to hear it,' she began. And stopped as Annie entered the room.

Coming to an abrupt halt, the maid said hastily, 'Beg pardon, my lady. I only wanted to say as they've sent up a bath for you.'

'Thank you, Annie. I'll be there in a moment.'

'Thank you, Annie,' countered Ralph smoothly, 'but you may go. Her ladyship won't need you.'

Elizabeth sucked in a breath and stared at him. He was never shy about admitting his desire for her or, indeed, introducing enjoyable variations. But this was something new. She said weakly, 'Ralph! That – that's --'

'It is, isn't it?' He released her to wave Annie back out through the door. 'But after these last days, I'm entitled to a reward, don't you think? And I reason that I can wash your back ... or any other part of you ... quite as well as Annie. If not better.'

Parts of Elizabeth were already waking in anticipation; an anticipation caused less by his words than the low, seductive tone in which he uttered them. Since she didn't know what to say, she said nothing at all but merely turned in obedience to his hands so that he could begin unlacing her gown. For a moment or two, he worked in silence. But presently he said musingly, 'I find it interesting that Lord Brandon knew Frances Pendleton five years ago.'

'You could call him Max, you know.'

'I shall call him Max when he invites me to do so. At present, the gentleman and I are barely acquainted.'

His fingertips skimmed her nape and on down her spine, leaving a fiery trail in their wake. Elizabeth swallowed and, feeling the gown slide away, stepped out of it. Ralph picked it up, tossed it over a chair and started work on her corset laces. When it didn't appear that he was about to say anything further, Elizabeth said, 'Why?'

'Mm?'

'Why is Max knowing Mistress Pendleton interesting?'

'Ah yes. Forgive me. I was distracted for a moment. It is interesting because of the timing ... the fact being that, five years ago, the lady was at the centre of a splendid scandal.' He stopped again to nip and then kiss the place where her neck met her shoulder. 'I don't suppose Viscount Malpas has ever crossed your path, has he?'

'No. What has he to do with anything?'

'A great deal. Frances was betrothed to him at the time. I was invited to the wedding – the kind of courtesy invitation I ought to have refused. I don't recall why I did not. I *do* recall arriving unpardonably late ... and was just stepping down from the carriage when the bride came flying through the church door.'

'*Did* she? Good heavens!' The corset followed the gown and his hands closed warm and firm around her waist. 'What did you do?'

'The only thing possible. I offered the use of my carriage so she could make good her escape.'

'Oh.' Elizabeth turned to look into his face. 'That was good of you.'

'Wasn't it?' A lazy smile glinting in his eyes, Ralph let his hands stray down her back to press her hips against him. 'You seem surprised.'

'No. Of course not. I just wonder...' The words trailed off as his mouth brushed her jaw and breathed hot temptation near her ear.

'You wonder if I had some personal interest in the lady?'

By now just a little breathless, she said, 'And did you?'

'No. But I'm flattered that you did not care for the possibility that I might have done. However ... what you are really wondering is why I did it.'

'Yes. Why did you?'

'Two facts were immediately clear. If she had wanted to marry Lord Malpas, she would not have been running. And since she *was* running it had to be because she had no other choice.' A playful tug at the tapes of her petticoats send them slithering to her feet. 'As I know to my cost, flight is not always the best answer ... but sometimes it is the only one. So I offered my carriage, she took it and that was the last I ever saw of her.' Stepping back, he drew her towards the dressing-room. 'And now, my lady's bath awaits.'

Unsure whether he was serious or not, Elizabeth said, 'Are you really going to – to --'

'Yes. Unless you object, of course. Do you?'

She supposed that she ought to. Allowing one's husband to bathe one didn't sound at all a respectable thing to do. But when one had been married less than six months ... and when one's husband had given up all the rakish pursuits rumour had once credited him with to become a model of fidelity, Elizabeth was inclined to think he was entitled to a few liberties.

She said, 'No. Though I'm sure I should – since I'm blushing at the mere idea.'

'So you are ... and most delightfully too.'

By the time Elizabeth had shed her shift and stockings and climbed hurriedly into the scented water, Ralph's coat and vest had also disappeared. Aware that he was looking at her, she shut her eyes and said, 'Stop that.'

'Stop what? I am merely enjoying a moment or two of anticipation.' He tilted his head thoughtfully. 'Why are you embarrassed? You know I find every inch of you beautiful. And it is not as if I haven't seen you naked before.'

'No. But on those occasions, you were naked as well.'

'So I was. If you want me to strip you have merely to say the word.'

She had to laugh. 'I know. But for now ... just your shirt, perhaps?'

Answering laughter gleamed in his eyes as he removed the shirt, tossed it aside and reached for the bowl of soft soap. Then he sat on a low stool behind her and said, 'Sit up.'

She did so and he surprised her by starting to massage the stiffness of a week's travel from her shoulders. Elizabeth couldn't repress a groan of appreciation.

'Nice?' he asked.

'Very. How do you always know just what I need?'

Something blossomed in Ralph's chest. It was a feeling that was becoming more and more familiar. A feeling which only his wife could produce and which delighted and terrified him in equal measure. He said, 'It's a knack I have. Relax.'

Sighing, she allowed herself to become boneless under his touch. Distantly, almost dreamily, she supposed that she ought to share her news before he worked it out for himself. But for the planned journey to Yorkshire, she would have already done so. His hands continued to work their magic and began to grow adventurous. Knowing where this would lead, Elizabeth reluctantly forced herself to concentrate before sensual pleasure overcame everything else.

Trying to sound casual, she said, 'You were very good with

Julian's trio.'

'I am glad you think so. I have absolutely no experience with children.'

'I know.' She paused. 'So the opportunity to practice will prove useful.'

His hands stilled and for a seemingly endless moment there was silence.

Finally he said distantly, 'What are you saying?'

'I am saying that in roughly seven months' time you may expect a happy event.'

Another long silence, broken only by the force of his breathing. Then his hands tightened on her shoulders and, in a tone she didn't recognise, he said, 'Beth. My Beth ... that is ... that is wonderful.'

Worried without knowing why, Elizabeth swivelled around to see his face, only to have him rise and step away, saying politely, 'This wasn't a good idea, was it? Rather selfish of me, in fact. I should give you your privacy. Please excuse me.' And he was gone, closing the door behind him.

Elizabeth sighed and relinquished all idea of lingering in her bath. But for that one glaring error, she might have put an unfortunate connotation on his sudden defection. But that would have been a mistake. She was always, *always* Elizabeth ... except in the moments of heightened emotion created by passion; the moments when his control over himself was at its weakest. And then she became Beth. *His* Beth.

During the time it took to dry herself and pull on a chamber-robe, she tried to work out what might possibly be wrong but could think of absolutely nothing. He ought to be delighted. If he wasn't ... well, if he *wasn't* he was going to have to explain why.

In the adjoining room, Ralph leaned against the window-embrasure and tried to subdue his unreasoning sense of panic. He reminded himself that one of his reasons for marrying had been that the earldom needed an heir. That had been all right in theory. Only now, Elizabeth would be the one providing it ... and women died in childbed all the time, didn't they? What if something went wrong? What if ... what if he lost her? He tried telling himself he was being ridiculous. Then he added the fact that, if he couldn't react more normally when she emerged from the dressing-room, she was going to think he wasn't pleased and be both confused and hurt – which simply couldn't be allowed to happen.

The door behind him opened. He squeezed his eyes shut for a moment and then turned to face her saying coolly, 'When I said it was wonderful news, I meant it. However ... exactly how long have you known?'

'You mean, how long have I been certain?' Elizabeth sat down, folded her hands in her lap and surveyed him calmly. 'About three weeks.'

'Three weeks during which you left me in ignorance. And two of those weeks knowing that we would be making the lengthy journey here. Then an entire, exhausting week spent being jostled about in a carriage. Ah ... and let us not forget the return journey we have still to make. Is it *totally* unreasonable of me to ask what the devil you were thinking?'

'I was sparing us an argument about whether or not to cancel our plans.'

'The decision on that being your sole prerogative, I suppose?'

'Normally – no,' she agreed, smiling. 'But on this occasion, I thought it best.'

'Did you?' Ralph could feel the panic edging close again and tried to force it away. 'Forgive me if I can't agree. Anything could have happened. You could have been taken ill. You – you might even have miscarried.'

'But I didn't. We are here and, as you can see, I am perfectly well.' Elizabeth wondered what he was trying to hide behind that screen of anger. 'It's all right, Ralph. There's no need to worry.'

'There will be no need to worry in seven months when you've got through this safely,' he snapped. And then stopped, appalled at himself. 'Forgive me. I am being overly dramatic.'

'You're certainly behaving very oddly. I thought you would be happy.'

'I *am* happy!'

'It doesn't show.' She decided that this might be a good time to stop making it easy for him. 'Are you annoyed because you think I've recklessly risked the life of your unborn child? Because if you are, allow me to inform you that I would *never* do so. This child means as much to me as it does to you. More probably – since I'll mind less than you if it is a girl.'

'That is not true,' he protested. 'A girl would be equally welcome.'

'Even though the very reason you married was to sire an heir?'

'That isn't true either.' Ralph could feel the ground slipping away beneath him. 'It may have been true in *theory* – you have met my brothers, after all. But it is not why I married *you*. You know it is not. As for the rest, you could not be more wrong.'

'Am I?' Relenting, Elizabeth rose and walked across to put her arms about him. 'Explain it to me, then. Tell me why, instead of rejoicing, you're reacting as if you're terrified.'

He held her close, his face against her hair and finally let loose the words, some of which he had been holding tight inside his heart for six months.

'Because I *am* terrified. I can't lose you, Beth. I ... could not bear it. Without you, I might as well be dead myself.' And wondering why it had always seemed so difficult when, in reality, it wasn't difficult at all, 'I love you.'

CHAPTER NINETEEN

The man Frances had called Grey leaned against the door and surveyed her with a faint, considering smile. Finally he said, 'I don't doubt it.'

'After all the tricks and games, you'd be an idiot if you did,' she snapped. 'And now, if you will be so good as to move away from the door, I am leaving.'

'If you want to go, I won't stop you. But would it help if I said that you're in no danger from me – that I mean you no harm?'

'I already know that. After all, Max will be here any minute, won't he? So you didn't need me as your lure, you see. He would have come anyway.'

'Of course. And despite how it looks, you aren't here as bait, Mistress Pendleton.'

'Really? Then why *am* I here?'

'Partly, so I could ask that very question.' He smiled and spread his hands in a gesture that was almost self-deprecating. 'I was curious. When I saw you at Brough, I was surprised. And when I realised that you'd continued travelling with Max after that, I was astonished. I couldn't help wondering why you'd risk your good name in such a way – or why Max would let you.'

'If you know anything about me at all – which clearly you do – you will know my reputation was destroyed years ago.'

'Was it? I'd debate that point. But even if you're right, it doesn't really answer my questions, does it?'

Like his smile, his voice was pleasant and with no hint of a Scots accent. He could certainly *pass* for a gentleman – though that didn't mean he actually *was* one.

She said, 'I'm not explaining myself to you. Why should I? And I'd advise you not to ask Max. He is more likely to knock your teeth down your throat than to sit and chat.'

'Then I'll have to depend on you to point out that you're unhurt and have not been threatened in any way, shan't I?' He gestured to a chair. 'Won't you sit?'

'No.' Frances folded her arms and eyed him coldly. 'If you want to talk ... why not explain what possessed you to meddle in my brother's life? And please do *not* suppose that returning our grandfather's watch exonerates you. It doesn't.'

For the first time, a faint frown entered his eyes. He said, 'Knowing I could return it, I took the watch to teach Sir Rufus not to leave his possessions lying around in public places. How was that meddling with his life?'

'It wasn't. But you didn't stop there, did you? You taught him an even more valuable lesson – that of not taking chance-met acquaintances at face value.'

The frown deepened. 'I did?'

'Yes. Is your memory usually defective?'

'No – nor selective, either. But in this instance, my recollections appear to differ from those of your brother. What did he tell you?'

Frances huffed an impatient breath.

'You promised to take him up in your carriage but then left without a word, knowing that he wouldn't rise in time to catch the Mail instead and would thus miss his appointment. Are you denying it?'

'I deny departing without a word. I left my apologies along with orders for Sir Rufus to be woken at --'

'Oh please! Do you really expect me to believe that?'

'Probably not – though it's the truth. But I can't prove it. I don't know if my instructions were carried out ... or whether, having drunk more than he was accustomed to, your brother slept through someone hammering on his door. But however it happened, the outcome was not my intention.'

'And I suppose you didn't pass yourself off as Lord Brandon either,' she remarked sarcastically. 'Something which you have been doing quite a lot.'

'Ah.' He had the grace to look slightly discomfited. 'Yes. I did do that.'

'Why?'

'I wanted to get his lordship's attention and, up to that point, wasn't sure I had it.'

'Well, dragging me into it certainly did the trick.' Setting aside the question of exactly how he had managed his seemingly chance meeting with Rufus for later, Frances decided to ask about the thing that had baffled Max and herself from the very beginning. 'How did you know that I had any connection with Max?'

'Forgive me. I'd prefer to answer that question when--'

The door burst open with a force that sent it crashing back and Max erupted into the room. In two strides, he had Grey pinned to the wall, hands around his throat. Over his shoulder to Frances, he snapped, 'Has he touched you?'

'No.'

He tightened his grip. 'At all?'

'No.'

'Then he can count himself fortunate.'

Turning steadily puce, Grey was making unpleasant wheezing sounds and clawing uselessly at the merciless fingers. Max stared into his eyes and said, 'I imagine I don't need to tell you what would have happened to you if you *had* touched her?'

Since neither speech nor nodding was possible, Grey attempted to signal his understanding by blinking.

'Good,' growled Max, shaking him so that his head bounced off the wall. 'Then this isn't a mistake you'll make again, is it?'

Deciding it was time to intervene, Frances said, 'Max ... if you don't want to kill him, you'd better let him go.'

'I'm a long way from killing him. He's still conscious.'

'Barely. And you won't get answers if he can't talk.'

Max swore under his breath and abruptly let go. Grey slithered to the floor, clutching his throat and gasping for air.

Ignoring him and slamming the door shut, Max pulled Frances into his arms and said, 'When I got back and found you gone, I thought --' He stopped, hauling in an unsteady breath. 'Well ... let's just say I don't want to feel like that again. So the next time you're invited to go off God knows where without me knowing – don't.'

'I won't. And I'm fine. He didn't touch me or threaten me or do anything he shouldn't.'

'So what *did* he want?'

'To satisfy his curiosity, he said.'

Aware that, behind him, Grey had managed to struggle partially upright, Max released Frances and turned to look at him.

'Well?' he demanded curtly. 'I'm here – which I gather is what you wanted. So get up and start talking.'

Levering himself awkwardly into a chair, Grey croaked, 'Give me a – a minute, will you?'

'No. We'll begin with your name. I'm assuming it's not Grey or any of the other aliases you've used. So what is it?'

His colour slowly and patchily returning to normal and still massaging his throat, he swallowed, winced and finally produced two hoarse syllables.

'Brandon.'

'Oh for God's sake!' said Max disgustedly. 'Believing your own lies now, are you?'

The man who was not Grey shook his head and tried again.

'Brandon. Sir Gregory ... Brandon.' And then, with an immense effort, 'We're related. Distantly ... but related.'

Seeing Max's expression of shocked disbelief and knowing that he needed a moment to think, Frances decided she might as well sit down. She said, 'If that is something else you can't prove, *Sir Gregory* ... I'd advise you to think very carefully.'

Another shake of the head and then, looking at Max, 'The family bibles ... ours and yours ... should support what I say.'

Frowning, Max said, 'How, precisely?'

Gregory risked a wary glance at Frances. 'I'll explain ... but some water would help. Could you ... the kitchen is through there.'

She nodded and went out. As soon as she had left the room, Max said, 'If this is another one of your impostures, stop right now. I'm in no mood to be patient.'

'I noticed.'

'So?'

'It's the truth.'

Max swung away towards the window outside which darkness was now falling. If it *was* the truth, it was one he had never suspected. Then Frances walked back in and, handing a glass of water to the man who claimed to be some sort of relative, said baldly, 'Max … there are five women and three children in the kitchen. They say they're his family.'

Max turned a hard gaze on Gregory. 'Are they?'

He took another sip of water, swallowed and said, 'Yes.'

'I see. We'll come back to that later – along with the question of family bibles. For now, just tell me in plain terms how you and I are related.'

'Do you know the family history?'

'Better than you, I imagine. Get on with it.'

'Our great-great grandfathers were half-brothers. You are descended from the bastard line … I from the legitimate one.'

For an instant, Max felt as deprived of air as the man who claimed to be his cousin had been. His immediate thought was it couldn't be true … then equally quickly he realised that it could. He said expressionlessly, 'You're descended from Ellis?'

'Sir Ellis,' corrected Gregory somewhat recklessly. 'Yes. And you from Gabriel.'

'I see. And is that what all this has been about? The fact that, five generations ago, a man disinherited his legitimate son in favour of his natural one?'

'Not in the sense that you probably mean it.'

'Good. Because if the answer had been yes, I'd have to point out that – after nearly a century and a half – you've certainly taken your time making an issue of it.'

'Every generation from Ellis to my grandfather has thought about challenging Robert Brandon's will,' replied Gregory wearily. 'All of them sought legal advice and all of them were told they hadn't a hope in hell of doing it successfully.'

'So you thought you'd try something different? Defrauding honest folk in my name? Blackening my reputation with my neighbours? What was next? Blackmail?'

'No. It was this.' He paused, making a half-hearted gesture. 'Getting you here.'

Max blinked. 'Getting me here? To what end?'

'Look around you. Pay a visit to the taproom. This sorry excuse for a tavern, coupled with every penny I can spare from my salary is all that is keeping the women and children in the next room from destitution.' Gregory stopped to take a breath and ease his throat with more water before adding bitterly, 'The situation was worsened when my elder sister was widowed last year, leaving my grandmother, mother, three sisters, two small nieces and nephew without the protection of a man. *I* can't stay here because they need my income.' He paused again and then added, 'The family has been moving from place to ever-cheaper place since before I was born and has ended up here ... where the next downward slide will see them without a roof over their heads at all.'

'All of which is very unfortunate,' responded Max slowly, 'but surely things need not have come to this? Ellis inherited an estate in Oxfordshire. What happened to that?'

'He and his sons ran it into the ground and my grandfather eventually sold it. My male ancestors were a feckless lot. I've tried to do better ... but I'm barely holding things together. All it needs is a hole in the roof or a doctor's bill and everything will fall apart.'

'And based solely on some very tenuous connection between your family and mine, you expect me to prevent that happening?'

'I ... with nowhere else to turn, I hoped you might help. Yes.'

An uneasy silence fell as one man stopped speaking and the other weighed what he'd heard. After a few moments, Frances said, 'Sir Gregory ... did you not think of simply *inviting* Max to come here?'

'Yes. But I had no reason to suppose he'd do it.'

'And you thought having folk send me bills for goods or services I didn't buy would soften me up and a week-long trek around the borders would finally convince me?' asked Max sardonically. 'No. Don't answer that. I'm already half-way to thinking you belong in an asylum. So let's try this instead. Where did you come by your information about my family? Most specifically, how did you learn something I hadn't thought *anyone* knew – namely, that there had once been some attachment between Frances and me? And please. Do us both a kindness and keep it brief.'

'Simon Greville,' came the succinct reply.

'*Simon?*' echoed Frances, shocked. 'But – but he died. In India.' And then, 'Oh. Is that where you met him? In India?'

'Yes. I work for the Company – as did he. I met him when his affair with a married lady in Calcutta became public, resulting in the Company transferring him to my office at Raipur. He drank. He bemoaned his lost love. And he talked incessantly ... sometimes, because you and I share a surname, about his friend, Max Brandon.' Gregory met Max's eyes. 'It was the first time I'd heard your name.'

'Let me guess,' said Max slowly. 'When Simon died, you volunteered to take his things to his family. And you passed the voyage going through his papers.'

'Yes. Among a good many unfinished letters was one to each of you.'

'Saying what?'

'Yours,' he said to Frances, 'had been begun not very long after he arrived in Calcutta and in it, he begged you not to marry some fellow called Archie – who wouldn't understand the concept of fidelity if it leapt up and hit him over the head. And yours,' he told Max, 'had been written much more recently. On the heels of endless ramblings about the pain and regrets of losing the love of your life, it informed you that Mistress Pendleton *hadn't* married Archie and that if she still meant anything to you, you should do something about it before it was too late.' He shrugged slightly. 'Once in England, it was a simple matter to establish that *neither* of you had married.'

Max exchanged a long glance with Frances. He said, 'Why in God's name could Simon never finish a letter and actually *send* it?'

'I don't know. But it agrees with what Lady Grantham told Mama.'

'Yes. I recall.' Max drew a long breath and then loosed it. Turning back to Gregory, he said, 'There are at least a dozen more questions I want answered ... but right now, I'm taking Frances back to the inn. If you wish to pursue this – and I suppose, having gone to so much trouble, you must do – you may call on me the day after tomorrow at two in the afternoon. I appreciate that you're desperate for help. I *don't* appreciate the way in which you've gone about getting it. And I'm not promising anything. But if you think you can explain your reasons in a way that makes any sense, I'll listen.'

When his guests had gone, Gregory sat for several minutes staring down at his hands before finally steeling himself to go to where his womenfolk were silently waiting. As soon as he appeared, his widowed sister stood up, saying, 'Well? Will he help?'

'Perhaps. Perhaps not.' His throat felt raw and the stiffness in his neck muscles made every movement of his jaw hurt. 'I don't know.'

'Did you tell him about Cousin Broderick?' she persisted.

'No. Not yet.'

'Why? It was the whole point, wasn't it?'

'No, Meg. It was only part of it.'

'But --'

'Just *leave* it, will you? I've done what I could. I'll see him again on Friday and bring up the subject of Broderick then. But the truth is that we're not his lordship's responsibility. And I'm not crawling on my belly in the hope he'll choose to make us so.'

* * *

For the first few minutes, Max and Frances walked back to the King's Head through the gathering twilight in silence. But finally she said, 'I hadn't appreciated how remarkable your brother's sketch truly is until this evening when I saw Grey – *Gregory* – properly for the first time. Leo has even captured his expression, for heaven's sake. Surely he won't waste a talent like that?'

'I've given up trying to predict what Leo will or won't do. He quit university after the second year to study art in Italy. But he has a knack with horses as well and has been practicing some fancy sort of equestrianism for months – though for some reason, I'm not supposed to know about that. All of which means that Leo is as likely to turn into a circus performer as he is a painter. Time will tell, I suppose.' Abruptly changing the subject, Max said, 'You said Gregory got you there to satisfy his curiosity. In which regard, exactly?'

'Mostly, he wanted to know why I'd stayed with you after Brough.'

'Did you tell him?'

'No. I asked questions of my own about his dealings with Rufus. And he told me a different, less spiteful, version of events.' She thought for a moment and then added, 'At the time, I didn't believe him. Now ... I wonder.'

Max's arm tightened about her.

'Don't be too sympathetic, love. He's plausible, I give you that. And naturally he's going to try to show himself in the best light. But as to how honest he is ... I'm reserving judgement on that for the time being.'

'You didn't go into the kitchen, Max. Even the children were just sitting there, still and quiet as mice. And the women's faces ... so bleak and resigned.'

Max took his time about replying. Then he said, 'I shouldn't have started this conversation. Do you think we might forget about Gregory and his family for a time? I've promised to listen to him again – and I will. But at the moment, I'm more interested in you and me and our wedding day tomorrow.'

Frances tilted her head to look up at him, her expression eager.

'You found somewhere?'

'Finding *some*where is easy. I was searching for somewhere special.'

'And?'

'And I found it,' he grinned. 'But that's all I'm saying. For anything more, you'll have to wait until tomorrow.'

Over a belated dinner, Frances made numerous unsuccessful attempts to persuade him to say more while Max enjoyed watching her, flushed and excited as a young girl. After so long, he still had difficulty believing that tomorrow he'd be allowed to love her with his body as well as with his heart and mind. And that she would go home with him to Brandon Lacey and they need never be parted again.

Eventually, after he had teased her long enough, he told her that the ceremony would take place at eleven the following morning and she should be ready to leave the inn fifteen minutes before that.

'So it isn't far away?' she asked.

'Not very, no.' He smiled at her. 'Afterwards, if the sun is shining, I thought I might ask the people here to make up a picnic basket and we could find a pleasant spot by the river. And after that ...'

'Yes?'

'After that,' he murmured, his voice low and a little husky but not without a note of laugher, 'we return here and make our union legal ... or in other words, you finally get to take me to bed.'

CHAPTER TWENTY

The sun did indeed shine and the sky was a brilliant canopy of unclouded blue. Wearing the green striped polonaise and with her hair more intricately arranged than usual, Frances descended the stairs to where Max, elegant in black brocade, smiled up at her. When she arrived beside him, he took her hand to place a hot, lingering kiss in her palm and said, 'You look beautiful, love. Dazzling, in fact. And now, if you're ready, we should go.'

There were so many words and feelings engulfing her that she couldn't say any of them. Nodding, she smiled back, took his arm and let him lead her to where Mr Miller waited in the open doorway. And then, from outside, came the bright, rapid sounds of a fiddle.

Catching his coachman's smug grin, Max said, 'Joe ... what have you done?'

'Nothing much. Word got out about your wedding and in these parts, couples walk to church to music – so last night the taproom was half-full of volunteers.'

Max groaned. 'And you couldn't resist picking one of them, I suppose?'

'Summat like that,' admitted Joe, cheerfully. 'Just be grateful I turned the piper down.'

'Thank God for small mercies,' muttered Max.

Frances laughed. 'I like it. He's playing a reel. We can dance our way to church.'

'Speak for yourself. *I* am going to march with the same gravity as any other condemned prisoner,' he retorted, dropping a swift kiss on her lips before she could retaliate. 'Now ... can we please go?'

'Reckon you'd better.' Peering into the street, Joe stifled a laugh. 'I've told the fiddler where you're going – so all you've got to do is follow him.'

Outside, a small crowd had already gathered and Max and Frances stepped out to a ragged cheer. Max bowed – first to Frances and then to the well-wishers. Flushing, Frances responded with a little curtsy ... and their audience applauded.

Then everyone fell in behind the fiddler and the procession began.

By the time they were half-way to their destination, the crowd had swelled to twice its original size. Men left their businesses and women their marketing; small children jumped up and down in time to the music and three dogs added to the general cacophony. Gripped by a sort of hysterical disbelief, Max looked down at Frances – pink with pleasure, half-dancing along at his side and clearly loving every minute of it.

With a crack of laughter, Max raised her hand and spun her beneath his arm. The audience roared its approval and Frances stood on tiptoe to kiss his cheek.

Then the fiddler took an unexpected detour.

Max tried to get the fellow's attention and, on his third attempt, succeeded in making himself heard. He said, 'This isn't the way.'

Without missing a note, the fiddler called back, 'Aye. It is. 'Tis for the water.'

'The – *what*?'

'The water,' sang out someone behind him. 'Ye mun go to the running water.'

This received a general chorus of agreement.

'The water,' said Max flatly, meeting his love's bright eyes. 'I daren't ask.'

The lane joined a wider road, down the centre of which ran a channel, little more than two feet across, of clear, shallow water running down towards the river. Here, everyone stopped.

'What are we supposed to do?' Frances asked Max.

'Ye've both to cross it,' offered a helpful voice. 'For luck, ye ken.'

Max looked at Frances, shrugged and stepped to the other side, offering his hand.

'Ha!' scoffed Frances. And, gathering up her skirts, she leapt over in a froth of petticoats. The bridal party cheered.

'Playing to the crowd, minx?' murmured Max.

'One of us should. What now?'

'Cross back,' came a medley of calls. 'Ye've tae come back again.'

'At least that makes some sense,' murmured Max. Then, without warning, he scooped Frances into his arms and jumped back across. This time there were whistles, shouts of encouragement and a frenzy of excited yapping. Too weak with laughter to struggle, Frances said, 'I m-might have known you'd show off.'

'I haven't. Yet. Showing off would be carrying you the rest of the way. But I won't.' He set her on her feet. 'It might be bad luck. Or it might look as if you're not willing.'

The fiddler, meanwhile, was heading back towards the crowd which parted obligingly to let him through and called the bridal pair to follow.

Grinning at Frances, Max said, 'What next, I wonder?'

'I don't know. I don't care. Isn't this *wonderful*?'

And looking from her happy face to those of their honest well-wishers, he said, 'Yes, love. It is.'

The remainder of the walk to the small, relatively modern kirk at the edge of town was accomplished without further diversions – though the crowd continued to grow.

Looking around at them, Frances said, 'Did you expect this to happen?'

'No. I thought it would be just you, me and Joe. I even asked the minister to find a second witness.' He gave her a little tug away from the church door. 'No. We're not going inside. It's this way.'

And behind the church, in a green, peaceful space dotted with daisies and surrounded by straggling bushes of wild roses, stood the remains of a much older chapel. Just a single, pointed arch of grey, weathered stone, garlanded with ivy and wild flowers. And a step beyond it was a smiling, black-clad minister.

'Oh,' said Frances, looking about her in delight. 'Oh Max. This is ... it's so lovely.'

'I'm glad you like it. Not exactly Kelso Abbey – but the next best thing.'

'No. Not the *next* best. It's *better*.' She squeezed his arm, then turned to find a young woman handing her a small bouquet of sweet peas and purple iris.

'And see? There's white heather for luck as well,' said the girl. 'Now, I'm Morag and I'm to be your maid and witness. D'ye have the sixpence in your shoe?'

Half-charmed, half-baffled, Frances shook her head. 'Should I have?'

'Och aye. 'Tis the custom.' And turning to the crowd, she called, 'The lassie doesna have her sixpence. Who'll lend her one?'

Half a dozen people volunteered but a brawny fellow wearing a butcher's apron barged his way to the front and solemnly handed Frances the necessary coin, saying, 'I'll no be needing it back neither. Ye mun keep it. For luck.'

'Thank you.' She smiled at him. 'That is extremely kind of you.'

He nodded, coloured in embarrassment and was promptly elbowed out of the way by Morag, who nipped the sixpence from Frances's fingers and knelt down to slip it into her shoe. Then, rising, she informed the assembled company that the lassie was ready.

'If all is now in order,' said the minister with tolerant humour, 'let there be quiet and peace. Will the bridal pair please approach.'

Frances took Max's arm and together they advanced to stand just inside the arch. Instantly, the hilarity of the last half-hour evaporated as if it had never been. Even the air around them felt different and both of them sucked in a sudden unsteady breath without knowing why.

'Maximilian Charles Brandon,' said the minister. 'Are you free to marry this woman?'

'Yes,' Max replied firmly. 'I am.'

'And you, Frances Amelia Pendleton ... are you free to marry this man.'

'I am.'

'Then turn now, each to face the other, and clasp hands.'

Morag stepped forward and relieved Frances of her flowers.

Smiling down on her, Max folded her hands in his. Dark grey eyes met gold-flecked blue ones in a shared and very private moment. This was the day that, for a very long time, both of them had believed would never come. That, against all the odds, it *had*; and that the love between them had emerged untarnished and stronger than ever ... made this moment one of almost unbearable poignancy.

Stepping forth with due ceremony, Morag handed the minister a length of red and green twisted cord.

Loosely winding it twice around their joined hands and tying the ends, the minister said, 'Maximilian and Frances ... this cord is a symbol of the connection between your two lives. As your hands are bound together by this cord, so too will your lives be bound together in marriage. But the knots of this binding are formed, not by these cords, but by the promises you make in your hearts and the vows you will now exchange, one with the other. Together as one voice, you will repeat those vows after me.'

'I pledge my love to you, and everything that I own,' he said.

And, looking directly into each other's eyes, 'I pledge my love to you, and everything that I own,' declared Max and Frances in unison.

'I promise to honour you above all others.'

'I shall be a shield for your back as you are for mine.'

'This is my wedding vow to you.'

Throughout each repetition, Max's voice remained low and steady while Frances's held the merest hint of a tremor.

'Remember,' the minister charged them sternly, 'that you hold in your hands the making or breaking of this union. And remembering that, now speak the final vow exactly as you spoke the other.'

'You are blood of my blood and bone of my bone.'

'I give you my spirit until my life shall be done.'

'I give you my body that we two might be one.'

Eyes and hands still locked, they remained seemingly frozen in a timeless moment which the minister eventually ended by saying, 'You may now withdraw your hands from the binding – without untying it – as man and wife together in the eyes of God and man.' Then, when they had done so, 'And you may exchange the nuptial kiss.'

Needing no further encouragement, Max pulled Frances into his arms and claimed her mouth in a long and extremely *thorough* nuptial kiss which provoked applause mixed with calls of good-humoured advice. But eventually he raised his head and whispered, 'At last. At long, long last. You cannot know how much I love you – how much I've always loved you.'

'I can because it's the same for me – and has been since the moment we met.'

With a slight shake of his head and still holding her close against his side, he offered his hand to the minister, saying, 'Thank you, sir. I – we – are grateful.'

'It was a pleasure, my lord. It has been some years since I was last asked to perform this particular ceremony – though I would again remind you of what I told you yesterday. However, my congratulations to you and I'll have the marriage lines delivered to you later today.'

When they stepped a little apart from each other, Frances was immediately surrounded by laughing townswomen and Miller stepped forward to seize Max's hand and clap him on the shoulder.

'Every happiness, my lord. I'm glad I was here to see this day.'

'So am I, Joe. In the absence of my brothers, you are the man I'd most want beside me at my wedding. And thank you for the damned fiddler. Frances loved it – that and having half the town turn out to cheer us on our way.'

'You'll need to lose 'em now,' observed Miller, glancing past Max to where half a dozen grinning fellows were waiting to shake his hand.

'I know – and that's something else you can help with.' Turning back to the impromptu congregation, Max said, 'My wife and I--'

And was forced to stop by a barrage of laughter, whistles and applause.

Holding up a hand, he began again. 'My lovely wife and I thank you for your company and your good wishes. If you return to the King's Head, my friend Mr Miller will instruct the landlord to provide food and ale so that you may toast our happiness.'

It was a further ten minutes before they were able to escape their well-wishers and slip unobtrusively away. As soon as they were out of sight, Frances removed the sixpence from her shoe and dropped it in Max's pocket, saying, 'Keep it safe for me.'

'Always.' He pulled her close against his side. 'Did you enjoy your hand-fasting?'

'It was perfect. The vows are beautiful. Simple – but beautiful. I had no idea.'

'To be honest, neither had I. When I asked the minister for it he was at pains to inform me that the hand-fasting ceremony was no less binding than any other. Convincing him that *binding* was exactly what I wanted wasn't easy. I had the distinct impression that he thought I was a wicked seducer.'

'You mean you're not?' teased Frances. 'That's disappointing.'

'We'll see if you're still saying that later,' he retorted, grinning. 'Somehow – though I don't wish to boast – I doubt you will be.'

Her breath caught and she flushed. 'Oh. Good.'

Max laughed and, reaching the riverside and a spot entirely screened from the road by trees and bushes, said, 'Here we are – our very own wedding breakfast.'

Frances looked at the wicker basket and the blanket spread out beside it – both of them being watched over by a groom from the inn. 'You arranged all this?'

'Did you think I couldn't?' Max tossed the groom a coin, thanked him and said he'd return the basket to the inn himself so there would be no need to return for it. Then, when the man had gone, he made Frances a very formal bow. 'Pray be seated, Lady Brandon.'

She sat and started to unlatch the basket.

'It will take me a while to get used to that. Lady Brandon is your mother.'

'It will probably take Mama just as long to become accustomed to being a dowager. Ah – good. A bottle of wine. What else do we have?'

'Enough food for a regiment, I think.'

Frances began unwrapping packages of tiny sandwiches, small golden pies, cheese, slices of rich fruit cake and, last but not least, a small bowl of candied cherries.

Max, meanwhile, poured two glasses of cool wine and handed her one, saying, 'To us, my love ... and the years that lie ahead. We've waited a long time for our happy ending, haven't we?'

'We have. But this isn't it. This is our happy *beginning*.'

'*Until life shall be done*,' he quoted softly. 'Yes. You're right. That's exactly what it is.'

While they ate and drank, they talked idly about the days – five years ago as well as more recently – which had led them to this one. And finally, whilst feeding Frances the last of the cherries, Max said, 'We'll set off home the day after tomorrow.'

'After your business with Gregory is concluded?' she asked hesitantly.

'Yes. After that.'

'Have you decided what you will do about him?'

'I don't know that I'll do anything at all. The fact that he's indirectly responsible for giving you back to me makes it difficult to remain angry. Equally, however, I don't feel particularly inclined to repair his family fortunes.' He paused and then added, 'It's odd. I expected some sort of villain – not a harmless fellow desperate enough to appeal to a complete stranger – and in the most ludicrously ramshackle way. But in the end, I suppose what I do or don't do will boil down to whatever he has to say tomorrow – both for himself and in answer to my questions.'

Frances nodded. 'Do you want to meet him alone?'

'No. Why would I wish that? And didn't you just promise to be a shield for my back?'

'Yes. Now you come to mention it, I believe that I did.' She gave him a mock-frown. 'Did you memorise quite *all* of our vows?'

'Only the important ones.' He pressed her down on the blanket and leaned over her, smiling. 'For example, there was also something about giving me your body.'

'That was a ... reciprocal agreement.'

'It was. And one I'm looking forward to honouring in full later. But for now ...'

And drawing her into his arms, he kissed her.

* * *

They returned to the King's Head somewhat earlier than Max had originally intended.

He had thought they could enjoy a gentle foretaste of what would come later. But when lazy kisses and caresses stopped being enough ... when Frances was stirring restlessly beneath his mouth and hands ... when he realised he was a breath away from taking things further than he should in what amounted to a public place ... he reluctantly tore himself from her hold and said ruefully, 'I think we'd better return to the inn before someone wanders this way and sees something we'd rather they didn't.'

Flushed and dishevelled, Frances laughed, nodded and began piling everything back into the basket. Picking it up in one hand and sliding his other arm about her waist, Max murmured, 'Since the half of the town who attended our wedding will by now have told the other half ... and if I look as delightfully rumpled as you do ... everyone we meet will only need one look at us to have a fair idea of what we've been up to in the last hour or so.'

Frances leaned her head on his shoulder. 'I don't care.'

'Neither do I. There won't be a man from eighteen to eighty who wouldn't like to change places with me.'

'Nor a female who won't want to be me,' she retorted contentedly. 'Aren't we lucky?'

'After the running water, the sixpence and the hand-fasting, I would certainly hope so.'

Frances twisted to look up at him. 'It *was* a lovely wedding, wasn't it?'

'It was ... though you'll have to pardon me for observing that the loveliest part of all is still to come.' He dropped a kiss on her brow. 'It took a certain amount of effort to stop just now. It will take even more if you tell me you'd rather wait until tonight – though I'll do it if that's what you want.'

'I don't.' She smiled without a hint of self-consciousness or embarrassment. 'You're not the only one who has been waiting five years.'

They were stopped at least a dozen times by townsfolk wanting to shake Max's hand and offer their felicitations. Max began to wonder if they would manage to get back to the inn before dark. But eventually they did and were able to run laughing up the stairs to their rooms and bolt the door behind them.

The laughter slowly fading from his eyes, Max simply folded Frances in his arms and held her for a seemingly endless, silent moment. Finally, he said slowly, 'I have wanted you so much and for so long ... I've dreamed and fantasised about this moment ... and now it is finally here, none of those imaginings can compare with holding you like this. Holding you and knowing that no one can part us ... that this is for always.'

Frances buried her face against his neck and felt happy tears stinging her eyes. She said, 'I know. Every now and then, I still catch myself not quite believing it.'

'So do I.' Without haste, he slackened his grip and lifted his head to smile at her. 'But I think we can do something about that. The only difficulty is that – with so many beautiful discoveries lying in wait – I can't decide where to begin.' Leaving an arm about her waist, he drew her towards the bedchamber which, until today, had been hers alone. 'However, I think we'll start with your hair. Yes – I know I've seen it loose before. But I wasn't allowed to touch.'

'And you wanted to?' She stood perfectly still while he plucked out hairpins and tossed them carelessly on the table beside her comb.

'Yes. Oh yes. Always.' Max ran his hands through the heavy, chestnut mass, loosening it with his fingers and lifting it to his face. 'Cool and soft ... like silk.' And with a sudden grin, 'Now, Lady Brandon ... your turn. What shall it be?'

'Your coat?' hazarded Frances. 'And cravat and vest and ...' She stopped uncertainly.

He stepped back and briskly discarded all three garments. Then, his grin widening, he said, 'Of course, I'm at a disadvantage here.'

She swallowed. 'You are?'

'Yes.' A good deal less briskly, he set about unhooking her bodice, punctuating the task with a series of butterfly kisses along her cheek and jaw. 'After all, you've already seen me without a stitch on.' He glanced up, his eyes full of mischief. 'Until that moment, I hadn't thought myself capable of blushing.'

'Blushing?' Frances continued untying his shirt, her attention riveted by each newly exposed inch of lightly-tanned skin and her voice correspondingly absent. 'You didn't.'

'I did. You were too busy admiring my ... posterior ... to notice.' And when her hands froze and she looked up opening her mouth to speak, he added kindly, 'Don't deny it, love. No one could blame you. I believe it to be a very superior specimen.'

She gave a choke of laughter. 'You have a superior *p-posterior*?'

'So I'm told. It's not something one can judge for oneself, after all. Trying to see one's own arse in the mirror strikes me as somewhat comical – not to mention vain.' He looked innocently into her eyes. 'What?'

Lost for words and still laughing, Frances merely shook her head at him.

'Atrocious? Outrageous?' he suggested helpfully, whilst slipping the overdress from her shoulders.

'B-Both!'

'I know. But I fear it's too late to change now.' In truth, Max wasn't sure how much longer he could keep the pace leisurely whilst simultaneously finding ways to seduce her into laughter. His blood was singing a loud and very insistent song. He thought – hoped – that perhaps hers was too. Certainly there was nothing of shyness or reticence in her reactions ... only an unmistakable glow of anticipation. But he wanted to be sure because this had to be better than merely good. It had to be perfect ... not just because it was *her* first time but because it was *their* first time together.

Less patient than he, Frances tugged his shirt from his breeches, indicating that she wanted it gone. Max obliged her and managed, while her hands mapped his shoulders and back and her mouth breathed temptation against his throat, to dispose of her stays and petticoats. After that, with his heart pounding in his chest, it was impossible not pull her against him and kiss her until they were both gasping.

Sensations raced through Frances ... each of them chasing the other too quickly to be caught and identified, like a fierce, unstoppable cascade. There was the hardness and heat of his body ... the texture of his skin beneath her fingers ... the hungry torment of his mouth. She had known that she wanted him physically as well as emotionally. She had not, she was discovering, had any idea of the reality. She didn't know if she was melting or drowning or about to burst into flames. She only knew that she needed his hands on her and hers on him; and that if that didn't happen soon, she'd die of wanting.

Stepping back a little and raising slightly unsteady hands to her shift, Max said, 'May I?'

'Yes. Oh – *yes*. Why are you asking?'

'Because,' he said raggedly, sliding the thin lawn from her and feeling his arousal spiral with every sliver of exposed skin. 'I'm trying not to rush you.'

'You're not. I'm not rushed.' The words came out in an almost incoherent tangle. 'I w-wouldn't mind being a bit rushed.'

'You wouldn't? Ah. Right.' Her chemise gone, he stepped back for the seconds it took to drag off the rest of his clothes and then stood quite still, allowing her to look at him while he gazed, hungry and awestruck, at her. She was all creamy skin, every delicious curve and hollow in exquisite proportion. He said humbly, 'God, Frances. How did I deserve you?'

He was so beautiful that she couldn't quite remember how to breathe. She said helplessly, 'That's silly. I ... love you. I – *oh!*'

This as he scooped her up and collapsed on to the bed with her, one thigh ending up between hers. 'And I, you. Let me show you how much.'

And then his hands and mouth were everywhere she had ever imagined wanting them, as well as places she had never imagined at all. Everything he had already awoken in her was suddenly intensified, bringing conflagration in its wake. Without thought or purpose but with ever-growing pleasure, she explored his body just as he did hers ... unaware that her uninhibited freedom and delight were straining Max's will-power every bit as much as her caresses. Finally, just when he was beginning to feel his control slipping, she gasped, 'I can't ... I don't ... Max ... please.'

'Yes, love. Yes.' It was a groan of gratitude. 'I'm sorry. Just this once. Never again.'

Slowly, steadily, he came inside her ... narrowly avoided exploding in the bliss of it ... and, for both their sakes, remained utterly still until his muscles were trembling with the effort of restraint and everything about her told him she was ready. And after that, pleasure piled upon pleasure ... and they tumbled effortlessly into joy together.

Max supposed that he must have dozed for a time because the next thing he knew, the light in the room had faded and Frances was gazing at him. He said, 'You're thinking.'

'No.' She smiled. 'I'm not capable of thinking.' And then, catching some small shift in his expression, 'But you are. What is it?'

'Did I hurt you? I tried not to ... but it's probably inevitable. Did I?'

'A little, perhaps. I don't remember.' The smile grew and one finger trailed lazily down his chest. 'If you need reassurance ... it isn't only your posterior that is superior.'

With a crack of laughter, Max hauled her on top of him. 'Thank you.'

'You are welcome.' She squirmed into a more comfortable position and felt something else shift. Her eyes widened and she decided to experiment.

'Stop that, you hussy!' He slapped a hand on her bottom.

'But do you – are we --?'

'No. Just because my body is showing renewed interest in yours doesn't mean that it must necessarily have its way. And regrettably, on this occasion – for your sake rather than mine – it isn't going to.' He saw the question forming and added simply, 'Once is enough for your first time, love ... so stop trying to tempt me and tell me if you're hungry.'

'Mm.' She let her head drop to his shoulder. 'Yes. Ravenous, actually.'

'Then I'll ring for them to send something up.' Tipping her unceremoniously back on the bed, he got up, glanced around at the litter of their clothing and decided against it. 'Stay where you are. I'll fetch my banyan. I've no intention of dressing in order get *un*dressed again.'

'Good.' Frances sat up, robed in nothing more than the wild tangle of her hair and not troubling to disguise the fact that she was enjoying the view. 'Just make sure you're decent when the maid comes – unless you don't mind her throwing herself on you?'

Max leaned over, kissed her and whispered, 'With the only woman I've ever truly wanted already naked in bed and looking enticing as Eve? Hardly. I'm all yours, love. Heart and soul, mind and body.' And wickedly, 'Every superior inch of me.'

CHAPTER TWENTY-ONE

Sir Gregory Brandon arrived at the King's Head a little ahead of time and was directed upstairs to Lord and Lady Brandon's private parlour. Gregory had heard all about yesterday's wedding. It was being talked of as the most exciting thing to have happened in Hawick since the town had woken up to find Lawyer Ferguson – always previously considered a good, upstanding Calvinist – drunk as a lord on the High Street and wearing one of his wife's gowns. Personally, Gregory hoped nobody had been idiotic enough to tell his lordship this. He doubted it was a comparison he would appreciate.

Gregory wasn't looking forward to the forthcoming conversation. At best, it would be uncomfortable; at worst, he'd end up feeling a fool. This, he reflected sourly, was what came of giving way to his eldest sister's incessant nagging and then launching without due consideration into an idea which, though it had seemed brilliant at the time, clearly hadn't been. It was also what came of swerving off at a tangent when he had become aware of a whole new alternative.

Then there was the fact that, deep down, he had never honestly expected anything to come of it. Five generations on, the degree of kinship between the two branches of the family was so remote as to be negligible. Max owed him nothing – so nothing was what he was likely to get. Really, thought Gregory dismally, he ought not to have let Meg talk him into doing anything at all. There had never been much chance of it ending well.

He knocked at the door, waited and was just about to knock again when it opened and Max – hair somewhat ruffled and minus his coat – gestured for him to enter, saying, 'Good afternoon. You are … admirably punctual.'

Since this merely reinforced Gregory's suspicion of precisely what he had interrupted, he flushed a little and said, 'I imagine that you are as eager as I to be done with this.' Then, bowing to Frances – now lit by an inner glow she hadn't possessed two days ago – he added, 'I understand that felicitations are in order, Lady

Brandon. May I wish you every happiness?'

'You may.' She smiled at him. 'And we thank you.'

Max shrugged his coat back on, pointed to a chair and said, 'Sit down.'

Gregory wasn't sure if it was an invitation or an order. Deciding to show that, whatever else he might lack, good manners were not part of it, he waited pointedly for Frances to be seated. She raised her brows at Max, unexpected laughter flaring in her eyes, before sinking on to the sofa.

Gregory also sat, looking anywhere other than at his sort-of very-distant cousin.

Max fixed his wife with the most repressive stare he could manage. She wanted him to laugh and he had very nearly done so. But he preferred to keep Gregory uncertain and a little on edge for the time being ... and allowing the atmosphere to relax wasn't going to achieve that. So instead of taking a chair, he folded his arms, leaned against the mantelpiece and finally said, 'I have several questions for you and I'd also like to hear your account of how and why you began all this. But first ... tell me about yourself.'

Gregory blinked. 'What do you want to know?'

'Where were you born ... what is your education ... how long you have been employed by the East India Company? That sort of thing.'

'I'm twenty-eight; I was born in Abingdon, Oxfordshire which is where the family moved to after my grandfather sold Steeple Park; and I was educated at a fairly superior grammar school – there'd been no money for Eton for the last two generations. University was also out of the question so when I left school I took a junior position with the East India Company. Ten years and several promotions have put me in charge of the regional office at Raipur.' He stopped as if unsure what else to say and then added, 'I'm not married or attached in any way – nor am I likely to be in the foreseeable future.'

'You have been in England for several months,' said Max. 'How has that come about?'

'I was granted extended leave because this is the first time in five years that I've taken any at all.'

Frowning, Frances said, 'You haven't visited your family in *five years*?'

'No – though we correspond regularly. But it's as I explained the other day. I can provide better financial help from India than I could if I came home.'

'You must be extremely well-paid,' observed Max mildly.

'Moderately,' agreed Gregory tersely. *Too* tersely, he immediately realised, catching the hint of scepticism in the dark grey eyes. He sighed and, seeing no help for it, said, 'It's true that I'm better paid by John Company than I would be in any position I could hope to find in England. But ... well, there are the bribes, you see.'

'*Bribes*?' echoed Frances, shocked.

'Yes. It's the system – the way everything works in India. When someone wants a supply contract or a recommendation for a relative, they offer a *gift* to whoever is in a position to help them get it.' He shrugged. 'Refusing doesn't stop them. Nothing does.'

For the first time since Gregory had entered the room, Max allowed the merest hint of a smile to surface. He said, 'Well done. I didn't think you'd mention that.'

'You *knew*?'

'Yes. I'm acquainted with several army officers who have served in India and they say it isn't even seen as corruption.' Finally deciding to sit down, Max joined Frances on the sofa. 'All right. I think it's time you explained why you suddenly began interfering in my life. I am assuming there must have been some sort of catalyst?'

'There was. It began when Meg's husband suddenly died, leaving the whole family even worse off and totally unprotected. Then three months after that, Cousin Ramsay finally stuck his spoon in the wall ... which turned out to be the last straw.' Gregory looked directly into Max's eyes. 'Broderick Ramsay. That name doesn't mean anything to you?'

'No. Should it?'

'He was our last living relative – or at least, the only one we knew of – and he wasn't exactly a cousin. The truth is, we never really knew *what* the degree of kinship was. The connection was through marriage – one of our Brandon great-aunts having married a Ramsay – and therefore a bit indistinct. But he owned a nice little estate in Northumberland and he was old and, having never married, childless. Five years ago, when my father died, Mother wrote to him asking for help. His reply was to send her ten pounds and instructions not to bother him again. But two years later, with things getting steadily worse, Mother tried again. She went to visit him ... and she took Kitty, my middle sister, with her. The result was that Ramsay took Kitty in as his nurse-cum-housekeeper.' Gregory's expression had turned dark and bitter. 'He never paid her a penny, of course – and he made sure she earned food and lodging a dozen times over in labour. But Kitty stuck it out for three miserable years because he was eighty-five years old and ill ... and because he kept promising to remember her in his will.'

He stopped speaking and stared down at the hands clenched on his thighs.

Finally, Frances said gently, 'And did he?'

'Oh yes.' His mouth curled in a derisive smile. 'He left her a ghastly portrait of himself. It had been painted when he was in his seventies but he'd insisted the artist make him look forty years younger. The result was grotesque. But it was in a very nice frame. Meg got seven pounds for it. Not much of a return for three years of Kitty's life ... but better than nothing.' He paused briefly and then, looking at Max, added, 'The old goat's money – what was left of it from buying endless *good* paintings – paid for the monstrosity of a mausoleum where he's buried. As for the estate ... that was bequeathed to what he called *the only relatives on either side of the family who are neither idiots nor wastrels.*'

Frances couldn't think of anything that could usefully be said to this.

Max could. Throughout the tale he had been wondering where it was leading and he was now fairly sure he knew. He said calmly, 'And which was that?'

'You really need me to say it?'

'Yes.'

Gregory gave a short laugh. 'Fine. It was left to the Brandons of Brandon Lacey. In other words – you.'

This time the silence felt heavy and airless. Frowning uncertainly, Frances waited for Max to respond. Eventually, he said slowly, 'I gather that you are talking about Alston Hall near Morpeth?'

'You know I am.'

'And you're aware of the contents of Mr Ramsay's will because your sister was present when it was read.' This time it wasn't a question. 'Did you never hear anything after that?'

'No. We were of no account, were we?'

'Not to your relative, it would seem,' agreed Max aridly. 'But – for whatever comfort it may be to you – I did not inherit his estate.'

Gregory froze and, just for a moment, seemed incapable of speech. Looking rather pale and as if the ground had been abruptly swept from beneath him, he said uncertainly, 'How can that be? Since it was willed to you, you must have done.'

'No. The only time I ever heard of Alston Hall was in a courtesy letter I received from a firm of solicitors in Morpeth. It informed me that I had been named as a beneficiary in the will of its recently deceased owner. If Mr Ramsay's name appeared anywhere in that letter, I don't recall it. What I *do* recall is that the solicitors had discovered that Alston was subject to an entail – which meant it wasn't your cousin's to dispose of.'

Yet again, Gregory seemed at a complete loss but finally he said, 'Then who --?'

'I've no idea. Presumably they're looking for a male Ramsay. If they can't find one, you may have some chance of making a claim. It can't hurt to write to them – or better still, visit in person.'

'All this time,' muttered Gregory blankly as if he hadn't heard, 'All this time, I've thought ... that is to say, *Meg* thought it and told me it was so and I - I *acted* on it. How stupid was I?'

'Your sister told you what she thought was true and you believed her,' murmured Frances, wanting to help. '*My* brother told me Lord Brandon had caused him to lose his chance of employment and *I* believed *him* – even though I ought to have known better.'

Max laid his hand over hers. 'Stop that, love. We're a long way past self-recrimination. And as for you, Gregory ... you were persuaded that I had something your family needed more and had more right to than I. That's understandable. What your cousin did, since he must have known about the entail, is less so – unless you and he suffer from the same deranged sense of humour?'

'I don't have --' began Gregory hotly before thinking better of it and saying colourlessly, 'I wouldn't know. I never met him. Whatever his reasons, they make what I've been doing these last weeks into an even bigger nonsense than they already are, don't they?'

'Ah. Yes. About that.' Max held the other man's eyes. 'I'd like to hear your version of what you thought you were doing and what you expected to achieve by it. I am speaking of the bills I didn't owe, the horse I didn't steal and the sculpture than could very easily have resulted in a duel. Well?'

'Some of it was to put your money into my pocket and the rest to ... to pique your curiosity.'

'It didn't pique my curiosity or anything else. It was just bloody irritating – as, I might add, was the tone of your letters.'

'Yes ... well, if I'd sounded like myself and politely invited you to join me on a mystery tour, I thought you'd give up and go home.'

'You appear to have thought a lot of things – very few of them sensible,' said Max cuttingly. 'However ... what were you trying to achieve?'

'To begin with, getting your attention and keeping it.'

'Ah. In *that*, you succeeded.'

'Yes. For what it's worth ... you have my apologies for the stratagems. All of them.'

'Words, my friend – and easily said,' came the grim response. 'Let's talk, for example, about what happened at Gilsland.'

'Gilsland?' echoed Gregory, looking baffled. Then, 'Oh. You mean the magistrate.'

'I do, yes. I also mean the unpleasant hours I spent in the

lock-up at Haltwhistle.'

This time the other man's jaw dropped and his neck turned red.

'Lock-up? No! That can't be right. Everything I told the magistrate was a complete fabrication! He'd have found that out easily enough. And even if he hadn't, he wasn't going to arrest a baron, was he? Or if he did, you'd have no trouble talking your way out of it.' He stopped, drawing an unsteady breath. 'You mean that you didn't?'

'I wasn't given the opportunity,' returned Max coldly. 'However ... why did you do it?'

'I – I had to deter you from trying to catch up with me before I was ready. That's all I intended – nothing more than that.' He shut his eyes and opening them again, said 'I suppose another apology won't help, will it?'

'Not noticeably, no. But let us move on to this week-long scenic tour of the lowlands ... that was for the purpose of getting me here, I think you said?'

'Yes. Well, that's how it was at first. But --'

'In which case, why didn't you end it the *first* time?'

'I'd intended to do that. Only then --'

'So why did you send us off to Selkirk, swiftly followed by Coldstream?'

'Max.' Frances laid a hand over his. 'If you want him to explain, you'll have to let him finish the occasional sentence.' And to Gregory, 'You were about to say that you changed your mind. Why?'

'I was already regretting letting it drag on by sending you to Selkirk, so I wrote *another* note telling you to stay in Hawick. Then I hung around because I was fairly sure you'd break your journey here – which would make it easy for me to put the new letter inside your carriage where you would be bound to find it before driving on.'

'Only you didn't,' observed Max flatly. 'Why not?'

'Because I saw the two of you together in the market and even from a distance I could see the way you looked at each other,' replied Gregory simply. And to Frances, 'I watched his lordship buying silly things for you – things you couldn't possibly want but which made you laugh. I watched you trying to drag him away when he pretended he was going to buy the parrot. And I thought ... I thought that perhaps something unexpected and *good* might be coming out of what I'd done ... and that giving you a few more days together might bring about a – a happy ending.' Restoring his attention to Max, he said, 'The old men were saying that the weather was closing in and the next day would bring a deluge, so I decided to take a chance. Of course, it all nearly came to grief when your coachman spotted me – but knowing the town better than you made it fairly easy to lose you. Then, instead of leaving the letter telling you to stay in Hawick, I rode hell-for-leather to Selkirk and left the one telling you to head for Coldstream.' He smiled crookedly. 'I remembered the Marriage House, you see.'

'Yes. You must have been disappointed that we didn't use it,' remarked Max dryly.

'I was. But it all worked out in the end, didn't it?'

The tone was so tentatively hopeful that Frances had to hide a smile.

Max wasn't noticeably amused. 'Is that what you think?'

'Well ... you're married, aren't you?'

'We are. And yes, you have played some part in bringing that about. But please don't try convincing me that it was all done out of the goodness of your heart. It was done to defuse any anger I might feel and to earn my gratitude. Wasn't it?'

There was a lengthy silence but finally Gregory said reluctantly, 'Yes. I can't deny that was part of it.'

Max eyed him with intense exasperation.

'All of this to gain my attention and get me here? Why, in the name of all that's holy, didn't you do it the easy way and simply *write* to me?'

'As I said before, I didn't know you.'

'You don't know me now, either.'

'I know you better than I did a month ago,' countered Gregory. 'I found out, for example, that you paid the goldsmith and the stonemason – which meant that you might have paid others as well.'

'I had to pay for the damned sculpture since my mother believed I'd bought it for her as a gift,' snapped Max. 'As for the rest, ordinary folk were paying the practical cost of moves that were aimed at me. I couldn't let that happen.'

'Most men in your position would have done.'

'Then obviously I'm not most men.'

'No. But I didn't know that to begin with. How could I? I expected you to be like every other gentleman of title, wealth and property. The ones who wouldn't spare a thought for a mere tradesman. I thought you'd be typical of your class.'

Frances gave a choke of laughter. 'Typical? Max? They broke the mould.'

'You exaggerate,' complained Max. 'I'm not a *complete* aberration.'

'No. You're just the man who goes hunting for hermits in order to annoy them by sitting down for a chat. The fellow who tells the tallest of tall stories and makes people believe them. The wretch who makes me blush a dozen times a day with his naughty innuendos.' She shook her head at him, still laughing. 'You couldn't be *typical* if you tried!'

He raised her hand and kissed it. 'But you love me in spite of it all.'

'Not in *spite* of – *because* of.'

'Thank you.' Max looked at Gregory. 'She is telling you that, despite indications to the contrary, I do actually possess a sense of humour ... though nothing so far has made me inclined to see the funny side as far as you are concerned. What happened to the bracelet, by the way?'

Caught unawares by the sudden change of subject, Gregory made a small spluttering sound and then said, 'Meg sold it.'

'Of course. I hope she got what I paid for it? Or no. Don't answer that. Just how close to complete ruin *are* you?'

'Very,' came the low-voiced reply. 'We are permanently flirting on the edge of it. Meg does her best to make ends meet but with eight mouths to feed and the tavern scarcely breaking even, nothing ever improves. All that happens is that they limp on for another week ... another month ... all the time knowing that they're only one unexpected expense away from disaster.' He hesitated, shut his eyes for a moment and then, opening them, said, 'I've no right to ask and, if I had a choice, I wouldn't. But if you could help ... even in a small way ...' He stopped again, flushing and looking both reluctant and embarrassed. 'Fifty pounds could make all the difference.'

'Even if I was prepared to give it – which, as yet, is by no means certain – thanks to our Scottish odyssey and a long journey home, I don't currently have fifty pounds to spare.'

'No.' Gregory's shoulders slumped. 'No. I suppose not.'

Frances looked at Max, her fingers tightening around his. Knowing what she wanted, he sighed and said, 'However ... I'm not saying no and I'm not saying I'll refuse to consider it. I'm merely pointing out that I can do nothing for you right now.'

The other man's eyes rose, a faint glimmer of hope dawning. He said haltingly, 'That ... that is exceptionally good of you.'

'After the trouble you've put me to? Yes. It is.' Max stood up, an earlier and probably foolish thought re-surfacing. 'The portrait of your Ramsay cousin. Do you still have it?'

'What? Yes. At least, I think so.'

'I'd like to see it. We'll call at the tavern in the morning before we start south. Have it ready, will you?'

* * *

After Gregory had taken his leave, Frances tried to persuade Max to explain his interest in Broderick Ramsay's portrait. He merely shrugged and said, 'Just an idea I had. It will probably turn out to be nothing. Then again, I can't help wondering just how awful the thing really is.' He pulled her into his arms. 'Now ... where were we when my extremely distant sort-of cousin interrupted us?'

She slid her arms about his waist and kissed his jaw. 'Can't you remember?'

'No. I have a truly terrible memory. You'll have to remind me.'

'Well, then.' Seeing an opportunity too good to miss, Frances pushed him down on the sofa and settled on his knee. 'We were sitting here like this ... and you were whispering naughty things in my ear.'

'Yes!' said Max happily. 'I think I remember that. What else?'

'You were trying to unfasten my gown.'

'Like this?'

'Just like that.' She batted his fingers away. 'But I told you we didn't have time for that because Sir Gregory would be here any minute.'

'Oh.' For a second he looked crestfallen. Then, brightening and again reaching for the hooks on her bodice, 'But that doesn't apply now, does it?'

'You asked me to remind you.' She slapped his hand away again. 'I'm reminding you.'

'I don't need reminding about this. I think I've got the hang of it well enough.'

'So I see.' This time she trapped the playful fingers and held them fast. 'We argued a bit. You said Gregory would be late – *I* said he wouldn't. So we made a wager on it.'

Max frowned and shook his head. 'I don't recall that.'

'No. That's why I'm reminding you,' came the patient reply. 'We agreed that if you won, I'd take off all my clothes, recline naked on the sofa and permit you any liberties you chose to take.'

Max hauled in an unsteady breath and said raggedly, 'God. I'm sure I'd have remembered *that*. Couldn't we -- ?'

'Pretend you won? Absolutely not. You didn't.'

'Oh.' He appeared to think about it. 'I hope my terms were equally ... interesting?'

'They were.' She smiled lovingly and stroked back his hair with her free hand. 'You said that if I won, you'd buy me a truly magnificent diamond necklace.'

And promptly found herself sitting on the floor with no idea of how she'd got there.

Standing over her, Max said, 'Not a chance. Even drunk as a lord or crazed with lust, that is not a thing I would *ever* say to you.'

'Damn,' said Frances mildly, somehow managing not to laugh. 'That's disappointing.'

'It *will* be disappointing if you mean it.' He held out his hand, pulled her to her feet and regarded her with almost imperceptible anxiety. 'Do you?'

'Not at all.'

The anxiety vanished.

'Good. Because I intend to deck you in lapis lazuli to match your beautiful eyes – though of course the stones would be hopelessly outshone.'

'Oh.' She felt suddenly breathless. 'Are we ... no. You're not still joking, are you?'

'No. I have it all planned,' returned Max, sweeping her back into his arms. 'And fortunately, I know an exceptionally talented goldsmith on Bond Street who will almost certainly be able to fulfill my exact requirements.' He grinned and kissed the top of her head. 'Someone else whose family and mine go back a long way, by the name of Maxwell.'

* * *

By the following morning when they arrived at the Green Man, Frances still had no idea why Max wanted to see a terrible portrait of a man he'd never met. She had, however, found the opportunity to ask him if he was truly concerned about having sufficient funds on hand to get them back to Brandon Lacey.

'Not desperately so, no. But I prefer to retain a safety margin in the event of accident or delay. Why do you ask?'

'It's just that I have a little money with me. Not quite ten pounds but --'

'No.' He smiled and folded her hand in his. 'We won't need that.'

'Oh. Then ... perhaps you wouldn't mind if I gave it to Gregory's family?'

'You don't need my permission, love. Do you want to?'

'Yes. I think I'd feel better.'

'Oddly enough, so would I.' He smiled wryly. 'But be discreet about it, will you?'

They found only Gregory and his widowed sister awaiting them in the empty and exceedingly run-down tap room. Meg curtsied and said baldly, 'My brother says you gave him a fair hearing. I thank you for that.'

'You need not,' replied Max. And looking at Gregory, 'I don't mean to be impolite but I'm hoping to be in the vicinity of Otterburn by this evening and will therefore need to be on the road fairly soon. If you still have the portrait, may I see it?'

'By all means.' Gregory walked behind the counter, reached down to pick something up and propped it up in front of him. 'We got the worst of the dirt and cobwebs off it but it's no less awful.'

Max and Frances stared at the canvas in stunned silence for perhaps five seconds.

Then Max breathed, 'My God. You weren't joking, were you?'

First glance said that the artist hadn't been without ability. The gentleman's blue satin coat and the lace at both throat and wrists were skillfully painted ... and the gentleman himself, some thirty-odd years of age. But a second look immediately revealed something bizarrely discomfiting. It was as if the artist had superimposed that younger face over one of a very old man ... and either by accident or design, had left the older one peering out from behind it. The pale blue eyes, behind their smooth lids, were small, mean and filmy with age; the thin, overly-red mouth leered rather than smiled; the fair hair was wispy and sparse with only semi-disguised strands of grey; and the hands didn't appear to have been altered at all, being mottled with age-spots and gnarled with heavy veins. The whole thing was, as Gregory had said, grotesque.

Frances, meanwhile, found herself feeling oddly uneasy – a sensation which only intensified when, having walked away from the portrait, she turned back and found those little eyes still watching her. She said, 'It's horrible. And the more you stare at it, the more horrible it becomes. I imagine it would give children nightmares.'

'It did,' volunteered Meg. 'That's why we put it in the attic.'

'God knows why you didn't burn it,' remarked Gregory.

Max, meanwhile, picked up the canvas to examine first the back of it and then the edges where it was attached to the stretcher. He said, 'Do you mind if I take it outside? The light isn't very good in here.'

'You can take it to Jericho for all I care,' muttered Meg. 'Nasty thing.'

While Gregory followed Max outside, Frances lingered to press a small purse on Meg, saying softly, 'It isn't much but it may help.'

Meg stepped back, shaking her head. 'It's kind of you to offer – but I can't take it. I feel badly enough about this whole thing anyway because Greg wouldn't have done it if I hadn't nagged him into it.'

'In that case, I owe you something.'

'You don't. How can you?'

'If your brother hadn't begun all this, his lordship and I would probably never have met again,' said Frances. 'I owe both of you the happiness I never expected to have ... and it is beyond price.'

Outside, watching as Max continued to examine the back of the canvas, Gregory said, 'What exactly are you looking for?'

'To be honest, I don't really know. I wondered about something but I'm reluctant to theorise and raise false hopes.'

Gregory shut the inn door behind them. 'Raise them with me.'

Max looked at him. 'It was what you said about the quality of the frame and Ramsay leaving your sister this particular painting when he'd spent untold money on what you called *good* ones. It's probably a stupid idea ... but it occurred to me that perhaps he had this atrocity done as cheaply as possible by re-using the canvas and frame of some other work he was perhaps not very fond of.'

Gregory drew in a slow breath. 'You're saying there could be another painting underneath this one? One that might have some value?'

'It's a possibility,' shrugged Max. And pointing to the edges of canvas nailed inside the rim of the frame. 'This patch of yellow here, for example.' He turned the portrait over. 'I don't see that colour anywhere in the actual picture. Do you?'

'No. No, I don't.' Gregory shut his eyes, then opened them again. 'But knowing our luck, it's just as likely that, if there *is* something underneath, it's equally worthless. And anyway – how on earth would one go about finding out?'

'I don't know,' replied Max. 'But if you'll trust me with it, I know someone who should.'

'You do? Who?'

'My little brother. I'm assuming that eighteen months studying art in Venice must have taught him *something*.'

CHAPTER TWENTY-TWO

With Cousin Ramsay stowed out of sight under the seat and Mr Miller, glad to be homeward bound at last, on the box, Frances settled in the curve of Max's arm and said, 'Do you really think there may be another picture underneath that awful portrait?'

'I don't know. I also don't know how possible it is to find out without destroying both pictures – assuming there *is* a second one. But there's nothing to be lost by asking Leo's opinion so I thought it was worth a try.' He glanced down at her. 'Did you give the widow your money?'

'Yes – though she was reluctant to take it.' Frances looked through the window and watched Hawick falling away behind them. 'How long will it take us to get to Brandon Lacey?'

'According to Joe, five days – and that's if we're lucky. Otterburn, then Newcastle where we'll pick up the Great North Road.'

'And after that?'

'Darlington, Thirsk, York ... and home.' He grinned. 'Since Sherbourne and Lizzie and Julian's children have all been there for some days now, Mama is *not* going to be pleased with me. But I hope bringing her a new daughter will spare me the worst of it.'

Frances toyed with his fingers. 'They'll be shocked, won't they – your family?'

'I doubt it.' What Max privately thought was that they would be *more* surprised if he went home alone. 'They'll just be disappointed about missing our wedding ... but that, as we've agreed, can easily be mended.'

Frances had been adamant that they would do whatever Lady Brandon wanted – even if it meant waiting until Arabella and Julian were back in England to hold a full-blown, formal second wedding. Max sincerely hoped it wouldn't come to that – because if anyone thought he was going to endure God only knew how many weeks of pretending *not* to be married, they had most certainly better think again.

But in the meantime, they had a five-day wedding trip ahead of them. It was a pity most of it had to be spent in the carriage ...

but at least it meant that he and Frances were blessedly alone. And he could think of several agreeable ways of passing the time.

The morning sped by in conversation, kisses and a great deal of laughter. When they halted at around one in the afternoon to rest the horses and seek sustenance for themselves at a tiny wayside tavern where the road they had been following since Hawick joined a wider one, they discovered that they had apparently arrived – quite literally – on the border to England.

'How do you suppose he knows?' Frances whispered to Max, when the ancient innkeeper told them that a few steps away from each other would put them in different countries. 'There's no milestone or river or *anything* to mark the place.'

'Since there's nothing for miles around except his tavern, I expect the border is anywhere he says it is,' shrugged Max. And to the coachman, 'How much further do you think, Joe?'

'Hard to tell since, as her ladyship says, there hasn't been a milestone for the last hour and more. But I'd reckon that we're about half-way – and the road'll be better from here so we should get to Otterburn by five. Six, at the latest.'

'Excellent,' said Max. 'Do you want me to take the reins for an hour?'

'No need, my lord. I'm good for a stretch.' Miller grinned. 'And I know where you'd rather be ... not as I blame you.'

* * *

Otterburn proved to be a small, sleepy place on the banks of a river. Having lost count of the number of rivers he had seen and crossed in the last eleven days, Max didn't bother to ask the name of this one. He simply ordered a bedchamber for Frances and himself, another for Joe, stabling for his horses and dinner. Then he looked forward to an evening with his wife while Joe relaxed with the locals in the tap room over a well-earned tankard or two.

It was the first time they had shared a room and Frances delighted in the new intimacy of being able to sit on the edge of the bed and watch while Max shed his shirt in order to wash and shave. She also discovered the unexpected pleasure of having her husband help her out of her gown and into a fresh one. This, of course, took a great deal longer than when she did it unaided since Max was unable to resist kissing and touching every bit of her that came within his reach ... which inevitably ended with him taking her to bed. They made love again after dinner and she fell asleep in his arms, her last waking thought being that surely life could offer no greater joy than this.

Max, waking to find Frances's head pillowed on his shoulder and her hair lying tangled over his arm, knew the same feeling of euphoric contentment at the thought that every day could begin like this. But for the day's journey that lay ahead of them, he might have been tempted either to let her sleep or to tease her awake with early morning love-making. As it was, he slid his arm from beneath her, dragged on his banyan and rang for hot water. There would be time enough for leisurely starts to the day when they reached their own home, and meanwhile, he thought, smiling to himself, he could tease and tantalise them both in the carriage.

It was a long day of largely uninteresting scenery – not, Frances blushed to recall, that either of them had seen very much of it. They stopped twice in places whose names she couldn't recall and drew into the busy, cobbled courtyard of the Old George in Newcastle at a little after five o'clock. Leaving Frances wallowing gratefully in a bath and telling her to save the water for him, Max took a pot of ale with Joe in pursuit of finding out what he could about the next day's journey. A country squire travelling in the opposite direction informed him that Darlington was some thirty-five miles distant but that the road was good and he'd made the trip himself inside seven hours with three stops along the way. Max bought the fellow a drink and then sauntered back upstairs to find Frances wrapped in a bath-sheet and still slightly damp.

'Ah,' he said, drawing her in for a lingering kiss before stripping off his clothes. 'A beautiful hand-maiden, waiting to scrub my back. I had no idea the inn supplied those ... but the idea ought to be taken up everywhere.'

Rivetted as she always was by his naked body, Frances watched him sink into the water and marvelled, not just at the sight of him, but by how comfortable he was in his own skin. He seemed to have no qualms about letting her see him as God had made him ... but then, she thought, God had done a spectacular job. As yet, she was somewhat less relaxed about her own nudity although she had never, right from the first, been nearly as embarrassed by it as she might have expected.

Now, seeing him lie back with closed eyes and aware of an overwhelming desire to touch him, she murmured wickedly, '*Only your back?*'

'Sadly, on this occasion, yes – unless you're happy to miss dinner?'

'Meaning that you're not, I suppose.'

'No.' He grinned at her. 'We newly-married fellows need to keep our strength up.'

And ducked as a wash-cloth came flying at his head.

* * *

On the following day at around the time Max and Frances were half-way to Darlington, a shabby carriage pulled into the yard at Brandon Lacey. Leo, on his way to join his mother for luncheon, was the first to see it – his immediate thought being to wonder if it was Max, returning in a hired vehicle due to an accident to his own. Then a young man he had never seen before descended to hand out a pinch-faced lady who said querulously, 'Why is there no butler opening the door? Are we to knock and be kept waiting? Atrocious!'

Leo knew a craven desire to slink round the corner and out of sight. Instead, inwardly groaning, he walked towards the unexpected visitors saying pleasantly, 'Good afternoon. May I help you?'

'Unlikely,' she snapped. 'I am here to see either Lord Brandon or his mother.'

God, thought Leo. *Lucky Max and unlucky Mama.* But he accompanied the ill-mannered dragon towards the door and said, 'My apologies. I don't recall Mother mentioning that she was expecting guests. I am Leo Brandon, by the way. And you are?'

'I am Lady Pendleton, young man – and this is my son, Sir Rufus. We are here --'

'Mama,' muttered Rufus, sliding an apologetic glance towards

Leo, 'I don't think --'

'I know that. If you did, I would have been informed of this disgraceful business much sooner.'

Deciding it was time to call a halt to this particular conversation until it could be held with some semblance of civility – assuming such a thing was possible with this female – Leo said swiftly, 'Please come inside, ma'am. Ah – Hawkes. As you see, we have guests. Please show them into the drawing-room and order suitable refreshments, would you? Do you know where I might find my mother?'

'I believe her ladyship is in the library with Mr Balfour,' replied Hawkes. 'Shall I --?'

'No, no. I'll speak to her myself, thank you.' And to the Pendletons, 'Excuse me for a moment, please. Hawkes will look after you – and Mama will be with you directly.'

Having made good his escape, Leo went directly to the library. Then, shutting the door behind him and leaning against it, he said, 'Now we *are* in trouble.'

Duncan stared at him, frowning.

Louisa said, 'What does that mean?'

'It means that Frances's mother and brother are here ... and, since Max *isn't*, there'll be questions we can't answer – which would be quite bad enough even if the woman *wasn't* a gorgon.'

'A gorgon?' echoed Louisa. 'Oh dear. Is she?'

'Yes. And a rude one at that. Hawkes is seeing to them but we don't have much time to come up with a story – even if we could think of one. And personally, I can't. Duncan?'

Mr Balfour shook his head. 'No. And there's no point in concocting something because the truth is going to come out eventually.'

'Of course it is,' agreed Louisa. 'I suppose we should have expected this. The only wonder is that it has taken so long. But I really had hoped I wouldn't be left with the task of telling Lady Pendleton that her daughter has been alone with my son for a fortnight.'

'I don't think you'll have to.' Leo detached himself from the door and laid his hand on the latch. 'My guess is that she already knows. So ... let's get it over with, shall we? If you hear sounds of murder and mayhem, Duncan, come and rescue us.'

In the drawing-room, Rufus Pendleton stared gloomily out of the window and tried not to listen to his mother's unceasing monologue of complaint and criticism. He had withheld the truth – or what he had eventually come to suspect was the truth – for as long as possible. But after Frances had been gone for over a week, he had run out of credible excuses and been forced to admit that, to the best of his knowledge, she was somewhere in Scotland and possibly with Lord Brandon. Inevitably, neither this nor the fact that he couldn't offer a logical explanation as to *why* Frances should be doing this satisfied his mother. She had demanded he escort her to Brandon Lacey.

So here we are, thought Rufus. *And it's going to be awful.*

Closely followed by Leo, Louisa entered the drawing-room and advanced on her guests, smiling valiantly.

'How do you do, Lady Pendleton? This is quite a surprise. I don't believe we have ever met, have we?'

'We have not,' came the clipped reply. 'As to it being a surprise – how *can* it be? Since my daughter and Lord Brandon have been cavorting about Scotland for some days now, I would imagine you must have been expecting me.'

'Cavorting?' murmured Leo. 'Max? *Really?*'

Her ladyship impaled him on a withering stare.

'This is no laughing matter! If my understanding of the situation is correct, it is utterly scandalous. So if you have nothing useful to say, I suggest you hold your tongue.'

Groaning quietly, Rufus laid a tentative hand on her arm.

'No, Mother – really! You mustn't --'

'Mustn't *what?*' she shot back. 'Don't be so feeble! If the tale about your grandfather's watch is true, this ridiculous affair is entirely your fault. Not that I should wonder at it. You've no more backbone than your father had.'

'May I suggest,' interposed Louisa coolly, 'that you sit down and allow me to pour you a cup of tea, Lady Pendleton? I understand that you are anxious but --'

'I am not *anxious*. I am *angry*.'

'Clearly. But that is scarcely productive, is it?'

'Neither is this conspiracy of silence in which *you*, ma'am, have been a part.'

'You are mistaken. There has been no conspiracy. We have merely --'

'Don't lie to me! You permitted your son to take my daughter off to God knows where and did not have the decency to inform me of it. That is inexcusable. Even more so is the fact that, to the best of my knowledge, you did not even insist on Frances taking a maid with her to protect her from your son's importunities. Does your family lack *all* sense of propriety? And do not attempt to placate me with a mouthful of trite excuses because I can assure you that they will not wash. I,' she finished wrathfully, 'am not an idiot.'

'No one supposed that you were,' returned Louisa crisply. 'But since hurling insults and accusations will not help, I suggest that you moderate your tone.'

'I shall speak as I see fit, ma'am! And if I discover that your son has debauched --'

'That's enough!' Louisa's spine stiffened and she fixed the wretched woman with an icy stare. 'Although I am willing to make allowances for your very natural concern, I will tolerate neither blatant rudeness nor the suggestion that my son is anything less than a gentleman. No – please do not interrupt. I would remind you that you are in my home – without, moreover, either prior acquaintance or invitation. So if you wish to discuss the situation, you had best sit down and recover some small degree of civility – otherwise I shall be forced to ask you to leave.'

Throughout the course of this speech, Lady Pendleton's colour had steadily risen until it reached choleric proportions ... and her sense of outrage was not lessened when Leo grinned and said simply, '*Brava*, Mama.'

Ignoring him, Louisa said inflexibly, 'Well, Lady Pendleton? What is it to be?'

With a tiny sound oddly resembling a snarl, her ladyship subsided on to the nearest chair in a flurry of black brocade.

'Thank you.' Louisa turned to her son. 'Leo ... why don't you take Sir Rufus to join Duncan in the library? The two of you can tell him the little that we know – along with everything that we don't. Her ladyship and I will get along perfectly well without you.'

'Oh, I've no doubt about that,' came the lightly amused reply. 'Come along, Pendleton. Let's leave the ladies to their tea while you and I hunt down something stronger.'

'Do not indulge in strong spirits!' ordered his mother as Rufus gratefully followed Leo to the door. 'You know you do not have the head for them and will likely --'

'Too late,' remarked Louisa as the door closed behind them. 'Now ... are we going to hold a civilised conversation or not?'

'If,' came the grudging reply, 'you are prepared to tell me everything you know.'

'Certainly. And you were not the *only* one kept in the dark to begin with. For the first six days after Max and Frances left here, I was under the impression that he was escorting her home and had taken the opportunity to pay some business calls on his return journey. It was only when the days wore on and I became suspicious that I demanded answers and finally learned the truth.'

'That is all very well. But what was Lord Brandon *thinking* --?'

'Since I haven't been able to ask him, I can only speculate. What I *do* know is that it was Frances who insisted upon accompanying him rather than the other way about. She wanted to recover her brother's watch. Max wanted to catch Grey – that's what we've been calling the fellow who stole it – because he has also been subjecting Max to numerous other problems and annoyances.' She shrugged. 'Frances could have returned once she had the watch ... but, presumably for reasons of her own, she chose not to do so.'

'Or was not *permitted* to do so.'

'If you are suggesting that Max is holding her against her will, this conversation is over.'

'It was merely a ... thought.'

'Dismiss it.'

Her ladyship huffed an impatient breath. 'Do you know where they are now?'

'No. The last we heard, they were in Hawick but that was four days ago. I am hoping that Max finally caught up with Grey there and is now on his way home. If that is so, he and Frances could be here quite soon.'

'In that case, Rufus and I will await them.'

'Yes. I thought you might.' Suppressing a groan, Louisa thought dismally, *She's expecting me to invite her to stay here, isn't she? And despite already having Lizzie and Ralph and the children here and not wanting to spend another moment with the unpleasant creature, I'm going to have to do it. But I'll let her wonder a while longer.* Holding the other woman's gaze with a very direct one of her own, Louisa decided to test her private theory. 'I presume you are aware there was some prior acquaintance between Max and Frances? Perhaps even a degree of attachment?'

'They met at the Grantham house-party,' said her ladyship dismissively, suddenly intent on smoothing her gloves. 'There could have been no question of any attachment because Frances was betrothed to Viscount Malpas.'

'Who she subsequently abandoned at the altar.'

'That – that came later. It was nothing to do with your son.'

'No?' asked Louisa gently. And thought, *You're lying. You also know a good deal more than I do about whatever happened between Max and Frances.* 'Then why *did* she do it?'

'Since her reasons have no bearing on the current situation, they are no business of yours. And we are straying from the point.'

'Which is what, precisely?' *As if,* thought Louisa angrily, *I don't already know.*

'Must I spell it out? Your son has thoroughly compromised my daughter. Naturally, I expect him to do the honourable thing.'

'Of course you do. And you think he'll need to be told that? He won't.'

'I am relieved to hear it,' conceded Lady Pendleton coldly. 'You cannot blame me for being concerned about my daughter's reputation.'

'I don't. But you must forgive me for observing that

Frances's reputation was … somewhat tarnished, let us say … when she fled from St George's on what should have been her wedding day.' Louisa rose and pulled the bell to summon the butler. 'If you and your son wish to wait for the truants to return, you may stay here – though we already have other guests. My niece and her husband, Lord Sherbourne are with --'

'*Sherbourne!*' echoed her ladyship, horrified. 'That murdering libertine? No. Impossible! I cannot – *will* not – remain under the same roof as that man!'

Louisa smiled cheerfully. 'Oh? That's a shame because his lordship is family so I'm hardly going to cast him out. However, all is not lost, ma'am. The Red Bear in Knaresborough offers very comfortable accommodation and is only a few miles distant.'

* * *

Leo and Rufus had been half-way across the hall when Ellie skidded to a halt beside them, clutching a kitten to her chest and saying breathlessly, 'Where's Aunt Louisa?'

'She's busy just now, pet.' Leo squatted beside the child. 'What did you want?'

'I want to ask if I can keep Flossie. Tom says I can't. But he said that about Figgy as well. Tom always says no to *everything*.'

'That's big brothers for you,' grinned Leo, stroking the kitten with one fingertip. 'And this is Flossie, is it?'

'Yes. *Can* I keep her? She'll be good, I promise and --'

'Ellie!' Tom came down the stairs two at a time. 'I told you not to go bothering anyone about that dratted cat.'

'I'm not bothering. I'm just *asking*.'

Tom rolled his eyes in despair and said, 'I'm sorry, Uncle Leo. I tried.'

'It's all right, Tom.' And to Ellie, 'You can keep Flossie while you're here, sweetheart. But what happens when you go home depends on Sir Julian, doesn't it?'

She beamed at him. 'That's alright, then. He'll say yes.' And she trotted off, sticking her tongue out at Tom as she went.

Leo stood up, laughing. '*Will* Julian say yes?'

'I expect so. He usually does.' Tom hesitated. 'Aunt Lizzie's still at the vicarage but his lordship is here and he says he'll take me riding if it's all right with you.'

'Of course. Tell him he needn't have asked.'

The boy grinned and dashed off. Turning to Rufus with a slight shrug, Leo said, 'Sorry about that – and, in case you were wondering, no. They're not actual relations, as such. But never mind that. Come and have a glass of something with Duncan and me ... and let's pool our resources – such as they are.'

As soon as the library door had closed behind them and he had shaken hands with Mr Balfour, Rufus blurted miserably, 'I'm sorry. About Mama, I mean. There's no stopping her.'

'As bad as that, is she?' asked Duncan whilst pouring glasses of Canary.

'Worse,' replied Leo, throwing himself into a chair. 'But Mama's more than a match for her.' And to Rufus, 'Is she always like that?'

'She has been since Father died and she found out about the debts. As for this business with Frances, I kept it quiet as long as I could but, well ...'

Handing him a glass, Duncan said, 'Have you heard from your sister?'

'Twice. The first time, she said the man I'd met at Stamford wasn't Lord Brandon at all but actually some fellow called Grey who Lord Brandon was trying to catch. But she'd got my watch back, she said ... so I thought she'd come home. Only she didn't.'

'And the second letter?' asked Leo.

'They were in Coldstream. Fran said they'd be going to Hawick as soon as the rain let up. She also said that Lord Brandon had promised to help me manage the estate better ... sending someone from here to advise about proper management and so on.'

Leo groaned. 'Not *again*. We haven't got Garret back from Chalfont yet. However ... what did your mother have to say about that?'

'I haven't told her,' confessed Rufus. 'I knew that if I did, she'd find ways of taking advantage.'

'Isn't she doing that anyway?' asked Duncan. 'Correct me if I'm wrong ... but hasn't she come here determined to force Max and your sister into marriage?'

Rufus flushed. 'Yes. She says Lord Brandon has no choice in the matter.'

Leo and Duncan exchanged glances. Leo said, 'Well, she may be right about that – though I can't see Max having his hand forced. Fortunately, if our suspicions are correct that's unlikely to be an issue. But enough said on that score.'

'Quite,' agreed Duncan. And then, 'Leo ... do you think Lady Brandon will feel obliged to ask Sir Rufus and his mother to stay here?'

'*What?*' Leo sat up with a jerk. 'Here? In the house? *God*. I hope not. No offence, Pendleton. But *really*, Duncan? With Sherbourne and Lizzie here, not to mention Julian's orphans? I daren't even *imagine* what Lady Pendleton would make of them.'

'Nothing good,' sighed Rufus. 'She never does.' And on a sudden explosion, 'I don't blame Fran for escaping and making it last as long as possible. I wish I could do the same. It's half the reason I've been trying to find employment – and the further away from Matlock, the better.'

'Max could probably help you with that,' began Duncan. And then, 'Ah. But you're going to be managing your estate, aren't you?'

'Yes. And it's only right that I should. Father left an unholy mess behind and I've been letting Fran deal with it because I had no idea what to do. But it's *my* inheritance and – and high time I took responsibility for it.'

'And I'll wager that those,' murmured Duncan, 'were Max's very words.'

'I believe so,' agreed Rufus uncomfortably. And went on to describe the position in which the family had found itself following the death of his father.

It was some half-hour later that a tap at the door was followed by a footman who said, 'Beg pardon, Mr Leo – but her ladyship says to tell Sir Rufus that his mother is leaving now.'

'Leaving?' Leo shot to his feet, grinning. 'Excellent. I'll come and see you off. Not that it hasn't been a pleasure meeting you, of course, but ...'

'I know. *But.*'

Out in the hall, while Hawkes waited beside the open front door, Lady Pendleton was busy issuing her instructions to Louisa.

'I shall expect to be informed the *instant* Lord Brandon returns. In fact, if my daughter is with him, I insist that they both call upon me *immediately*. I trust I make myself clear?' And then, noticing her son, 'Come, Rufus. We shall find accommodation in the town and await your sister's return there. Nothing will persuade me to stay in *this* house.'

'What a shame,' said Leo cheerfully. 'Why not?'

'She won't share a roof with …' Louisa stopped. '*How* did your ladyship put it?'

'I said,' snapped her ladyship clearly, 'that I would not remain in the same house as a murdering libertine. And I will not.'

Leo's jaw dropped. He stared at Lady Pendleton. Then, like Rufus and Duncan, he stared at the figure in the doorway behind her.

'Then you had better remove yourself forthwith,' advised the Earl of Sherbourne quietly, 'because here I am.'

The next few moments plumbed the abyss of embarrassment for everyone but the woman who had caused it. *She* merely spun on her heel, shoved his lordship aside and exited without a word. Following slowly in her wake, Rufus paused beside Sherbourne to say awkwardly, 'I beg your pardon, my lord. She – she's not --'

'Rufus!' screeched his mother. 'Come away *now*!'

And two minutes later they were gone with the door closed behind them.

Louisa let loose a strangled breath and finally found her voice.

'Ralph … I am desperately sorry you had to hear that. It was inexcusable.'

'Was it?' A pulse throbbed in the earl's jaw but his tone remained perfectly level. 'Are you quite sure about that?'

'Oh my dear! *Yes*. Of course I'm sure.' And to his complete astonishment, she crossed to enfold him in a hard hug, saying, 'I wish you hadn't heard it – truly, I do. But I can't help being immensely grateful to you.'

'You are? Why?'

'Because if it hadn't been for you,' replied Louisa, releasing him, 'we'd have had that ghastly woman as a house-guest – and I would probably have been driven to smothering her with a pillow.' She paused, looking despairingly at Leo. 'I have been hoping and *hoping* that I was right in thinking that Max and Frances fell in love years ago and have spent these last days discovering they still feel the same. But if they marry ...'

She stopped and simply shook her head.

'If they marry and the gorgon behaves like that with Max,' observed Leo calmly, 'he'll toss her out on her ear. Alternatively, you can just hand *him* the pillow.' Then, differently, 'Come and let me pour you a brandy, Sherbourne. You look as if you need it – and it's the least we owe you for ridding us of the old witch.'

CHAPTER TWENTY-THREE

Two days later, Max and Frances awoke in a large, comfortable bed at the Old White Swan in York.

'We'll be at Brandon Lacey in two or three hours,' he said, his fingers trailing lazily back and forth over the lovely curve of her waist and hip before roaming on to find the inviting dimple at the base of her spine. 'Home at last. It feels ... odd.'

Lying on her stomach across his arm, knees bent and toes pointing at the ceiling, Frances turned her head to look at him. 'I thought you would be glad.'

'I am glad ... mostly. But this fortnight with just the two of us ... I find myself regretting that it's over.' Max did not tell her that he could have shortened their journey by a full day simply by pushing on for a further seven or eight miles beyond Thirsk. He had thought of it, of course. But once they got home, life would intrude more or less immediately so he told himself that there was no harm in stealing just one more day. 'However ... we've had our escape, you and I. And I wouldn't have missed a minute of it.'

'Nor I.' She turned and kissed his chest. 'I still think you should have let your family know that we're on our way. Just arriving without warning – particularly when Lady Brandon has guests --'

'You're going to have to stop calling my mother Lady Brandon, you know. It'll confuse everybody if there are two of you. And the guests are family.'

'Even Lord Sherbourne?'

'Even him.' The exploring fingers grew more adventurous and he heard her breath catch. 'Stop worrying, love. No one is going to be prostrate with shock. In fact, I'd be surprised if they haven't been half-expecting us for days. And as for our Grand Announcement ... I'm looking forward to seeing their faces.'

Not for the first time, Frances reflected on how lovely it must be to have a family one could trust absolutely and without question. Concentrating on tracing the muscles of his arms and shoulders, she said randomly, 'I love you. Have I ever mentioned that?'

'I believe you may have hinted at it from time to time ... but it bears repetition.' Max moved, propping himself on one elbow in order to give himself easier access to the parts of her body which gave both of them most pleasure. 'As does this, don't you think?'

'Yes.' She gasped as his hands grew more enticingly intimate ... and responded with a caress of her own that elicited a low growl of appreciation.

They had made love numerous times since their wedding and though every occasion was a little different to the others, all were equally joyful and mutually satisfying. She had never imagined that physical union could be such a perfect expression of love ... and the sensations that he could create in her body still had the power to astound her. Now, for example, he touched a spot that had her writhing helplessly against him – which, in turn, caused him to say raggedly, 'Do I ... have your whole attention?'

'Yes.'

'No more fretting about the day ahead?'

'No. *Oh!*'

He nipped at her breast and, on something resembling a shaky laugh, said, 'Excellent. I wouldn't like to think that my ... my efforts were going unappreciated.'

* * *

After love came breakfast, during which Max announced that, before setting off on the final leg of their journey, they were going to buy her a wedding-ring.

Frances's breath leaked away. She understood why this hadn't previously been possible and, much though she wanted it, felt impelled to say, 'But what of the cost? It can wait a little while --'

'It's waited long enough. Briggs & Hackett on Goodramgate know me and will send the bill to Brandon Lacey in a couple of days.' He smiled at her and kissed her fingers. 'I want you wearing my ring when we get home. And it will be interesting to see if anyone notices it before we break the news.'

Encouraged by Max, Frances chose a lightly-engraved ring of Welsh rose-gold ... and spent most of the final seventeen miles admiring it and being mercilessly teased as a result.

It was a little after three o'clock when the carriage finally pulled into the yard at Brandon Lacey. Max grinned and squeezed her fingers. 'Ready?'

She nodded. 'I think so.'

He hopped down and offered her his hand while calling, 'Joe – you have my undying gratitude for everything you've done these past weeks. I'll catch up with you later.'

'No rush,' agreed Miller laconically. 'Ah. Looks like you've been spotted already.'

Hawkes already had the door open and through it rushed Louisa and Leo with Mr Balfour strolling casually behind them, while Elizabeth and Ralph Sherbourne lingered at the top of the steps.

'Max!' Casting herself upon her son's chest, Louisa said, 'Oh God – Max. *At last*!'

He hugged her, kissed her cheek, sent Leo a grin and said, 'Did you think we'd got lost?'

'That and many other things,' retorted Louisa, releasing him to greet Frances. She folded the girl's hands in a warm clasp and said, 'My dear ... I don't know why you went off with Max like this but I'm immensely relieved to see you back, safe and sound.'

Frances managed a small curtsy. 'Thank you, my lady. That – that's kind of you.'

Leo, meanwhile, was gripping his brother's hand and simultaneously slapping him on the back. 'Grey seems to have led you a merry dance. I take it you *did* find him?'

'We did – or more accurately, he found us.' Aware that Frances was showing a tendency to lurk half a step behind him, Max retrieved her hand and placed it firmly on his arm. 'But it's a long story, so do you think we might go inside and tell it sitting down?'

'Of course,' said Louisa. 'Hawkes, have someone bring in the luggage from the carriage, please – and we'll take tea in the drawing room.' Leading the way into the house and smiling at Frances, she said, 'From the little we know, it appears that you have been travelling almost constantly. Are you completely exhausted?'

'No, ma'am. Not at all. I … well, I have enjoyed it.'

'That's the spirit,' murmured Leo. 'And how about you, Max? Had fun, did you?'

'From time to time.' Knowing that Leo was building up to his annoying best, Max met Mr Balfour's gaze and said, 'My apologies, Duncan. I didn't expect it to take so long. Has my absence created any problems?'

'Nothing that Leo and I couldn't deal with,' shrugged Duncan.

'Really? I'll have to take a holiday more often --' And then stopped as the children came hurtling down to greet him.

'Oh dear,' sighed Louisa. 'At this rate, we'll never get through the door. Lizzie, dear – come and lend a hand, will you?'

Laughing at the attempts of his mother and cousin to calm the children's enthusiastic welcome, Leo captured Frances's hand and towed her up to the door. 'You'll have to meet Lizzie later … but for now, come and say hello to her husband.'

Faint amusement glinting in his eyes, Ralph allowed Leo to make the wholly unnecessary introduction and bowed over Frances's hand, saying, 'A pleasure, Mistress Pendleton. As you may imagine, we have all been awaiting your return with a great deal of … anticipation.'

'Y-Yes,' she agreed. And in the instant Leo's attention was claimed by one of the children, added hastily, 'My lord, I've always wanted to thank you for what you did that day.'

'No need,' he murmured, 'and certainly not now. Ah.' He paused, his gaze resting on her left hand. Then, smiling reassuringly at her, 'Don't worry. I am the soul of discretion.'

Once everyone was assembled in the parlour and tea had been brought, Leo said impatiently, 'Come on, Max. Tell us where the devil you've been all this time and who Grey *really* is and what you did when you caught up with him. Everything.'

'I will,' promised Max. 'Everything, right from the beginning. But before I do, I have something much more important to say.' He stood up, drawing Frances with him. 'I imagine there has been some speculation about this lady and myself … and whether, on our return, you might expect us to announce our betrothal. If such has been the case, I'm afraid we're going to disappoint you.'

He paused, watching in particular the faces of his mother and brother. 'In point of fact, Frances and I were married six days ago in Hawick ... for which we hope you'll forgive us.'

There was a brief, stunned silence. Then everyone spoke at once and Louisa literally flew across the room to embrace first Max and then Frances. She said, '*Forgive* you? Oh – my dears! As if there is need for that! I am delighted for you – truly, I am. And for myself, too, since I've finally been provided with another daughter.' Her eyes a little too bright but still smiling, she drew Frances into a second embrace and said, 'Welcome to the family, my dear. Come and meet your new cousin while the gentlemen congratulate Max.'

The second the ladies moved away, Leo hauled Max into a bear-hug and buffeted him on the shoulder again. 'That was quick work, brother.'

'Quite the opposite,' replied Max cryptically. 'How long before Mama realises we've robbed her of a wedding?'

'Not long. And when she does she'll likely ask you to go through it all again.'

'I know ... whereupon Frances will insist we do as we're told.'

'Under the cat's paw already, are you?' asked Leo provocatively.

'And enjoying it immensely. You'll understand when it's your turn.'

A glance across the room assured Max that, as well as his mother and Lizzie, Frances was also surrounded by the children, apparently set on making the acquaintance of their new aunt. Satisfied, he turned back to find Mr Balfour and Lord Sherbourne waiting to offer their congratulations and, accepting Duncan's hand, said, 'Lots of ruined abbeys in your part of the country, aren't there?'

'Thanks to the heathen English, yes.'

'And rivers. A good many of those, too.'

Duncan shrugged. 'Yes. Well ... it rains.'

'I noticed. Three days in bloody Coldstream.' Max gave a sudden laugh. 'But it was worth it. Wait until you hear about our wedding.' He met Ralph's eyes and shrugging slightly, added, 'Not over the anvil ... but not exactly St George's, Hanover Square either.'

Smiling faintly but choosing to ignore this clue, Ralph said smoothly, 'My felicitations, Lord Brandon ... and my very best wishes for your future happiness.'

Accepting the offered hand and taking advantage of the low-voiced argument currently taking place between Leo and Duncan, Max said bluntly, 'Frances wants to thank you, my lord. As do I.'

'She has already done so – though thanks are unnecessary. But I'll admit that I am surprised.'

'Surprised that she told me about it?'

'No. Surprised that she remembered it was I - the occasion being both brief and exceedingly fraught.'

'Nevertheless, Frances remembers it with gratitude and, I think, some affection.'

'Then I am sufficiently rewarded.'

Max opened his mouth to reply but stopped when he heard Leo mutter forcefully, 'No, Duncan. Max needs to know.'

'Know what?' asked Max.

'Your mother-in-law called on us a couple of days ago. She's at the Red Bear with Rufus, breathing fire and waiting for you to turn up.'

'Is she indeed?' asked Max. And smiling grimly, 'Good.'

'You wouldn't say that if you'd met her. She's appalling. I think the only one of us she *didn't* insult was Duncan – and that was only because he stayed out of her way.'

Max merely shook his head. 'I'll deal with her tomorrow. For now, don't tell Frances and see to it that no one else does either. I won't have her day spoiled. Ah – here's Hawkes with the champagne. And I thought everybody wanted to hear about our travels and how we finally unmasked Grey?'

A little later, when the children had been sent to enjoy a picnic tea in the garden and all the adults were enjoying a glass of chilled wine, Max began his tale from the recovery of Rufus Pendleton's watch at Brough. And since he was unable resist the opportunity to tease Frances, he said, 'The annoying thing is that Grey was actually *there*. Frances recognised him in the garden and came flying inside to tell me but I was --'

'Not quick enough,' she cut in, shooting him a repressive look. 'By the time we got outside again, he was nowhere to be found.'

'Did you *really* think I was going to tell them?' whispered Max, looking aggrieved.

'I wouldn't put it past you. Just tell them about Gilsland. And behave yourself.'

He grinned, resumed the tale ... and was interrupted again almost immediately when Frances digressed to Hadrian's Wall. Max sighed, waited and picked up the thread again. The story of his arrest was greeted with outrage by Louisa and Elizabeth and a good deal of laughter from Leo and Duncan. Max managed to get as far as Hawick and their second sighting of Grey but was prevented progressing to Coldstream by Frances's enthusiastic description of Kelso Abbey ... swiftly followed by another detour for the Marriage House. Consequently, by the time he got them back to Hawick, Max simply rang for more champagne and said, 'I give in, love. We'll come back to Grey in a minute. First, tell them about the wedding.'

Holding tight to his hand and pink with remembered pleasure, Frances recounted everything. The fiddler ... the well-wishing townsfolk ... the running water and the sixpence; and finally, the simple yet beautiful ceremony which had joined Max and herself in matrimony. When she stopped speaking, there was a moment of complete silence before, blinking away a tear, Louisa said, 'It sounds ... it sounds quite lovely, Frances. And very special. I would have liked ... indeed, I am sure we would *all* have liked to have shared it with you.'

'We missed you,' said Max. 'Of course we did. But having had the devil's own time persuading Frances to say yes, I wasn't going to chance her changing her mind.'

Frances tucked her hand in his and shook her head. 'I wouldn't have.'

'You say that *now*,' he agreed smugly. 'But that's because six days of marriage have shown you what you would have been missing.'

She choked over her champagne and turned scarlet.

Over the scattering of laughter Louisa ordered him to stop embarrassing his wife and get on with telling them about Grey.

'Well, then,' said Max. 'The first thing to say is that his name isn't Grey. It is Sir Gregory Brandon ... and he is our very, very distant sort-of cousin.'

This produced another but very different silence.

Then, 'He told you that and you *believed* him?' asked Leo incredulously.

'Yes. For the benefit of Lord Sherbourne and Duncan, I should explain that the Brandon family tree split in two some hundred and forty years ago, each branch being subsequently descended from a pair of half-brothers. Our branch goes back to the illegitimate son of Robert Brandon ... the other, to the legitimate one.'

'Ellis,' said Louisa faintly. It was not a question.

'Yes. Ellis ... who appears to have justified his father's decision to disinherit him in Gabriel's favour ... and whose descendants have followed unerringly in his footsteps. The downward slide of the last century-and-a-half has left five women and three small children trying to scrape a living from a crumbling tavern while Gregory, the only man of the family, props them up with his earnings from the East India Company.' Max paused, shrugging slightly. 'What all this boils down to is that Gregory isn't quite the villain we expected.'

'Perhaps not,' remarked Mr Balfour slowly. 'But his situation is none of your making and neither is it your problem.'

'He knows that.'

'So what does he want of you?' asked Louisa.

'Brandon Lacey?' demanded Leo, not entirely facetiously.

'No. He's realistic enough to know there's no chance of that.' Max shrugged slightly. 'But he does want help ... and is desperate enough to hope I might give it.'

'*Desperate*?' echoed Leo. 'Demented is more like it. He wants your help and thought annoying the hell out of you with idiotic pranks and then playing hide-and-seek all over Scotland was the best way to go about it?'

'He believed a direct approach would be ignored. His goal

was for me to see his family's circumstances for myself ... and provoking me into tracking him would do the trick. There is a certain shoddy logic to that, I suppose – difficult though it may be to believe.'

There was a long silence into which Ralph finally said thoughtfully, 'I am guessing that you have not refused.'

'No.' Max gave a slightly crooked smile. 'I haven't. But that isn't because I've seen his family's plight and understand the problem. I haven't refused because, purely by accident, his actions have brought me a gift I thought was lost to me.' He lifted Frances's hand to his lips. 'My wife.'

'Oh,' said Louisa helplessly. 'That's different.'

Speaking for the first time, Elizabeth said, 'That sounds like the beginning of a whole other story.'

'It is,' agreed Frances. 'Max and I fell in love and agreed to marry five years ago but my parents had other plans for me and went to great lengths to make them succeed. In the end, my only way out was a very public flight from the altar ... as Lord Sherbourne knows better than anyone since he loaned me his carriage so I could escape.'

'Ralph!' said Louisa admiringly. 'How perfectly *splendid* of you!'

Laughter stirred in the earl's eyes but he inclined his head and said, 'Thank you.'

'Unfortunately,' continued Frances, 'Max didn't know. Because all his letters to me and mine to him ended in my mother's hands, he believed I was married and *I* thought he had forgotten me.' She paused, smiling a little. 'So you see ... it's thanks to Gregory that, after five wasted years, we have found each other again. And that makes everything different.'

'Of course,' said Louisa promptly. 'Of course it does.'

'So what *will* you do about Gregory?' asked Duncan of Max. 'Send him money?'

'Some, perhaps, as an interim measure.' He rose and went to pull the bell. 'The *real* need is to remove those women to somewhere less disreputable where they can do more to help themselves. But in the meantime, there's another possibility –

remote though it probably is.' He stopped and waited while a footman brought in the portrait of Broderick Ramsay and placed it where everyone could see it. Then he said, 'Duncan ... you'll remember the letter about Alston Hall?'

'The entailed property in Northumberland? Yes.'

'This is Broderick Ramsay, the fellow who willed it to me – though whether from ignorance, confused wits or deliberate spite, I don't know. Despite Ramsay being a kinsman and one of Gregory's sisters having given the old man three years of unpaid labour, Gregory believed Alston had come to me ... while all his sister received was this. Needless to say, it was a very sore point and partly responsible for Gregory's recent antics.' Max glanced across at his brother. 'Leo ... what do you make of it?'

Rising and prowling to some three feet from the painting, Leo stared at it with a sort of fascinated revulsion. He said, 'Truthfully? I'm relieved to hear that you didn't pay money for it. Who in God's name painted it?'

'I've no idea and it's of no consequence – though the unfortunate artist was instructed to make a very old man look forty years younger. Just take a look at it, will you? A really *good* look.' Max tapped Mr Ramsay on the nose and said, 'I'm told that he collected art. I'm also told that this was originally in a good quality frame.'

'Ah.' Leo shot him an arrested look. 'You think something is hiding behind it?'

'I thought it might be a possibility, yes.'

Leo picked up the canvas, turned it over and scrutinised the back for several moments. Finally he said, 'You may be right. Certainly that bit of yellow doesn't belong ... but it would need the removal of a couple of square inches of surface paint to be sure. Not that ruining this horror could be anything but a blessing.'

Leaving Frances telling Louisa and Elizabeth what little she knew of Gregory's family, Duncan and Sherbourne strolled over to examine the picture. Duncan said, 'What on earth possessed the man to insist on being painted like this? It makes him look evil.'

'It does,' agreed Ralph, 'but I suspect that is because the artist was having his revenge. And rather cleverly, too. Is there really some possibility of there being another painting behind this one?'

'There may be,' replied Max. And to Leo, 'Can you do whatever needs to be done?'

'Yes – or at least, I'm happy to take off enough paint to determine whether or not there *is* something behind it. But if there's the remotest chance we're uncovering a masterpiece, I'll hand it over to old Brentworth in York. He's got years of experience with this kind of thing and will do a much better job than me.'

'Where would you start?' asked Ralph with interest. 'And how is it done?'

'The bottom right-hand corner is the obvious choice in the hope of uncovering a signature,' replied Leo. 'As for how ... gently and with patience, using turpentine and pieces of soft linen. I have to break down and gradually remove the surface paint without impairing what, if anything, lies beneath. If there isn't anything, we'll know quickly enough because I'll be down to bare canvas.' He looked at Max. 'Do you want me to do it?'

Max nodded. 'Yes. Gregory won't want the portrait back unless you find something – so the sooner we know the answer, the better.'

* * *

Late that night, Max drew Frances into a warm, passive embrace and said, 'We seem to have got away with it so far, don't you think?'

'Got away with what?'

'Our Scottish hand-fasting.' He settled her a little more comfortably on his shoulder and stroked her hair. 'It won't last, of course. Mama is probably hatching a plan right now.'

'I shan't mind. I love your family. I wish mine was as nice.'

Deciding that this was as good a cue as any, Max said, 'Yes ... about that. Your mother and brother are in Knaresborough.'

'*What?*' She broke from his hold and sat upright. 'How do you know?'

'Leo told me just after we arrived and I spoke to Mama about it this evening. I didn't want you to know until I could tell you myself and in private. They came here a few days ago and your mother tried to intimidate mine. I rejoice to say that she failed.'

Frances gave a heartfelt groan and flopped back down beside him.

'Oh God. I'm so sorry. I can just imagine it. I suppose she was unbelievably rude?'

'Yes – but that isn't your fault.' He pulled her back into his arms. 'Stop worrying.'

'I can't. And neither would you if it was your mother. She must have got the whole story out of Rufus and --' She stopped, suddenly shaken by a faintly hysterical laugh. 'She'll have come to demand you make an honest woman of me – which, after everything she did to separate us, is cripplingly ironic.'

'Isn't it? And better even than that is the fact that we have pre-empted her.'

'That won't help.' Frances buried her face against his throat. 'I'll have to go and see her tomorrow morning.'

'No. You won't.'

'Of course I will. If I don't, she'll come here and --'

'She won't. And neither will you visit her,' said Max flatly. '*I'll* do it.'

'No. That wouldn't be fair.'

'Hang what's fair, sweetheart. I shall deal with her. Indeed, as I said to you once before, I shall *enjoy* dealing with her.' He smiled with grim anticipation. 'And by the time I've finished with her, I think you'll find that she'll no longer be a problem.'

CHAPTER TWENTY-FOUR

On the following morning, Max strolled into the Red Bear in Knaresborough and, after exchanging a few general pleasantries with Daniel Clegg – the current landlord and, like Joe Miller, another man with whom Max had shared some youthful adventures – said, 'Are Lady Pendleton and her son still here, Dan?'

Mr Clegg's face closed up.

'Aye. And I wish they weren't – or *her*, anyway. The old battle-axe has my maids scampering about morning till night with daft errands and she does nowt but complain.' His eye brightened hopefully. 'Any chance of your lordship taking her away?'

'No. But if you're lucky, she'll leave of her own volition after I've spoken to her.'

'Ah. Like that, is it?'

'Yes. Where is she?'

'My best rooms,' growled Mr Clegg. 'And she's in. Rang down for tea not ten minutes since – then sent it back saying it weren't hot enough.' He grinned suddenly. 'If you can get rid of her, there'll be ale and one of Betty's meat pies in it for you.'

'I'll see what I can do.' Max set off towards the stairs and then turned back, smiling. 'Congratulate me, Dan. I'm a married man.'

'*Married*! Since when?'

'A week ago.'

His hand was immediately seized in a crushing grip.

'Every happiness to you, my lord – and to your lady. *Every* happiness.' Mr Clegg beamed at him. 'Well ... that's a turn up and no mistake.'

'A bigger one than you think,' replied Max with a sigh. 'The battle-axe is my mother-in-law.' And before Mr Clegg could speak, 'See we're not disturbed, will you?'

The door to the Pendletons' rooms swung open the instant Max knocked on it and Rufus stood staring at him, bafflement changing slowly to comprehension. Swallowing hard, he said,

'Lord Brandon?'

'Yes.'

Rufus remained apparently rooted to the spot. 'How d-do you do, sir?'

'Rufus!' snapped a sharp, irritable voice. 'If that stupid maid is here with more excuses, tell her that I wish to speak to Clegg. Immediately!'

'N-No. It isn't the maid. It's ...'

He stopped as Max moved him firmly aside and stepped into the room, saying, 'Good day, Lady Pendleton. I believe you've been expecting me.'

She rose from the sofa, the frown that Max suspected was habitual deepening into an expression of angry accusation. 'Well. And about time, too. What do you have to say for yourself, sir? And where, pray, is my daughter?'

'I have a great many things to say, ma'am. And Frances is at Brandon Lacey where she will remain until I have said them.'

'You are impertinent. You also over-reach yourself. The fact that you took her with you on this scandalous escapade – and for what possible purpose, I cannot imagine – is already the outside of enough. And now, when you finally deign to face me, you do not bring her with you? Your behaviour has been disgraceful in the extreme and you should be thoroughly ashamed of yourself. But before we discuss how to mend matters, I demand to see my daughter. You will return to Brandon Lacey immediately and fetch her.'

'Not a chance,' said Max flatly. Throughout her tirade, he had looked at the pinched mouth with its lines of discontent, the crease between the narrow brows and the chilly emptiness in the faded blue eyes. As for her voice, it grated like a fork across the bottom of a cooking pot. He couldn't see anything of Frances in her anywhere. 'Whether you like it or not, you will have deal with me first.'

'*Deal* with you? I have no wish to *deal* with you, Lord Brandon. I wish only to hear how you intend to undo the harm you have done.'

'I'm sure you do. Unfortunately, your wishes are of

absolutely no consequence to me.' Then, before she could recover from her splutter of outrage, 'Pendleton, it will be best if you leave your mother and me to speak privately. But --'

'You will leave when I say so, Rufus – and not before.'

'But first allow me to assure you that the promises I made to Frances, with regard to yourself and your estate, were genuine and will be honoured – regardless,' he glanced briefly at her ladyship, 'of other considerations.'

Rufus flushed. 'That is v-very good of you, my lord.'

'What are you talking about?' demanded Lady Pendleton. '*What* promises?'

'I should further inform you,' continued Max as if she hadn't spoken, 'that your sister and I were married a week ago in Scotland. If you wish to offer your felicitations, feel free to call at Brandon Lacey – now, if you like. I'm sure Dan Clegg will lend you a horse.'

'Married!' echoed Lady Pendleton, before Rufus could open his mouth. 'Without my permission or knowledge? And in *Scotland*?'

'She doesn't need anyone's permission. And since marriage was what I understand you came here to demand, I don't believe you have anything to complain about.'

A cold, hard smile bracketing his mouth, Max watched the expressions chasing each other across her ladyship's face. Shock, affront, anger and then calculation. Finally, she said, 'You may go, Rufus. By all means, call on your sister and tell her that, although I am appalled at how this marriage has come about, I will see her presently in order to decide how to present it to the world in the best light. Now – go.'

With a wild look and a nod, Rufus slid from the room, closing the door behind him.

'You may be seated, Lord Brandon,' Lady Pendleton informed him regally. 'As you say, there are matters to discuss – most notably this Scottish wedding of yours.'

Max remained standing and, inclined to humour her for a little while before coming to what he considered the crux of the matter, said mildly, 'What of it? It wasn't performed by a blacksmith, if that's what worries you.'

'I am pleased to hear it – though it makes little difference. If it comes to light that you married in such a *furtive* way, the fact that you and Frances have been travelling around alone together for days on end will *also* become known – and that cannot be allowed to happen. People would naturally conclude that you'd *had* to marry her.'

'Was not that your own point?'

'Do not be obtuse, sir! It may be the truth but I will not have the world sniggering behind its hand at my daughter and waiting for a seven month babe.' She paused briefly and then said, 'There must be another ceremony, as soon as it may be arranged … something private, with only the families present and then an announcement in the *Morning Chronicle*. Yes. Your mother and I will put our heads together over that. Perhaps some tale about a long-standing attachment …'

'There's an original idea,' murmured Max.

'What did you say?'

'Nothing. Please go on. I'm sure you have some thoughts on what else must be done to salvage the situation.'

'Yes. Frances's position in society must be re-established. You must take her to London as soon as possible – having first furnished her with a suitable wardrobe, of course. You will also – since I doubt you have a London house of your own – see to hiring one in a good part of town,' said her ladyship, warming to her theme. 'But first and foremost, settlements must be drawn up. Under the circumstances, I shall expect you to be generous.'

And now we come to it, thought Max. He said, 'I'm sure you will. *How* generous?'

'That may depend on whatever promises you have already made to Rufus.'

'Your son's lands are failing. He needs to learn how to manage them better so that, in time, they may return to prosperity and full production. I can help with that.'

Lady Pendleton gave a dismissive snort.

'That is all very well, I'm sure – but it does not address the real issues.'

'Which are what?'

'The carriages and horses were sold when my husband died and Pendle Hall has been allowed to fall into a state of dilapidation. These things and others require immediate attention. Lord Blandford had agreed to a sum of twenty-five thousand pounds in the event of Frances's marriage to his son. I don't imagine a mere country squire such as yourself can equal that ... but what might you manage?'

'For you and your house and your stables?' asked Max softly. And deciding it was time to take the gloves off, 'Not a penny.'

For a second, she looked at him as if she had misheard. Then she stood up saying, '*What* did you say?'

'Was I not clear? My apologies. What can I manage? For Frances, anything she wants and everything I own. For you ... not one penny.'

Colour stained her face and neck, her expression one of shocked disbelief. Then she gave a discordant laugh and said, 'You are being ridiculous. Of *course* you will make a settlement.'

Max shook his head.

'Not the sort you have in mind. I will make it possible for your younger son to attend university and I will give Rufus the help he needs with the estate. If capital is required for that, I shall provide it. But I shall insist on strict accounting ... and not one penny of it will be available to you. If you require new furnishings, gowns and a carriage, they will have to wait until your son is in a position to provide them out of estate income. It may take a little time. But if he applies himself, it will happen.'

There was a long, poisonous silence before she whispered, 'That is iniquitous!'

'It is what you deserve.' He impaled her with a look that Frances would not have recognised. Suddenly everything he knew about this woman caused temper to roll through his chest like thunder. Controlling it with an effort, he said, 'Sit down.'

'I do not take orders from you!' she snapped. 'You *will* make a settlement. I shall see to it – in the courts, if I must. But for now you may leave.'

'*Sit down.*' He waited until, almost without realising it, she had done so. 'I shall leave when you have explained what the hell you thought you were doing five years ago when you forced Frances into a betrothal you knew she didn't want.'

Another silence while Max watched her finally begin to realise where this might be going. Her high colour faded, leaving bright spots behind on either cheek. Looking through rather than at him, she said coldly, 'I did no such thing. It was an excellent match and Frances had agreed to it.'

'*Had* agreed to it. Past tense. During the last two weeks at Westlake, she repeatedly told you she no longer wanted it – that she would not, in fact go through with it. So you sought a way of making sure that she did.' He paused for a second to steady his breathing. 'The means you chose is beyond my comprehension. She is your daughter, for God's sake – yet you had no compunction in drugging her into compliance.'

'*Drugging* her? What nonsense is this? Of course I didn't drug her! If this is what Frances has told you --'

'It is what she's told me and I don't doubt the truth of it for a minute. I remember how she looked that night. Confused and blank like a sleepwalker. I should have known something was wrong. I am ashamed that I didn't. But who would believe a mother could do that to their child? It's like something out of a damned novel.'

'It would be if it was true but it is not. You are raving!'

'And you are lying. What did you put in that glass of wine?'

'Nothing!' She strode away to pull the bell. 'Go. Or I will have someone toss you out.'

Max laughed. It wasn't a comforting sound.

'Good luck with that.' He regarded her over folded arms. 'You and your late husband really tried, didn't you? The betrothal contracts signed ... the wedding brought forward with almost indecent haste ... oh, and let us not forget the premature notice in the *Morning Chronicle*. You probably thought nothing could go wrong. The disappointment when, despite all of this, Frances still managed to thwart you must have been killing.' He waited and when, for once, she didn't speak, added, 'What? Nothing to say? Or are you waiting for someone to answer the bell? They won't, you know.'

'I refuse to listen to any more of this. If you will not leave, I shall.'

'And go where? To your bedchamber? You think that will stop me? We can have this conversation there as well as here. Or how about downstairs in the coffee-room? Only think how delightfully public that would be.'

'You are completely insane,' she said, a slight betraying tremor in her voice.

'*I* am?' he asked. 'You are the one who didn't scruple to destroy her daughter's life.'

'I – I did nothing of the kind. This – all of this – is quite ludicrous.'

Max looked at her in silence for a moment. Then he said ominously, 'What did you do with the letters? And don't waste time in continued lies or denial. I know everything now. *All* of it. You made sure Frances's letters to me were never sent and that mine never reached her. So what became of them?'

'I – you had no business writing to a lady who was betrothed to another man. None whatsoever. It was highly improper.'

'Ah. Burned them, did you? But I'll wager that you read them first. And if you did, you knew ... even before Frances jilted Archie ... you knew that she and I were in love with each other. And you knew my intentions were honourable.'

'If your intentions were *honourable*,' snapped Lady Pendleton, seeming to recover some of her composure, 'you would have approached her father with an offer. You did not.'

'With betrothal to Archie still hanging over her head? How could I? And what good would it have done? You wanted Archie and his money. You wanted it so badly you'd have done anything to get it. You didn't care about Frances. You didn't care that she'd be married to a man who'd have been bedding the chambermaids before the honeymoon was over and wouldn't even have been discreet about it. After all, what was Frances's happiness when set against that twenty-five thousand pounds?' The temper he'd thought he had under control ratcheted up a notch. '*God*! You make me sick.'

'And where were you after she left Lord Malpas at the altar?' she spat spitefully. 'You didn't exactly come riding to the rescue, did you?'

'Because, thanks to you, *I didn't know!*' He hurled the words at her. 'I believed that thrice-damned newspaper announcement. I had no reason not to. I never saw the retraction and I thought … I thought I'd lost her.' He shut his eyes for a moment, unprepared for the sudden, searing pain memory brought with it. 'I stopped writing then. There seemed no point. But Frances *didn't* stop, did she? She went on writing letter upon letter. If you had let one of them reach me … just *one* … I'd have been there in a heartbeat. But you didn't, did you? Partly because it would have meant admitting what you'd done … and partly, I would guess, to punish her for depriving you of Archie's money.' He eyed her with icy contempt. 'You robbed us of five years. But for an odd trick of Fate, those five years might have been a lifetime. Frances may eventually forgive you for that. I doubt if I ever will.'

'I see.' She looked back at him, head high and brows raised in mocking enquiry. 'That is going to make this marriage of yours a trifle awkward, would you not say?'

'No. It isn't going to be awkward at all. If Frances wants to see you, I won't try to stop her – not ever. She has had enough of being controlled and manipulated. She will not have more of it from me. But you should not expect to be welcome in my home. And if you wish to see your future grandchildren, you had better achieve some semblance of courtesy … even if normal human kindness is beyond you. They will have one grandmother who will love them so they won't miss one who can't.'

Lady Pendleton continued to stare at him … perhaps recognising that, in this, he was and always would be a formidable opponent or perhaps trying to find a way through his defences. He couldn't tell which. And so, because he felt physically drained and suddenly wanted nothing more than to walk away from this woman and go home, he said, 'I hope that makes the position quite clear?'

'Perfectly.' She stood up and faced him defiantly. 'But I still insist on seeing my daughter and shall remain here for one more day. Tell Frances to call upon me tomorrow without fail. Good day, my lord.'

* * *

He returned to Brandon Lacey and found his brother-in-law in the stables on the point of departure. He said bluntly, 'You may tell me to mind my own business, Pendleton ... but I'd advise you to make yourself master in your own house. If you don't, your mother will make your life – not just difficult – but a misery.'

'I know. I just don't know how to make her stop.'

'You develop a thick skin and learn to stand your ground. Say no ... refuse to listen to her or walk away ... be as rude as she is, if necessary.' Max saw the look of doubt in the younger man's eyes and added, 'I don't pretend it will be easy. But hold on to the thought that, in a few years' time, you'll meet a lady you will want to marry. But if your mother is still behaving like a harridan, she'll probably turn you down. Now ... with regard to your other problems, I'll send one of my fellows to assess them. He'll talk to you, bring me back a report and we'll take it from there. Will that suit you?'

'Very well indeed, my lord. Thank you.'

'No need for thanks. And you'd better get used to calling me Max.'

* * *

Learning that Frances and his mother were entertaining Rob and Ellie in the drawing-room, Max went directly to the library. Raising his eyes from his book to take a long, thoughtful look at him, Lord Sherbourne said, 'I am guessing your morning did not go well.'

'That is putting it mildly.' Max reached for the decanter. 'I don't normally drink brandy at this hour. Will you make it a trifle more respectable by joining me?'

'Why not?' Closing his book and laying it aside, Ralph accepted the glass he was offered. 'Relatives can be the very devil, can they not?'

Max slanted a glance at him. 'Your brothers? Or the Reverend Marsden?'

'Oh my brothers, without a shadow of doubt.' A faint smile

dawned. 'I find a tendency to turn every conversation into a sermon vastly preferable to downright idiocy. But I believe Elizabeth's mama and sisters enjoy having her to themselves ... and it suits me to indulge them.'

'Very diplomatic.' Max downed the brandy in one swallow. 'I, on the other hand, have just told my mother-in-law I won't have her in the house. And now I have to tell my wife that I meant it ... and also that the wretched woman wants to see her.'

'Ah.' Ralph contemplated the untouched contents of his glass. 'Might I make a suggestion?'

'By all means.'

'Wait until you feel a little less ... raw. You will handle it better.'

Max looked at him. 'The voice of experience, my lord?'

'Very much so.' He took a sip of brandy. 'You will have been told what Lady Pendleton called me. Have you no questions?'

'Should I have?' shrugged Max. 'I am presuming that, if there was any truth in it, Lizzie would know – not to mention Rockliffe.'

'Elizabeth knows ... those parts which were fit for her ears.'

'And Rockliffe?'

The earl's mouth twisted in a wry smile. 'The parts that were not.'

'Then there's no more to be said. If it helps, when Rock told me you were to marry Lizzie, he also said you were a better man than he'd supposed. So since you're part of the family, do you think we might dispense with the formalities?'

Ralph rose and offered his hand. 'I would be honoured.'

In the drawing-room, Rob was practicing a new piece which he was determined to perfect before Julian returned; Ellie sat on the floor, teasing her kitten with a ball of twine; and Frances and Louisa were deep in discussion over what appeared to be two different lists. Rob continued doggedly playing but everyone else looked up when Max appeared and coming quickly to her feet, Frances said, 'Thank you for telling Rufus to call.'

'I assumed you would like to see him. And I wanted him out of the way during my interview with your mother.'

'Yes. He said as much. How was it? Was she *very* rude to

you?'

'I think the honours were about even.'

'Ah.' Seeing the darkness in his voice reflected in his eyes, she said, 'Well, you can tell me all about it later. Your mama and I were just considering the various ways in which we might hold some kind of wedding celebration for the family. What would you think about a church blessing – perhaps performed by your uncle – followed by a belated wedding breakfast?'

'That sounds about right.' He dropped down on his haunches beside Ellie. 'What do you think? Shall we have a party when Sir Julian comes to take you home?'

She beamed and nodded. 'Can I be a handmaiden again and wear my pink dress?'

'I'll be upset if you don't. I might even cry.'

She giggled. 'Silly. Gentlemen don't cry. Even Tom doesn't.'

'Well, Tom's very brave. But what if he met a dragon?'

Ellie's eyes grew round. 'A dragon? With wings and claws and – and fire?'

'Yes.' Max leaned towards her, whispered something in her ear and then added, 'But you mustn't tell anyone.'

'I won't.' The child put her arms around his neck. 'And *specially* not Uncle Leo.'

At which point, the door was flung open, drawing every eye and creating an abrupt silence. Even Rob stopped playing.

Lacking both coat and cravat, his hair standing on end and paint on his fingers, Leo had brought a distinct odour of turpentine with him. His gaze settled on Max and, in an oddly strangled voice, he produced just three words.

'I've found something.'

CHAPTER TWENTY-FIVE

Max released Ellie and stood up. 'There's a painting under the other one?'

Leo nodded, his expression a mixture of terror and wild elation. 'Come and take a look. It may be nothing but ... well, you and Frances should see for yourselves.' He hesitated and added 'You won't mind not joining us, Mama?'

'Not at all. I saw quite enough of your Mr Ramsay yesterday, thank you.'

'Where have you put it?' asked Max, taking Frances's hand in his.

'The ghost's room,' replied Leo tersely. 'I've been ... using it for a while.'

'The ghost's room?' echoed Frances, amused. 'You have one of those?'

For the first time in several hours, Max knew an impulse to smile.

'A ghost? Possibly. As to this particular room, we called it that as children because it was always cold – but that probably has more to do with it being situated on the north-east corner of the house with windows on two sides than to any phantom presence.'

Led by Leo, they climbed two flights of stairs to a gallery in one of the oldest, least-used parts of the house. And there, entering the so-called ghost's room, they stopped dead.

With the exception of the bed, all other furniture had been removed. And around the room, bathed in merciless northern light, a dozen or so portraits were propped against the walls ... all of them glowing with depth and vitality.

Turning slowly, Max said, 'Leo ... how long have you been painting in oils?'

'I don't know. A year, perhaps? It doesn't matter.'

'Not *matter*? For God's sake! Even *I* can tell that these are too good to just be hidden away up here.'

'Some of them, maybe. But never mind that now,' said Leo impatiently, still brimming with tension. 'Come and look at this –

down here at the bottom. What do you see?'

Looking even less pleasant than it had yesterday, the Ramsay portrait sat on an easel close to the windows. Max and Frances peered obediently at the place where some three square inches of the gentleman's blue coat had been removed to reveal a patch of dark ochre.

After a moment, Frances said uncertainly, 'Are those letters?'

'Yes,' agreed Leo, radiating tension.

Max leaned closer to squint at a row of six capital letters which were almost as dark as the background upon which they were painted. He said, 'A magnifying lens would be useful. But it looks like C ... I ... A ... N ...V ... S? And then ... I don't know. Is that a T or an F?'

'It's an F.' Sounding suddenly much less sure of himself, Leo said, 'If this is what I think it is, it will be an F.'

'And what *do* you think it is?' asked Frances.

'I ... *God.*' He groaned. 'I'm scared to say it in case I'm wrong.'

'Well, let's work on the assumption that you're not,' said Max prosaically. And when no reply was immediately forthcoming, 'Leo ... just spit it out, will you?'

'The F stands for *fecit* meaning --'

'Meaning *made* or *made by*,' cut in Max. 'Yes. I daresay I remember as much Latin as you do. But made by *whom*, for heaven's sake?'

For a long moment, Leo merely stared him, breathing rather hard. Then, 'Tiziano Vecellio. Titian. I think ... I think it's a bloody *Titian!*' And before either Max or Frances could react, he snatched up a scrap of paper and a piece of charcoal and scrawling upon it, said rapidly, 'The V is actually a Romanised U ... so what we have is CIANUS.F. I was working from right to left, you see ... and when I uncovered the C, my hands were shaking too badly to go any further. But if those letters are preceded by T and I, it will read Ticianus.F. Made by Titian.' He looked up at Max. '*Now* do you see?'

'Not yet.' Max glanced around the room. 'Turpentine, I think you said. Where is it?'

'Over there. But I can't --'

Max scooped up the turpentine and a bit of rag lying near it. 'Fine. *I'll* do it.'

'Don't you dare!' Leo dived at the bottle, only to have Max pass it to Frances and stand his path. 'Don't be an idiot, Max – you've no idea what you're doing! You could ruin it!'

'Probably. But at least we'd know, wouldn't we?'

Leo groaned. 'Alright – *alright*! I'll do it. There's some clean linen over there. Pass me that ... and stay out of my way. It'll take a while.'

'We'll wait,' said Max calmly. 'And pass the time studying *your* work.'

Leo muttered something that sounded suspiciously like a curse.

Leaning on her husband's arm, laughter in both eyes and voice, Frances whispered, 'That was wicked of you.'

'It worked, didn't it? And I knew he'd never let me touch it.' He stopped, studying the portrait of a young man. 'That's Adam.'

'Your brother? Oh. I thought he'd be dark-haired like you and Leo.'

'No. He's blond like Belle. Leo ought to put him in the gallery with the rest of the rogues.' And dropping a kiss on Frances's brow, 'Remind me to show them to you. Gabriel's there ... and everyone says I look exactly like him.' His attention moved on to another picture. 'Good God – it's Julian!'

'Don't touch that,' said Leo sharply. 'I did some work on it yesterday and the oil won't be properly hard yet. It's for Belle's birthday.'

'She'll love it. You've captured him exactly.'

Frances absorbed dark green eyes and a shy, sideways smile which made her want to smile back. She said, 'He looks rather lovely.'

Max groaned. 'You hear that, Leo? Lovely. And she hasn't met him yet.'

Leo gave a brief laugh, started to say something and then froze, staring at his handiwork. 'I think I've got the I.'

'Excellent. Find the T and we can go downstairs and share the good news.'

'It still might not be genuine,' warned Leo. 'It might be 'school of' or a studio copy of one of Titian's originals ... or even just a simple fake, painted last year. The signature alone isn't enough to tell us it's genuine. But if it is ... if it *is*, there's a chance it may be one of the lost ones.'

'Lost ones?' asked Frances quickly.

'Mm. Titian died in the 1575 Venetian plague epidemic. He was in his eighties by then and he'd been the most famous and sought-after artist of his day for sixty years – so his work had earned him a fortune. At the time of his death, there were reputedly over a hundred paintings in his studio, most of them unfinished. But Venice was in chaos. With scores of people dying every day, violence and looting took over ... and I don't suppose it helped that the corpses were being collected by convicted felons.'

Leo stopped talking to concentrate on what he was doing so Max said idly, 'You seem to know a lot about Titian. Did you study his work particularly?'

'Yes.' His brother sent him a brief glance redolent with pity for his ignorance. '*Everyone* studies Titian.'

Catching Max's eye and seeing that he was about to say something provoking, Frances said quickly, 'Finish the story about the lost pictures.'

'What? Oh – right. As I said, there should have been a great many canvases in the studio,' replied Leo absently, 'but by the time things settled down and someone went there to look, there were only a dozen or so left. Needless to say, with no proper inventory, it was impossible to know exactly what was taken or what happened to them. Stolen paintings would probably have been sold on and could have ended up anywhere.' He flashed a sardonic grin over his shoulder. 'But as you can imagine, there probably isn't an art expert or collector anywhere who hasn't hoped to find an unknown Titian one day.'

'And the chances of this being one of them?' asked Max.

'Not high ... but not impossible either.' Leo stepped back and stared at his handiwork. Finally, he said weakly, 'It's here. Ticianus Fecit. Oh God. It could be real.'

Frances and Max crossed to stand beside him. Max dropped

a hand on his shoulder and said, 'Breathe. And tell us what happens next.'

'I'll take it to Brentworth and ask him to remove the rest of Mr Ramsay. Once that's done and we can see what we've got, we'll need an expert to determine whether or not it's genuine.' Leo looked round, his eyes brilliant. 'If it is … if it *is* there's no saying what it could be worth.'

'Then let us hope,' remarked Max, 'that it does prove genuine … and that, knowingly or otherwise, Ramsay left something to Gregory's sister after all. And also, that once in possession of a small fortune, Gregory proves less financially inept than his ancestors.'

* * *

Thanks to the excitement about Leo's discovery and the necessity of everyone trooping up to the ghost's room to see it for themselves, it wasn't until later that night that Max was finally alone with his wife.

In the days since their wedding, they had formed a nightly ritual. Having shed his coat, vest and cravat, Max helped Frances out of her gown and stays – a process which naturally took rather longer than necessary; and then, while she sat before the mirror clad only in chemise and petticoats, he set about unpinning her hair. It was a part of the day he would be sorry to give up, as he must when she acquired a maid, which was why he'd been putting it off.

Sliding his fingers through the silky chestnut mass and on across her shoulders, he drew a deep breath and forced himself to broach the subject that had been lying in wait all day.

'Your mother wants you to call on her tomorrow.'

And Frances, who had spent the intervening hours waiting to hear what had been upsetting him, said calmly, 'Yes. I was expecting that.'

'Will you go?'

'It has to be done, don't you think? And now, while she is here, is the ideal opportunity.'

'Yes. I suppose so.'

She leaned back against him and sought his eyes in the

mirror.

'Max ... what happened this morning?'

He settled his arms about her and bent to kiss the top of her head. Finally, he said, 'She behaved exactly as you predicted she would. Her first decree was that Scotland is not to be mentioned because people will naturally assume I got you pregnant and *had* to marry you.'

Frances groaned and shut her eyes.

'If only she knew! But the truth would never occur to her. She always thinks the worst of everyone so naturally she imagines that others do the same. What else?'

'We're instructed to have a speedy and private second wedding to be arranged by herself and my mother, after which I'm to take you to London and re-establish you in society. But first, she asked how much I'm prepared to pay for the privilege. Did you know that Lord Blandford had promised your father twenty-five thousand?'

'What?' She spun round on the stool to face him. 'No! That – that's insane.'

Max sank to his knees in front of her, took her hands and bent his head over them.

'Not really. Even five years ago Archie was gaining a very unsavoury reputation. His father probably thought marriage might settle him ... or if it didn't, as least he'd *be* married and to a lady of suitable pedigree.'

'You make me sound like a horse,' Frances objected.

'To Lord Blandford, you might as well have been. As for your mama, she wants money for the refurbishment of Pendle Hall. She also needs a carriage and pair and probably numerous other things she didn't have the chance to mention before I said I wouldn't give her a penny.' He looked up at her. 'I can't apologise for that. I *enjoyed* saying it.'

'I don't blame you. But she knows that you're going to help Rufus, doesn't she?'

'I don't believe she considered either that or my promise to fund William's university education adequate payment,' he replied dryly. 'She is the most monumentally selfish woman I've ever met ... and she doesn't deserve to be called a mother.'

'I know. And when we were children, she wasn't one. We were brought up by nurses, then a governess for me and a tutor for the boys. I was of no interest until I was old enough to be presented and married. Rufus has only become interesting since he inherited ... and I'd guess the reason she wants me to take my place in society to make it easier for her to find an heiress for him to marry.'

'A suitably biddable girl she can dominate, no doubt.'

'Yes – but that is Rufus's battle to fight. You were telling me about this morning. And nothing you've said so far is what was troubling you when you first came back from Knaresborough, is it?'

'No.' He sighed and stood up, drawing her with him. 'Can we do this somewhere more comfortable? Preferably somewhere I can hold you?'

'Yes.' She towed him towards the bed and when she was lying in the curve of his arm with her head on his shoulder, said, 'Now. Tell me and let us be done with it.'

'I confronted her about that damned betrothal ball and the fact that she had withheld our letters. If she'd admitted what she had done instead of continuing to deny it ... if she had shown a shred of compassion or remorse, I might have reacted differently. But she didn't. She behaved as if it had been *nothing* – as if the consequences of her actions had been of no importance at all. So when I let myself contemplate the pain she'd caused and the years she had stolen ...' He stopped, his breathing not quite even. 'I said some very harsh things. Harsher than I'd intended. The only thing in my head was how different everything would have been if, when Archie was no longer a factor, she had posted just *one* of your letters to me. So I told her that although I wouldn't prevent you from seeing her if you wished to do so ... she would never be welcome in this house.' He shut his eyes. 'I'm sorry.'

'You're sorry about saying *that*?' asked Frances blankly. 'Why?'

'Because I ought to have been more controlled. And because, on something as final and far-reaching as that, you had a right to be consulted.'

'Oh. Well, I'll remember that for the future.' Smiling, she tugged at the laces of his shirt so that she could slip her hand inside it. 'She would never come here except to make demands or mischief ... so you didn't say anything I wouldn't have said myself.'

Max shifted, propping himself on one elbow to look into her face.

'Do you mean that?'

'Yes.'

'Even though my behaviour is likely to make your visit even more unpleasant than it might otherwise have been?'

'I doubt I'll notice the difference. And it will be a very short meeting during which I'll merely echo your sentiments and point out that, if she wants a relationship with us, the remedy is in her own hands. Ten minutes should do it. Five if she's not inclined to listen.' Her fingers explored his chest and she drew one foot invitingly up his calf. 'Now ... can we forget about my appalling mother and think of other things?'

Max smiled at her, one hand taking a leisurely journey from shoulder to hip.

'Yes. Now we're home, I can finally begin spoiling you. Clothes first, I think. And perhaps a horse?'

'Oh *please*! It's been so long ... and to be able to ride with you again as we used to would be wonderful. But why should you think you need to spoil me?'

'Mostly because I'll enjoy doing it and you're long overdue for a little spoiling. And because ... yes, because you suggested thinking of other things just now.'

Frances hid a smile against his shoulder. 'Ah. You have something in mind?'

'Yes. Don't you?'

* * *

Frances described the following morning's meeting as being neither particularly acrimonious nor productive and added that she had informed her mother that if she wanted a rapprochement, it needed to begin with an apology for her former behaviour. Immediately afterwards – and reluctantly accompanied by her son – Lady Pendleton left Knaresborough for Matlock. Although he didn't say so, Max hoped she'd taken fleas in both ears with her.

Eight days passed. Frances settled happily in amongst her new family and was borne off for a shopping expedition in York by Louisa and Elizabeth. Plans for the blessing ceremony and wedding-breakfast were completed then put aside, pending the return of Arabella and Julian. Leo produced a pretty grey mare for Frances's sole use and Max ordered a fine saddle of embossed Spanish leather. Tom had daily riding lessons with either Leo or Ralph and progressed to simple jumps. And Ellie and Rob, wanting to know if Sir Julian was *ever* coming home, started to become mildly fractious.

On the ninth day, a coy note arrived from Silas Brentworth in York, announcing that the painting was now stripped down to its original state and inviting Leo and Lord Brandon to his studio to view it. Leo spent the whole of the ride to York speculating on what the restorer *hadn't* said and what they might expect to find. After ten miles of this, Max simply told him to shut up. They would find out soon enough.

Mr Brentworth, it turned out, was almost as excited as Leo. When his visitors were standing in front of the easel on which the painting rested, he whipped off the cloth that covered it, saying, 'Behold, gentlemen – the *Penitent Magdalen*!'

For an instant, Leo knew a small flicker of completely illogical disappointment. Then he looked – really *looked* – and understood the old man's elation. He said weakly, 'Oh. It's not … it isn't …' And stopped.

'You see it, don't you?' demanded Mr Brentworth eagerly. 'Tell me you do!'

'You'd better tell me as well,' remarked Max, faintly amused. 'What I see is a not very flattering portrait of a female clutching her shoulder and rolling her eyes up to heaven. If there's something remarkable about it, I'm afraid it escapes me.'

Mr Brentworth looked at him as if he had committed the worst kind of sacrilege.

Leo cleared his throat and said, 'Titian painted numerous

versions of the *Penitent*. They fall into two categories. The earlier ones were nude, with rose-gold hair and little background detail. The later ones were clothed, with darker hair and some kind of landscape behind them. This ...' He stopped, drew an unsteady breath and then said, 'This isn't either of them.'

'What does that mean?' Max studied the portrait, mentally adding up what Leo had said. He supposed that the mass of rippling hair *could* be called rose-gold and the background was largely indistinct. But the woman wasn't nude. Her ample breasts were concealed in some sort of blue robe and which gave him the feeling that, if he touched it, it would feel like silk sliding over warm flesh. 'That this is a copy by another artist?'

Leo and Mr Brentworth exchanged pained glances.

'Not at all,' said the restorer. 'Although it will still have to be verified, I am convinced that this is a rare – a *very* rare find indeed.'

'It's the robe,' offered Leo. 'See how it has been painted? How different it is to the rest of the composition? This is how Titian painted in his old age – using his fingers as often as his brush. So what Mr Brentworth and I are thinking is that *this* was one of the earlier *Penitents* ... and that Titian added the robe long after it was originally painted.'

'Which would mean,' added Mr Brentworth, 'that it was still probably in his studio at the time of his death.'

'Making it one of the so-called lost ones?' hazarded Max.

'Yes – though sadly we can never be certain.' The old man eyed the picture with rueful longing, sighed and then, resuming a business-like tone said, 'Since I understand your lordship's intention is to sell the painting, I have taken the liberty of writing to Eustace Crosby-Lynch and Viscount Newbury. Both are experts on and collectors of Titian's work – and both, if satisfied with the *Penitent's* authenticity, will undoubtedly offer to purchase it. They will be here on Friday. Mr Brandon ... perhaps you would care to be here when they come?'

'Wild horses couldn't stop me,' said Leo promptly.

Once on the road back to Brandon Lacey, Max said, 'Frances has a final fitting for her riding-dress on Friday. Doubtless either

Mama or Lizzie will go with her so take the carriage and escort them, will you? They can shop while you're at Brentworth's.'

'Fine.' And with a sideways glance, 'What do you intend to do about Gregory?'

'Nothing until we see what Friday brings. There's no point in raising premature hopes.'

'And afterwards?'

'With any luck, pass on the glad tidings along with a substantial sum of money. What else?'

* * *

Louisa and Frances returned from their shopping trip laden with parcels and in perfect charity with each other but none at all with Leo who had refused to tell them what had happened at Mr Brentworth's studio.

'Not a word until we get home,' he said with annoying loftiness. 'I'm not having the news spread piecemeal through the house before Max knows.'

By the time the carriage had been emptied of packages and Frances had changed into a blue taffeta *robe à l'anglais*, Leo had everyone except the children gathered before the *Penitent Magdalen* which he'd seen the wisdom of bringing home with him.

After kissing his wife's hands and telling her she looked beautiful, Max said, 'So, Leo ... you have our undivided attention. What was the verdict?'

Leo stretched the moment of anticipation out as long as he dared before finally saying, 'I don't know.'

There was a universal groan into which Louisa said indignantly, 'What do you mean – you don't know? After keeping Frances and me on tenterhooks all the way home --'

'That was *because* I don't know. Not the final outcome, anyway.'

'Cut line,' said Max impatiently. 'Is it a genuine Titian or isn't it?'

A slow triumphant smile provided the answer before Leo said simply, 'Yes.'

When the collective expressions of pleasure and excitement

had died down he related the rest of what he knew.

'Old Brentworth was cannier than I realised when he chose Crosby-Lynch and Newbury. They're arch-rivals apparently and, having agreed that the *Penitent* was genuine, they immediately embarked on a bidding war. Newbury started the ball rolling with an offer of five thousand. An hour later, it had reached twelve … and by the time I left to meet Mama it had topped seventeen and they were still at it hammer and tongs.' Leo gave a laughing shrug. 'I took it away in case they started a tug-of-war with it – not to mention the fact that I thought money ought to change hands before it disappears into somebody's private collection.'

* * *

The next day brought a triumphant Mr Crosby-Lynch with a bankers' draft for the full amount of twenty-three thousand five hundred pounds. When he had gone, bearing the *Penitent Magdalen* with him, Max stared disbelievingly at Leo and said, 'Twenty-three thousand for a *painting*? Is he *insane*?'

'Not as insane as fellows who throw twice that away at the card table in one sitting,' returned Leo. 'Crosby-Lynch has bought something which will never be worth less than he paid for it – though to be fair to him, that's not why he wanted it. Avid collectors are a breed apart, you know.

'So it would seem.' Max stared at the bankers' draft in his hand. 'I can't trust this to the Mail – or even to an express courier. I think … yes. I'll send Duncan with it. It's high time he paid a visit to his family, anyway.'

'What will Gregory do with the money, do you think?'

'Put it to good use, one would hope. A new home for the women and children and some solid investments to provide regular income? On an amount like this, he could even give up his position with the East India Company and stay in Scotland. Thankfully, however, what he does now is none of my business.'

CHAPTER TWENTY-SIX

Two days after the excitement over the painting, a complete furore occurred when, without any prior warning, Arabella and Julian arrived just as everyone was about to go in to dinner. Watching them being nearly knocked off their feet by Ellie and Rob while Tom stood two feet away grinning from ear to ear, Louisa said, '*What* a good thing we let them out of the attic this evening so Belle wouldn't suspect how badly they've been treated.'

And then, over a great deal of laughter, came a complete mêlée of welcome with more hugs, kisses and hand-shaking – accompanied by a barrage of questions which, amidst the chaos, went largely unanswered.

Aware that, throughout this, Frances – looking flushed and pleased but faintly uncertain – had retreated a little way to stand beside Ralph, Max allowed it until the room quietened a little. Then, putting his arm about her waist and drawing her towards his sister, he said, 'You probably won't remember, Belle ... but a few years ago you sent me off to a house-party with an instruction to bring you back a sister. Granted, it's taken a while – but here she is. My wife ... Frances.'

Arabella stared at him. Finally, she said, 'You're married?'

'Yes.'

'*Already*?'

'Yes.'

'Without waiting for Julian and me to get back and *be* there?' She slapped her palms against his chest so hard that he, and also perforce Frances, took a step back. 'How *could* you? I'll never forgive you!'

Max grinned. 'Yes you will. And it wasn't just you and Julian. Mama and Leo weren't there either – or anyone, in fact. We ... I suppose you might say we eloped.'

'Oh.' Arabella looked from him to Frances and then back again. 'That's different then.' And finally giving way to the laughter that had been building inside her, she grasped Frances's hands and said, 'Don't mind me. I'm not *really* angry at all – just wildly disappointed about missing it. It sounds very romantic. Was it?'

Frances nodded and, looking up at Max, said, 'It was ... perfect.'

Seeing what was in that look, Arabella nodded and squeezed Frances's fingers.

'I'm glad. And I'll want to hear every single detail – as well as why, if you and Max fell in love years ago, it's taken until now for you to marry – because he knows how much I wanted a sister. But we can talk of all that later. Now, I'd like you to meet *my* husband.'

Bowing over Frances's hand and giving her his usual shy, sweet smile, Julian offered his felicitations and then, turning to Max, said, 'I was looking forward to the day you would finally walk down the aisle. I had a special programme all planned.'

'Yes, I'm sure you did,' laughed Max. His lack of appreciation for parts of Julian's repertoire had become a regular joke between them. 'But all is not lost. Mama and Frances have planned a sort of ceremony-cum-wedding breakfast which can finally be held now you're back ... and I'd be very surprised if your name doesn't feature on a list somewhere.'

Dinner was a merry and somewhat noisy affair. Since everyone wanted to know about Julian's concerts, Arabella was forced to postpone questions about her brother's sudden marriage for another occasion and supply all the details she knew Julian would not.

'He gave two concerts in Paris and a third at the Chateau de Chantilly. At the end of the first one, the audience refused let him leave the platform for a further half hour,' she said, proudly. 'He had to play encore after encore and even *then* they weren't satisfied.'

'Did they pay you extra, Julian?' asked Max, laughing.

'No. But I didn't mind. It was the best kind of audience.'

'Which is what?'

'Musicians.' Julian laid down his knife and sent a diffident glance across the table. 'The hall had a seating capacity of over three hundred and, despite what he'd heard from London, the impresario doubted I could fill the place. So he offered cut-price seats to students from the conservatoire and the other music schools and ... well, musicians generally.' He hunched one shoulder and added simply, 'They came.'

'They came,' echoed Arabella, 'and the following day, Julian's name was *everywhere* so tickets for the other concerts were immediately snapped up. It was the same in Vienna. Julian played at both Belvedere and the Schönbrunn.' She sighed. 'Vienna is *so* beautiful. It makes London look shabby by comparison. And Viennese ladies are every bit as elegant as the ones in Paris.'

'And how did *you* find the ladies, Julian?' asked Leo with seeming innocence. 'You know the ones I mean. Those who come to ogle you, rather than listen to the music.'

The dark green gaze grew faintly baffled. 'Do they? I hadn't noticed.'

This produced a ripple of laughter into which Arabella said, 'It's true. He really *doesn't* notice.' And in a darker tone, 'But *I* do.'

From her seat across the table, Frances could easily imagine how, with a different sort of gentleman, this might be a problem. As well as being perfectly beautiful and endearingly modest, the virtuoso earl seemed largely unaware of the world around him and remained completely undisturbed by Max and Leo's merciless teasing. Fortunately, Ralph Sherbourne eventually put an end to this by asking about future engagements and thus gave Frances the opportunity to say, 'I seem to be the only one who hasn't heard you play, Lord Chalfont – and I'd very much like to, if it's no trouble?'

This produced more laughter interspersed with groans and remarks about trying to *stop* him playing. Julian shrugged and, leaning back in his chair, waited until he could get a word in. Then, bathing Frances in his singularly beguiling smile, he said 'I'll be practicing tomorrow and you're welcome to listen if you wish. But please don't call me Chalfont. I may be stuck with the title but I don't have to use it. Julian will do.'

* * *

Three days later on the afternoon before the celebration of Max and Frances's union, one final guest arrived. Wandering into the house and finding it apparently deserted, he sauntered through to the library in pursuit of his brother's voice.

'No,' Max was saying, 'I will *not* spend this evening at the Red Bear drinking myself silly. I'd like to enjoy tomorrow and --' He stopped abruptly, his gaze alighting on the new arrival. 'Adam! This is a welcome surprise – and brilliantly timed.'

'A surprise?' Tall, fair-haired and with a sword strapped to his hip, Adam Brandon strolled across to embrace his older brother. 'Didn't Mama tell you she'd sent word?'

'No. Did you know, Leo?'

Leo shook his head. 'She probably wasn't sure he'd get here.'

'I nearly didn't – which is why it's taken me so long,' said Adam, crossing to exchange a brief hug with each of his brothers. 'So, Max ... an old married man?'

'Married, yes – but less of the old, if you don't mind. And take that damned sword off before you send the ornaments flying. You know Mama doesn't like you wearing it in the house.'

'I've never yet sent anything flying that I didn't want to,' remarked Adam as he reluctantly discarded the sword and deposited it in a corner. 'However ... aside from news of your extremely precipitate nuptials, Mama's somewhat garbled epistle suggested you've had some excitement while I've been away. Something about a fellow from the other branch of the family and a possible masterpiece hidden beneath a terrible portrait?'

'It's a Titian,' began Leo ... before Max cut him off saying, 'Stop. It's long story which can wait until Adam has let Mama know he's here.'

'Well, he can't do that now,' objected Leo, reaching for the decanter. 'She's upstairs with Frances and Belle and Lizzie making secret female preparations for tomorrow. It'd need a brave – or stupid – man to interrupt them.'

'Then I won't.' Adam sat down, accepted the glass he was offered and lifted it in a toast. 'Your health, Max, and that of your bride – and every happiness to you both.'

'Thank you.'

'I don't suppose I need to ask if it's a love match?'

'You don't and it is.' Max continued to lean against the desk. 'How was the fencing academy and Paris in general?'

'The academy was instructive and Paris was … interesting. I managed to get a ticket for Julian's first concert, by the way – though I wasn't able to get near him afterwards.'

'Mobbed, was he?' grinned Leo.

'Worse than that night at the Pantheon. And rumour had it that seats for his two subsequent recitals were sold out before they'd even been printed.'

Max eyed Adam sardonically.

'Fascinating as all this is, I believe I was asking about *you*.'

'There's not that much to tell,' came the careless reply. 'I practiced, did a bit of tutoring from time to time and met friends. What else can I tell you?'

Whatever it is you're deliberately not saying, thought Max. *But as usual it's a waste of breath asking.* And let Leo hold the floor with an animated account of finding the Titian.

* * *

On the morning of what she had come to regard as her second wedding, Frances sat before the mirror while Louisa's maid turned her hair into a work of art and listened to Arabella grumbling about the Reverend Marsden.

'There ought to be music – and there *would* be if Uncle Josiah wasn't so stubborn about holding the ceremony in the chapel. It's a *blessing*, for heaven's sake. And if Julian and I could get married in *Rockliffe's* drawing-room, surely Uncle can pray over you in ours?'

Since, when approached by Louisa and Arabella over the question of music in the chapel, Julian had proved every bit as unmovable as the reverend, Frances had to smile at this. Staring at them as if they were quite mad, he'd said, 'You want the harpsichord moved here for the ceremony, then back upstairs for later? No. Even if moving it didn't upset the tuning, the temperature in here certainly would. So no. Absolutely not.'

Arabella was still muttering when the maid left the room. With a more important decision to be made, Frances laid two gowns on the bed and said, 'Which one, Belle? I can't make up my mind. I want to wear both of them.'

'At once?' grinned Arabella. And then, glancing incredulously at the gowns, 'You can't decide between a gorgeous figured silk ball gown and a dimity polonaise? *Really?*'

'Really. The gold silk is the most beautiful gown I've ever owned. But the polonaise is the gown I wore for our *actual* wedding and I thought that Max might …' She stopped. 'But no. You're right. Today is for the family – so the gold is a better choice.'

'It is,' agreed Arabella, 'and the colour will look wonderful on you. But there's nothing to stop you changing into the other later, if you wish. Now. Let's get busy – unless you *want* to leave Max wondering if you're coming?'

'I don't and he wouldn't – wonder, I mean. Besides, we're already married.'

'So you are.' Arabella settled the gold over-gown on Frances's shoulders and began tightening the laces. 'And I gather he's enjoying wedded bliss far too much to have a maid spoiling his fun.'

Frances flushed and laughed. 'There's only one way you could possibly guess that.'

'Yes. And, like you, I have no complaints. Neither does my maid, since she's rarely required to wait up for me. You might drop a hint in Max's ear because relying on Mama's girl to do your hair will become tiresome. There. All done.' She stepped back and regarded Frances with bountiful satisfaction. 'You look stunning. Max is going to expire on the spot.'

* * *

An hour later, downstairs in Brandon Lacey's rarely-used chapel, the family and a few close friends were gradually taking their seats amidst a profusion of flowers.

Max muttered, 'It's colder in here than the ghost's room. If Uncle Josiah treats us to one of his interminable sermons, everybody's teeth will be chattering.'

Leo slanted a grin at him. 'If it's Frances you're worried about, I'm sure you know ways of warming her up. But if you need a few tips --'

'From you? I don't think so. But I'll give *you* one. When your turn comes, run off to Scotland. It's a hell of a lot more fun.'

His gaze on the rear of the chapel, Leo's immediate reply was a low whistle.

'Turn around and tell me you still mean that.'

Max turned ... and felt his breath leak slowly away. Frances stood beside Adam, one hand resting lightly on his sleeve and her face alight with laughter at something he was saying. Most of her hair was piled up in an intricate arrangement involving small, white flowers and a single glossy curl lay against one shoulder. As for the gold gown, completely devoid of trimming and shimmering in the candlelight ... it revealed inches of creamy skin and molded her upper body in a way that made Max's mouth water. He almost groaned.

Beside him, Leo grinned. 'Changed your mind, have you? Thought you might.'

Max didn't hear him. Frances was walking towards him, her eyes locked with his and holding a smile that he knew was just for him. He smiled back, suddenly not at all sorry that they had agreed to do this. She deserved a beautiful gown and to be surrounded by a loving family, even if it was only hers by marriage. But as she reached his side and he took her hand, his mind's eye was full of a very different picture. A vivid image of a girl in a simple green gown, her hair tussled by the breeze, laughing aloud as she danced along a Scottish street on the way to her wedding. And he knew that, special as today was, that other memory was the one he would most cherish.

Frances was also remembering their wedding day; the simple, honest vows they had exchanged and the love in Max's eyes as he had made them. He wore that same expression now and it made concentrating on the Reverend Marsden's prayers and blessings difficult ... so she stopped trying and, tightening her fingers on Max's, concentrated on him instead. And then, seemingly in no time at all, it was over and they were being surrounded by the loving congratulations and good wishes of their family.

As they made their way upstairs, the music that had been missing earlier filtered down to them. Julian, it seemed, had slipped out ahead of everyone else and was playing the bridal party in with something fluidly lyrical by Mozart.

Frances smiled up at Max and said, 'I'm glad we've shared our happiness with your family by doing this ... but I can't help feeling a little sorry we weren't able to repeat the vows we made in Hawick.'

'Me, too.' Smiling back at her, he raised one hand to lightly trace the curve of her cheek. 'Perhaps we could make them to each other later?'

She nodded. 'Yes. I'd like that.'

But first there was an elaborate meal to be lingered over ... speeches and toasts to be made ... and a great deal of laughter. Holding tight to Max's hand, Frances looked about her and silently blessed Gregory. Thanks to him, she had a mama-in-law who was sweet and warm and as different from her own mother as it was possible to be. She had a sister, two new brothers, a brother-in-law and female cousins. And more than any of that, she was married to the man she had loved for what felt like all of her life. For an instant, the magnitude of it threatened to overwhelm her; but then Max embarked upon the haggis story and Duncan was teasing her about being an ignorant Sassenach ... and the feeling vanished.

Louisa asked Julian to play for them and he wandered amiably off to the drawing-room, leaving the rest of them free to follow as and when they chose. But hearing the first haunting notes of a piece he remembered from the Wynstanton House concert, Max pulled Frances to her feet saying, 'Have you heard him play this before?' And when she shook her head, 'Come, then ... and take my handkerchief.'

She might have laughed, except that the Johann Christian Bach *Andante* was already weaving its spell ... and by the end of it, she was glad of the handkerchief. When the applause died away, she said simply, 'That was beautiful, Julian. Thank you.' And more softly, to Max, 'Now, I think. But not here.'

* * *

Alone in their rooms, they faced each other with clasped hands.

'I promise to honour you above all others,' said Max.

'I shall be a shield for your back as you are for mine,' replied Frances.

And together, smiling at each other, 'This is my wedding vow to you. You are blood of my blood and bone of my bone. I give you my spirit until my life shall be done. I give you my body that we two might be one.'

Curling an arm about his neck, Frances pulled him down for a kiss which, since his fingers were already busy with the laces of her gown, turned rapidly into something more. Something which made her forget everything until they had somehow made it to the bed and she became aware that, unlike her, Max was still half-dressed. Since assembling words into a sentence seemed too difficult, she sought to remedy the problem herself.

Max let her struggle for a few moments and then, on a ragged note of laughter, brushed her hands aside to shed the rest of his clothes. And when he came back to her, all heated skin and hard muscle, Frances closed her arms about him with a small glad sob that was almost lost in his own rumble of approval.

He knew her body now; knew what pleased or aroused her most ... knew how to bring her to shuddering fulfillment several times in succession or how, sometimes, to draw the pleasure out until neither of them could wait any longer. He was also aware that she was quickly learning some delightful tricks of her own. But most of all, he exulted in the knowledge that she wanted him as fiercely as he wanted her. Lovemaking had never been like this ... nor had he ever imagined that it could be.

Floating in layer upon layer of exquisite sensation, her bones dissolving and her blood running in molten channels, Frances whispered helplessly, 'I love you ... love you and love you and *love* you. And this ... when we are together like this ... I had no idea.'

'Nor I.' Lacing his fingers with hers, Max joined their bodies on a subterranean groan of mingled relief and bliss. 'Nor I.'

Much later, lying sated but still entangled, Max licked a drop of sweat from her shoulder and, locating a scrap of coherent thought, said, 'I should move. I'm crushing you.'

'I don't mind. I like it.'

Given that her palms were wandering dreamily over his backside, he liked it too. But he rolled heroically away and let her snuggle at his side. Eventually, he said, 'We can go to London in the autumn, if you'd like that. You don't have to be trapped here all year round.'

'I'm not trapped. Whatever gave you that idea?'

'The fact that I've deposited you in the midst of my family without ever asking you what you wanted?'

'I want this,' she said seriously, propping herself on one elbow so she could look at him. 'Just this. You, more than anything in the world ... but your family as well. They've been so kind – and I hope that, in time, they will come to love me.'

'I don't think you need have any fears on that score.' Max smiled at her. 'As for me, I never knew happiness like this was possible – and without you, it wouldn't be. You fill my heart and make my life complete.' He stopped, frowning slightly. 'Well ... *almost* complete.'

'Only almost?' Suspecting he was about to make one of his more outrageous statements, Frances gave a heavy sigh. 'That's very disappointing. What is missing?'

Max echoed her sigh and said reluctantly, 'The hermit. I can't be *completely* content until --'

And, shaking with laughter as Frances whacked his stomach with her pillow, 'I'm sorry – I'm sorry! But you started it with your fake, hermitless grotto. How could I help falling head over heels in love with a girl who offered me something like that?'

Printed in Great Britain
by Amazon